Conjuring A Grim

Book One of the Draxmere Academy of Conjuring Series

M.N. Lash

Conjuring a Grim

M.N. Lash

Table of Contents

Content Warnings

Before you even begin to flip through the pages of this book—read this list. This is a dark fantasy/romance that involves several dark elements. Those include:

—Lack of emotions/feeling (The character believes herself to be monstrous/bad because of these issues but I am NOT trying to portray people with these issues as such)

—Graphic death (murder, accidental, in the process of dying)

—Graphic violence/gore

—Dead parents/family

—Divorce

—Self-harm/suicidal thoughts

—Infertility issues (including miscarriages/ectopic pregnancy)

—Sexual activities

—I insult Florida quite often in the first few chapters…

PLAYLIST

Chapter 1 — Evil by Melanie Martinez

Chapter 2 — Ain't No Rest for the Wicked by Cage the Elephant

Chapter 3 — Explorers by Muse

Chapter 4 — Nothing Is As it Seems by Hidden Citizens, Ruelle

What You Know by Two Door Cinema Club

Chapter 5 — You've Got a Friend by Carole King

Chapter 6 — PSYCHO by AViVA

Chapter 7 — Pain by Three Days Grace

Chapter 8 — Choke by I DON'T KNOW HOW BUT THEY FOUND ME

Chapter 9 — Play with Fire (feat. Yacht Money) by Sam Tinnesz, Yacht Money

Chapter 10 — Little Girl Gone by CHINCHILLA

Chapter 11 — Control by Halsey

Chapter 12 — Shadow by Livingston

Chapter 13 — bad idea! by girl in red

Chapter 14 — Love and War by Fleurie

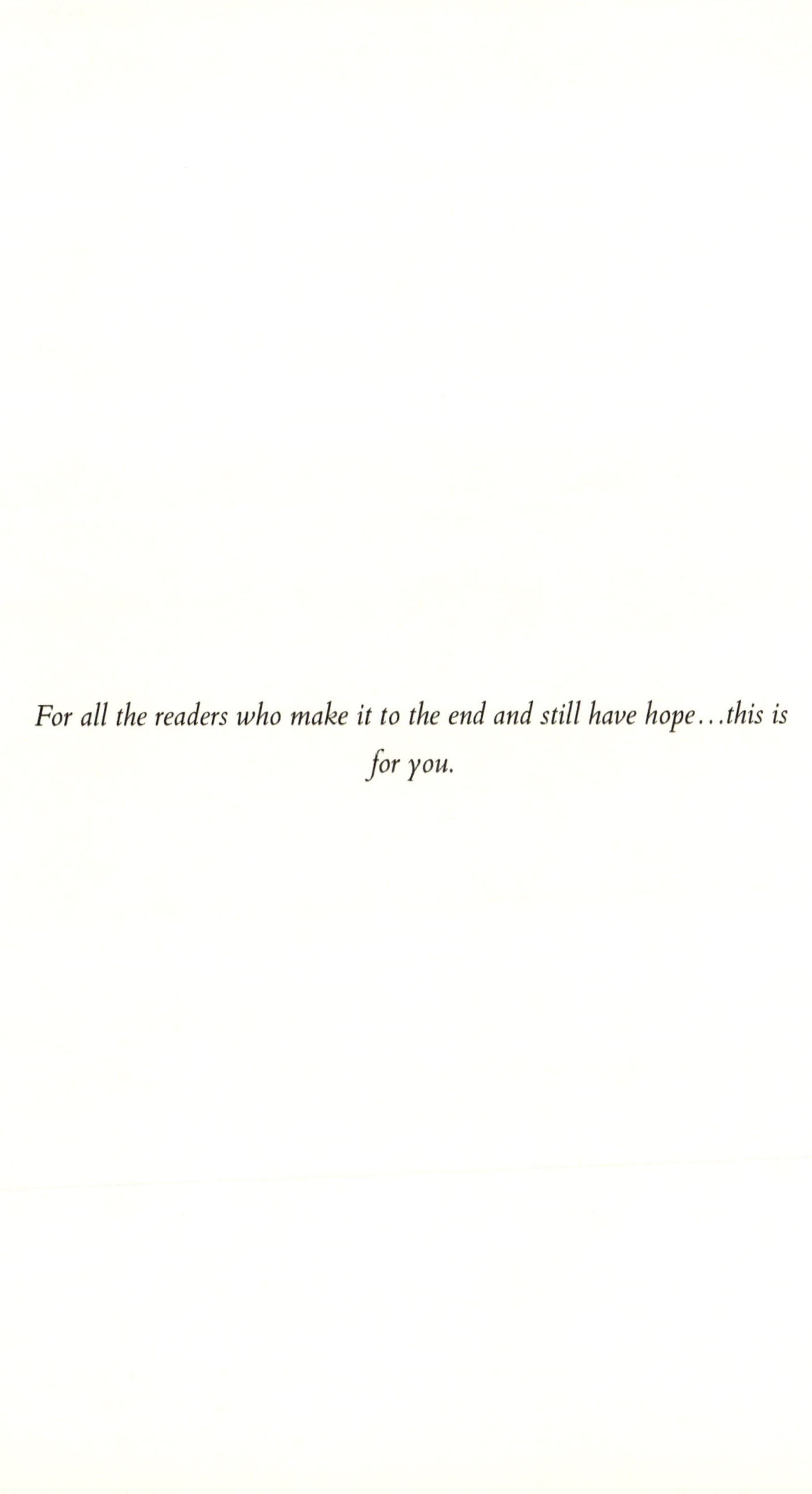

For all the readers who make it to the end and still have hope…this is for you.

PART ONE
AZALEA JINX AND THE HUMANS

CHAPTER 1

"Retrieve a child of jinx, or be forlorn.
Retrieve a child of jinx, and a savior will be yours."
-Prophesy found inside Seer Arabella Cane's prophetic journals,
106 B.G.

My story doesn't start with a happy memory because I haven't had one of those in over fifteen years. Not a single one.

I know I was happy at *some* point; I haven't always felt like a blank sheet of paper waiting to be written on. I remember some of those emotions, remember what it meant to *feel*.

Maybe when I met my ex-husband, Neil, I thought I was happy, or perhaps I thought he would be the one to give me happiness. But, honestly, how am I supposed to feel anything except misery in this miserable state surrounded by such miserable people?

For most, Florida is a vacation state, a place to go when you want to do something fun or lounge around on a beach, but when you live here, you realize how horrible things are. The people are certifiably insane, with the bonus of having extremely violent streaks. I can't even begin to count the number of times I've been threatened or approached by creepy old men who are trying to pay for some truly disturbing things.

Also, this place is hot. Like, unbearably hot. It's one of the reasons I chose to stay here: I want extremes. I'm beginning to think that the heat isn't for me, though. Maybe if I go somewhere unbearably cold, that's what will fix me. Because, clearly, the heat isn't doing it. I would love some snow and ice, I would love frozen fingertips. Anything to feel *something*.

It's not that I don't feel, the problem is the only emotions left inside of me are ones that I don't want controlling me. I don't feel remorse and have most certainly never felt regret, but emotions like anger, jealousy, and boredom reign my sentimental spectrum. When those are the only things you can feel, you become desperate to find something good: desperate enough to try every drug, to sleep around with anyone who sparks your interest even though you are married, to drink every type of alcohol in existence. Desperate enough to kill.

My therapist says I should accept the fact that I will never feel again. She even believes I never felt anything at all. *But I did.* The diagnosis I receive most often is sociopath, though I've also been told I'm bipolar, have depression, and am a psychopath…among other things. I've been offered countless medications, medications I was willing to try early on in life. None of them worked because I am not what people think I am. *That's* why I'm so fucked up. Knowing I can be more than this shell, this husk…it's made me the exact kind of desperate I don't need to be. Which is why I'm here, in this store, attempting to make my heart race with something that will make me feel good.

I push my cart a little farther in front of me, doing my best to pay attention to my surroundings. It's hard when there are people everywhere; it's distracting. They don't only fill this store, but also this city. I thought Orlando could be different from Miami because it's a landlocked city, which means no beaches and no bitchy people occupying those beaches, but everywhere in this cursed state is the same. There are too many people and not enough room for me.

When I moved here a couple of weeks ago, it was only because it was the first place to pop into my mind. I don't like beaches, or people who do like beaches, so I thought coming here would improve my mood. I was wrong. Hardly anything can excite me anymore, and this city is no exception. If I am being truthful with myself, it was all just an attempt to run away from my memories of Neil.

I stayed in Miami for so long because it is where I was born, despite my hatred for it. It connected me to the past I don't remember, to the parents I don't miss. But it's also where I met Neil. He was a transfer student in our last year of high school, having just moved to allow his mother a fresh start. She ended up becoming some big-shot hotel manager and made a decent living after an ugly divorce. It was a *true* fresh start, unlike the sham of one I'm attempting here.

We talked about it next to her son's dead body.

Most people who are high school sweethearts break up pretty quickly, don't they? They go to college and find themselves or something, right? Or maybe find the larger variety a college campus has to offer. Either way, that's not how it happened for us. I guess we got married too fast for that.

Neil and I were engaged by nineteen and married by twenty. Neither of us even thought about college. Neil got a job interning with his mom, and I worked as a bartender at their rival hotel chain. Life was good…I guess. The money was great, but the constant sexual harassment? Not so great.

I shove past an elderly couple, mumbling insincere apologies under my breath even though *they* are the ones standing in the middle of the aisle. People tend to do that in thrift stores. This is the first time I've been in this particular one, and it's a little underwhelming.

I frequently thrift. Being in a new city, I was looking forward to trying new stores. People like this ruin the hunt. I mean, do they just have no spatial awareness?

Neil would not have apologized. He probably would have flipped them off and moved along. My lips turn up at the thought. He didn't care much what other people thought of him. Not that I do, but…I think I have trained myself to be a little nicer. I wear a mask a majority of the time, especially when it comes to social settings. I learned fairly quickly that other people have big feelings, even if I don't, and I honestly don't like dealing with the aftermath of hurting them.

One of the first things that drove me to Neil was that bad boy attitude. He didn't look like one, not by a long shot, but when he opened his mouth…I was a goner. Blonde hair, blue eyes, muscles, no tattoos, no piercings: he looked like the typical jock/golden boy type, but he wore these cool band shirts, talked about a variety of music and books our classmates had never heard of, and rode a motorcycle to school every day. To teenage me, that was as bad as it got.

When I married Neil, I didn't think much of it. It was like a formality; it felt like something we were supposed to do, and it felt right. By the end of the first year, I knew it wasn't. I wasn't happy and neither was he, but we were both good at pretending. Quite frankly, I should have never started dating him. Much less married him. It was selfish of me, but I was selfish enough to not care. Why? Well, there's one major flaw about me that I never got around to telling Neil about.

I'm cursed.

And I don't mean cursed in a hoodoo voodoo kind of way. I mean legit cursed. Hence the last name, *Jinx*. When we married, I took his last name: Wilder. Azalea Wilder just doesn't sound as good as Azalea Jinx, though. Not that it matters now. Technically, I'm a widow and am, once again, Azalea Jinx. I would have become a Jinx again, anyway, seeing as we were almost officially divorced by the time he died.

I'm not sure what, exactly, pushed us over the edge. We just weren't right for each other anymore. Neil was happy here, happy with his mediocre life in Florida surrounded by mediocrity. But I wanted to leave. Not necessarily to travel, but to *go* somewhere. Anywhere. Preferably somewhere cold.

He tried to tell me I was never going to be happy with anything in life if I wasn't happy with myself. He was probably right. But how was I ever going to find happiness if he was holding me back? He didn't want to leave, he didn't want things to change. He wanted me to be a doting and loving wife, wanted me to give him kids and raise them while he was off working. I couldn't do that. I think the no-kids thing was too much, in the end. He didn't know about my curse and didn't understand my urgency. If he had, everything would have fallen apart.

I wasn't surprised when he died; everyone around me always dies. Like I said, I'm cursed.

My parents were brutally murdered when I was five years old. Then, poof, I'm put into the foster system. I barely remember my parents, so I can't say I'm sad about the whole situation. I do remember every foster family, however. At first, I was placed with an aunt. But she fell down the stairs at the age of fifty-three and died, too. Then it was a great-grandmother of some sort who was pushing ninety. Honestly, my curse was probably doing her a favor. By that time, I had forgone being happy, and even my sadness was draining away. The next foster was a distant cousin, but she choked on something or another and ascended to the celestial plane within weeks of my arrival. Her death mattered little in my mind, as I could no longer form attachments. I couldn't love anyone, including myself. On and on it went until, eventually, no one was willing to take the emotionally damaged kid in anymore. No actual family, anyway.

The social worker I was assigned to never revealed the truth to my foster families. The only information they received was that I had dead parents and no family to speak of. My curse didn't pass them by, though, despite their ignorance. Luckily, not everyone I encountered died. There were a few house fires, some kids with broken bones, and most often near-deaths. So, yeah. It got to the point where I was only making it mere months before being swapped into another family. Good thing there's an endless amount of people in this state, huh?

My curse warned me over and over and over again that I was not allowed to love, not allowed to have close friends, not allowed to have family, and especially not allowed to have a relationship. It is a burden I carry on my shoulders, a heaviness that weighs me down. Death and I may be friends, but it's a toxic relationship. One only I suffer the consequences of. I stupidly let myself believe otherwise, had convinced myself I had this grand opportunity to fall in love, to have someone fill my emptiness. And now Neil is dead because of it.

Neil was too young to die, but he did. Dying at twenty-two years old? It's a tragedy, plain and simple. But the way he died? It made the situation ten times worse. He was hit by a car while crossing the street, and the officials tried to comfort us by saying it was fast. As if that's any comfort. Just because I wasn't in love with him didn't mean I wanted him to die. I cared for him, in my own way. Even if that care was just a selfish thing meant to benefit me. Dying in that way…it was a damn shame.

Being a twenty-two-year-old widow is kind of funny, in a macabre sense. I should have been a twenty-two-year-old divorcee, which is just pathetic. Instead, I got to stand next to a dead body and listen to a dozen handfuls of people tell me how great the man I was separated from was and how they understood my pain. But they didn't understand anything about him and me, and I will have to take that information to my own grave.

Neil had life insurance; a small blessing. It was enough to cover the cost of his funeral and his burial, but that was about it. The last thousand or so left I used to move here. I couldn't afford to move across the country like I dream of, so I decided to stay in the all-to-familiar state. I was in a rush to leave Miami. I had to get away from the stuffy city that held me in its damp grasp. I needed new scenery, new people, new everything. Neil wasn't the emotional booster I had hoped for, so I went looking for something that would be.

Unfortunately, it all still feels the same. Sure, I don't have to look at the fridge we bought together or the couch I lost my virginity to him on. I don't have to walk the same street he died on, and I don't have to look at all of the places we would visit together. But everyone here looks and acts the same. It all just feels like one big joke. I sold every single item I owned to start over here and, really, I'm right back where I started:

Desperate to have the one thing that may never be returned to me.

I found a job as a waitress pretty quickly, but I don't get the same tips a bartender does. It was so easy to trick drunk people into paying me more, and I never felt the least bit guilty. But, hey, how much money can you place on not having drunks grabbing your ass and their wives throwing drinks in your face? It's barely enough to make ends meet at this point, but I can't bring myself to care. It's still better than being around everything that reminds me of him. Reminding me of the failure that the whole situation was.

Now that I don't have to worry about Neil screaming at me for it, I can start saving every extra penny to *really* leave. To go to the cold and lonely place I dream of. To never worry about death following me again. One day, I'm going to do it.

I'm going to escape.

I blink away all of my foggy thoughts, deciding to focus on the task at hand: refurbishing my apartment. These thrift stores are the only efficient way to do it within my budget, not that I mind. I like a good thrift haul. Old books, old clothes, old trinkets. There are just certain items that call to me, that provide me with this tiny rush I will do anything to obtain. Everything I find is a thrill, especially when it's a good deal. Lately, it's the only thing that has sparked the spot within me that I think used to be filled with emotions. Damn, that's pathetic. And maybe a little psychotic.

Ah, here it is. The furniture section. I wrinkle my nose at the floral couch that greets me, ignoring the stained wooden dresser next to it. There's a cute kitchen table that looks a little Gothic, but…ah, yeah. Two hundred dollars is not in the budget. My eyes trail to the mirror propped up against one of its legs.

Immediately, I feel the familiar tug, the stirring in my chest that occurs when I find objects that call to me. It's a large standing mirror, one that had clearly been someone's DIY project. Whoever did it knew what they were doing, though; a professional crafter. Some of the shiny black frame still pokes out from beneath a jumble of moss, mushrooms, and flowers that adorn it, hinting at its identity before becoming this masterpiece. The butterflies dancing across it look so *real*. I can't stop myself from reaching out to touch it, can't help but lift it into my arms. I abandon my empty cart to head to the register, not even bothering to check the price tag. This mirror is calling to me. It is meant to be *mine*.

Maybe I'm drawn to it because I have its replica tattooed on my thigh.

Neil always thought I was odd for the strange tattoos inked into my skin. I don't think I'm odd at all. Strange things happen to me a lot, and I truly believe there are no such things as coincidences in this world. I have had dreams about every tattoo that adorns my body, inspiration for the pieces of art I have chosen to forever be a part of me. I've only ever had the privilege to see my dreams in real life a few times before, and I know better than to ignore signs such as this.

The lady at the register barely looks at me as I approach, only glancing at the white tag briefly before pushing a few buttons. The machine beeps a couple of times, annoying both me and her. Finally, after a much too long silence, she calls for a manager over the radio.

"What's wrong?" I shift my feet, lowering the mirror gently to the ground. Has someone already bought it and has yet to pick it up? There were no 'sold' tags placed on it. I didn't miss a sign or something, did I?

"Price discrepancy." She shrugs, popping a bubble in her gum before looking me up and down with a sneer. "Your hair is weird."

"Thanks, I guess?" I reach up absentmindedly to touch it, twirling a purple lock around my finger. Currently, I have it streaked with two different colors. A few chunks colored amethyst purple, a few my natural dark brown. I run my finger through my bangs, fixing them across my forehead neatly like they are supposed to be. I guess picking up the mirror dislodged them. I wouldn't necessarily call my hair weird, especially considering the amount of actual weirdness I see every day, but to each their own I suppose. I've had worse insults thrown at me over the bright colors I put in my hair.

"What's the problem?" The manager, I'm assuming, approaches with a forced smile. He glances between the employee and me, suspicion in his eyes. It's not an unusual reaction to my appearance. Colorful hair, septum and eyebrow piercings, covered in tattoos? Recipe for trouble, obviously.

"Price discrepancy." The lady repeats herself. I glance down at her name tag, which reads "Hannah".

"Tag labeled wrong?"

"Yeah, the computer is pulling up the price as one hundred ten, but the tag says twenty-five. That can't be right." Hannah's bland eyes squint over at me.

"That's a pretty large difference." The manager turns to me again, eyebrows raised and hands crossed across his chest. "You didn't switch tags, did you?"

"How could I have? These are the stickers that rip apart when you try to remove them. No damage, see?" My heart begins to pound as I point to the sticker, realization dawning. I'm about to get this mirror for way, way less than it's worth. Shit, this is *exactly* what I was searching for today.

Sometimes, when items like this call to me, I get anywhere from seconds to minutes of my heart racing in only the best of ways. I've felt pangs of excitement, pangs of joy, pangs of giddiness. It's the reason I continue to thrift, the reason I stay on the hunt for those special items. And this mirror? This mirror is one of them.

"Yeah, you're right. Huh. Well, someone fucked up the stickers, I guess. Probably Lucinda. She's as dumb as a box of rocks." He scratches his scrappy beard, reaching out for the register. "Well, anyway, sorry for the trouble. We honor the stickers. Here, I'll authorize a price change." He doesn't seem to want to change the price, but his fingers begin to move despite the bitter attitude.

I watch in utter astonishment as he reaches over and swipes his employee card, typing in the new number. I'm practically shaking with shock as I pull out my wallet, slipping the girl a twenty and a ten. The manager sighs in resignation, leaving us to handle the rest of the transaction. Soon, my change is in my wallet and I am walking down the street toting a genuine grin and an enormous mirror.

My new apartment isn't far, and I don't own a car, or know how to drive, so I walk at a leisurely pace. With so many people crowding the streets, I don't want to risk bumping into someone and breaking my new prize. But no one touches me the whole way back. Some gawk and glare, but none get close enough to worry about endangering the mirror.

I struggle to pull my keys out of my pocket, silently thanking myself for choosing an apartment on the ground floor. My hands are slick with sweat, my body aching from the effort it took to walk what should have been fifteen minutes—with my slow pace, it was more like thirty. But I manage to get the key out after wiping my palms on my shirt, drying them enough to grab it and slip it into the lock. I kick the door open with a grunt, listening to its creak as I begin to shove the mirror inside. It's a tight fit, but fit it does.

I take it to my bedroom, which is just a corner in this studio apartment, and place it next to my closet, grinning again as I step back to admire its beauty. *It's perfect.* There aren't a whole lot of things in this room that scream "me", but this is one of them. It's the perfect height, standing at around five and a half feet. It's perfect because it's only a few inches taller than me, meaning I can see my whole body in it at all times. Staring into it now, I can see my shoulder-length waves, my dark brown eyes, the gap in my two front teeth, and even my squishy cheeks.

Well, maybe this mirror is a little too perfect, considering it has no problem showing me all of my imperfections. I frown at the sunburn on my shoulders, at the freckles dancing haphazardly all over my body. I'm so tan you would *think* the fuckers would disappear, but no. They are still here, prominent features beneath the flaky red skin. Florida's sunshine is the one positive thing it can offer, and it still has no use to me.

I sigh, turning away from the new piece of furniture. The brief excitement I had has faded, replaced by the nothingness that resides within me. I suppose now that the high is over, I should make something to eat and shower, preferably before the storms hit tonight. By the time they reach me, I plan on being laid out in bed and ready to fall asleep to the soothing noises rattling around outside.

CHAPTER 2

"You will find the jinx in a mirror of duality,
only then will redemption become a reality."
—Recovered notes from the prophetic journals of Seer Scott
Killinger, 032 A.G.

Thunder reverberates throughout the room, a single bolt of lightning flashes in the night sky outside of the tiny window across from me. Usually, storms like this all but ensure I will be out like a light but, for some reason, I am still awake and staring at the ceiling as if it is the most interesting thing in the world.

Another boom of thunder shakes the bed, and I mutter profanities under my breath as I throw the black comforter to the end of the mattress, swing my legs over, and push myself up. It isn't hard considering I'm only a few inches above the carpet; a bed frame isn't in the budget right now.

My feet pad across the harsh carpet and toward the fridge for some water, and I cringe with each rough touch. I probably shouldn't walk around barefoot in this place. The carpet looks dirty and unclean, and I wouldn't be surprised if there is mold hiding underneath. This apartment was one of the only ones I could afford on my own, so…the mold should keep itself hidden. Out of sight, out of mind, right?

I pause just as I am about to pass my new mirror, a small smirk breaking out as I look it over. Twenty-five dollars! It's utter madness, and yet, I pulled it off. Without putting in much effort, might I add? All it took was a half-hour walk and a little heavy lifting.

I reach out to touch it one more time, still chasing the memory of that rush. Just as my fingertips graze the mirror, another bolt of lightning cracks across the sky. I jump, pulling away and shaking my hand. I swear it just shocked me! Maybe the moss carries friction inside of it?

I carry on with my journey to find water, leaving the mirror behind for a moment. When I come back, there's something different about it. Its new vibe is making the hairs on the back of my neck stand at full attention. It's the same feeling you get when you know a man is following you through the store, watching your every move, and trying to find out if you're alone. Yeah, that kind of creepy vibe. But I shrug it off, draining my glass before falling back into bed with an amused grunt.

As if anyone can see me through a *mirror*.

Getting ready for work is always a depressing event.

I hold my uniform in front of me, frowning at myself in the mirror. Long skirt, long sleeves, and an ugly little apron to go along with it. I hate it; it's not flattering whatsoever. But it pays the bills, so…

I begin to rid myself of my pajamas, pausing after I pull on the skirt. Something flickers above my shoulders in the mirror, catching my attention, and I squint to get a better look. Is that…is that a pair of *eyes*? There's a familiarity to the eyes, and I'm certain I have seen them before. I spin around, shoving my shirt in front of me like a weapon. I expect to see somebody within mere feet of me, only…

No one is there.

I turn back to the mirror, laughing unamusedly at myself. Fuck. That weird, creepy vibe isn't going away now, is it? I know that there is no possible way there was a pair of eyes in my mirror. *I know it.*

Fucking hell.

Has becoming a widow made me crazy? Why does that always happen? It isn't much of a stretch to think I could be insane, honestly. Is that the next step after becoming empty inside?

I suppose acknowledging I have a problem is the first step to solving that problem.

Despite my reassurances that there are no eyes in the mirror, I can't forget them. I must have a damn good imagination because they were *detailed*. Throughout the day I get flashes of long, blond lashes, of green irises with a pinch of gold around the center, of a singular brown dot in the left eye. Fuck, why were they so *vivid*?

"Thank you!" I chirp to a customer absentmindedly, taking the cash from her hand. "I'll bring back your change."

"Don't bother. Have a good one." Once she is gone, I glance at the bill and the cash. Four dollars and twenty-one cents is my tip. Fucking bitch; that was an eighty-dollar tab. I shove the cash into my apron with an angry sigh, rolling my neck as I stretch. Better than nothing, I guess.

Today has been horrible. It's been a splurge of meaningless interactions, followed by horrendous tips. I think I've made maybe thirty bucks since coming into work six hours ago, but this brings the total to thirty-four dollars and twenty-one cents.

I grab the last empty plate and glass from the table, attempting to slip into the kitchen. I find the entrance blocked by other waitresses all crowding around the computer there.

"Excuse me," I snap irritably, shoving my way through the crowd. I don't see the foot that thrusts out in front of me until it is too late.

Laughter bubbles up around me as I am flung to my hands and knees, followed by the distinct sound of glass shattering. Fucking hell. My hands land in a mysterious liquid on the tiled floor, my knees ache as I glance up. Yep. The plate and cup I had been holding are destroyed, the little pieces they became scattered across the ground.

"Whoops. Sorry, Azalea. Didn't see you there!" a waitress by the name of Lacy says from behind her hand, blinking down at me innocently. Some of the girls may even believe she *is* innocent, but I've seen right through her from the moment I arrived in this hell hole: It's probably why she hates me so much already. Everyone hates the person who sees right through them, the person they can't lie to.

"Azalea!" a new voice barks.

I turn away from Lacy's cold gray eyes and blindingly red hair just as the girls scatter. I sigh, pushing myself up to a squat and rocking on my feet for a few seconds. Then I jump up, dusting my hands on my skirt.

Fuck it all.

"Sorry, Phillip. I tripped."

I have found over the years it's best not to plead your case, best not to argue when someone thinks they're right. It's easier to blend in and be forgiven that way. I don't care about being right or wrong, anyway. It doesn't matter, in the end. The only thing that matters is who has power in the situation and, currently, that isn't me.

"Yeah, I see that. Clean this mess up and go home. You've been off your game all day. I'm not sitting around waiting for another catastrophe to happen here."

"Yeah, alright, I'll just—" I gesture meekly to the mess, grabbing the broom from his outstretched hand. He's right, unfortunately. I *am* off my game. And it has nothing to do with me and everything to do with the paranoia my mirror gifted me this morning.

It doesn't take much effort to clean up the mess, to remove any signs of broken pieces. Soon it's almost as if they never existed in the first place.

Just like the eyes in my mirror.

I shove my hands down into my apron, pulling out all of my tips in Phillip's office. He cashes me out, dutifully handing me what I am owed. As soon as I am able, I'm ripping off that ugly apron and stomping out the door. Two doors down is a tattoo shop, one I've never been to or seen reviews on. But those eyes are haunting me. Not necessarily because I saw them this morning, but because I saw them last night, too.

It took most of the day, but I realized at work why they were so familiar. I dreamed of them, my mind providing vivid imagery of them attached to a faceless body in a far-off place. They are embedding themselves into my brain, and I know the only way to get them out of my head is in a place like this. It's the only way any of my dreams escape my mind: through ink.

"Got any availability right now?" I question as I push into the shop, glancing around the mostly empty space.

"Yeah, actually. You're in luck. I think Don has a couple hours before his next client. Let me ask if he is willing to take you. What were you thinking about having done?" The green-haired girl gestures me forward with the twitch of a finger, pulling out some papers from within her crowded desk.

"This." I plop down a napkin with a drawing of the eyes on it, one I had done in a fevered state on my break with colored pencils.

"How big?"

"I don't know, maybe three inches? Here, let me show you where I want it." I roll up my skirt, pointing at the one empty spot on my right thigh. "I want it to fill in this empty spot here." Right between the dragon and the large Gothic-looking castle, right below the strange image of a mermaid holding a wolf.

"Ah, yeah. I gotcha. That's definitely doable today. Fill out these papers real fast. I'll be right back."

"Cool."

I do as she asked, filling out paperwork with my name and address along with consent forms, confirming I'm not pregnant, on drugs, or drunk right now. When the receptionist comes back, a grumpy bald man is trailing behind her. He glances down at my drawing, back up at me, and takes a puff from his vape.

"One hundred and it's yours."

"Done." I hand them my card, plus most of my tips from today as payment for *his* tip. I don't send him home with the many coins jingling in my apron that even I don't want.

The tattoo takes a full two hours, but I was lucky. The guy is a perfectionist and a damn good artist. He took all of my tips on the coloring, turning areas a little more green or adding touches of gold upon my request. They fit in perfectly among my other tattoos, staring off into the distance with intent. They may have seemed creepy in the mirror, but I've turned them into something not so terrifying.

Not that I can actually *be* scared.

"You a witch or something?" Don slides his chair across the ground as he begins to clean up his station, preparing to wipe my leg. This is the worst part for me. The needle I barely feel, the pain a distant touch. But the paper towels? They mark the end of a session, the end of a brief period where I feel more than empty. That's more painful than any needle could ever hope to be.

"Nah. Just dream like one," I say, glancing down at the tattoos splattered across my legs. A lot of people assume I'm a witch. I have so many spell-like words, so many symbols, so many *weird* things on my skin. I don't know what all of the words mean, don't know what the symbols represent, but I dreamed of them, so I put them here, taking them from fantasy to real life. It's the only way they will get out of my head and out of my dreams.

Neil always called it my version of a dream journal.

"Well, you're good to go. Come back whenever." He grins as he wipes my leg. I don't ask him to wrap it: I prefer airing them out and coating them in lotion. Sometimes I have weird skin reactions to that latex stuff most places use.

Night has fallen now, but I don't mind walking alone in the dark: I carry pepper spray and know way too many defensive moves. Mostly, people tend to leave me alone, anyway. There's no particular reason I'm aware of, so maybe I'm just lucky. Maybe I'm not pretty enough to bother with, or my resting bitch face is a deterrent.

"Good evening, Azalea!" a neighbor two doors down calls out with a wave as I approach my door. I try to smile shyly to hide my annoyance, waving back and pushing my bangs out of my eyes. I don't remember her name, but I do recall her nosiness.

"Thought you would have been home by now," she continues despite my lack of a response, blowing cigarette smoke in my direction.

See? Nosy.

"Worked a couple extra hours, needed some more money for new furniture." I fake a light laugh in response, picking up my pace. I can see her lips press together lightly as she thinks, and I decide not to give her a chance to respond. I'm unlocking the door and slipping into my apartment before she can determine it is a lie.

"Ugh. Home sweet home." I practically crawl toward my bed, stripping off my uniform as I go. At least tomorrow is my day off.

I can wash this disgusting, smelly outfit and maybe even get the oil stain out of my skirt.

My skin prickles in awareness as I pass the mirror, but I ignore it. I need a shower and fresh clothes to even think about this again. So, that's what I do. By the time I'm pulling a clean sleeping shirt and pajama shorts out, I feel much better. I finger the fluffy fabric on my thighs, glancing over my shoulder at the "I heart Neil" graphic stretching across my butt in the mirror. I snort, shaking my head. I really shouldn't be wearing these, but…well, he's dead, so it's not like he can care about it anymore.

I turn around, fully facing my beautiful mirror once more. I went on the internet during dinner and found several forums talking about hidden cameras in their used items, so that's what I'm going to look for. Maybe that's what is setting off the alarm bells in my mind.

I gently run my hands along the moss, pressing my face close as I feel for any abnormalities. I feel every nook and cranny this thing has to offer, praying I'm wrong about this. So far, I am. Could there be a camera hiding behind the glass? I've heard of things like that happening in those bed-and-breakfast places you rent through an app. I may be seeing a mirror, but a camera may be seeing *me*.

I take a deep breath, trying to remember what I'm supposed to do. Should I knock on it and see if it is hollow? Isn't there some trick that involves pressing your finger to it or something? Fuck, what is that rule? I should start paying more attention to those crazy posts people put on social media about these exact types of situations.

I reach out, tapping my knuckles lightly against the glass. No, it doesn't sound hollow. Tentatively, I press my finger to its center. Now what? What's the next step?

"Ah—!" My scream barely comes into existence before it's snuffed out. The surface of the mirror ripples like water as a hand stretches out to meet mine. The rough, calloused hand grips my wrist, tight and painful. I don't have time to jerk away. The hand tugs on mine harshly and I am tumbling, crashing through the mirror in one horrifying moment.

Plummeting toward the impossible.

CHAPTER 3

"The first known Grim sighting occurred 2024 years ago, believed to have been created by a necromancer and a Seer who performed unsanctioned experiments. Once the Grim came into existence, an evil plagued this world with it. Thus, from that point on, any time that passed would be known as After the Grim (A.G.) The years before are simply Before the Grim (B.G.). We hope to one day be rid of these terms altogether and to peacefully rejoice when the Grim no longer rules over us all."

—*A Guide to the Charmed* (current edition), written by Glamourist Elias Kasper in 1907 A.G.

This is fucking disgusting.

The sensation I am experiencing is like treading through a thick liquid, or maybe struggling to get out of a riptide. I can still feel the calloused grip on my arm, and I swing as I attempt to dislodge it. I scream as I struggle, gurgling in the absence of air. Am I really about to drown in a mirror? Is this how my cursed life ends? In a cold, wet, sticky substance?

After what seems to be an entirely too slow death, I emerge, gasping for air, on what I can only assume is the other side of the mirror. I should be wet and dripping, should at least have evidence of that awful substance on my clothes or in my hair, but I am utterly dry.

I trip and fall as my assailant releases me from their grip. I clutch my throat with both hands as I cough, struggling to breathe. I feel this horrible, slimy thing sliding around inside of my throat, assisting in my breathlessness as it occupies a large majority of the space in which it is confined. Ah. There's my evidence. A giant glob of silver goo is now on the floor, freshly dislodged from my esophagus. Damn, that's disgusting.

"Should have closed your mouth." The cold, sneering voice brings me back to reality. I snap my mouth shut, head jerking up as I sneer right back. Those eyes…I would recognize them anywhere.

"Where am I? Who are you? Did you seriously just fucking kidnap me?" I pull myself up to a standing position, chest heaving. I can barely look at him, can hardly allow myself the pleasure. Because it *is* a pleasure.

I already knew about the gorgeous green eyes, but the rest of him? Yeah, that's gorgeous, too. His hair might be considered less blond and more white, and it's styled in one of those ways meant to exude the 'no effort' effect despite everyone knowing it most certainly did. Sharp features, a crooked smile, perfectly white teeth. Oh, and tall. However, most people are tall compared to me. Neil was only about five and a half feet, but this guy? He's probably pushing six feet. And *fuck* is he huge. With just a glance, I know that I do not want to get on his bad side. Though considering I have been kidnapped, I might need to put up a fight. Maybe I should think about my options here, because, well, he *is* hot. And not in a 'cute sorority boy' or 'rugged country boy' way like the majority of guys in Florida. No, he's cute in a 'will wreck your life and you will be the one apologizing to *him* for it' kind of way.

"Jaymes Bloodgood, at your service." He does a dramatic bow, peering at me under those luscious lashes in amusement. His uniform crinkles with the movement, a black suit of sorts with a strange logo printed on the jacket pocket. For fuck's sake, did he really just bow? And is that a dragon wearing a crown on his suit jacket?

"Like 'blood is good'?" I attempt my best vampire accent while holding up fingers for teeth, adding on, "You know, 'bleh bleh bleh'?"

I should hold my tongue here, considering I was just kidnapped and all. Shouldn't I be more panicked? I definitely should be. Though, to be honest, he'll probably just die soon and this little problem will be solved. That's on him for not researching a girl whose last name is literally Jinx.

I glance around as he stays silent, taking in my surroundings. I pause, squinting at the familiar environment. This is my room…but not. Everything here is slightly out of place. Almost…mirrored. And everything has this weird shine to it as if to warn me they aren't real. A mirrored room after being dragged through a mirror? How original.

How did he pull this off? Shit, there *was* a camera in that mirror! And I definitely hadn't imagined his eyes watching me. He had to have drugged me to keep me calm, and that would explain what's happening right now. There's no other way I could hallucinate the mirror-travel.

I ignore the silver goo on the ground that contradicts this version of the story.

"You're going to die, you know?" I shrug confidently, deter-minedly. If he plans on keeping me hostage here, he might as well know the truth. Maybe he will have the good sense to return me where he found me whenever he realizes I am serious.

"We all die." He brushes it off easily, stepping around me to glance out the window. "And don't worry, I've been told about your issues." I follow his line of sight, heart dropping with the first hint of fear I've had in a very long time. Wherever I am, it isn't Florida.

"Where am I?" I repeat my earlier question, voice cracking despite my best efforts.

There is snow outside. Actual snow! The sun is barely visible behind gray, gray clouds. We seem to be high up; there are rows upon rows of trees down below alongside rather large buildings. I can see people walking around out there, groups crossing over paths, entering and exiting buildings in patterns. In the distance, the trees begin to drop, as if this place sits up on a high hill. If I hadn't been kidnapped, I would be thrilled. This is the exact type of environment I have been desperate to find. Small, secluded, cold.

It's a dream come true, and a nightmare come to life.

"Welcome to the Draxmere Academy of Conjuring."

"Academy of Conjuring? Is this some kind of fancy mental asylum or something? Fuck, is that why I'm imagining all of this crazy stuff? What kind of drugs did you give me? Was it the nosy fucking neighbor who turned me in?"

Maybe he didn't kidnap me after all. That would be a relief, considering how attractive he is. He's definitely my type…if I was allowed to have a type, that is.

"It's a school." Jaymes scoffs, turning to face me again. "A very prestigious one. One you have been graciously accepted into despite not being qualified. If it were up to me, I would have let you continue to rot in the human world. But it wasn't, so here we are."

"The human world?" A forced laugh bubbles up, disbelief filling my features. Okay, maybe I was wrong on all accounts. Maybe this is a prank show of some kind.

"Okay, where are the cameras?" I spin around, throwing my hands up dramatically. Surely, they have to be here somewhere. Wherever they are, they hid them well. I'm not sure why I was chosen for this, but at least it'll make for a good story down the road. *Hey, do you want to hear about the time I was kidnapped for a prank show?*

"Cameras? No, I don't think you quite understand the situation." The genuine annoyance on his face halts my tracks, uncertainty swirling inside of me. Yeah, he's being serious. He fully believes whatever bullshit he's about to spew.

"Alright, explain it to me then, fucker." I'm getting angry now. It's the one true emotion I still have a grip on, and it loves to make an appearance. And I mean, *fuck*, he did kidnap me!

I think.

"Based on your reaction, I am assuming that you haven't heard of Draxmere. Surely you have heard of Conjurers? You can't be that daft, can you?"

"Well, I—"

"Dear Grim, you are that daft." He scowls, interrupting my nonanswer. "How you made it this far, I'll never understand."

"Shut the fuck up and give me the crash course," I hiss back, annoyed.

Jaymes pauses, pursing his lips in annoyance before saying, "Draxmere is a school where the species known as the Charmed go to hone their abilities. Most of us are pretty good with our powers by the time we make it this far, but there is always room for development. In our time here we learn to increase the strength of those powers, increase range, and increase the magnitude of what we do. It's done through Charms, through practice, and through lots of skill. You'll find some of your classmates possess more power than others. The amount of power we possess is known as Charm Levels, and those levels differ between individuals.

"Humans attend high school and then go to college, right? This is our college. Well, a college where you would be earning an advanced degree. Students start around your age and typically have graduated and accepted high-paying positions by twenty-five. You have been accepted into this school, and will be allowed to study and hone in on your abilities here should you have enough.

"So, no, there are no cameras. No, I did not kidnap you. No, I did not drug you. What you have seen so far is real, and you haven't seen half of what this campus has to offer. Unfortunately for us both, I was chosen to retrieve you. Now, if you will follow me, I can take you to the Dean. She has requested to see you upon arrival and will provide more information." Jaymes spins on his heels, turning toward the door. He walks out at a brisk speed, not concerned with whether or not I actually follow him.

"Wait!" I sprint after him into the hall, ignoring the snickers and laughs that follow. Shit, I'm still in my "I Heart Neil" shorts!

Jaymes doesn't bother to turn around or acknowledge me, only continues at the same quick pace. Doesn't he realize I need more than a few seconds to process this kind of information? I'm still pretty sure I've been drugged. I had to have been. Because this talk of powers and the human world? It's all a lie. A beautifully crafted lie coming from even more beautiful lips. What does he get out of this, anyway? And why am I still chasing after him? What is *wrong* with me?

"You're confused and have no other options," Jaymes states in a bored tone. Shit, I said that out loud.

"*Fuck you.*" I pant. I really don't need to make the pretty kidnapper angry. Really, really, really don't need to.

As we continue down the hall, I come to the understanding that this place is gigantic. I half expect to see moving staircases or ghosts flying through the walls based on Jaymes's description of the place. Everything is normal, though. Well, as normal as things can be in a supposedly magical school.

I wish I had been smart enough to attempt to remember the path, smart enough to think about retracing my steps. By the time the thought enters my mind, it is too late. We are already getting farther and farther away from the witnesses hanging out in the halls.

The inside of this school is mostly stone, which I find rather odd. It's a cold and slated gray, with faux torches posted every few feet. Weird tapestries hang between the gigantic array of doors, the weirdest being a topless mermaid slamming her luminous tail into a skeleton that's holding a ball of flame. Chandeliers hang above us, dramatic and gauzy, but bright.

After passing what seems to be a hundred doors, we begin to descend a spiral staircase that comes straight from a movie: Sleek black steps accompanied by a black handrail with swirling floral patterns. Little stained windows show me glimpses of the outside world on our way down, dozens upon dozens of snowflakes coming in and out of my vision.

We descend close to three flights of stairs before hitting the bottom and turning to exit through a giant hole in the wall. After only walking a few more feet, Jaymes stops abruptly.

"Here we are. Dean Delarosa's office." He rolls the 'r' in her name playfully, smirking at me. "Have fun, human. Don't let her eat you on your way out."

I throw my hand up at his receding figure, flipping him off. He returns the favor.

I turn my attention to the large door in front of me, raising my hand hesitantly to knock. This door looks like all the others: black, wooden, and old. The only difference is the name tag on the front reading "Dean's Office". Not even her name is present here. But this is where Jaymes said to knock, so I let my knuckles tap against the wood. I receive an answer before I can lift my hand a second time.

"Come in!"

The female voice is strong, authoritative, and in control. Once upon a time, I would have gulped and panicked as my nerves cascaded down in a flurry. But it's been a long time since I've had to deal with teachers and principals, and they no longer have the same effect on me they once did. If this is even real, I mean. I'm still not convinced there isn't a camera crew following me around secretly. Slowly, I open the door and enter the room.

"Uh, yeah, hi? You're supposed to be the Dean, right? The one who wanted to see me?" I glance around in surprise at my surroundings, the first thing catching my eye is the small size of the room.

For a Dean, her office is tiny. There's enough space to fit a long desk, a few filing cabinets, a couple of uncomfortable-looking chairs, and a glass cabinet full of little trinkets. Papers litter the wall-length mahogany desk in a disorganized pile, a couple of monitors blinking toward the Dean. With a flourish, she pushes all of the papers to the side and pulls herself out of a brown cushioned chair with a bright smile. I can't help but flinch back in surprise at the sharp teeth that flash inside of her mouth.

"Dean Delarosa, at your service." She bows the same way Jaymes had, amusement twinkling in her eyes.

"Right. Well, I'm—"

"Oh, I know exactly who you are. Please, have a seat." She gestures between the two chairs in front of her desk before plopping back down into her own. Black curls bounce off of her shoulders with the motion, sharp black eyes watching me carefully. My own eyes trail to her unblemished, tattoo-free, honeyed skin, and I make a noise of appreciation. Reluctantly, I listen to the pretty woman and take a seat in the chair on the right, thinking of its resemblance to a chair my great-grandmother had owned as I do so.

I blow my bangs out of my eyes, saying, "Um, okay, listen. I think this is some kind of misunderstanding. I get it, you guys think this is a funny joke or whatever. I don't. I don't know how you guys pulled a prank of this magnitude off, but you must be some high-end show with a great budget. Also, you can't just fucking drug and kidnap people. You'll be lucky if I decide not to press charges or sue. This is not okay—"

"A joke, hmm? What, do you think that this is some reality TV show? That someone's going to pop out and point at all the hidden cameras as soon as you start to believe us?"

"Well, yes, actually. That's exactly what I think." That or I'm officially losing my mind.

Her harsh laugh sends a chill down my spine, and it's what finally forces reality on me: this isn't an elaborate prank.

"No, my friend. No, this is not a joke. I wish it were, for your sake. But luck is on your side, I do believe, because you are blessed by your genetics."

"Yeah, now I really know you have the wrong girl. Look, can't you just, like, wipe my memories, send me home, and make everything fine? I won't tell anyone about any of this, because no one would believe it anyway. I swear I won't tell."

I know it must sound cheesy, but what else am I supposed to say? They seriously fucked up by grabbing the wrong girl and I'm about to fall into some deep shit when they realize it. I'm a good fighter, but how can you fight off magic people? Easy: you don't. You just beg for your life and hope they don't want to play with you.

"Your parents died when you were five." She leans back, popping a mint into her mouth after the matter-of-fact statement. Her wolfy smile reappears, and another shudder racks through my body with it. Maybe Jaymes wasn't joking about trying not to get eaten.

"Yeah, and? How do you know about that, anyway?" My defenses rise as I watch her pull a file out of one of the drawers in her desk, plopping it down neatly in between us. The *thwack* reverberates in my ears, my eyes wide as I stare down at the folder. "Does that say 'Jinx'?"

"Oh, yeah. Lots of information on mom and pops in here. Information about their death and the daughter they left behind. They made quite an impact on our community. I remember them well. A strange pairing, albeit a powerful one."

"Well, then, I'm glad *someone* remembers them." It's barely a whisper, my eyes unable to stray from the bold lettering on the file.

"You don't remember your parents?" Dean Delarosa sits up straighter now, eyes crinkling in confusion. "You don't know about us at all? About your prophesies?"

"Why would I know about a magical college that kidnaps people or their supposed prophesies?" I can't stop the gurgling, disbelieving laugh that escapes me. Is she for real right now?

I continue to laugh, despite it not being genuine. As long as I pretend to find it funny I won't have to find it terrifying. If that could even happen, anyway. Fear is an emotion I can live without perfectly fine, so I'd rather not have that be my first toe-dip back into the world of feeling.

"I thought that when you were talking about it being a joke TV show you meant you felt like getting accepted was a joke. Like you felt unworthy to be here. Now it's clear I was mistaken and that I have misunderstood the situation entirely."

"You had a guy kidnap me from my apartment." I screech angrily, laughter dying out abruptly. "And you think I was just like 'Oh, wow! I've finally been accepted into college!' Why would that have been my first thought? I didn't ask to be here. I certainly didn't apply. How did you even find me?"

"We were informed many years ago by our Seers that we would need to 'retrieve the child of Jinx', so we did. We had to if we wanted to ensure your prophecies would come true. We didn't—I didn't realize you would be so woefully uneducated about our world, our people. But that's okay. I can still work with that. We will train you as a proper Conjurer, mark my words." She goes from confused and worried to sure and determined in a matter of seconds. Like I am an untrained dog she is ready to beat discipline into.

"Fuck to the no. Seers? Conjurers? Prophecies? I don't know what the fuck any of that means, lady, but I'm not staying here. I want to go home."

"Oh, is there someone waiting for you at home?" She crosses her arms across her chest, raising an eyebrow expectantly. "Well, go on. I'm waiting."

"I'm not telling you anything about myself." I don't plan on willingly admitting all that waits for me is a miserable little apartment in an even more miserable city. That I have no friends, no family, no lover. That not even a houseplant waits for me. She doesn't need to know about any of that.

"That's okay. You don't have to. I can see the look in your eyes, and I've read the notes Jaymes provided after he surveilled you these past days. There's *nothing* in that world waiting for you, is there?" I look away, hating the satisfaction in her voice. "I don't need the details. I don't want to pry. You are an adult and I will treat you as such, but answer me this: Do you feel hollow? Do you feel like you aren't satisfied with your life? Like there is something more that you just can't find? Do you feel like there's something inside of you that no one else has? Does it keep you away from people? Do you prevent yourself from making meaningful connections because, well, what's the point? You are different from everyone and *no one* will ever understand, so why bother trying? Does any of that sound familiar? Am I getting close to hitting the nail on the head?"

I take a deep breath as I try to hold in my anger, try to control the urge to leap across this desk. Was I signed up for some preemptive therapy session or something? The Dean read me like an open book. How? How does she know all of those things? Things that hide deep inside of my mind, dark thoughts that I have hidden almost my whole life? Thoughts that have led me to do crazy, stupid things. I've held a gun to my head just to see if I could still be scared, have stood on tall buildings to see if my heart would leap. I didn't do any of it because I wanted to die, but because I wanted to *live*. I could never figure out why no one else had the same empty thing that burrowed itself down inside the hole it had carved within my chest.

But she knows all about it.

Is it because she is right? Is it because I *do* belong here? Does everyone here feel the same things as me?

Reluctantly, a single word passes across my tongue. "Yes."

"We would all feel that way in the absence of our powers, Azalea. The human world stifles them and hides them away. It's one of the things we train for here at the Academy. The human world possesses this natural sort of barrier, a shield of sorts. It can be worked around, but not without training. That's why we teach you how to control your powers even through repression, so when you are sent on missions to the human world, you don't have to feel that way. Or, at least, you don't have to feel it for long. You are a Conjurer, Azalea.

"It's time for you to find out exactly what that means."

CHAPTER 4

"In the jinx shall lie
a curse of death exchanged for a breath of life.
Bring her here for the fresh air,
bring her here for her soul to repair."
—Prophesy found on Dean Delarosa's desk in 2020 A.G., unknown
origins

I'm given little to no time to process what being a Conjurer means before Dean Delarosa continues, a hopefulness to her voice I am not willing to accept.

"Magic is the thing you've been looking for your whole life. A power that completes you, that fills the crater inside of your chest, something no human could ever understand. It's probably why you weren't able to make many friends."

"I couldn't make friends because I killed them all." I blurt out bitterly, pursing my lips. It isn't a lie, but I shouldn't have said anything. Now she has another vital piece of information to use against me.

"Ah, yes. Your curse. Seers haven't been able to see much about you, we assume because of your distance, but that is one thing that was mentioned. The curse of death, I believe they called it. I have my theories on that."

"Oh?" I perk up, interested. Maybe the curse isn't because of something I did, like I so often like to believe. Maybe all of those deaths aren't completely my fault after all.

"I believe it was your powers manifesting in the human world. They struck out at the nearest target, slowly eating away at the small amount of Charm Levels humans possess as they tried to keep you alive. Charm Levels make up the essence of our two species; without that essence, our lives are forfeit. The human world, while not harmful to their kind, greatly diminishes a Conjurer's levels. If you are there too long, your levels slowly drain away. So the more often someone was around you, touching you…"

"The more power I took from them," I whisper, shocked. The deaths are definitely my fault if that's the case. Unknowingly lashing out at them with some strange, deadly power just to strengthen mine? Yeah, that's for sure on me.

"Don't let it drag you down. It's not your fault your parents abandoned you in the human world." She smiles reassuringly, as if she hadn't just insulted my parents.

"They didn't abandon me. They were fucking murdered. Should they have seen that coming? Should they have consulted a Seer that day to prevent it?" I'm not sure why I'm defending them: I didn't know them. But, well, I guess they *are* still my parents.

"Yes. How very right you are. I'm sorry, I should have been more considerate. The Reapers finally found them after all those years on the run, and unfortunately, living in the human world left them unequipped to deal with such strength. I was very sad to hear about it."

"T—the Reapers?" My parents' murders had gone unsolved. They were brutal and gory, the assailant leaving only enough pieces to identify them, but there was no evidence. Not a trace of DNA anywhere on the scene. Is this why? Did something or someone from this world cross over to kill them? And if so, why?

"I guess it's time I explain to you what, exactly, a Conjurer is and what we are training for, hmm?"

"Yeah, that would be a great start. Probably should have led with that," I murmur in disbelief.

"Our people are known as the Charmed," she says slowly, as if speaking to a child. "Our world, much like the humans, does not have a name. We just are. But to us, they are the human world. Some of us refer to our world as the Charmed world, just to keep things simple when discussing the two. To humans, our world is unnamed as well. This is simply because they do not know of our existence, and we will do everything in our power to ensure they continue to remain unaware.

"Conjuring is the type of magic we perform. Hence, a Conjurer. Now, not all of us are good Conjurers or even powerful ones. For many, it is a learned skill. Like…sports. Some have a natural ability, and once they've trained up a little, that ability is increased to tremendous heights. And, well, some people are simply just not good at sports, despite the amount of training provided."

"So, where do those people go? If they can't make any progress, they aren't of use at a school for powerful Conjurers. So what do you do to them?" I expect her to tell me they are used as slaves, tortured, or even murdered. Instead, she laughs.

"We don't *do* anything to them. They just choose a more peaceful career path. We need people for lots of different jobs, just like humans. Not all jobs require competence in magic."

"Okay," I say slowly, blinking up at her in confusion, "Then why am I here? I'm certainly way below the level of competence in magic required for a school like this, considering I knew nothing about this place until a few minutes ago. I understand my parents have something to do with it, but how do you guys even know I have any sort of usable power?"

"Let me finish explaining, and I will tell you everything you need to know about your place at this school." She gives me a pointed look that convinces me to shut my mouth; I don't want to upset the magic lady with extremely sharp teeth.

"Where was I? Ah, that's right. Draxmere is where you go when your abilities have proven to be more than average. We aren't the only school to choose from in this world, but we are the best." There's a twinkle in her eyes, a prideful gleam.

Probably the most expensive, too, I think bitterly.

"So, what do we have to offer? What can you learn that you didn't already know? Well, the answer is quite simple: all kinds of things. We first place you into classes with others who share your type of power, but you are allowed to mingle with others during Basic Combat Training, Charm Development, and Faction meetings."

"The fuck are you guys doing basic combat training for?" I blurt out, slapping a hand over my mouth immediately afterward to silence myself. "Sorry, continue," I mumble behind the hand.

"That's alright. I know the humans only send their young to train for war, and that they must sign up for said training. You have yet to sign up, so you don't understand. Trust me, everyone here knows exactly what they have agreed to do. They understand they have a high chance of dying younger in this career field. It's a sacrifice every single one of us is willing to make. Wipe the incredulous look off of your face and let me tell you why.

"First, I would like to elaborate on the types of power we Conjurers possess. I will start with Shifters like me: I am a werewolf." Dean Delarosa pauses to stand, her body and head shaking at an unnatural speed as she begins to shift. Her body seems to vibrate, moving so fast my brain can't comprehend the movement. I only see her blurry form, and it changes from human to wolf in the blink of an eye. The black fur is shaggy with tight little curls, her eyes still very much human. She snarls lightly, snapping sharp teeth at me playfully. In another blink, she is back to normal, sitting back down as if it never happened.

What the actual *fuck*.

"Come, why don't we take a little walk around the grounds while I explain things to you?" She gathers a few papers in her hands before rising, heels clacking on her way out. I stumble behind her, eyes wide as we move into the hallway.

"This is the East wing. Our first stop on the tour is the pool room." She flings open a door to our right, gesturing inside.

I'm hit with a wave of humidity, the temperature similar to that of the typical Florida weather I'm accustomed to. My mouth pops open as I stare at the Olympic size pool inside with a group of damn mermaids gliding around inside it. A large neon sign hangs up at the back of the room, advertising a sauna. I'm not sure why they need one when the room is already the same temperature as hell.

"Don't worry, the pool isn't always full of sirens." She chuckles, shutting the door abruptly and carrying on.

"Oh, yeah, I was really concerned about that," I whisper, shaking my head in disbelief.

"Where had I left off? Oh, yes. Shifters. Also in the Shifter group are the vampires, the sirens, and the plain old shifters. Vampires won't suck your blood without permission, don't fret. Sirens won't lure you to a watery death…unless you deserve it. And the regular shifters? They just turn into anything they can think of: beast, insect, person. They are rarer among our people and treasured. Don't be alarmed, they won't hurt you either. Their classes tend to focus on enhancing their senses, on teaching them *how* to hunt, and how to be *useful* on a hunt."

"Does transforming like that hurt? I mean, your whole bone structure just changed. Surely that hurts?" If I possessed more than some residual annoyance and a shit load of anger, my reaction to seeing a fucking werewolf and sirens in a big-ass pool might be more fearful. As I am, I'm not entirely concerned about this new development. I mean, if aliens are real, why can't this shit be?

"Not at all." She laughs airily, amusement gleaming in her dark eyes. "It's instinct. The first time hurts a bit, but then our bodies take over our minds and we know exactly what to do and how to feel. Quick and painless. The more times you do it, the better it feels."

"Okay. Great. But I'm not one of those. I mean, wouldn't I have felt symptoms by now? Died from lack of blood intake?" I am met with another laugh.

"How about I finish explaining the other types of abilities you can have? Shifters aren't the only options." Dean Delarosa opens a second door, showing off a black-walled room that has a strong bleach odor emitting from it. A large operating table sits in the middle of the room and tools line the shelves on the wall. A singular light bulb swings from a rope in the middle of the room, moving on an invisible breeze. I'm pretty sure I see blood stains on the white-tiled floor, as well as a weird glob of goo hovering over the large drain under the table. If I had to describe this place in one sentence, I'd describe it as a serial killer's wet dream. The only explanation I receive for this room is a hushed "for the necromancers."

"The second type of Conjurer is known as Glamourists. They fall a little lower on the chain Charm Level wise, but they are incredibly useful. They can change how things look, can make you see what they want you to see, hear what they want you to hear, and smell what they want you to smell. A good Glamourist can control all five senses, but most can't do more than two or three. Moreover, some can take over whole rooms while others only change the appearance of singular objects. The amount of time they can hold such vivid scenes can vary, too. Their classes focus on increasing their times, capacity, and ability to use more senses."

"So, this can all be an illusion right now?" I raise my eyebrow slightly, rushing after her as she abruptly spins on her heel and begins a path back to the West Wing.

"Exactly! You're getting the idea. I won't escort you down the whole wing, most of the rooms are empty and awaiting use. Ah, this is the place where your combat classes will be held. I'm fairly certain it is in use right now, however, so we will move along."

"Um. Right. Okay." I barely get to glance toward the closed doors she vaguely gestures at as her steady pace thunders on.

"The next type of Conjurer would be the Necromancers. I know this particular ability sounds cursed or morally wrong, seems scary and untoward, but they aren't as creepy as their namesake sounds.

Generally, Necromancers are only allowed to raise the dead when necessary, and they aren't allowed to keep the dead here for long periods. Most Necromancers need the dead to be fresh, but the more skilled ones can raise the deceased months after the fact. That's why their classes are used to hone that skill and to teach proper interrogation techniques. Necromancers are wonderful tools in investigations and often find information on mysterious deaths, or vital information they were hunting for on missions. It's an extremely useful talent, though not very common. It's how we got so much information on you and your parents, actually."

"Somebody raised the bodies of my dead parents?" I wrinkle my nose in distaste, poking my head in the new room Delarosa stops at. It's empty. White walls, white floors, white ceiling, and zero objects inside.

"For the Glamourists to practice. And, yes, they did. Your parents went on and on about their precious daughter, but they refused to tell us where you went. They paid someone to take you and hide you if something were to happen to them, and that person did their job well. We don't have access to human records and don't have a way to track people down reliably. Alas, it was meant to be. Everything happens for a reason, you know."

"So they say." I swallow hard, not wanting to think about how many pieces they had to put back together to be able to speak to my parents.

Delarosa ignores me, jumping back into her speech. "Seers are very common here and rank high on the totem pole. Although we as a population hold many, most don't make more than a few important predictions in their lifetimes. Seers see snippets into the past, the present, and the future. The stronger ones can even read auras. It's a very exact science, and not often do their predictions make sense right away. Their classes teach them how to focus on that thing inside of them, teaches them new and different methods to read those distant sightings. They are also taught how to examine those predictions in attempts to become better, and faster, at understanding a sighting. I'm sure you can understand why we value them so greatly, especially since they can tell us who may die or who may lose battles. It's all extremely interesting. I've taken up prophecy reading as a hobby myself."

"What a…*fun*…hobby."

"This is the cafeteria, but it's closed." She waves another hand at a set of doors, then takes a sharp right into a hidden exit. She swings the door open, gesturing for me to follow. I scoff, shaking my head with a frown. What kind of tour is this? She's skipped over half of this floor alone!

"Fuck, it's cold." I begin to shake as soon as we exit the building, but Dean Delarosa waves her hands in a few funny gestures and moves on. I don't have time to be amazed by my sudden warmth despite the snow falling around us.

"Enhancers are a special kind of magic. Though they hold no specific magic of their own, they do exactly what you might expect: they enhance the abilities of those around them. Enhancers typically can only focus on one or two people at a time, but that's why they are put on the most powerful teams. Even if they can only help their Illuminoor, that itself is a major advantage in battle. The stronger ones can help many more people at the same time and may even hold the ability to borrow some of that enhanced power. Yes, that's exactly as it sounds; they may be able to give themselves a new power. It's a very coveted power, and it's rare to have one at such strength. We have one here on campus."

"Good for them?"

Dean Delarosa leads me out into a courtyard, a beautiful fountain its centerpiece. A dragon shoots water out of its mouth, wings raised and tail lifted. There is a long brick driveway circling it, dipping down the side of a very large hill and blocked by gates. There seems to be one way in, one way out. If you aren't traveling through mirrors, that is.

I turn to look at the school itself, eyes wide. It's giant, probably closer to the size of a castle than a school. It seems to be mostly one building, the East and West wings turning sharply to dive behind it. Most of the school is built of a deep gray stone, but the darker red bricks that make up the driveway are found in inconsistent sections throughout. It's almost as though patchwork had been performed, and the workers decided to give the place some pizzazz.

I take a moment to admire the huge, brightly lit Gothic windows every few feet, and I see movement behind several of them. My eyes trail to a large stone staircase that leads to the giant entrance, where a group of students linger. The door there is something akin to what you would see draped over a moat, except in a double-door format. I tilt my head back to find several spots on the roof reaching up to make breathtakingly tall and pointed peaks. A large, luminous clock in the distance sits on a singular tower. I can hear the slight ticking from here, and I dread the sound it will make when it hits the hour.

"Alright, alright. No time to linger. Come, come. We still have a back courtyard, too."

"Wha—Okay, wow, I'm coming."

Delarosa is already striding off, humming as we make our way back to the door we exited from only moments ago. Can she slow the fuck down? Will she not let me have any time to appreciate the magical school I was *just* introduced to?

Delarosa jumps back into her speech, promptly ignoring my incredulous look. "Finally, there are the Elementalists. Yes, that is exactly as it sounds. These Conjurers possess power over one of the four elements: earth, fire, air, and water. However, there are two additional elements humans do not recognize in their world: light and shadow. Though they are grouped in with the basic Elementalists, they are given specific names and wield a great amount of power here. They are our biggest assets in this war.

"Light Wielders are most commonly known as Illuminoors whereas Shadow Wielders are known as Dimineers. They form two halves of a whole and complement each other in all the best ways. Because of their association with Elementalists, this group as a whole is among the most popular and most bountiful. Even if you don't possess the power of Light or Shadow, you have been indirectly associated with those who do. Their classes train these wielding skills and teach them how to wield properly and without destruction. Some will wield more for longer, while others will only be able to hold a simple flame. You have to be skilled when using your element unless you wish to set your partner on fire during battle. Control is important in this group."

The Dean walks straight through the first door and right out another, leading me to another set of grounds. This one is just as magnificent, just as beautiful.

I can't begin to comprehend how large the maze in the center is. The tall hedges stretch toward the heavens. I can't see beyond its entrance, can't tell what lies at the center if anything. I spot two small buildings on the other side, one near the East wing and one near the West. They seem more like huts compared to the school itself, but maybe that's because of their distance from me. Benches dance across the courtyard, along with beaten-in paths littered with shiny rocks. My gaze falls on the many statues haphazardly placed in alcoves, large open areas, and near hedges. Fuck, those are intricate.

"What's in the middle?" I question breathlessly, watching in awe as students emerge from its entrance.

"That's not for me to tell." She chuckles wickedly before leading me back inside and passing off her papers to a student absent-mindedly. "Now let me answer your question about Basic Combat Training: What the fuck do we need that for? The answer is simple: Reapers. Reapers were us at one point—normal people with normal powers—but they became corrupted. They dove too deep, traded their soul with the devil, and became the monsters we know today. Most Reapers were Conjurers with limited abilities, people who could barely perform their abilities or who would never be able to hold an ability-driven job. So, they seek out the Grim, the creature who creates them and has done so for centuries.

"Our world revolves around who is the most powerful, around strength and abilities. But power corrupts. Remember that, Azalea. You cannot exceed your limitations. As I said, most who turn are practically powerless. It's hard to survive in a world as harsh as this one without that strength to rely on. They believed they had no choice, that the only way for them to be powerful was for them to steal said power.

"The Grim preys on weakness and uses those desperate people, making a deal with them for his own sick needs. He turns them into these mindless drones in hopes of taking over our world *and* the human one. The creatures he creates no longer have a heart, a body, or a mind. All they want is absolute power, and they will do anything to have it. So, where do you think they find that power?"

"In us," I whisper, wishing I could feel as horrified as I should.

"In us." She agrees gravely, whisking us back into her office and taking a seat at her desk. "The stronger we are, the more power they will be able to consume. They target those of us with higher Charm Levels, feeding off this special thing living inside of our bodies. They will literally *rip* you apart, piece by piece, to squeeze every last drop from you. Ultimately, it is the ability of the Illuminoors that kills them. The Dimineers, however, trick them into walking right into carefully placed traps. The Reapers seek out darkness, so we use that and their obsession with power to hunt them. The Illuminoors and the Dimineers work in tandem to take down our enemies.

"This is what we are training to fight for, why we are willing to sacrifice our lives. If it means protecting the rest of our species, then that is what we are going to do. The Grim himself has evaded capture for centuries, so these creatures of his are never-ending. The deaths will never stop. If we don't fight, then who will?"

"What do they want with the humans? How are you guys even traveling back and forth?" I don't want to stop and think about the gravity of what I am being told, about the decision I will inevitably face at the end of this meeting: stay or go.

"All humans have a little power inside of them, but as I said before, their world stifles it. They have no idea they harbor any sort of power. Usually, those with higher Charm Levels manifest as Seers. They are the ones you know as fortune tellers or witches. They tend to be people who claim to have great intuition or who can tell the type of person someone is through a simple feeling they get. That power inside of them, while not strong, is still present. Unfortunately, they make for easy targets. Why come fight the highly trained and lethal guys when you can hop over there and have a feast without having to fight at all? That's why we continue to fight for humans: They don't know how to fight for themselves.

"As to how we get back and forth? Well, that's what Shadow Walkers are for. Shadow Walking is a type of Charm anyone can learn to perform, but it is hard. Usually, only those with strong Charm Levels can succeed at it. This ability creates gates between the worlds: little portals we can walk in and out of before closing. That's why I sent Jaymes to fetch you. He's been training in that particular skill over the past year and it was excellent practice for him."

"Oh, so kidnapping me was a premeditated thing. Good to know for the legal documents I'll be filling out later." I avoid her eyes, still processing.

"I am truly sorry about that, Azalea. I thought you were expecting us. We didn't know the circumstances you were in. As I said before, the Seers have had a hard time predicting anything about you."

"But they did see me? Here?"

"In a way, yes. They predicted your arrival very early on, and we were told the only way to find you would be through that very specific mirror. Our artifact retrieval group found the one in the human world years ago, but we were told very specifically not to retrieve it yet. Not until after it had been found by you. Even then, that prophecy was a little vague and a lot hopeful. But we were sure that it would work. Its match is here in this world, and that had to be the way you crossed. We don't question the prophecies of the Seers, even when they don't make a ton of sense. Maybe your powers are too weak after so long in the human world, maybe you wouldn't have been able to pass through without the help of an extremely powerful object. We can only speculate.

"We were never able to find your exact location, you see, so it was the only way. Jaymes has been keeping an eye on that mirror for months, waiting to find you. Yesterday, he finally did. None of us knew what you looked like, how tall you were, what your name was. It was pure luck that our Seers had descriptively described a man by the name of Neil who was associated with the jinx. Not the Jinxes, just the jinx. Since that's what most prophecies refer to you, as we took a leap of faith. Jaymes saw the name on your shorts and knew this might be our only chance at finding you, so he took it. I'm sorry in doing so we have frightened you."

I don't correct her, not wanting to explain how remarkably not fearful I am of this situation, despite wanting to be. Mostly, I'm overwhelmed by all of the information and concerned for my mental health.

"The Seers have referred to the child of Jinx as a savior for more years than we have been able to track, so it was important to us that we found you. I won't tell you that you are meant to save the world, I don't want you burdened with something that may not be entirely true, but you are important, and you are meant to save us in one way or another. Will you defeat the Grim? Will you keep our people from war? Will you save our school? It's all entirely unclear. I hope I'm not scaring you with all of this chosen one talk."

"A magic Seer said that I would come through a magic mirror? A magic guy pulled me through said mirror because he has a special magic that he decided to practice on me? Seers who claim I am a savior of some sort? Yeah, those things definitely freak me out a little less," I settle on saying.

"I know this is a lot of information to take in at once. Most of us grow up in this world, and I don't think I've given a crash course like this before. I swear, I'm almost done."

"Oh, are you?" I scoff in disbelief.

"This last part is important information, okay? Our people are divided into two factions: Light and Shadow. Just like the powers. Though the Elementalists work in tandem, these factions do not. They are supposed to, but politics is not a fair or nice game. Hence why the Elementalists prefer to go by different names altogether.

There's been a lot of discord between the two factions as of late, a lot of blame being placed upon one another. By the end of your first year here, you will choose a side for yourself. I, myself, am a member of the Shadow Faction and have not regretted it a single moment in my entire life. Even if we are being ostracized right now. But I won't get into that, it's much too complicated a discussion.

"Now then. The 'government' talk is out of the way. I suppose all I have left to tell you is *why* you are here." She makes air quotes and rolls her eyes when saying "government" as though she thinks it's a ridiculous concept.

"It's because you think I have some kind of power, that I'm some savior. I get it, but I don't think—"

"Your parents were alumni of this school." She interrupts with a small smile, nodding her head as I gape in surprise. Maybe I shouldn't be. I didn't know them, after all.

"My parents? At this school?"

"Oh, yes. Very, very popular here. Your mother was an Illuminoor in the Light Faction, your father a Dimineer in the Shadow Faction. A very sweet, although heavily judged, love story. They were some of the most powerful Conjurers this school has seen in a very long time. Other than Jaymes and his friends, of course."

"And you think that, because of them, I'm going to be very powerful, too?" I mutter under my breath, tapping my fingers against the desk rapidly. This is why I am here. Not because they were worried about my disappearance or even because they thought I deserved to know of my heritage. No. It's because my parents were some kind of hotshots and they want me to be one, too. They need me to be powerful if I am to be a true savior.

"We know you will be. That much has been made clear by the Seers."

There she goes with the prophecies again. Supposedly *vague* prophesies that hardly told them anything other than they needed to find a powerful Jinx child to be their savior.

"I don't have powers. I don't. Do you understand? I don't have powers!"

My body seems to vibrate as anger heats me, my head shaking fervently. I would know if I had powers. The only thing I *do* possess is a death curse and an inability to care about anything but myself.

"As I said, I know it's a lot to take in. Your parents—"

"Are dead and didn't leave a single hint about something like this!" I bark, running a hand down my face. "Why was I left in the human world if I had powers, huh? Why would they take me there unless I was powerless? Why would they have allowed themselves to die there, away from everything they've ever known?"

"They ran off before you were born. We don't know their reasons, and I won't speculate." Dean Delarosa shrugs helplessly, watching me through a pitying gaze.

"I had a family, though. To be fair, most of them did die because of me, but—"

"Your human records are fake, Azalea. None of those people were *actually* family. Only humans willing to help out a little girl in need, along with the extra stipend offered by the person your parents paid to hide you."

"Fuck. How can you sit there so calmly? This is fucking insane!" My fingers don't stop their rapid taps, my feet following as I try to just *think*.

"My world isn't the one getting flipped upside down." She smiles sadly, reaching out to stop my hand.

"No, only I get that pleasure."

"Azalea, I have presented you with all of the facts, and you will learn more over time. You will find your power, learn to perform Charms, and gain more muscle than you ever thought possible. But you will also be filling that empty hole inside of you that has been longing for this, for more than what the humans had to offer. You won't be a fraction of yourself any longer."

"You're about to make me choose, aren't you? Fuck. Right now? I have to decide right now?" My eyes widen, a small squeak escaping me as I try to think of ways to prolong this. She is. She really is. I can see it written all over her face, can see the pain behind those eyes at forcing this upon me.

"Do you accept the offer to become a student at Draxmere Academy of Conjuring?"

Shit.

After that giant information overload, she thinks I am ready to make a decision as huge as this? I didn't even know the Charmed world existed a few hours ago, didn't know that I was part of anything bigger than the Florida population. But I am, aren't I? According to her, anyway.

What am I supposed to do? If I say no, will they let me return to the life I know? The one where snarky bitches trip me at work and I barely get any tips? The one where the only things I can afford to buy are preowned and the only apartment I can find is shitty? The one where everyone around me dies and something inside of me will continue to ache for the rest of my sad, lonely life?

Here, I may be able to feel again. Here, I may be able to fill the empty chasm in my chest. Here, I may not have to be alone anymore.

Honestly, there's only one right answer.

"Yes."

"Perfect!" She cheers, standing and clapping wildly. "Oh, you have no idea how excited I am. Your parents were legends. Absolute legends. And you will be, too, I just know it! Our savior come at last."

"What happens now?" I question wearily, flinching at her happy shouts proclaiming me a savior. It's not like I had much of a choice.

"Now I will provide you with a few supplies. Here is a uniform. That's your size, right? Oh, and a satchel! A few of your basic books are in there, but once you find out your type of power, you'll get more. Pens, notebooks, that sort of thing, too. Oh, and here! It's a book entitled *A Guide to the Charmed.* It updates itself every year, so it is all good information. I think you will find it most helpful." Dean Delarosa begins grabbing things from around the room and shoving them into my arms, enough to make me struggle as I attempt to stand with the heavy weight of it all. I ignore the slight insult as she hands me their version of an "Are you an idiot?" book, a beat and worn copy that seems to be well-loved.

"And how am I going to do that? Find out my type of power, I mean?" I shift as she hands me the last item, arms burning already.

"Oh, your trial is tomorrow morning. A little test of sorts to find where you are best suited. Lucky for you, our semester just started a couple of weeks ago, so you won't be behind for long."

"And if I don't possess any power after all? Or I'm not as strong as you hope I will be?"

"Then you get kicked out." She shrugs nonchalantly, clapping her hands again before gesturing for me to follow her. "Oh, trials are so much fun! I can't wait to see which one of your parent's powers you inherited!"

"Yeah. Me either."

I feel more numb than usual following behind her, every cell inside of me taut and ready to flee. I'm not meant for this world, that much is obvious.

But maybe this world was meant for me.

CHAPTER 5

"A new friend you must make,
a formed bond you cannot shake.
With the jinx, a friendship will bloom,
with the jinx you will meet your savior or your doom."
—Prophesy spoken to Demi Lockwood by Seer Shiloh Bar in 2023
A.G.

I blink away the blurriness in my eyes, glancing around as I try to remember where I am and what happened. I'm in my room, and I almost laugh at the incredulity of it. My affliction must finally be altering my mind beyond repair if I could dream something so real, something I was so willing to believe.

I jump at the pounding knock at the door, and rub my eyes once more as I sling myself off of the bed and into a standing position. I almost fall back down as I get a good look at my mirrored room with the weird sheen.

Fuck. Should I be glad I'm not going crazy after all?

"I'm coming! Hold on. Geeze," I shout as the knock sounds again, stomping toward the door and throwing it open in a fury.

A small girl pushes her way inside, a large, locked box swinging in her hand as she cries out, "Oh, I'm so glad you are awake! We have such a busy day planned! I hope you were able to sleep well. Dean Delarosa told me how overwhelming this whole situation has been for you. If it had been me, I would still be on the floor weeping."

As she pushes past, I notice that she is shorter than me by several inches at least and dressed in a school uniform with sleek black heels. Her hair, a shade of brown resembling chocolate, is braided and streaked with a rainbow of colors. I'm entranced by her doe-like eyes, which are a similar hue of gorgeous brown with long lashes and eyelids coated in smoky shades. I take in her cute heart-shaped face, big cheeks, and small nose as she glances around my private space. But her skin is what really attracts my attention.

Her natural tone is a dark shade, but spots of white are splattered across her body. Her face, her hands, her neck, her legs, her arms. Everywhere has a small amount of discoloration, though the majority seems to be on her arms and legs. Her pointed ears startle me, glistening jewelry scattered up and down their length. There's also a small dot on her nose, a tiny stud that's barely noticeable. When she opens her mouth to speak, two pointy canines greet me behind plump, glossy lips.

"Oh, my Grim! How rude of me! Hi, I'm Demi Lockwood. Vampire Shifter." She points to her fangs with a happy giggle. "I've been sent to prepare you for the upcoming ceremony, and also to provide you with a friendly face."

"The welcoming committee. Got it."

"Something like that." There's a secretive spark in her eyes, a sneaky smile, and it reminds me all too much of my nosy neighbor back home. "You have an accent of some kind."

"Yep. I'm from Florida. Can't live there without gaining a little bit of a southern twang." Despite my best efforts to not have one. "Well, thanks for welcoming me, I guess. If you don't mind now, I'll just…" I gesture vaguely to my hanging uniform: a short black skirt, white blouse, and black vest.

"Oh, no. Don't put that ugly thing on yet. Let me give you a little makeover first. It would be a shame to spill any of these products on the uniform on your first day. They're real sticklers about the whole uniform thing. I don't want to get you into trouble."

Demi waltzes into the adjoining bathroom as though she owns it, and I hear the clunk of her big box hitting the counter.

"Um, okay, listen—"

"Come on! Sit down on the toilet. I'll have you all dolled up in no time. And don't worry, I'll have those bangs nice and trimmed up so they are out of your eyes."

"I don't really think—"

"Sit down." Her soft, kind voice changes. No longer a sweet and innocent young woman, she has become a harsh and angry lady. I can't help but flinch at the sudden change, abruptly reminded that she is a vampire. Has she come here for a meal? Delarosa said the vamps won't attack me, but who knows? Not that I'm scared, but I'm not sure I want to deal with the effects of blood loss right now. I've donated blood before and it always leaves me queasy.

Reluctantly, I enter the bathroom, sitting down as told and swiping my bangs out of my eyes.

"Sitting down," I mutter bitterly.

"Sorry!" Her voice changes back to its normal chirpy tone. "I shouldn't have gotten mean with you. I just really want to be your friend. I do all my friends' makeup and hair. It helps us bond."

"Seriously? That's the story? That you just want to be my friend? Yeah, okay. I know what this really is, Demi."

"What are you talking about?" She stops rifling through her things to turn and glare at me, hands on her hips with a raised brow.

"I'm the new girl. I'm interesting until I'm not, right? You're just trying to dig up some dirt and get a read on me. I get it. I've been the new girl before. I'm not interested in having friends, though. Especially not fake ones. So go back to the others and tell them I'm ugly and have three heads or something. That shit doesn't bother me."

"Listen, Azalea. I'm sorry if I am coming off as insincere, but I'm not, okay? I don't care what skeletons are hiding inside your closet, and I'm certainly not going to tell anyone about them. Just relax. Delarosa told me the human world has done you no favors, and she was right. I don't know how humans treat each other, but that's not how I plan on treating you, okay? You're in a new place, confused, overwhelmed. You need a friend. I thought I could be one for you."

I would have been skeptical if she didn't have tears pooling in her eyes. Fuck. Now I've offended her; that always makes things so awkward. "I'm sorry." I clear my throat and look away, hoping it sounds sincere enough to believe. "You're right. Please, go ahead. I'm not good at doing makeup on myself, so I would love to see it done right."

"And your hair." She sings with a bright smile, and I can't help but be drawn to those deadly little teeth. "Don't worry, I don't bite.

Unless you want me to." She smirks slightly, snapping those shiny white teeth playfully.

"No, thanks. I'm good right now. I'll let you know if I get in the mood for some blood-sucking."

"Ah, you may warm up to me yet, Azalea Jinx. Alright, close your eyes and relax. Tell me about yourself. You said you lived somewhere called Florida? Is that an exciting place?"

"It can be for others. In my experience, it was hot, overcrowded, and everyone was rude."

"Mmm, and who is Neil? Some kind of celebrity or something you like? Don't look surprised, I saw those shorts, girly. I think everyone in the entire school did." She laughs a little as something cold touches my face, the tickle of a brush following.

"My ex-husband," I say sourly. My cheeks heat with anger as I think about Jaymes dragging me out of my room in my pajamas and parading me down the hall. I'm definitely going to have to burn those shorts now.

"Ooh, juicy. Alright, you have to tell me more. Is he hot? Good in bed?"

"He was very hot. Great in bed, too." I can't help but laugh, something I rarely do. Demi has a contagious energy, the kind that swallows you up and holds you tight.

"Then why the breakup? If they are good in bed, you have to hold on to them. It's a rare find." She giggles again as more items clink around.

"We didn't. Well, we were going to. We had been separated for close to a year and were ready to call it quits. But he died before I could do the honors of serving him with divorce papers." Or vice versa.

I'm not sure why I'm telling her any of this, but it isn't like I'm a super personal person. At this point in my life, it's just something that happened. It's only been four months, but it feels like a lifetime. I guess because I haven't loved him for a while, if I ever did, and I had been expecting his death for years. Our relationship always had an expiration date, I just hadn't known when it would be.

"Ah, I see. Well, if it's any comfort, most people around here don't get the chance at divorce, either. We marry, breed, and die young. The hazards of our workplace and all."

"How young are you guys breeding?" I mutter, surprised.

"Oh, it depends. Forty is the average age of death for Conjurers, so most people try to be done with kids by then. Some students fall pregnant while still here, but for most of us, it's in the year or two after graduation. People who don't attend Draxmere are much, much sooner. If I were to give an average range, it would probably be between sixteen and twenty-five. Got to repopulate and all." She carries on cheerfully, unperturbed by my shocked gasp.

"What the fuck? I mean, to each their own, but *everyone* has kids that early here?" Neil and I had attempted to have our own kids soon after marriage, so I'm not judging, but that's not necessarily standard practice in the human world. A lot of people wait until well into their thirties. These people have multiple kids by twenty-five and prepare for death soon after! Who even raises these kids if they all just die right after?

"Yeah. We kind of die fast because of the Reapers. So, if we want to keep up the population…we have to start fucking now." I can feel her infectious grin, and I can't help but let out a surprised laugh once more. "You'll learn that pretty quickly. Everyone accepts that they will more than likely have short lives. So, we live life to the fullest. You'll probably get a lot of sexual offers in your time here. My advice? Take a few of them. It helps you to relax after the crazy amount of shit we do every day. I would wait on the pregnancy thing until after graduation, though. That way you can get through all the schoolwork. Basic Combat Training is a no-go when pregnant, and you need it to graduate. Besides, this type of work plus a kid? It's tough. Too tough."

"And if I don't want kids?" The way she talks about this is so nonchalant, as if it's expected. I guess in this world, it is.

"Well, you might find it a little harder to find a long-term partner, then. Especially guys. They practically drool over the thought of having an heir." I can hear the eye roll in her voice and the slight snort that follows. I haven't been on the hunt for a new relationship these past months, and I don't plan on starting that hunt now. If she is serious about this whole kid thing…well, no one will like my unwillingness to have kids or my lack of ability to have them.

"Don't need a partner. Just got out of a long-term relationship, remember?"

"Well, just aim for good sex then, yeah?" We laugh together, and I find myself more and more willing to like her.

"I'll think about it." My mind flashes a brief image of Jaymes, one I immediately shove away. No way would I even *consider* fucking that asshole. No way.

"You're already thinking of someone, aren't you? Oh, yeah. You definitely are. I see it on your face! Spill!"

"The guy who picked me up yesterday was hot, that's all. I don't want to fuck him, though. He was extremely rude. Just hoping they all look like that here." It'll make my stay here more bearable if there's at least *some* eye candy. I don't often feel arousal, but I can admire beauty.

"Ah, Jaymes Bloodgood. Best to stay away from him and his posse, if you want my opinion."

"His posse?"

"Yeah, there are four of them in total. We call them the Gravediggers. They're all smoking hot with amazing bodies, but they're dangerous. Extremely so."

"The Gravediggers? What kind of fucked up group name is that?"

Demi ignores my comment, saying, "Yeah, all four of them are Shadow Walkers. That is, people who can use a Charm to travel to the human world. Did Delarosa mention that? Anyways, that's crazy, right? We've never had so many in the same class. We typically only get up to two. Their little group is going to do big things, though. We can all feel it, and the Seers have said as much."

"Uh-huh." There it is again: the Seers said it, so it must be true. I'm not sure if I want to be one or if I hate them.

"There's Jaymes Bloodgood, who is an Illuminoor. Then there's Arlo MacLaren, a Werewolf Shifter. Shayde Glover, a Dimineer. And last but not least, Nox Emerson, an Enhancer."

"Aren't those abilities kind of a big deal? Their group sounds just a tad overpowered." An Illuminoor and a Dimineer? Not to mention their own personal Enhancer. And *all* of them are Shadow Walkers?

"Maybe. They're also all part of the Shadow Faction, and it scares the crap out of the Lights. They like to spout a bunch of conspiratorial bullshit about the Shadows overtaking them so they can hold singular control. It's all kind of fucked right now. And we have to choose!"

"Yeah, I've gathered that. You don't beat around the bush about things, do you?" She's told me important details about this world already, ones that I needed to know to fit in. The popular groups, what guys will want from me, and how the politics are coming into play. And why? Why not leave me in the dark to fend for myself? I wouldn't have befriended myself, wouldn't have told myself shit. But maybe that's because I couldn't care less about helping anyone else.

"Why should I? Like I said, we don't have long to live. Why would I offer you the disservice of sweet little lies? You don't know anything about our world, so I might as well be upfront about it all. You'll fit in quicker that way."

"Well, thanks, I guess." I'm not sure what else to say to her. She is insanely honest, and I've never met anyone like her before. I can already tell that just from the mere fifteen minutes I've been in her presence.

"Back to the boys. I have to tell you, Jaymes is cute, but please stay away from Arlo. I'm calling dibs on him. Things don't usually work out well between vamps and wolves, being natural enemies and all. But still. Dibs." I crack my eyes open to see her face break out into a flush, red coating her cheeks and neck.

"You just told me not to get involved with any of them!"

"Yeah, but I'm saying especially don't get involved with Arlo. He's got a girlfriend right now, anyway. Jaymes, too. So both of them are kind of off the table. And Shayde is a little terrifying and a major player. The girlfriend he has right now is an absolute psychopath, from what I hear. One of my friends said that she attacked her for looking at him too long, so maybe Nox is your best bet. He's cute, shy, and nerdy. That your type?"

I shake my head with a snort. "Not at all."

Demi is doing a great job at getting my mind off of this weird change. She knows what to say, what to do. I'm sure that's why she was the one sent to welcome me.

"Ah, well. No matter. I'm done here. Just need to put some gloss on you. But I am curling your hair, too, 'kay? Great. Sit still so I don't burn you."

"Okay, geeze." I huff as she begins to chatter away once more and do my best not to move when I hear the distinct sound of hair being cut. The snips are fast and efficient, and Demi is moving on before I can even open my eyes to peek.

"The Gravediggers practically run this place. Everyone is terrified of them, and no one would dare go against their wishes. They are just too powerful, you know? They will run the world one day, and we all know it. Most of us don't want to get on their bad side because it isn't likely they will forget it when they take over the Shadow council."

"So students just listen to everything they say without question? All because it's assumed they'll be on this council one day?"

"Oh, yeah. Staff too. We all bow to them. It's been that way since they showed up last year, and I've heard it was like that at all of their previous schools, too."

"That's fucked up." I shake my head, then cry out when she burns me with the curling iron.

"Hold still!" she hisses before continuing to feed me tidbits of gossip and more information about how things work here. "Want to know why they're called the Gravediggers? Good, because I'm telling you. They're called that because they can, and will, bury you to get what they want. They don't care about you, or me, or anyone else here. They have an agenda, and they will do anything to stick to it. Their one goal is to become the leaders they were destined to be. It's all about power here, babe. Especially to men like that."

"I'm not going to blindly follow orders from a group of guys like some lost puppy." I don't have the heart to tell her I'm not good at taking orders, either.

"Azalea, sweetie, heed my warning: Listen to the Gravediggers. Listen to them and everything will be golden. Everyone will be friendly to you if they are." I only huff, pressing my lips together tightly.

By the time Demi is done and I am sliding on a uniform, I can hear strings of curses about how late we are. She shoves a grain bar into my face, telling me to eat it on the way. I'm not fond of the strawberry flavor, but it's the only thing I've had since someone brought me dinner last night. I know if I don't eat now, I won't get food for hours, and that will just put me in a bad mood.

"What kind of test is this?" I question as Demi's surprisingly strong grasp encircles my wrist and she practically drags me down the same hall from yesterday. Every once in a while she stops abruptly, waving with bright smiles and friendly hello's to students we pass.

"Oh, don't worry, Azzie. It's not the kind of test you can flunk. Don't be nervous. It's exciting to find your power. Most of us know what we are going to be, but it's still fun. Our tests are usually performed around age twelve, though. It's cool to see someone your age doing a test. We are all so excited!" She drags out the 'o' in 'so' and squeals to prove her point.

It sounds as though it isn't going to only be me and a professor present at this test. I'm not sure I want a ton of people watching me take this test, nor do I want them judging my ability or my lack of one. I open my mouth to tell her so, but she begins shouting at another friend. More introductions, more forgotten names.

I wish I could make myself more friendly, wish I could bring myself to try and fit in here. But I'm not interested in making friends. I'm already putting Demi in danger, even if Dean Delarosa says otherwise. I'm the one who has been cursed her entire life, and I am the one who has seen what happens as a result. I can't let down my guard just because these people *suspect* my curse will be cured here.

"Don't be nervous," Demi repeats after we descend the three flights of stairs, making a beeline for a set of double doors at the other end of the hall. I'm pretty sure it's the combat classroom Delarosa showed me yesterday. "Your parents are legendary here. They had some crazy Charm Levels; you will too."

I swallow hard and nod, even though I don't agree at all.

My "legendary" parents have been mentioned multiple times, but I never knew those people. They are a distant memory, something from my past that has been idolized in my brain. They never seemed real. But coming here, learning I've possibly inherited something so important from people I rarely think about? I'm not sure how I'm going to live in a reality where they will occupy space inside of my mind. And what if living so long in the human world completely drained me of any type of power? What if I never had any to begin with since I wasn't born here? What if the Seers are wrong and I'm not the savior they have been counting on?

The possibilities of what could go wrong are endless, and I don't want to believe any of this until I see proof in the form of my very own powers.

CHAPTER 6

"When the time comes for your Placement Ceremony, do not fret. You will, more than likely, receive one of the gifts bestowed upon your parents. You will rarely be awarded a power outside of your familiar line, and it's even rarer for you to not receive a power at all. The Placement Ceremony is meant to be an exciting time, so children must not fear the unknown. All that is meant to be, will be, as they say."
—*A Guide to the Charmed* (current edition), written by Glamourist Elias Kasper in 1907 A.G.

Once Demi and I finally make it to those distant double doors, she pushes them open with a dramatic flare. She flounces in first, skirt swaying as she leaves me to sit with a group of girls in the bottom row on a set of bleachers.

I take in my new surroundings, noting the similarities to the typical American gym. Except, this isn't the type of gym you see in public schools. This is the type of gym you pay a membership to, the type with fancy equipment and special qualifications to even be considered before allowing you to enter. The only outlier is the bleachers flanking two sides of the room opposite one another.

The equipment has all been pushed to the side, leaving behind drawn-out marks on the hardwood floor to show exactly where they had been. I was right; this *is* the Combat Training classroom.

I take a hesitant step forward, eyes flickering to the almost-full bleachers on the left side. The right is bare. My gaze trails to a handful of colorful orbs floating in the middle of the large room. I keep my eyes on the white stone walls behind them, refusing to look anyone in the eye as I force myself to approach them.

Dean Delarosa waits for me in front of those orbs, a tight-lipped smile on her cherry-red painted lips. She gestures for me to enter the circle the orbs have formed, so I do. I ignore the students whooping and hollering on those shiny gray bleachers, ignore the ones still piling in to watch the spectacle.

"Welcome, Azalea Jinx, to your Conjuring Test. Each one of us holds a special type of power within us, one that separates us from others of our kind. Let's find out together who here your powers belong with." A practiced speech if I've ever heard one. Delarosa smiles brightly now, gesturing toward the orbs. "Approach each orb with caution. Sometimes they will glide toward you, some may even produce sparks. It all depends on you. Whichever orb reacts to your presence will represent the power you hold. Don't be frightened; they won't hurt you."

I nod, taking a shaky step forward to the black orb directly in front of me with the image of a skull inside. I am practically touching it, I am so close, but nothing happens. I frown, moving toward the white orb on my left, which holds a clock. It, too, refuses to move. I reach out to touch a blue orb filled with fire, letting out a noise of surprise as it explodes into five more orbs. Each one is the same color, but they hold different images. A cloud, a flower, a wave, a sun, and a moon. None of them so much as quiver at my approach. I can't help but feel a little disappointed, knowing the sun and moon must represent the light and dark powers my parents held. If I didn't inherit their abilities, did I inherit anything?

With a sigh, I approach a brown orb, the image of a mirror reflecting my own disappointment. I huff as it, too, denies me the pleasure of a power. I take another hesitant step toward a yellow orb that holds lightning bolts inside, but none come out to strike me. Taking that as a sign that I haven't been chosen to represent its power, I move to the last orb. This one is red, with a wolf snarling inside. I'm not as surprised this time when it divides itself, producing three new orbs. One with a mermaid, one with a set of fangs, and one with a human. Actually, it's probably a Conjurer meant to represent those who shift into anything. Not that it matters; the Shifters don't want me, either.

Not a single damn orb has reacted to me. No moving, no sparks. By the time I am reaching for that final Shifter orb, I begin to hear laughs and snickers. Heat creeps up into my cheeks as I feel my anger rising, and I can't seem to force it away.

"Maybe I should just leap at them?" I question wearily, jumping toward the black orb abruptly. It jerks away from me, refusing to allow me anywhere near it. I stumble only slightly, lunging toward the white one in frustration. It, too, evades me. All of the orbs seem to have an understanding of the situation, and they simultaneously move away from me in an attempt to put an even greater distance between us.

I really am cursed.

"Fuck all of you!" I spit out at the orbs quietly. "Fuck you right up your little orb—"

"Maybe you really are powerless!" I snap my head toward the source of the shout, ignoring the howling laughter that follows. My eyes fall to a redhead next to Jaymes in the middle of the bleachers. The laughter is accompanied by whispers and the pointing of fingers. If I could feel embarrassment, this would be the embodiment of that feeling.

"I told you she didn't belong here. She's only human, after all. Didn't live up to the family name, did you, Jinx?" Jaymes's voice is cold and loud. He smiles at me darkly, tapping his wrist as if saying my time is up. I clench my teeth while watching him, anger rising and crashing like waves. If I could, I'd knock that fucker's teeth right out of his head. I'd—

Loud gasps and a few screams interrupt my violent thoughts, and I gape in shock as a blue orb slams into Jaymes at a ferocious speed. He topples backward, groaning as his head slams into the empty seat behind him. I cover my mouth to hide my vicious laugh, eyes wide in delight. A few cheers rise from a group to his left, the girls surrounding Demi, and they whistle and cry out in excitement.

"A Dimineer like your father!" Delarosa shouts, beaming. So that's which orb had hurtled itself into Jaymes for me. "Excellent! How exciting to add another Elementalist to our school! I must say, that's the strongest I've ever seen the orbs react! Congratulations!" She claps ferociously, and students hesitantly join her.

I can't help but sigh in relief: I can stay here after all. Hopefully for free since no one ever mentioned a cost for tuition.

"I guess I do live up to the family name, huh, Bloodgood?" I call, grinning like a madwoman. Then, the most spectacular thing happens. Another blue orb hurtles at Mach speed toward him.

Jaymes has just gotten himself righted, pulled back into a seated position by his friends. The moment they release him is the moment the orb knocks him back once more. This time I allow the laughter to escape me, as does the entire room. Only the Gravediggers are unamused by this turn of events.

"It isn't funny," the redhead snarls, snapping his sharp teeth at everyone. That must be Arlo, the werewolf Demi has a crush on. "Both Light and Shadow have chosen her. Don't you think that's odd?"

Silence settles across the room like a cool blanket.

Confusion and chaos swirl within the crowd, suspicious eyes falling on me. Is it weird to have two powers here? Would it not make sense to have two? Do they not inherit one from each parent? Surely that isn't so strange?

"Calm down, everyone. Calm down!" Dean Delarosa jumps in as the students begin to rise, their panic quickly changing to anger. Groups of students are screaming at each other, at me, at the Dean. I search for Demi, my friendly face, but she has been swallowed by the small crowd of students who have begun to descend upon me.

Before I can turn and bolt, Delarosa grabs me by the elbow and tugs me along after her. I stumble at first, but right myself quickly. Clearly, it's in my best interest to get out of here. The students are getting angry and out of control all too fast.

But why?

"I don't understand," I say as another professor holds the doors open, slamming them shut behind us within seconds of our feet crossing the threshold. "Why is everyone so mad?"

"Azalea, it is very rare to have two types of powers. It is even rarer to have both the Shadow *and* Light elements."

"Rare, but not unheard of?" I question uncertainly. There's got to be more to it than rarity. Those students were prepared to *attack* me. It was clear to both me and Delarosa—their thoughts written in the hard lines on their faces.

"I've never heard of it." She admits, glancing down with guilt and worry. "Not to say that it has never happened before, though. I'll do some research and find out more."

"I don't—"

"Azalea, those two powers are exact opposites of each other. Light and dark? The moon and the sun? They are completely different elements. I'm not sure how you can hold them both within you. They represent very different things, very different people. I'm not sure how that may affect you as a person in the long run."

"But why were they so mad? Surely that's a me problem? I mean, they weren't just mad, Dean Delarosa. They were *furious*."

"Do you remember how I told you yesterday that our world revolves around power and who has more of it?"

"Yeah, I remember that part quite clearly."

"Power is *everything*, Azalea. And you've just shown everyone in that room that you have a whole lot of it."

CHAPTER 7

"If you find yourself alone with a Reaper, do not engage. Until the Charmed reach adulthood, they are unable to come into their full powers. That being said, it is not unusual for a child to find themselves cornered by a Reaper who sniffed out their untapped potential. If this happens, run. Run and do not look back."
—*A Guide to the Charmed* (current edition), written by Glamourist Elias Kasper in 1907 A.G.

"You should have seen everyone's faces, Azzie! Especially the Gravediggers. They were *pissed*. Honestly, if I didn't like you before, that performance alone would have secured you a friendship with me. It was great! Nothing ever rattles those guys." Demi prattles on as she once again does my makeup and hair.

I'm not sure if I should be expecting her from now on or not. I'm not complaining, though. This is two mornings now where all I have had to do is sit down and listen instead of going through the motions of getting ready. Having a sort of friend is…nice. Even if things can't stay this way for long.

"Well, I'm sure my face was equally as horrified," I respond, thinking back to the whole debacle. "Though, I still don't entirely understand what the big deal is. Delarosa said it isn't necessarily unheard of for someone to have two powers."

"It's rare, Azzie. The Gravediggers themselves don't even hold two powers. Not a single one of them. They're jealous, plain and simple. And after yesterday…it wouldn't be a big leap to say that you've made yourself some powerful enemies."

"What the fuck do you mean *enemies*? That's a little extreme, isn't it?"

"Not here, it isn't. It's going to take you some time to adjust to our ways, but…yeah. Things aren't going to be easy for you, Azzie. A stranger coming from the human world with a shit load of power and a rare ability combo? Yeah, that makes you enemy number one. You are nothing without your power in this place, babe. The more, the better. I know Delarosa has told you this multiple times already, but I will, too, if it's what makes you finally understand. Yes, our larger goal may be to take down the Reapers, but in all reality, you can and *will* be targeted by some people if it means they remain at the top. Not everyone is in this profession because they want to save lives; some are only here to make a name for themselves.

"Remember how I said yesterday the Gravediggers have ruled over this school for a full year now, and that they ruled the schools they attended before this one for even longer? Well, I forgot to mention that every Conjurer in this world knows their names. They are used to being above everyone else, used to being elevated to a level only the Grim rises above. As soon as you learn to control those abilities of yours, you'll soar higher than they ever will be. And that makes you a gigantic threat to them and this empire they are creating."

"I don't want to be anyone's enemy, much less theirs. Can't we just, like, ignore each other and pretend one another doesn't exist? That's my preferred method of dealing with people I don't like."

"Nope. Won't happen." She laughs nervously, her hand twitching against my face as she falters. "Listen, Azalea. Hear me. Do not antagonize those men, okay? They are crazy powerful. I may like Arlo, but I also know what he is inside. What all of them are. They only care about each other. They don't care about me, or you, or anyone else in this damn school. They will do whatever they have to as long as it ends with them being the strongest Conjurers here. Some people are going to be in awe of you, and may even give you the same treatment the Gravediggers receive, but don't count on the Gravediggers being in awe, or even count on them wanting you to stay alive for the greater good.

"I've heard they are vying to be the youngest council members in Shadow Faction history. To do that…they are going to have to jump through a lot of hoops. Prove themselves in ways the others didn't have to. You're a giant red flag waving in front of them. Don't make them believe you are a problem that needs to be taken care of. If anything, prove to be an asset."

"What do you mean by 'taken care of?'" My heart beats a steady pace as I ask, my mind forming an answer before she can. "Oh. You mean they will kill me."

Her nod is the only confirmation I get.

I'm sure hearing that is supposed to spark terror within me, maybe provoke me into watching my back every time I leave this room. But I'm not terrified, and I don't plan on becoming paranoid, either. Mostly, this is annoying. Fucking asswipes think they rule over the whole place, huh? Well, they aren't going to rule over *me*.

"Do you even care?" Demi gapes down at me with a barely contained surprise, blinking rapidly at the calm expression on my face. I guess she doesn't see the reaction she expected there.

"Why would I?" I know she has gone out of her way twice now to warn me about these guys, but they sound like a group of spoiled punks who get a kick from scaring their fellow students. Unfortunately for them, I won't be one of those students.

"Are you for real right now? Fuck, Azalea. Do they not teach you that dying is bad in the human world?" She sets down the brushes that are in her hand, crossing her arms across her chest as she glares down at me.

"Well, yeah, but dying doesn't scare me. Nothing does."

"Nothing scares you?" She arches a brow, but I can only shrug. How do I explain this emptiness inside of me? How can I tell her the only things I feel are not worth feeling?

"Nothing scares me, nothing excites me, nothing keeps my heart racing. It's just how I am." I settle on saying.

"Oh. Oh, I see."

I wrinkle my nose in disgust at the pitying look that overcomes her face, the sadness leaking from her eyes. That's the look my first, second, and third therapists gave me, too. It's how I knew something was seriously wrong with me.

"You see?" I raise an eyebrow, glancing to the side as she brushes her tears away with a poised delicacy.

"It's not your fault, Azzie. You weren't meant to live so long in the human world without being able to use your powers. We have Charms, plus training, while being raised that help us sustain our abilities here. We are given every opportunity to discover ourselves. But you weren't. So all of that repressed power? It's damaging. It slowly eats away at you and has done so for many, many years, by the sounds of it. It would have kept going until you were dead. You weren't always unfeeling, were you?" The question doesn't sound much like one.

"No." I think I felt things for Neil. At one point, he was this hopeful beacon. Until he wasn't. Until he was nothing more than a pawn in my game, a player I was willing to use until there was nothing left if it meant I would finally win.

"It's your powers. Damn, it's a good thing you are here. You would have destroyed yourself over there. What a waste of power that would have been." She shakes her head sadly, as if that's what matters: my powers being gone and not necessarily me.

Delarosa said a similar thing about my powers yesterday, had told me that they were the likely reason behind my curse. If those two are right, then maybe I made the right choice deciding to stay here after all. I *want* to feel. Even if all I get is pain. Pain is better than the emptiness.

"I have to attend classes today, right?" I change the subject, watching her flutter around the bathroom.

"Yep." She pops the 'p' as she starts on my hair. "I have your class schedule here. Sorry about all the wrinkles and tears. I had to write it quickly and shove it in my pocket."

Demi digs through her box of goodies, then pulls out a thin sheet of paper with scratchy writing and an emblem pasted at the top. A dragon wearing a crown, holding a shield. Inside of the shield is a giant 'D' nestled on a bed of roses. The dragon's tail snakes up around the bottom, resting just below those roses. It is beautiful and dangerous, exactly the type of symbol I would expect Draxmere to have.

"Basic Combat at eight." I read aloud, my eyes raking over the list. "Charm Development at nine-thirty. Light Specialty Training at eleven. Lunch at twelve-thirty. Shadow Specialty Training at one thirty."

"Monday through Friday." Demi grins, patting me on the shoulder. "Don't worry, your muscles will build quickly. And it won't hurt so much after a few weeks."

"I'm not worried about my muscles, or about being sore," I say, and it's true.

"But you are worried about something?"

"Not worried. Just curious about the people I have to share these classes with. Are they all going to be like the Gravediggers?" If everyone hates me, so be it. I'm an outsider and always will be in their eyes. Worrying about it won't change that fact.

"There's a lot of confusion when it comes to you and your abilities, Azzie. Everyone is arguing about you and where you belong, about hidden motives and lies. Some shout tales of unfairness, others shout stories of you being the savior we have been waiting on. A few even tried to argue that it was a trick, that you don't actually have two powers."

"How would I even know how to trick you guys, much less have a reason to? I knew nothing about this world before coming here. Not much time to prepare such a well-crafted lie and the magic trick that accompanied it." Surely people aren't that gullible?

"Ah, that's where the argument is. Some are trying to say that you *did* know about this world before yesterday. They've theorized that you work for the Grim and he has been training you to destroy us. Yeah, I know, don't shoot the messenger and all. Most of us know it's a load of B.S."

"Fuck 'em all." I shrug, standing abruptly.

"I guess I'm done." She huffs, passing me my uniform. "You don't have to prove anything to anyone, anyway. Hey, want to hear something crazy?" I sigh as Demi bounces around excitedly, slinging my pants off and replacing them with the skirt that's too short for my body type.

"I have a feeling you would tell me even if I didn't."

"Listen to this! Yesterday, a Seer came forward claiming she prophesied about your return years ago, she just didn't realize it was you. She had proof in her journals, in entries written like three years ago or something. She had written all kinds of crazy things about you. Though, from what I heard, it was all vaguely referencing you. Like, everything just said the jinxed one. She said almost all of them depicted you as some kind of savior, but she didn't know who or what you were saving.

Delarosa snatched that journal before anyone else got a chance to look at it. No one has seen this chick since yesterday, so my theory is they are doing major damage control. Whatever is in that journal, they don't want the rest of us finding out." Demi is whispering conspiratorially, laughing lightly.

I don't want to be anyone's savior, and I don't plan on living up to that reputation anytime soon. "They can keep their journals. I'll decide my future on my own, thank you very much. Hey—what's this?" Distracted, I tap on the pin now attached to the breast of my uniform's vest.

"That is the symbol for the Light and Shadow Wielders. You guys get a different one from the other Elementalists so you are easily identifiable on the battlefield."

The pin has a sun in the middle with a crescent moon overlapping it. Little rays of light shine from behind it, and a gaggle of stars encompass them in the general shape of a circle. A sun for the Lights, a moon for the Shadows. I suppose the stars are meant to represent our abilities working together, the need for those two elements to combine to become a greater creation.

"Every type of Conjurer has a symbol like this?"

"Well, duh! Mine is here!" She points to her pin, a mermaid with bat wings holding a baby wolf. Kind of odd, but I can understand the basic symbolism. Actually…I have a tattoo on my leg of a mermaid holding a baby wolf. Were my dreams trying to tell me about this place all along? "The Glamourists have this framed, oval mirror with a hoard of butterflies inside. It's pretty cool because they flicker in and out like an actual glamour would. The Necromancers have a skeletal hand holding an anatomical heart, which is kind of freaky if you ask me.

"The other Elementalists have this sort of stacked design, one layer a row of flames, the next a row of mountains, then a row of waves, and topped off by a row of wind gusts. All of it is surrounded by these little lines kind of boxing them in. Then there are the Enhancers, who have a sword with lightning bolts protruding like wings. And, umm…oh! The Seers. They have a pair of hands holding a crystal ball with roses inside."

"Oh, okay. So all I need to do is look at these pins, and that will tell me someone's ability?"

"Yeah, basically. Usually, they all hang out in groups with similar powers, so you can tell cliques apart pretty easily. Werewolf Shifters are the worst about forming these secretive groups. Ugh. Basic Combat Training and Charm Development are supposed to help us mingle and find friends outside of the stereotypical groups we stick with, but…only a few of us make that kind of effort. You'll see."

"Great." I wiggle the white blouse over my head, the vest slipping on after. I don't bother to tuck in my shirt like Demi does, opting instead to have it fall loosely over the top of my high-waist skirt.

I notice the school emblem is now slapped proudly onto my skirt pocket, its dragon glaring menacingly.

"Should we be dressed for Basic Combat Training like this?" I question, gesturing vaguely at the outfits that are not at all meant for fighting.

"Nah, we have locker rooms with outfits to change into and out of. Here." Demi tosses a package at me, and I catch it clumsily. "Eat that. Bring a water bottle, the school should have provided you with a reusable one. I don't recommend a big breakfast right before training yet. Don't worry, I'll bring you those little toasted treats every morning." She winks, turning to flounce away.

I reach out and grab Demi's wrist before I have much time to think about what I'm going to say or what her reaction might be to it.

"Don't you have any other friends to hang out with? Anybody that isn't the new girl who literally has to be given multiple explanations on basic things like a child?" She has spent the last two days entirely with me. Why? Why spend so much time with me? Why plan on being here more? We hardly know each other.

"Trying to get rid of me?"

"No, I'm just genuinely curious. I mean—"

"It's okay, Azzie. Yes, I do have other friends. Lots of them. But they don't need me right now: you do. Besides, I've been waiting for you. I'm sure you are getting sick of being told that, but it's true. A Seer friend told me this, once. She said 'befriend the jinx and all will be well. Your savior or your doom only time can tell.' And preceded to give me three more prophesies about you that year.

"I took those pretty seriously. All of your prophecies refer to you as the jinx or the jinxed. Once Delarosa pieced that together a few years ago, I knew exactly what you were going to mean to me. And now there's all this talk of you being a savior! Who am I to deny our destiny?" Demi lets out a soft little laugh, a happy twinkle in her eyes.

Maybe she has been waiting for me in the same way I have been waiting for this place.

"Alright. I suppose I can accept that. Though, I don't think it will ever get easier listening to people talk about what Seers say as if it's some kind of decree. As if there is no changing fate once they've said their piece."

"Stick around, Azalea, and you will learn to accept a lot of things."

"That's not ominous at all."

We laugh together, and with a jolt, I realize I am feeling a hint of something new: *happiness.*

CHAPTER 8

"Among the humans, a savior will live,
safe and sound with all four limbs.
But in her heart she cannot feel,
only Conjuring can help her heal."
—Prophesy recorded inside student Seer Allia Jordan's Prophetic
Journal, 2023 A.G.

The locker rooms are smelly and cold, just like I imagined.

Demi pushes into the small room with me, grinning and holding my hand as she pulls me toward her locker. "Everyone, this is Azalea Jinx! Here, the locker next to me is free. I took the liberty of putting your training clothes inside."

Around thirty girls linger inside in various states of undress. Their chatter and laughter dies out upon my introduction.

I stumble behind Demi and into the middle of the room, reaching toward the locker she indicated. Two benches lay between us and another row of lockers are against the wall. A few girls watch from underneath their eyelashes as they tie their shoes. I ignore their beady eyes, pulling out the clothes Demi had said were there. Black, black, and, oh, look at that! More black.

"Thanks, Demi."

The room reluctantly resumes its chatter, but I can still feel the stolen glances and outright stares as I change. I know what they see: the girl with vivid chunks of amethyst purple in her hair, imperfect tan skin covered in sunburns and an outrageous amount of tattoos, and an oversized body not prepared for training. I forgot how things are as the new kid, how the stares can make you self-conscious. I've been that kid enough times to know the novelty fades over time, though. I can only hope that remains true here, because I may have to use my new powers to explode a few eyeballs if this goes on too long. I'm not sure I can do that but, well, it may be worth trying.

I stay quiet as I follow Demi and the other girls out of the locker room right at eight when the extremely loud gong from the clock tower sounds. We trail into the gym from the night before, except this time, the training equipment is all back in its proper place. Large machines and heavy weights are littered around, some I recognize as treadmills and moving steps. I spot a giant rope hanging from the ceiling in one corner of the room and a rock climbing wall in another. What truly catches my attention is the giant mat placed off to the side, similar in size to a boxing ring's floor.

A large group of guys emerge from the other side of the room, and I stumble after the others as we all gather around that large mat in one fluid movement like a school of fish.

I try not to look for the Gravediggers among the men, but I can't help myself. I find them quite easily, annoyance rising when I see that all four are already watching me. I shiver underneath their stares, but not in fear; in anticipation.

"Alright, Conjurers!" A giant man claps his hands in the center of the mat to draw our attention, muscles bulging with each movement.

It only takes one glance to understand this man's qualifications. He's covered in scars, the light marks a stark contrast on dark skin. His bald head shines in the bright lights above us, but his beard seems to be long and full. He watches us with deep brown eyes, sharp gaze flicking between each of us like we are ants he is preparing to crush beneath his boots. I see a Necromancer pin gleaming on his tight shirt, which could easily be mistaken as a speck of dirt on his giant body.

"We are going to be sparring again today. I think we are going to start with…you, new girl. Step up. What's your name?"

"Azalea Jinx," I sigh as I push my way through the group of girls, pulling my hair into a high ponytail as I walk. *Sorry, Demi.*

"Right. Jinx. I'm Grey Donovan. Do you know anything about fighting? Had any training?"

"Sure. A little." It's an understatement, but I'd rather show than tell.

"Mmm. I'm sure you do." He glances me up and down with a scoff, likely noticing my lack of visible muscle and larger stature. "Alright. Well, let's see you fight, and we will go from there. The Gravediggers are attending classes with you first years to help you get your sea legs, so to speak. So, if you need extra help, I will assign one of them to you. But for today, your partner is going to be…Stella Stargrove."

Hoots and laughs erupt from behind me, accompanied by gasps and cries of outrage. Stella must be good, then.

A girl steps forward, hands on her swinging hips as she approaches. Swinging with her is long, straight, blond hair, and her piercing gray-blue eyes bear into me. Her steps are confident, her smirk arrogant. I don't see a pin on her to identify her ability, but most of us aren't wearing them right now. She's built like a stick, thin and breakable. The idea she could beat me is laughable. I'm around two hundred pounds, curvy and thick; I could sit on her and win.

"It would be my pleasure to be her partner today," her purring, sticky sweet voice replies.

I follow Stella onto the mat, mimicking her movements as we plant our feet onto the firm cushioning. Fists are raised and legs are stepping back as we begin an age-old dance.

A whistle blows without any shaking of hands or talk of luck. "Begin!"

The circling continues for a few more seconds before she speaks. "I hear you know my boyfriend." Each word is a quiet hiss, though a smirk still haunts her thin lips.

I dodge an advance, and her flying fist retreats to her side in a flash. "I'm sure I don't."

"Jaymes Bloodgood? You know, the guy who saved you from that hellhole you called home?"

"Oh, you mean the guy who kidnapped me?" She swings again and I barely dance out of the way, stumbling slightly as frustration creases across her plain face.

"Listen, bitch. I'm only going to say this once: back off. I don't care how powerful you are or how special you believe yourself to be. He doesn't want you. He never will."

I almost laugh at the absurdity of it. Jaymes and I had spoken all of a few minutes, not counting the time he yelled out in front of half of the school that I was a fraud. What about those interactions has her scared? Or is it just my power she thinks will tempt him?

"Why the fuck would I want your boyfriend? Keep the prick."

I am the first to swing this time, faking with my left hand and swinging with my right. The distraction works; my fist meets her cheek, the force of the hit sending her stumbling back in surprise. I am annoyed far too greatly by the way she howls, her lithe body racing forward angrily in retaliation.

I am quick to step to the side, sticking my leg out at the last second. She trips over it, falling to the mat hard. Her head bounces as I leap, putting all of my weight into the attack. Stella struggles underneath me, trying to crawl out from the damning position. Somehow, she manages to throw an elbow back into my ribs, leaving me wheezing and tilting off her body. She's out before I can blink.

I cry out when a foot hits my ear, a ringing sound filling my head. I push myself to my feet, off balance and reeling. Stella leaps toward me again, catching her arm around my neck and attempting to drag me down from behind. I choke and sputter briefly, reaching up to clasp her elbows in my hands before using her momentum against her. Her body flips over mine, flinging down onto the mat painfully. I hear the breath leave her body, hear her whimper as she shakily pushes up onto her hands.

I'm on her before she can rise.

I pin her arms down underneath my knees, grabbing a handful of perfect blond hair. I slam her head down over and over and over again. I don't stop until that shrill whistle sounds again, knocking me out of my dazed stupor.

I stand and retreat, blinking rapidly at the warm liquid on my hands. Stella's face is bloody, her nose bent at an odd angle. I don't feel guilty about the bruised and bloody face I left behind, nor do I feel satisfaction. It happened, I did it, and it doesn't make me feel anything new.

It's a damn shame.

"Well, well, well. I underestimated you, Jinx. Great job! Someone take Stargrove to the medics!"

A couple of girls race to Stella, glaring at me as they pass. I shoot a small grin over my shoulder, winking at Demi before walking back toward her. I receive cheers and claps on my back as I go, my performance enough to make me worthy of their praise.

"How did you do that? Stella is usually one of our best fighters! She is so fast and agile, it's hard for a lot of people to avoid her. But you pinned her down like it was nothing!"

A girl next to Demi gapes, her head shaking in disbelief. Her auburn curls bounce with her, brown eyes boring into me. My gaze trails after the freckles dancing across her cheeks and forehead, following it down to the pale skin of her arms before flicking back up to her eyes.

"I tried a lot of hobbies in the human world. I took self-defense, boxing, karate, Kung Fu, Jiu-Jitsu, and a ton of other martial arts classes. It's all muscle memory at this point. Oh! And street fighting—great way to get tattoo money—my favorite and preferred style." I plaster on a grin, remembering those nights in abandoned buildings with cheering crowds and the smell of blood permeating the air. I abandoned those nights to flee to Orlando.

I don't remember every single class I took.

I must have tried everything and learned every technique. Most of them didn't stick, only vague memories left where technique should lie. But they all had one thing in common: they were attempts at making myself feel. I thought the pain would work, the soreness, the burning muscles, the blood.

It didn't.

I bounced from hobby to hobby over the years, hoping *something* would excite me.

Almost nothing ever did.

"Putting my experience aside, that girl is built like a twig. I'm, like, triple her size. I'm sure her size assists in speed, but it does nothing against brute force. And, obviously, she's used to being on the offensive. My defensive moves tripped her up too easily. Also, Stella was leading with her emotions. It cost her in the end. That's the best you guys can do?"

"Wow! I didn't know humans could be so cool. Hey—"

"Alright, knock it off with the human insults, *Genevieve*." Demi cuts her off mid-sentence.

"Just Ginny." She corrects with a sniff from her large nose, exposing a long neck as she glances me over with one hand on her jutted-out hip. "Ginny Brady. Nice to meet you, Azalea Jinx."

Her thin lips purse in annoyance at Demi as she reaches a hand out, and I clasp it in mine to give it a brief shake as I truly take her in. Ginny has a harsh kind of beauty, with a wide forehead, sharp cheekbones, and a jawline that could cut someone. I notice a Glamourist logo embroidered on her shoe and take note of her long legs accompanied by wide hips.

"Um, yeah. You too."

Everyone continues to stare at me, even as Professor Donovan starts yelling out more pairs, even as he forces us into drills and formations. I wish the burning in my muscles bothered me as much as Demi said it would. I wish meeting all of these beautiful people would spark a light inside of me.

Unfortunately for me, only darkness lives there, and even fighting can't fix that.

CHAPTER 9

"Charming is an exact science, albeit a simple one. To perform the advanced Charms listed in this text, we must remember the basics we learned as children. Without control over simple Charms, you cannot perform Advanced ones, so don't bother trying unless you wish to harm yourself or others."

—*Advanced Charming* written by Roman Emerson, 2001 A.G.

"Welcome back to Charm Development, students! Alright, turn in those essays I assigned on Friday."

Mumbles and groans follow that statement, but everyone moves to grab their papers from inside their bags. I glance around awkwardly, tapping my feet underneath my desk. Honestly, I'm incredibly annoyed after the long walk through the back courtyard to get to this tiny little building on the edge of campus.

Ginny had escorted me here, leading me out of another one of those doors I never would have noticed on the bottom floor of the main building. Then we walked a fucking mile up a slight incline to get here. I didn't even have time to look at the pretty flowers or the immaculate maze outside! Maybe, instead of staying in this class, I can go do that instead.

I'm staring at the door, plotting my escape, when the professor approaches and taps on my desk. It grabs my attention, her gentle smile drawing me in.

"Um, hi?"

"Hello, Azalea Jinx. I am Professor Canmore. Obviously, I don't expect an essay from you. However, I do expect you to read the first four chapters of your textbook, *Advanced Charming*, to get caught up and for you to write a paper on each one. I'm sure any of your new friends will help you with the things you get confused about. I know Charming is new to you, and it can be hard to understand without knowing the basics. Please, let me know if you need any help with your studies." Her smile seems more sinister now, her back turning to me slowly.

Professor Canmore is a plump, older lady; a surprise considering all of the Conjurers I have met are in immaculate shape. Her gray hair is cut short, barely grazing across her neck and forehead. What really makes her seem so sinister is the crooked nose, her prevalent wrinkles, and her eyes which are black like a crow's. If asked to describe her, I would say she looks like the witch in movies who lives in a hut in the middle of nowhere.

Something about her is setting me on edge.

"Today we will be learning the Transportation Charm. Now, who can tell me about it?" Only a few students raise their hands, and she allows a guy in the front row to answer.

"It moves you small distances, around teen feet max. Its sister Charm, the Transference Charm, can move you to much greater distances. It's not complicated, but it requires a ton of focus. Plus the correct hand movements, of course."

Canmore claps her hands excitedly, grinning brightly at him. "Correct! Now, Azalea, something you need to know about Charming is that you have to have *intention*. Without intention, nothing will happen. You have to believe in yourself and your abilities. In other words, you need to have confidence. You must concentrate on exactly what it is you are trying to do. We don't use words to cast a Charm. They aren't like the witch spells humans think we do, yeah? We use our bodies to do the work for us. An easy acronym to remember those things is BIC. Body, intention, confidence. Now, class, watch me."

Her hands move wildly as she speaks, her voice fluctuating in and out of dramatic displays. Her eyes flutter shut as those hand movements stop abruptly at the end of the speech, her body stilling unnaturally. After a full minute of silence, Canmore claps her hands together, pushing them in a circular, clockwise motion. Then she opens them up, swishing them down in a cupping motion.

Canmore disappears right before our eyes, reappearing in the back corner of the room next to an unsuspecting student. She screams out in fright as the other students whoop and cheer for their professor.

"Envision your destination, see it clearly in your mind. By this time next week, I expect you all to do this multiple times within a minute. And, yes, you will be tested on it. Now, pair up folks! Time to practice."

"Want to be my partner?" Ginny asks from beside me, smiling shyly as the room erupts in a clatter of noises.

"Sure," I agree, sending her my own hesitant smile back. Shy people are always reassured by other's shyness; they don't like to feel alone in their anxious thoughts.

The two of us stand along with the others, helping to push desks toward the back of the room before standing in rows across from one another.

"Alright, I know this is your first Charm. So, my best advice? Believe in yourself." Ginny's face is serious and determined: she wants me to succeed. I nod along to her words, closing my eyes tightly. I *can* do this. I have to.

"Don't be upset if you don't get it on the first try, most people don't. Just do your—" Her voice fades from my consciousness, along with the ones surrounding us.

I think about Ginny and her pretty auburn hair, think about the space in front of her. I think about the white tile and picture that foot-by-foot square directly in front of her feet. My hands move on their own, my mind calm and focused as I clap them together. I don't worry about not being able to perform the Charm; if I'm truly powerful, then I can do it. My hands form that perfect three-hundred-and-sixty-degree circle, opening and cupping sharply before swooshing down in the same way Canmore had shown us.

It doesn't feel silly to be doing this; it just feels *right*.

Ginny screeches as I pop up in front of her, her hand flying to her chest in surprise. She had been mid-sentence, mouth opening and closing as she tries to comprehend what happened.

I laugh, my heart racing in the best way. Fuck, that felt good. The rush of power is not like anything I've ever felt before, like a shot of adrenaline straight to the heart.

It's there…then it's gone.

I frown, rubbing my chest. I ache for more, ache for the missing thing in my life I need to feel *alive*. Apparently, Charming isn't the solution. Even if using my powers feels like a temporary high.

"Wow. That was cool," I say with a shaky voice, glancing down at my body. Yep, all of it is here. The room has fallen into silence, all eyes on me. Again. How many times is that today?

"Excellent job, Azalea! Brilliant! Aiming to be my star pupil, I see!" That sinister smile returns, something dark hiding in Canmore's gaze.

"Thanks," I say, unsure of what to do now.

"Alright, my turn, show off." Ginny smiles, giving me a light shove to encourage me to walk back to my spot. I do so, watching her try, and fail, for forty-five minutes afterward to transport herself to me. So far, only me and two others have managed to do it. Another thing to put me on the enemies' radars, I suppose.

"Alright, class. That's enough for today. We will try again tomorrow! Practice, practice, practice in the meantime!"

We gather our things silently, and I follow Ginny out of the door. Demi is waiting to greet us, her smile bright and friendly. She blabbers on about her Shifting Specialty Training class, telling us about some new trick or another she learned from her professor. I try to listen, I really do, but I'm distracted by the four boys off in the distance.

The Gravediggers.

Four people I should absolutely stay away from.

For some reason, I have a feeling I won't be able to.

"Miss Jinx! Come, come!"

I sigh as I hear another excited professor call my name. She watches me approach the area where my Light Specialty Training class is hovering in the courtyard of the West Wing, and I outright groan when I spot Jaymes standing beside her.

"Yes?" My eyes flicker to Jaymes's slight smirk apprehensively, weariness in my tone.

As the Light Specialty Training professor approaches, I notice her gray-streaked brown hair is pulled back in a tight bun, most likely to help tighten some of the wrinkles against her tan skin, which exposes her older age. Despite my assumptions about that age, I notice a small ring hanging from her eyebrow and a tattoo curling above her chest: a floral pattern of some sort. My eyes travel down the rest of her face, past her blue-gray eyes, to the tiny scar on her bottom lip. Is it a scar from an old piercing, or possibly a battle scar? I've never seen someone her age with tattoos and piercings, and it gains her a tidbit of respect from me.

"Let me introduce myself before we get started, hmm? I am Professor Battle, and I will be instructing you in your Light Wielding abilities. And how exciting it is to teach a student as promising as yourself! I will be teaching you what I can but, unfortunately, you are very behind. Most students have at least the basics down, but you…don't. And I'm not sure how fast we will be able to teach you without some one-on-one training. So, Jaymes here has volunteered to help you out! He's light years ahead in his own class, which makes him the perfect tutor! And I know you two have already met, so that's always a bonus.

"This first week I want you two working on catching up. I've not gotten very far into the teaching aspects of this class yet, as we are all in very different places ability-wise, and I'm still getting a feel for everyone and what I think they may be capable of. But this week is the last week for that, so I need you to work extra hard to catch up with your peers. Any questions?" Professor Battle speaks fast and fervently, grinning brightly when she's done.

"Nope." My questions can't be answered by her.

Why did Jaymes volunteer to teach me? Why is he taking time out of his day that could be spent elsewhere to help me? Shouldn't he be trying to sabotage me or something?

"Great! Alrighty, off you two go. Who's next?" A line has formed behind us, and we are quick to leave the scene.

"Are you actually going to teach me anything?" I can't wrap my head around this. Aren't he and his buddies supposed to be intimidated by my power? Why the fuck would they want to help me learn how to use them?

"Of course I will," he snaps impatiently, spinning toward me sharply and invading my personal space. "I may not like you or your presence here, but that doesn't mean you should be defenseless. You have no idea what's out there, Jinx. I wouldn't even wish *you* death at the hands of a Reaper."

"That scary, hmm?"

"Terrifying. I've seen what they can do firsthand. You don't want to be their next meal." His eyes seem haunted as he speaks, the ghost of a memory forming. He blinks and that vulnerability is gone, replaced by a hardness I am becoming accustomed to.

"Alright, then. What am I supposed to do?" I haven't used my Light or Shadow abilities yet. I know I'm both halves of a coin, two parts of a whole: I get it. What I don't get is how I'm supposed to wield them.

"Close your eyes."

I cock my head, rolling said eyes. "Why would I do that? Am I supposed to trust you aren't going to kill me in such a vulnerable state? Because I've been warned you will attempt to do so."

"Why would I kill you?" He looks genuinely bewildered, scoffing in distaste at me. "That would get me kicked out of school. Code of conduct and all. Now, if you were to die in your sleep mysteriously…well, that wouldn't be my fault."

The small tilt of his lips gives him away.

"Gotchya. You won't kill me with witnesses around. Good to know. Guess I'll need to find someone to warm my bed at night, then."

"Are you expecting me to volunteer?"

I shake my head slightly at the dry monotone in which he delivers that statement.

"Didn't I just say it's *you* I have to worry about sneaking into my room unsolicited at night? If you're a creep, just say so."

"That's not what I meant," he growls, clearly annoyed.

I send him a sly smile, one I hope unnerves him. "Alright, closing my eyes now," I say, deciding that I don't give a fuck if he does try to kill me in front of all these witnesses and gets himself kicked out of school.

"I'm going to touch you, okay?"

"Touch away. Just don't expect me to not rub this in your girlfriend's face."

I feel his callused hands brush gently against my arms, trailing their way up to my shoulders. They crawl up my neck, to my cheeks, stopping in their tracks. His hands are warm and large, covering my entire cheek. The tips of his fingers graze my hair, digging in if only slightly.

His breath comes next, minty and hot against my skin. One day, I might be able to feel that terrifying pit of attraction deep in my stomach that a touch from a man who looks like this brings. I'm glad I can't feel it now, truthfully. Being aroused during training would fucking suck.

"Focus on where our skin meets. Think about that thing inside of you that feels different, that you know no one else has. The creature living inside of your abyss. Tug on it, like a leash. Call it to you."

I listen to Jaymes, taking a deep breath before diving down into the empty spot inside of me. Except…it isn't empty anymore. I reach and dig, urging the creature inside to rise, and it does. Two little spheres dance around in there, not creatures at all but beautiful orbs that are eerily similar to the ones from my test.

"What the fuck?" I hiss, eyes flying open. "What are those?"

"They are representations of your powers, dumbass. Now close your eyes."

I slam them shut again, annoyed. "Sorry, I didn't realize I wasn't allowed to ask questions, *dumbass*."

I ignore how tightly Jaymes digs into my skin at the verbal jab, instead focusing on the task at hand. I'm quick to think about reaching out and snagging the bright one, imagining my hand clasping around it while somehow feeling the burn it leaves behind. It struggles at the intrusion, bouncing around in that imaginary hand.

"Why won't it just come?"

"You aren't letting it. Relax, Azalea. Use my touch to anchor you. I'm going to send some of my Light inside of you, okay? It'll encourage yours to come out and play, convince it that it is safe in your hands."

I gasp, arching my back as his power abruptly enters me. It seeps through my cheeks, burning through my veins as it searches for my Light. It explodes inside of that dark pit, illuminating every inch of me. I feel it burning through my body, blinding my cells, spreading my molecules. But it works. The bright sphere in my imaginary palm relaxes, easing into me before beginning to grow.

It grows, grows, grows, until my pit is alight all on its own. Until I am providing the light in the dark, brightening every nook in my emptiness. Jaymes's Light has fled, allowing room for mine to continue to expand. And oh does it do so. It warms my entire body, spilling out of my skin like ink from a bottle. Dripping like water after a storm. A brief spark of joy is ignited within me, and I enjoy it while it lasts.

Just as fast as it exploded, the Light is sucked back inside. It cozies back up in its home, content and ready for me to pull from. I can still feel it, a strange and airy presence I've never experienced before. It's like a piece of my puzzle has clicked into place or as if I've let loose a breath I never knew I was holding. Genuine laughter bubbles inside of me, pouring out in one big gush.

"Wow. I didn't know *that* was inside of me!" My eyes fly open again, and I see the creases at the corners of his eyes, noticing the pursed lips.

I suppose he didn't like what he saw.

"You have an unusually bright light," he says, hands falling back down to his sides.

"Okay, great, but now that I've found it, how do I use it?"

"I'll teach you the first thing a child learns, yeah? Since you're still on that level and all."

"Fuck you. I need you to teach me, I don't need you to commentate."

"Alright, whatever. Hold your hands out. Like this." He cups his hands in front of him, gesturing for me to do the same. Then he reaches out, covering my hands with his own. "Just focus, like you did when you were in Charm Development this morning. Think about bringing it to the surface. Be confident. I'm going to shoot another bit of my power into your hands, and I want you to encourage yours to meet it. Ready? Three, two, one."

I jerk when I feel the invasion again, his Light sparking into my palms. My Light rises with intent, ready to tango with its newfound friend. I struggle to control it, pulling as it pushes. I don't pull back hard enough, my grasp releasing as it bursts free and blinds us both. I fall back, landing hard on my ass. I groan and blink away the fuzzy dots in my vision, cursing myself for the lack of control.

"How am I supposed to control that?" I screech, annoyed with myself, my power, Jaymes, *everything*.

"With lots of practice. Don't worry, princess. You'll get there."

"Call me princess again and I'll kick your balls up your throat."

"Maybe I like it when you get violent, Jinx," he purrs with a smirk, dusting himself off as he stands.

"Freak," I mutter angrily, pushing myself up, too. "Now shoot your poison in me again."

CHAPTER 10

"Conjurers are volatile creatures and are often found to be jealous, angry, and violent. Recent studies have shown that this is linked directly to Charm Levels. Those with higher Charm Levels tend to be more possessive, more confrontational, and more hostile. Despite this being the case, high Charm Levels are coveted among the Charmed."
—Article entitled "Conjurers and Power Dynamics", written by Elementalist Tod Dallary, 1956 A.G.

The cafeteria here is unlike any I've seen before; though, I must admit, I've only seen a handful of the cheap, public ones.

The room is gigantic, with long bars of food stretching across in multiple rows. One holds deep red drinks in glass bottles, neat labels pasted on their fronts that I can't read but suspect detailed blood types; the vampires crowded around fuel those suspicions. Another bar is stacked high with only red meats, some still raw and bloody. The one next to that has sushi and fish of all types: grilled, fried, and raw. Directly across from those, a respectable distance away, has only leafy greens with no bright colors. However, from what I can see, there are color-coordinated bars located in the rows following.

There is even a bar for desserts only, with cakes and brownies lined up on trays in the center of the room. It goes on, and on, and on as far as my eyes can see.

"Where is the normal food?" I question wearily, raising an eyebrow at Demi. I'll eat a salad and sushi, but, truly, I can't be expected to have that all of the time. Red meats are okay, but the blood oozing off some of the platters is a turn-off.

"Oh, don't worry. The normal items change every day, there should be lots of foods you are accustomed to in the human world. There are lots of delicious things to choose from; these are mostly specialty items. It's us Shifters who need most of the food in these front rows.

"I recommend the dessert bar to start with; sugar helps with power depletion. Come on, we just have to dive a little deeper to find something you'll like." Demi tugs me along, laughing and waving at the vampires we pass at the blood bar.

"Do you…eat regular things?" I'm not sure if that's offensive to ask a vampire.

"Of course, silly. Blood is like…like insulin for a diabetic! I need it, but not all the time, and only if my body is telling me so. I had a bottle this morning for breakfast, so I won't need any until this afternoon, probably. I can make it longer than that if I don't use a lot of power from now until then."

"What kind of power do Shifters have? Besides being able to Charm, I mean?" They seem to be highly valued, but I'm not sure what, exactly, that value is.

"Ah, not much. The ability to shift *is* our power. Increased speed, increased strength. And a Siren's voice? Ooh, you don't want one of them getting in your head. Basically, we exist to assist our assigned teams in the field, but we can't take down a Reaper on our own. We are certified distractions. We can force a Reaper into submission, allowing the Illuminoors and Dimineers to do all of the important work."

"So…you have, like, a vampire form?"

"Sure. It's a little scary, though, so I'll show you another time. Our faces crack and turn into this hideous beast. It's the worst part of being a vampire because I look so *ugly*. At least werewolves look like cute puppies."

"We are not cute puppies," Arlo snaps playfully from in front of us, turning to grin at Demi. "We are ferocious beasts who can rip you apart in a single bite."

"Yeah? You'd have to catch me first," she bites back with a smirk, hand planted on her hip.

"I'd love to chase you, little vamp." He grins back, bending down to invade her space. "Want to play sometime?"

"No, thanks, Arlo." She laughs, a blush staining her cheeks.

When he steps forward, I notice his height, which is a great difference for Demi but seemingly still on the shorter side for a man. With him this close, I have a chance to observe more than just the distinctive red curls and lackluster height.

Arlo is much more handsome than I originally thought. His messy red hair flops into his large face, brushing against his bushy eyebrows. His hazel eyes are alluring, the size and shape oddly resembling a dog's. His nose is long and sharp, but not in a way that overtakes his entire face. My gaze is drawn to the pointed white teeth hiding under curved lips; sharp and deadly, just as he claimed. His jaw is as sharp as his teeth, the lower half of his square-like face hidden underneath a stubbly beard. When he smiles at Demi,

I notice a single dimple on his left cheek, which is all too adorable for a man as dangerous as he. I also can't help but notice the muscles underneath his white shirt bulging, but I'm not shocked by this revelation. Practically everyone here is fit; I suppose it's a perk to the whole monster-hunter occupation they're training for.

"There you are, sweets!" a voice chimes from the crowd, and Demi practically deflates.

"Come on, Azzie. I know you're hungry. Let's leave the wolf to his meal."

Arlo frowns at Demi's back as we leave, a questioning look in his eyes that flickers to me. I shrug, even though I know that grating voice must have been his girlfriend. Obviously, Demi didn't have talking to her on the agenda today.

"Wow." I gape as she pulls me along, taking in everything and nothing all at once. The amount of food is a little overwhelming, honestly. As well as the bars full of drinks, some of which look suspiciously alcoholic.

"I know, it's a lot. What's your favorite food?" Demi's voice knocks me back into the moment.

"Oh. I don't know, actually. I just eat to eat, usually. Not because I particularly like it."

"Are you for real? Azzie, that's awful. It's that human world stuff, I swear it tastes like cardboard. I know they have less sensitive taste buds, but come on." She rolls her eyes, approaching a bar dedicated to fried foods.

"Okay, I know fried foods aren't great for you, but we truly deserve them after the insane workouts we did this morning. Fried chicken, raven, frogs, and ooh they even have bat wings today!" Demi is practically salivating at the sight of fried bat wings.

"Should you be eating bats?" I gag at the mental image of eating raven, frog, *or* bat wings.

"Oh, it's fine. Really, it's just the wings. They're collected humanely after their bi-monthly sheds, not chopped off. And they grow back! Besides, they're delicious. You have to try one!"

"Since when do bat wings grow back?" I refuse to commit to trying one.

"Oh, right. Human bats aren't quite the same as ours. Well, I promise, they don't mind. Since they only shed bi-monthly, this is considered a delicacy. Nab one while you can!"

I will absolutely *not* be doing that, but I don't say so to Demi who piles five onto a plate.

I end up choosing fried chicken and a heap of fries: a normal, human-like meal. Demi chooses a soda for me, something called Batty Cola. She claims it's delicious, and that it has a nice sting to it. I have to admit, I'm not sure a sting can be considered nice.

Demi leads me away from the chaotic chatter around the bars, and we enter the portion of the cafeteria with tables in an adjoined room. Most of the tables I spot are round, but there are a few booths off to the side. The theme in this room also seems to be black: black tablecloths, black chairs, and black booths. Occasionally, gray shows up, too, but overall, the room seems a little depressing and a lot creepy. As I'm glancing around the gloomy atmosphere, I notice a large rectangular table in the center of the room, long enough to fit about twenty people.

That's where the Gravediggers sit.

Two of them are propped up on the table like kings ruling over their kingdom, girls littered around in the seats near them and standing nearby. Each one is more desperate than the other to score a spot at the clearly exclusive table, attempting to catch the eye of at least one boy. I roll my eyes at Jaymes when he looks up at me, sending him a pointed middle finger as I follow Demi to one of the booths on the outskirts of the room.

Ginny greets us warmly, three women flanking her in the long booth. Triplets, by the looks of it. All average-looking brunettes with soft round faces and warm brown eyes. One has a mole on her left cheek, the second has one on the right, and the last is missing one altogether. All three wear Shifter pins, but they don't look particularly wolfy or much like a vampire.

"This is Reese, Wren, and Willow Thatcher." Ginny points to each girl in turn, eyes lingering on Willow for far too long. No mole, left mole, right mole: easy enough.

"Azalea." I press my lips together, dipping my head lightly in greeting.

"Jinx," Wren says, leaning forward with a curious gleam in her eyes. "The new girl with two powers. We know who you are."

"Everyone does," Willow chimes in with a shy smile.

"Yeah, I've gathered that by now." I'm not sure what else to say, my annoyance flickering to the surface. Demi is the first to sit and I follow suit, and the silence only brief.

I thought making friends would be awkward, especially after that initial encounter. I thought that I wouldn't know what to do or say, that my infliction might turn them off. I was wrong.

No one seems to notice there is something wrong with me. I laugh and chime in where it's warranted, finding myself relating to these people I barely know. It's a strange sensation, one that I'm hoping I can become accustomed to.

"So, wait, you're telling me—"

"Azalea Jinx." The six of us stop speaking, turning toward the harsh voice at the end of our table.

"Oh. It's you. Uh, Silver? Seller? Sorry, I can't quite remember. No offense, it's just my first day and all. Lots of new people." I remember her name, of course. But I do have a sense of humor, and watching her face redden triggers it.

"I told you to stay away from Jaymes, so why am I hearing about you two hanging all over each other during Light Specialty Training?" Her sharp eyes watch me murderously, expression furious. If jealousy could turn you green, she would be a nice emerald shade by now. Two copies of her flank her sides, arms crossed across their chests menacingly.

"Did you ask him about it?" I plop my last fry into my mouth, turning my full attention to her. I notice the Elemental badge on her chest, though I can't be sure which element she possesses. Not that it matters.

"Well, no, but—"

"Listen, Solar. I'm not interested in you or your boyfriend. Jaymes is a great teacher, and I'm not going to give that up because he has a crazy girlfriend. Now, I already handed your ass to you once today. I think you should just cut your losses, tuck your tail in, and be on your way. Have a good one." I turn away, flicking my eyebrows up at the others in a 'can you believe this shit' way.

"Azalea, maybe you should—" Demi is interrupted by screeching and laughter, accompanied by the cold and wet liquid suddenly sliding down my head.

"Oops. My hand slipped and I spilled my drink. Thanks for catching it, Jinx."

I'm up faster than Stella can blink, eyes flashing in anger. She stumbles back in surprise, the two girls beside her following suit. Bullies like her tend to try and assert their dominance in frustrating ways like this, and I've experienced similar situations more often than I care to admit on my first day of school. Unfortunately for her, I've never been a fan of bullies.

"Oh, shit." I barely hear the words leave Ginny's mouth, barely register Demi tugging on my shirt to pull me back. I am too busy leaping at Stella, tackling her to the ground.

This fight is much different than the one this morning, namely because Stella puts up a bit more of a struggle.

The two of us are rolling around, pulling hair, and swinging fists. Skin slaps, screams erupt, and neither of us loosens our grips. I'm able to gain the upper hand when I am swinging on top of her once more, using my weight to pin her down and stop the momentum. Her freshly healed bruises begin to reform with each swing of my fist, her friends screaming and pulling at my hair and body. I rear back and hit them, too, knocking the breath out of one and causing the other to fall. I ignore their following shrieks of pain, turning back to Stella's bloody form.

It's an unfamiliar face who finally pulls me away, dark hair and light eyes finding their way into my line of sight.

"Impressive." The tall man drawls as he pulls me up and away, helping me back into my seat. I plop down with a huff, glaring at his beautiful face. With a start, I realize he's even better looking than Jaymes, and probably has the most beautiful face I've seen in this place…or ever.

My gaze travels over dark hair that is layered and long, noting the ends that land just past his shoulders. It curls in those longer places only slightly, the rest falling in neat waves. My eyes are drawn to ears that glisten with piercings, shiny silver balls in his right eyebrow, and the multiple dark tattoos inching above the collar of his shirt and peeking out from his rolled-up sleeves. I see the upper half of a sun and a moon, a dragon's head peering out from his wrist, and fragments of things I don't recognize. One is eerily similar to a tattoo I own: a half-hidden castle beneath his right sleeve.

I try to ignore the angles of his face, almost diamond-like, while also trying to ignore the softness that most people in this place don't possess. Everyone here has been sharp, sharp, sharp. But he is soft in all the right places, smooth and hypnotizing. I can't help but notice the large scar stretching across his right cheek, honey-colored skin puckering into pink. His hooded, light green eyes still refuse to move away from me.

Wait, no, I do recognize this guy. I've just never been close enough to see more than dark hair and staggering height.

He is one of the Gravediggers. Their Dimineer, according to his pin.

"Is it?" I question with a raised eyebrow, wiping blood off of my lip and pushing my bangs back into place. He watches every move in silent judgment, eyes staying on my lips before dipping lower to the ripped buttons on my blouse. This uniform hadn't fit well in the first place, and the spacing of the gaping buttons had left small holes between the fabric where my breasts pulled them apart. I suppose getting into a fight encouraged them to flee the scene altogether.

"Stella's used to being the biggest bitch in the room. Guess she has some competition now."

"Major competition. You know that saying 'fuck around and find out'? Yeah, she found out." I snort unattractively, turning away and effectively dismissing him.

Demi and the others stare at me with wide eyes, fear hidden in those simple gestures.

"I'm helping your professor in Shadow Specialty Training," he remarks slyly, and I can see the hints of a grin out of the corner of my eye. "Let me walk you there."

"No, thanks. Demi's got it covered."

"Oh, no, Azzie, really—"

"Demi's got it covered," I repeat, turning back to the Shadow Wielder and smiling sweetly. "I'll see you there."

"Yes, you will." He shoves his hands down into his pockets, cocky grin gone. He gives me one last glance over before turning and stalking away, whistling as he goes.

"That Stella chick is insane. Are fights like that common behavior around here?" I comment, attempting to defuse the tension between the girls. "Really, what are the standards here?"

Willow is the first to break the silence, shaking her head in exasperation. "No, you're just really pretty and Jaymes is nonstop watching you. The Gravediggers tend to make girls act like they have no common sense. Also, you are a crazy good fighter. Seriously, what did that human world teach you?"

"I took a lot of classes. And most of them weren't for beginners." I shrug, dabbing my lip again. It isn't the first time I've had my lip split open and certainly won't be the last.

"Azalea, I warned you about the Gravediggers," Demi pipes in, gazing at me worriedly as she chews on her upper lip.

"I can handle those dicks."

"No, you really can't."

Demi watches me for several long seconds, finally releasing a loud sigh and looking up toward the vaulted ceilings. Then the chatter begins anew, and the triplets begin spilling all of the juicy details about Stella and her relationship with Jaymes.

According to them, Stella has an on-again, off-again type of relationship with Jaymes. Mostly off, by the sounds of it. She's insane, jealous, and a powerful Fire Wielder; hence the temper. They blab on and on, whispering how they suspect she must be good in bed, because why else would he keep someone like that around?

I find my eyes drifting back toward the Gravediggers, watching Jaymes curiously. The triplets raise a good question: why keep her around? He didn't bother to come to her rescue and isn't comforting her now. He probably didn't even ask if she was okay. So why is she fighting so hard for something that is obviously not working?

Jaymes's gaze finds mine as if summoned by my thoughts, our direct eye contact unwavering for several minutes. Then Demi shakes me, pushing me out of the booth and warning me about being late. I grumble, breaking the contact as I stumble up.

I sling my book bag over my arm, glancing one last time over my shoulder at the boys. This time, four sets of eyes meet my own. Smiling slyly, I turn back to Demi and discreetly throw another middle finger their way.

Go to hell, Jaymes Bloodgood, and take your friends down with you.

CHAPTER 11

"In her darkest hours, she'll crave
a sinner, a monster, a digger's grave."
—Prophesy recorded inside student Seer Allia Jordan's Prophetic
Journal, 2023 A.G.

Shadow Specialty Training starts suspiciously in the same way Light Specialty Training had.

Professor Slateman—a bulky man with kind blue eyes, large ears, and balding brown hair—called out to inform me I needed to catch up, and claimed one Shayde Glover had volunteered to teach me. Unfortunately, Shayde Glover is the hot Gravedigger I practically told to piss off less than an hour ago.

"Is teaching me an excuse to put your hands all over me?" I question as we separate ourselves from the rest of the class.

"And if it is?"

I shrug, holding my hands out like Jaymes had shown me this morning. "I'd say it's a good excuse."

"I hear the 'but' in there." He chuckles, batting my hands down.

"But don't expect to do it outside of training. I'm not interested, and I can tell you are."

The expression that came over him when he watched me approach earlier can only be described as one thing: hunger. I can tell when men like him want me; working at a bar for years will provide you with that sort of skill. I also know how to get rid of untoward advances. Nip them in the bud, hard and fast, and don't let their fantasies grow. He'll move on faster that way; they usually do.

"Got it. No uncouth touches *outside* of training."

"Wait, no, I meant—"

"I'm just joking, Azalea. Relax. I'm not going to do anything you don't want me to. Seriously, though, put down your hands. The fuck was Jaymes teaching you?"

I had stuck my hands out again expectantly, but I quickly drop them again. Are Shadow and Light Wielding taught that differently?

"He just…zapped me and my Light appeared."

I watch as he plops down onto the grass, leaning his back against a tree and stretching out. "Yeah, I'm not doing that. Trust me, darling, you don't want any of my darkness."

"Um, okay. Then what am I supposed to do?"

"Come here." He gestures to the spot next to him, patting the grass gently. "Don't worry, I won't bite unless you beg for it."

"Get over yourself." I huff, sitting next to him anyway. "Now what?"

"Impatient much? Listen, Shadow Wielding isn't the same as Light Wielding. Everyone has light inside of them, something bright and worthy of life. It could be your hope, your joy, your dreams. There is something there that, quite literally, lights you up.

It's not hard to find, and it's a natural, harmless quality. Shadows aren't as harmless.

"Not everybody possesses a deep darkness or something that drags them down. And if they do, most people don't like to admit it. If you possess the shadows, *they* possess *you*. You have something inside of you for them to clutch onto, to deem you worthy of holding their gift. So, that's what we are going to do first: find your darkness."

I rub my chest absentmindedly, searching for that black pit inside of me. Except, now, it isn't a black pit. All I can find is a blinding white light, one that burns the imaginary hand reaching down. I can't make it far enough, can't see what to grab.

"Fuck. I saw it today, my Shadow powers. But now..."

"The Light took over, didn't it? Are you a goody-goody at heart, darling?"

"I don't know who I am at heart," I admit, slumping over. My head hits my pulled-up knees as I huff out in anger. "I didn't know Wielding would lead to so much soul searching."

"Yeah, I heard about your human world sickness." After seeing my surprised expression, he tacks on, "Delarosa may have mentioned it to us when she asked us to help train you."

"She asked you to help train me?" I don't ask who "us" is because I know exactly what group he belongs to.

"Well, yeah. I know we don't look the part, but we are pretty smart. We know a thing or two about power."

I shake my head, snorting. I knew they were smart: they had to be to hold such a high status among their peers and their community. "You don't look dumb. You look..."

"Handsome? Hot beyond measure? Like I make panties drop to the floor with one look?"

"Well, I was going to say you look like you actually give a fuck about all of this life and death stuff with the Reapers, but never mind. I refuse to compliment arrogant assholes."

"Ah, sorry. I just can't help myself. Arrogance is a silent disease, one not recognized by many. No one will ever be able to heal me or my inner asshole." He sniffs once playfully, hiding a smile.

"That explains it, then. My apologies. I shouldn't make fun of such a serious condition."

"How kind of you, my darling."

"Alright, enough with the flirty 'darling' bullshit. Tell me what to do. I actually want to learn something." I shift uncomfortably, not liking this weird banter. It reminds me of Neil, and I will not be repeating that mistake.

"I told you already: find your darkness. Close your eyes and answer some questions. Not aloud, if you aren't comfortable doing so." I do as told, laying flat on my back and closing my eyes tightly. "Have you ever done anything bad before?"

"A few things," I say, not mentioning the illegal fight clubs or the nefarious amount of drugs I was on at one point. Oh, or the armed robberies, the carjacking, the assaults…

"Probably nothing serious, though. I bet fighting is your main offense. From what I've seen today, you seem to have a fighting spirit. That's good in a Shadow Wielder. You'll need it."

"Yeah, mostly fights and cussing like a sailor," I quip, gulping the lie down as easily as air. "I've never felt compelled to do something truly horrible."

When I fought, it was because the other party agreed to fight. Most of the things I did were for money, or to make my heart beat to a different tune. It's not as if I went out killing every night; that's as truly horrible as it gets in my mind.

"Sure, you've never felt compelled, but would you? Would you kill someone to save another life?" It's as if he reads my mind, jumping straight into talk of murder. "Would you use an innocent person to find and kill the monster you are hunting? Could you use your bare hands to take a life? Could you look them in their eyes as you murder them? Those are the questions you need to answer, Azalea."

"Why? What does murdering people have to do with those beast things we hunt?"

"You'll be surprised, Azalea, at the lengths those beasts will go to to seem human. Answer me. Will you kill?"

I wish I could say *no, absolutely not.* I wish I could be an innocent little girl who would never dream of harming another so irrevocably. But I can't. I'm desperate to feel human again, desperate to be this person everyone keeps telling me I will become with enough time. I don't give a shit about the savior stuff, and right now, I don't think I could feel even a slight amount of remorse for killing someone. Obviously, it's ethically wrong, and I do have a sense of morals. I'm not going to go kill Stella because she hit me. But…if I had to kill her to save Demi? I would. If I had to kill a human to also take down a Reaper? Yeah, I'd probably do that, too.

If what the Charmed claim about Reapers is true, then how could I not? One life versus a hundred? It's an easy decision to make. Especially for someone who didn't have to think more than a few seconds about their answer.

"Yes."

I feel the darkness rising before I see it, my eyes flashing open in surprise. Shadows seep out of my hands, coating the grass in a cloudy darkness. It spreads far and wide, covering all of the trees in a fifteen-foot vicinity.

Shayde grins from beside me, a wicked gleam in his eyes as he claps dramatically. I find myself smiling back, laughing in excitement, intoxicated off of the brief buzz Wielding had created. In those seconds my heart raced, my stomach fluttering in desire as I watched him. Then it's gone, replaced by the numbness that's always lying in wait.

"Congratulations, Azalea Jinx. You *are* a Shadow Wielder."

Shayde proceeds to show me how to reel them in, how to cast them to the length and space I desire. He doesn't train me like you would a child, doesn't coddle me or tell me I can't handle things. He just teaches me what he can and chides me for the things I can't accomplish. In a single hour, I feel more than I have felt in at least ten years, and a loose tendril inside of me is close to snapping. The more of those that snap, the closer I am to becoming myself again.

Whoever she is.

PART TWO
AZALEA JINX AND THE CHARMED

CHAPTER 12

"Though we are told killing is fundamentally wrong, we must understand that Reapers are not people. Not anymore. It is okay to kill a Reaper; expected, even. When the time comes, do not hesitate because they were once Charmed like us. That is not who they are anymore, and they will never be one of us again."
—*A Guide to the Charmed* (current edition), written by Glamourist Elias Kasper in 1907 A.G.

After four weeks of classes, I'm still hopelessly behind.

Everything is easy for my classmates; no one has to try very hard to succeed. But I *do*. I have to learn all of these amateur moves, these Kindergarten abilities, as well as the advanced, college-level ones.

Charming is what I've proven to be best at. It's the most natural to me, the most fluid. It's almost like a performance, a song only I know the beat to. My body moves and flows like it knows exactly what to do; like I am nothing but a conduit for the power inside of me. I suppose that's all I am, though. My Light and Shadow wielding, however? Well, let's just say I have a lot of room for improvement.

Jaymes insists on treating me like a child, and I am forced to watch others in my class perform these amazing feats as I hold his hand and wait for his power to help mine along. He doesn't trust me to do anything on my own, not like Shayde does. Shayde meets me halfway, pulls out my inner darkness, and urges it to merge with his own. He doesn't have to hold my hand, doesn't have to shove his abilities down my throat. The Shadows are already there, ready to take over. I suppose that's the heart of my problem: these powers overwhelm me.

Maybe I should be easier on myself, maybe I shouldn't grow more frustrated each day I fall even more behind. But I can't stop myself. There's this urgency in everyone here, this importance I can't shake. Every day we are given reminders of death, of hopeless fights, of a world taken over by the Grim and his Reapers. I don't know what he looks like, or even what powers he holds. I just know that everyone is terrified, and they think I should be, too. I know that I need to push myself harder, to prove myself to be stronger.

If I try hard enough, eventually I will be able to feel the same fear everyone else does.

"Are you okay, Azalea? You look a little…serious. That's not usually your vibe." Demi jabs me in the ribs, her bubbly voice penetrating my thoughts.

Her tiny, cute fangs poke into her bottom lip as she smiles up at me, and I can't help but admire her beauty. If I was on the hunt for potential suitors, Demi would be high on my list. But I know I will never be on hers. Honestly, I don't even want to try to be anything more. Ever. Returned emotions or not. Her friendship is a blessing I definitely don't deserve. Her guidance has helped me this past month in more ways than one, and I know she wants the same thing as me: to get my lost emotions back.

"Sorry. Just thinking about how behind I am. Again."

"Ah, don't worry, Azzie. You're a dual Wielder, probably the strongest one we have had in decades. You are doing fantastic for learning so much already. You're a fast learner, and you have improved significantly faster than most of us do. You won't be behind forever."

Her smile is meant to be comforting and reassuring; I wish I could feel that reassurance. Mostly, I just feel annoyed. A feeling that only increases as Shayde approaches.

"Azalea," he purrs, hands buried down into his pockets as per usual. "Got a minute?"

"No, actually, I—"

"Of course she does, Shayde!" Demi looks at me with wide eyes, shaking her head rapidly as she mouths "'Don't make them angry."

That's one thing she hasn't let up on: her fear of the Gravediggers. I've tried to tell her they aren't as bad as they seem, but she is petrified. I think there is something deeper there, something more serious than she lets on. Whatever it is, she can't, or won't, talk about it.

"Perfect. I have a proposition for you." Shayde reaches out for my arm like it is natural, as if he has every right to touch me so casually. I shake his hand off roughly, glaring to prove a point. He only chuckles darkly, glancing at Demi with a raised brow. She scurries off, leaving us alone.

Fucking traitor.

"What do you want?"

During class, I'm friendly with Shayde. We talk as classmates do, occasionally diving into deeper topics to help me control my abilities—nothing too personal, nothing I wouldn't tell anyone else—but those talks never extend outside of class. Never publicly. I assumed it was because the Gravediggers didn't want the others to know they were friendly with the competition. Their reputations were on the line, after all.

"Ah, no need for hostility." He clicks at me like I'm a misbehaving child, eyes gleaming with amusement. "I think you're going to like what I have to say."

"I rarely like anything you say, Shayde."

"You wound me, Azalea Jinx."

The way he says my name always leaves me with an odd feeling. It's seductive and secretive, and he always makes it slow and purposeful. He's not made his lust for me a secret and, similar to Demi, if I wanted a relationship, I would search for one with Shayde. Just that whisper of my name would have me on my knees begging for more. But I can't, and I won't, and I've made that abundantly clear to him.

"Spit it out, Shayde. I've got things to do."

"You don't anymore."

"Oh, yeah? Why's that?"

"If I could escort you to my bedroom, I could—"

"I don't want to hear any sexual shit, okay? I have work to do." Studying, practicing, and attempting to feel something that hasn't been in my emotional arsenal for over a decade: it's what my free hours are dedicated to nowadays.

"You are coming with me and the boys on a mission. You know, the ones only second-years are allowed to go on? The ones where we get hands-on experience in taking down a Reaper? Yeah, one of those." His smirk is infuriating, his hand reaching up to twirl a lock of my hair even more so. "See? I told you that you were going to like what I had to say."

"Are you serious? *I* get to go on a mission? Like, actually go?" I gape up at him in surprise, dropping my previous attitude. If he is being serious…this is huge. I am going to see a Reaper for the first time, not just listen to someone describe them from a textbook. Will I get to fight one, too? Fuck, this is what I need.

Something dangerous.

"Yeah, I'm fucking serious. You down? Because we are leaving in…approximately ten minutes." He glances down at his watch for confirmation, amusement smeared across his face.

"Of course I'm down! Do I need to bring anything? Where are we meeting? Where are we going? Is it somewhere in the human world? Who is going to be there? Is—"

"Shh." His hand is suddenly over my mouth, his face inches from mine. His dark eyebrows are raised mischievously, light green eyes delighted. With an amused chuckle, he closes the distance and licks my cheek in a singular long, slow stroke.

"What the actual fuck, Shayde!" I jump away, wiping the leftover saliva away in disbelief.

"I just wanted a taste of you, little flower. You taste as sweet as you look." He laughs, turning away and taking a few steps forward. Then he pauses, glancing back at me over his shoulder with a lazy smile.

"Go put on some fighting gear. We will be in your room in ten minutes, so I would suggest you're dressed before then. Or don't be. Really, we won't mind either way."

He ignores the series of curses that follow him, casually strolling away without a care in the world. The farther he gets, the faster reality sinks in.

I've got to make it back to my room *now*.

I take off in a run, waving Demi away as she turns to run after me. She's much faster than I could ever be, and could easily catch up if she wished, but she chooses not to follow. I appreciate her staying out of my way when asked; it's refreshing to have a friend who doesn't constantly feel the need to butt in where she isn't needed.

Luckily, Demi and I hadn't been very far from the dorms. We had just finished lunch, and the cafeteria is located on the bottom floor of the dorms. Very convenient for us students, even more so for me at the moment.

My room is on the East wing of the third floor, the farthest door down. That means I only have three flights of stairs and a long hallway in my way. I'm not much of a runner yet, and I can only pray this short run won't make me hurl my lunch right back up.

Our rooms unlock with a touch of our hands, convenient and fast. No struggling with keys, no shaking as you drop them in your rush, and no making small talk with annoyingly nosy neighbors.

My room is disgusting. Clothes are slung everywhere, trash littering the floor. I wave my hand frantically in a sweeping motion, taking advantage of the cleaning charm, also known as the Scouring Charm, Demi taught me earlier this week. The cleaning charm works its magic, making its way around the small room in a flurry.

I don't bother to watch as the trash flies into a bin, or as the clothes begin to pile up in the hamper. I only snatch a pair of thick, black leather leggings out of the air, along with a black tank top. I stumble out of my uniform, pulling the tank top over my head as I bend over to dig around my closet for the thick, Charm-infused vests we are supposed to wear. I've been given two, but neither seems to be in plain sight where I should probably be keeping them.

The Charmed mainly wear thick pants, vests, and large belts that can hold half a dozen daggers, along with a handful of smoke bombs. The daggers hold a small amount of Light within them, the smoke bombs a hint of Shadow. They won't kill a Reaper, but they hold enough power to wound and distract in emergencies.

"Impressive." I jump at the sound of the familiar voice, along with the familiar word. Dammit! I never shut my door.

I turn my head to find Shayde and Jaymes in my doorway, Jaymes watching the flying objects in an obvious attempt to not look at me. Shayde, however, isn't as gentlemanly as that. I roll my eyes and scowl at his blatant ogling, stepping into my leggings and wiggling them up in a hurry.

"Appreciate the view now, Shayde, because you'll never see it again."

"Never say never," is the only response I receive as they cross the threshold, Arlo and Nox popping up from behind them.

I don't bother with hello's as I pull my hair up, glancing over at the clock when I finish: it just hit ten minutes. They are early.

"Anyone going to tell me where we are going or what we are doing?"

"No." Jaymes is the one who speaks up, approaching my mirror lazily.

"Is that why you got here early? Need to get a little self-appreciation in before the mission? Maybe say a few affirmations before we go?" I pull on my vest, buckle my belt, and shove on my boots in rapid succession, avoiding the gaze of the four men standing in my room.

Nox is the only one who appreciates my humor, his buzzed blond hair poking up just above Jaymes's shoulder. His thin lips lift and he coughs behind a dark hand, blue eyes shining. I don't pay much attention to Nox, usually, but he is just as handsome as his friends. I guess I avoid him because he has always seemed shy, unsure, and a lot colder than the other three combined.

"Shut up, Jinx." Jaymes scowls at me before turning back to the mirror, closing his eyes, and reaching out for it. The other three surround him protectively, shielding him from my sight. When he reappears, my mirror is shimmering with an unearthly color.

"What is so special about my mirror?" I gape at the newly created portal, blinking at the beautiful substance that now dons its surface.

"It was made by a Charmed." Nox is the one to answer, honest and quiet. "These kinds of things are way easier to make a portal out of. Trying to create one out of normal objects takes a lot more power and a lot more energy. Tons of items like this are in the human world; it's how Jaymes found you so fast. This mirror and the one you found are embedded with certain powers from our world. Lots of power-infused objects make their way to the human world, actually, and most of them have nothing to do with portals."

Is this why I was so attracted to the most random things in thrift stores? Were they items that had been laced with some kind of power from this world, items that called to a Conjurer like me?

"Don't tell her anything else about portals, Nox," Jaymes demands, glaring at his friend. "She isn't ready."

"You'd be surprised by what Azalea is ready for, Jay. Maybe you'd realize that if you would do more than parlor tricks in class—"

Shayde begins, stopping abruptly as Jaymes pushes his chest against Shayde's.

"We aren't having this argument again. Especially not in front of her."

"You guys have been arguing about me? Seriously?" My eyes flicker between the two men wearily.

How many times have they had this argument and why? Why does Shayde bother? Why does Jaymes not want me to learn? I rub my temples in annoyance, already over this trip.

"Oh, they argue about you all the time." Arlo pipes up helpfully, grinning at me playfully. "It's very amusing."

"Arlo," Jaymes grinds out, tilting his head towards the portal. "That's enough. You go through first."

"You always make me go first," he gripes despite stepping forward. He walks through the portal with ease, disappearing from my room in a blink. Nox steps through with a wink within seconds of Arlo's departure, and Shayde's exit afterward is quiet and unnerving.

"Your turn, Jinx." Jaymes pushes me toward the portal, raising his eyebrows expectantly when I hesitate.

"The only other time I've been through a portal is when you pulled me through one. What do I do? Is it the same?"

"How about this time I just push you through instead, hmm?"

"Jaymes, no, do not—" My protests are sent to deaf ears.

Jaymes shoves me hard, sending me tumbling into the portal. I'm swallowed by the jelly-like substance, coated in its slimy residue. I can't scream or open my eyes. I can't tell if I am moving, can't tell if I am making any progress through the empty space. Time is still, I can't breathe, and my heart is slowing exponentially. Maybe

I should learn more about portals because if this is what they do to me, I need to learn how to overcome it.

I pop out of the portal back first, sucking in air loudly before choking and sputtering it back up. I tumble back, unable to stop myself. I fall into someone and we both hit the ground, clothes dry and untouched. I groan, blinking up at a blue sky and a bright sun. The Charmed world is perpetually gray, so we must be in the human world.

Home.

"He pushed you, didn't he?" Shayde's voice comes from underneath me, his tone lacking its usual playfulness.

"Of course he did." A new voice now, a woman's.

The owner of that voice appears before me, hand reaching out for my own. I take it, allowing her to pull me up and off of Shayde. The first thing I notice is her taller stature and plump figure, something unusual for a Conjurer in our field. Her cropped black hair frames her circular face perfectly, her tan skin rivaling my own. I glance down and notice a large engagement ring on the hand clasped in mine, the large jewel in the middle the same deep green as her eyes. A pin decorates her outfit, declaring her as either a Dimineer or an Illuminoor.

"Of course I did," Jaymes responds gleefully from behind her. I glance over just in time to watch the portal on the wooden wall behind him disappear. "Nice to see you, Alice."

"Charming as always, Jaymes. Alright, kids. Let's do a quick debriefing."

Alice can't be more than five years older than us, but she still looks at us as if we are wild toddlers. She gestures for us to follow her, and we do, approaching a small group of Conjurers. A woman with an Elemental pin, a man with another Dimineer/Illuminoor pin, another man with a Shifter pin, and the last man with a Glamourist pin. A useful team, one that looks like they know how to handle themselves. All stand with arms crossed: rigid, serious, and unyielding.

"Well, Azalea, you are one very lucky girl. It's not often a first-year gets to come out on the field with us. The boys here asked us to include you today, said you've never seen a Reaper. They send high praises about you and your abilities and seem eager to train you. So, that's what we are going to do. Today you get to finally see what all the fuss is about."

"Where are we? Are we back in the human world?"

"Ah, yes. You were raised here, right? We are, in fact, in the human world. Near the Gulf of Mexico, on the edge of a place called Louisiana. We are currently located in an abandoned cabin, probably only a few hours away from that gulf. Unfortunately, today's trip is not meant for swimming and sand castles."

"I've never been to Louisiana," I say quietly, glancing around the cabin.

It is falling apart, near ruination. The wood is rotted, the ceiling is caved in, and vines dance across every surface. The floor isn't in a much better state. A dusty table is pushed into the corner of the large room, a recliner with giant holes and a moldy smell next to it. Overall, I'd say this place is truly and utterly abandoned.

"Not much to see here. We are at least a hundred miles from civilization. This is near a popular camping sight, which is why the Reapers are attracted to the area. Dark, secluded, and easy prey. It's a Reaper's wet dream."

"The humans…would…well, would anyone recognize me if they saw me? Like, my face hasn't been plastered on the news or anything, right?" I've had lingering questions about that all month. What did they think happened to me? Did anyone care?

"Oh, no. They took care of that the moment you were rescued." Shayde answers this time, hand brushing against mine. I turn to squint my eyes at him, noticing he has pulled his hair up into a bun. "They cleared out your room, sent the landlord an email from you stating you were breaking the lease, and another to your employer informing them of your early retirement, so to speak. It wasn't very hard to make sure no one looked for you."

"Oh. Well, okay, then."

It doesn't bother me that it was all too easy for me to be kidnapped and never seen again. It should. I should be angry at the world, angry that no one cared enough to look for me, but the only person I can be angry at is myself because I made it that way.

"Continuing on." Alice looks pointedly between us, clearing her throat and starting again. "We have pinpointed the Reaper's exact location to be somewhere in this area based on suspicious deaths and local legends. We have already cleared the woods surrounding us of any humans, so it is safe to perform Charms and use our abilities.

"Now, Azalea, I know you haven't used your powers here in the human world before. You may find it a bit more difficult because it's a natural repellent of said powers. So, if you find yourself unable to perform under pressure, don't stress about it. It happens to the best of us.

"Alright. Any questions? No? Perfect. Shayde, you and I will be calling the beast here. Everyone else, stay quiet and nearby. Wait for my instructions on whether or not you can participate. That means you, too, rookies. You're here to observe, not to kill."

Jaymes wraps an arm around my waist, pushing me into the nearest wall and pinning me in place with his arms. I open my mouth to yell at him, my head tilting back so I can look into those dark green eyes. I barely get a glance at his worried expression before everything turns dark.

Shayde and Alice work in tandem, their inky darkness overtaking us. I attempt to form my own shadows despite Alice's instructions not to intervene, the weak tendrils crawling across the ground and toward the horde. I'm not sure how much they help, if it all, but I send them out in waves anyway. They flutter and fluctuate, building and dying, never growing stronger than the tiny tendrils I first created. Alice was right; it is much harder to control them here.

After around the thirty-minute mark, I stop trying altogether.

Jaymes's warmth engulfs me in the same way the darkness does, his breath tickling the top of my head as we wait. I shift uncomfortably a few times, but he refuses to release me. He continues to cage me, to protect me. I'm not sure how I feel about it yet, but I know I can't risk yelling at him or shaking him off. This moment is too important, this mission too dangerous. I don't know what is about to pop out of the shadows, and I can't risk giving our positions away.

I'm too desperate to see a Reaper.

After an hour, it finally appears. I see movement in the shadows, small little twitches inside them. Then I hear a guttural groan, the sound making my breath catch. The groan is a signal, the darkness disappearing and replaced by the blinding light of the sun.

My eyes burn at first, and I have to force myself to keep them open and readjust quickly. As soon as they do, I see it. I see it and I understand exactly why Shayde wanted to know if I would kill someone if it meant protecting the Charmed.

It's because Reapers don't look like monsters at all; *they look like us.*

Don't get me wrong, there is something…off about the creature. From a distance, it would seem distinctly normal. But this close, I can see every flaw that marks it as a Reaper.

Its skin is almost gray, and its eyes are almost completely black. Those eyes are also sunken in with dark bags underneath. I squint harder and notice that the skin isn't *just* gray. I spot multiple areas on its body that are darker than others, similar to bruises, with skin falling off like scabs. I turn my attention to Shayde only briefly, watching as he slinks back against a wall to watch the Reaper.

When I turn my gaze back to the creature, I notice that it is wearing clothes, clothes that are filthy and covered in rips. I almost gag when I notice black veins throbbing underneath the surface of its bald head, and wince when it smiles at us menacingly. That smile reaches up to the tips of its ears, stretching across the full length of its ugly face.

It's unnerving at best, terrifying at worst.

Though its face looks scary, I notice that its body appears small and weak, with a bloated belly that seems ready to pop. I watch in utter horror as its abnormally long mouth opens to show off multiple rows of sharp, discolored teeth. The noise that escapes that mouth will forever haunt my memory. It's a war cry full of anger and hate, a sharp sound that penetrates us all. I frantically look between the professional killers who watch on while standing as still as statues, a scream escaping my lips unwillingly as the Reaper takes one final glance around and leaps.

Jaymes turns sharply, flipping around so his back is against me. I grunt as I am slammed into the wall once more, the air leaving my lungs all at once. Jaymes's hands light up, head snapping around as he takes in the situation. There's no way he can get a shot in, and, even if he could, he had been instructed not to. So, we watch as the team dives in.

Shayde's shadows curl around him lazily. His hands are crossed over his chest and one foot is propped against the wall. He seems to be bored of the situation entirely, not concerned in the least about the horrors about to unfold before us.

Alice takes a step toward the Reaper, but it is she who it chooses to attack first. It snarls and snaps its teeth at the Dimineer, hissing into her fearless face. Alice digs a dagger out from her belt, shoving it into the Reaper's ribs just as the Shifter turns into a wolf. I stifle a cry in Jaymes's back as the wolf leaps at the Reaper with a terrifying roar, tackling it to the side and allowing Alice to crawl out of the way. The Reaper is fast, though, and within only seconds it has the wolf by the throat and is slinging him around like a chew toy. The Shifter is flung into the nearest wall before anyone can intervene. The small cabin shakes around us.

The Glamourist forms illusions that look like us to distract the Reaper as Alice attempts to drag her damaged body to him. I can see that her leg is bloody and bent at an odd angle, but she seems to be gritting her teeth through the pain. In utter horror, I watch as the Reaper ignores the glamours entirely, leaping for the Conjurer. I scream again when another Conjurer is tackled, my ear pressing against Jaymes's back just as his heart begins to race.

Alice is down with a major injury, and the Glamourist seems unable to reach his belt, which means he can't pull out a dagger or smoke bomb. The Illuminoor is next to the Shifter, attempting to drag him outside before the Reaper realizes that there is a limp, unconscious man ripe for the picking.

"Jaymes—" I start, heart racing with something I hardly recognize: *fear.*

"I know, Azalea," he whispers reassuringly, sighing as he runs a hand through his almost-white hair. "Stay here. Please, don't move."

I watch as Jaymes darts over to Alice, Arlo sharp on his heels. Together, they help her up and assess the damage. They speak in harsh whispers before Arlo transforms into his wolf form: a large, red-tinged beast twice the size of the Reaper. I turn to see Nox near the man under the Reaper, his strong body unnaturally still as he uses his Enhancer abilities. I'm not sure who, exactly, he is targeting with his enhancements, but I can only hope he is successful.

I press my back further into the wall as Arlo tackles the Reaper, pinning its arms underneath him and ripping at its neck. The Glamourist grunts painfully as soon as he is released, pulling himself away from the Reaper just as the Illuminoor comes bounding back in. I wrinkle my nose as the smell of blood begins to permeate the air, along with a noxious scent emitting from the Reaper's freshly ripped-open belly. Guts and blood don't escape this wound like they would on normal people; no, only a foul black goo seeps onto the floor.

I almost sigh in relief as the Illuminoor approaches with brightly lit hands raised, preparing to end things. That is until I notice the second one.

"Jaymes!" I scream as loud as I can, pointing with a shaky hand toward the open door.

He turns a second too late, the beast already attacking.

I don't have time to watch the first Reaper be blown to bits by Light. Instead, I find myself stepping away from the wall and leaping into action. These things are faster and stronger than I could have ever imagined, despite their weak appearance. It is stupid of me to join in on the chaos, but I do it anyway.

This Reaper is different from the first one: its skin is smoother and intact, and it's missing a bloated belly. This one seems entirely too normal, with only its inhuman smile and outrageous roars giving it away.

I stumble into action, striking out with my Light clumsily and blasting a hole through its arm. I watch numbly as the limb falls to the ground, twitching and oozing the same black goo I noticed before. What I didn't notice earlier? The black goo is fucking *sizzling* on the ground. I may have been aiming for the chest, and I could have used a little less sizzling goo in my life but, well, that'll work, too. I manage to create enough of a distraction for it to loosen its grip on Jaymes, its head turning toward me instead.

Jaymes releases a burst of Light that brightens the room, a hole ripping straight through the Reaper's chest as a result. I watch in utmost delight as the creature falls to the ground, crumbling into a pile of ashes before us. Jaymes strides forward and puts his hands on my cheeks, eyes searching my own. Something warm and wet coats his hands, staining my cheeks and dripping down onto my neck.

This strong and insanely powerful feeling overcomes me as I try not to think about what that mysterious liquid could be. It's overwhelming, and I shake as my heart begins to race while my head lightens. I feel…happy, satisfied, and in control for the first time in over ten years; I hardly recognize the foreign emotions.

Is this it, then?

Is this the thing that I have been missing?

Is killing going to make me whole again?

Chapter 13

"There will be no end to the Reapers
until the reaping comes to an end.
There will be no way to survive
until a savior learns to live."
—Prophecy recovered in the prophetic journals of Abraham De-
lowosky, 377 A.G.

All too quickly Jaymes is ripped away from me, his body flying in a perfect arc across the room. I let loose a blood-curdling scream, hands reaching up to cover my mouth as I fall back into the wall once more. Jaymes's body hits the ceiling before crashing back down, a loud groan escaping blood-coated lips. Debris rains down from above us, dust and wood hitting the ground as the ceiling attempts to cave in.

"Azalea!" Shayde's panic has my head spinning, and I take a few shaky steps back and away from the wall as I notice the Reaper only feet from me. It's another normal-looking one. Its all-to-human nose tilts up as it sniffs the air. Just as I go to take another step away, the Reaper's empty gaze hones in on the blood adorning my cheeks.

I reach out a hand and touch the beast in a panic. My Light escapes, blasting a hole straight through its heart in one uncontrollable burst. I gasp as its body blasts apart as though it never existed in the first place, its ashes raining down like snow.

If I thought watching these things die gave me intense feelings…well, that was *nothing* compared to the rush of adrenaline that shoots through me now. The very cells I am made of are on fire, the very molecules inside those cells bouncing around in excitement. The world is clear for the first time, my heart clenching and my body doubling over from the pain. I drop down to a crouching position to help ease the ache, clutching onto my chest with one hand and pressing the other against the wall for balance.

I can feel *everything*.

Shayde is the first to reach me, his body dropping down next to mine. I shake as his eyes begin to inspect me for injuries, worry written across his features. I can only watch in silence as he tears off a section of his shirt, wiping at the blood on my cheeks with a gentleness I don't deserve. And when he touches me…another new feeling lights up inside of me: *desire*.

I crave him like a pregnant woman craves weird foods, like a vampire craves blood, like I crave emotions. I need him the same way I need air.

My breathing becomes heavy, my skin sensitive, my stomach fluttering, my core throbbing. I almost let out a moan upon feeling his next touch, the gentle caress on my cheek almost too much to bear. With a sudden jerk, he drops the fabric, placing a hand over my mouth before the treacherous noise can escape. His eyes light up in brief amusement before darkening, his hooded gaze raking over my shaking body before performing a Scouring Charm.

"Are you okay?" Jaymes asks from behind us, his voice weak and his arm bent at an odd angle. He reaches out with his good arm, attempting to touch my cheek, too. I watch in shock as Shayde smacks it away, releasing me from his grip. I almost collapse from the disappointment, then take a shaky step forward as I attempt to close the distance between us once more.

"No physical injuries," Shayde answers for me, meeting Jaymes's eyes briefly. "But I think I should take her back; she's shaking like a leaf. You guys got the cleanup covered?"

"Yeah, take her back, man. This may have been a bad idea." Nox shakes his head from beside us, glancing around at the large piles of ashes left behind: the only proof of the Reapers' existence in this small space. "Three Reapers..."

"For such small hunting grounds, it's very odd," Alice agrees from nearby. "I should have known there was more than one when the first came in looking like that. It was definitely malnourished, the runt of the litter if I had to guess. I'm sorry you guys got caught up in this. There was only supposed to be one..."

"You're lucky we were here," Shayde says pointedly, eyes glued to mine. "I'm getting Azalea out of here. She's a little shaky. Shock, probably."

I should be more concerned about the injured Conjurers, more worried about what happens now. But I'm fucking tired of all the things I *should* feel. Right now, all I can think about is Shayde, and I'll be damned if I stick around and allow that lust to slip right out of my grasp.

"Ah, it happens to everyone the first time. Don't let it bother you, kid. You did a good job, even though your control could use a little work. Our powers tend to be uncooperative when learning how to use them here the first few times; you either put too much energy into it or not enough. Either way, you got the job done, and you'll get better the more often you practice. Well, go on and take her back; the rest of us can handle this," Alice says, pulling herself into a seated position. I watch as Jaymes approaches her, the room suddenly doused in an iciness I don't care to stick around for.

I don't have to worry about getting out of the gloomy atmosphere for long. Shayde doesn't hesitate after being told we can go, his hands moving to form a portal in the same spot of wood we entered through. I marvel at the sheer amount of power he holds, at his ability to still form a portal after blasting nonstop shadows to fill an entire room for an hour. My lost thoughts prevent me from paying attention to his movements and the secret of forming portals, but I don't have any fucks to give at the moment.

I focus on the way his lips part open slightly, on the way his muscles flex as he works. I've never felt attraction so strongly before, never wanted anything as badly as I want him right now. I can tell he knows what I want and can see the same urgency reflected in his every movement.

Shayde and I stumble through his portal, his lips on mine before we even emerge. This time, my lack of air isn't brought on by the icky substance I could drown in.

I barely manage to suck in fresh air before I am picked up and slammed into a wall, the portal closing shut abruptly behind us. Not once do his lips leave mine.

My hands search for him in desperation, pulling on his hair, his shirt, his pants. Any skin I can reach, I touch. Somehow, Shayde seems just as desperate as me. Everywhere he touches leaves a pleasant tingle, my skin heated and aching.

"I've never...I've never felt..." I pant, trying to communicate this absurd feeling in words. But how can I?

As someone who doesn't feel...this...this is electrifying. Better than any drug I've ever tried. Better than being under a tattoo needle, better than the sting of a piercing, better than the pain left from a fight.

This is a kind of addiction I will never be able to recover from.

"It's the power use," he groans against my lips as my hands brush over sensitive areas, his own hands masterfully undoing my belt and pushing my vest off of my shoulders. "It's releasing some of those feelings it has been repressing for so long."

"Fuck." I moan, grinding against him in a shameless haze. "Is it supposed to feel so strong?"

"The adrenaline," he murmurs, pulling off my shirt in one fluid move and removing my bra. "Just the adrenaline gives me a rush. But both combined? Well, I imagine it feels pretty fucking good." He chuckles darkly, pinching a nipple harshly.

"I really shouldn't be doing this," I think aloud, pausing to moan as he sinks his teeth into my neck.

"You have to tell me now if you want to stop, Azalea. I'm serious. Tell me now. This is your last chance." Shayde is practically growling at me, squeezing hard on my breasts in a punishing way.

"I don't want to stop."

I'm not sure if I will regret this tomorrow, not sure if the high will fade and this will feel like a fever dream, but I don't care. To feel this way...I want it to last as long as possible. I don't want to let it go. And if being with Shayde is what makes me feel this way? How can I possibly deny that after spending half my life looking for it?

Shayde lets out a deep, guttural growl before the rest of our clothes fly off and our shoes are thrown into corners. His hands are touching me everywhere, and I feel *everything*. The feel of his skin on mine is intoxicating, a sensation I'll never be able to replicate. His touch is lightning, his kiss a resurrection.

I am alive.

We don't bother with pleasantries. No gentle kisses, no kind words, no foreplay. I whimper at the sight of him lining himself up to my entrance, screaming in pleasure when he pushes in with one hard thrust. Shayde fills me up completely—thick, long, and punishing. And now that I finally have him inside me, I begin to die over and over again just so he can breathe life back into me.

Shayde fucks me hard and fast against the wall, but he doesn't stop after the first orgasm like most men I've been with do. He doesn't stop after the third, either. He takes me against the wall, the table, the counter, and eventually the bed. Each orgasm rips through me like a tornado, taking everything and anything in its path and leaving behind only pieces of what was there before. Each time I think my mind is finally clearing, his fingers begin to expertly roam, or he thrusts in just the right spot. It goes on for so long that my limbs become numb, my brain a puddle of mush.

It's the best sex I've ever had, and I can't stop myself from aching for more once it's over.

"Fuck," Shayde grunts as he falls beside me, eyes closing as he pants heavily.

"Fuck," I agree breathlessly, mourning the desire and happiness that are already beginning to fade.

"That was…"

"Don't. Don't say it, Shayde. Don't get all touchy-feely on me. You know I can't reciprocate any of that." I've mentioned my emotional issues on more than one occasion during Shadow Specialty Training. Already, my burst of emotions is practically gone. Already, I am turning back into the shell I was before.

Will I remember this feeling? Will I ever be able to get it back?

"But that was *amazing*! That was—" His eyes pop open, surprise and bewilderment filling them. They almost seem soft and hurt, as if he can't believe I don't feel the same things he does.

"It was temporary madness. And it might always be this way. Did you really expect anything more?"

"No, not before, when you denied me every chance you got. But now, after that? I don't know, Azalea, I thought that maybe you would want—"

"I don't want anything more, Shayde. You shouldn't either. Isn't that your whole thing? That you're a player or womanizer or whatever?" I haven't heard of him being with anyone the whole time I've been here, except a crazy girlfriend Demi mentioned on my first day. But Demi told me exactly what to expect from him, and I don't think I will be any different. Unlike those other girls, I don't hold delusions of changing Shayde.

He shouldn't hold delusions of changing me.

"Or whatever." He shrugs, all hints of that vulnerability gone. "You're right. Sorry. Just the heat of the moment, I guess."

"I wish I could offer you more," I say, not bothering to apologize. He knows I can't mean it.

I stand abruptly, beginning the hunt for my clothes and the awkward process of redressing. I don't bother putting the vest or tool belt back on, only scooping them in a pile to carry. I don't even examine his room, refusing to look at all of the personal things that make this place his.

"We're going to do this again, right?" Shayde is still lounging on the bed, arms behind his head as he watches me. My eyes rake over his naked body one last time, committing every hard muscle and every inch of his dick to memory. When my eyes make it back to his face, a satisfied grin awaits me.

"Maybe," I say with a shrug, pulling on my boots, "If I feel like it."

"Don't worry your pretty little head about that."

"About what?"

"About feeling things. I will make you feel more than you ever knew possible, Azalea Jinx."

I don't bother replying, because the truth is undeniable: he already has.

CHAPTER 14

"You'll know the end is near
when students begin to disappear.
When Reapers begin to hunt in groups,
it's time to hunker down and protect the youth."
—Prophecy found inside Seer Arabella Cane's prophetic journals,
106 B.G.

Hookups are usually awkward, especially when they involve someone you see every day. But with Shayde…it just isn't. He doesn't allow it to be.

There have been times when he has set out to embarrass me, but not out of malice or anger. It's his way of flirting with me, which has increased tenfold. If I thought he had been flirty before…well, he has cranked up the charm now. He wouldn't have to work so hard if I were anyone else.

The memories of his flirtations leave me feeling empty some days, and on other days, I can almost feel a tiny spark trying to ignite inside my chest. One I often think of is when, only a week after our hookup, he tried to trick me into falling back into bed with him.

I pant as I finish my laps around the gym, wiping sweat off my forehead and adjusting my wet bangs. I crouch, put my head between my knees, and close my eyes as I try to take a few breaths for myself. My body is past the point of breaking and in desperate need of recovery. Shayde chooses this moment to crouch down next to me, all but reassuring me he is no woman's peace.

"Hmm. Are you a quitter, little flower?"

"I finish—"

"Don't lie to me. I know all too well what that magnificent body of yours looks like when you can't take anymore."

"How do you know I couldn't take anymore?" I scowl, biting at the bait.

"Want to head to my room and try again to see how much you really can take?"

"Fuck off, Shayde Glover, and don't come back until you've exerted some of that pent-up energy on someone else." My words are hostile despite my heart's attempt to race. And, fuck, do I wish it would stop palpitating when I'm in his presence; it's uncomfortable and weird.

The worst one came only a few days ago, leaving me panting and wide-eyed just thinking about sex.

"You know you have some really interesting tattoos," Shayde says as he approaches me at lunch, his head tilting toward my exposed arms. My friends fall into a shocked silence, but Shayde continues as though they aren't even there. "Want to know my favorite? It's the tiny heart on your left breast. You know, the one that looks like a mole?"

"How the fuck did you even notice that?" I sputter out, shocked. How am I supposed to ignore him when he does things like this? When he's constantly bringing up specific little things about my body he shouldn't

know? Things he shouldn't have noticed or cared to remember? Things Neil didn't even care enough to know?

"Want to know what else I noticed?" The shit-eating grin on his face forces a squeak out of Ginny, who I promptly ignore as she knocks over a glass of water after leaning too far forward in an attempt to hear better. My brown eyes are trained on Shayde's green ones, my heart attempting to pick up its pace but failing.

"Not really." I hold my breath when he leans in, lips brushing against my ear.

"I noticed the noises you made when you came, and I think about them quite often. Every day, multiple times a day, in fact. The memory of you and those noises haunt me, Azalea Jinx, and I can't wait until the day you banish my phantoms."

I know that he doesn't want me to be his girlfriend. He wants sex. The issue is, without any emotional ties, that's all it will be: sex. Not lust, not desire, certainly not love. I can't get involved unless I know feelings are involved, too. I'm not interested in meaningless sex that I can't even enjoy properly. I've had enough of that for a lifetime, and it never did me any favors.

With Shayde on my mind, my eyes begin to search for him among the crowd of students. I know he is here somewhere, and I can picture him approaching just to whisper something highly inappropriate in my ear because, well, that's what he always does. Some days I think I might cave, just to see if I could feel something without needing that extra rush of emotion the fight brought on. But I know deep down that I won't. That this bottomless pit inside of me will eat and eat, yet never be satisfied. So, I don't give in.

He doesn't either.

"Who are you looking for?" Ginny questions from my left, nudging me playfully. I shake my head, ignoring her as I continue my perusal.

"Shayde Glover, obviously," Demi pipes up from my right. "Didn't you know? She has a thing for him, despite my many warnings against it."

"I don't have a thing for him," I interject, turning to glare at her.

"Oh, but he totally has a thing for you." Wren giggles from the seat below me, Reese wiggling her eyebrows beside her.

"Yeah, he has those 'I'm going to devour you' type of bedroom eyes every time he looks at her," Willow confirms nonchalantly, adding, "Plus, everyone knows he's obsessed with you. He watches you all day and talks about you to anyone who listens. He hasn't dated anyone since you showed up, either. That's some serious commitment from a man like Shayde."

"Stop." I groan, putting my head in my hands.

I hate this kind of chatter. I don't want to encourage Shayde, and I certainly don't want him to think me talking about him with my friends means I'm one step closer to giving in. We fucked one time! Once! And I'll never hear the end of it.

I knew it was a bad idea.

"Maybe you should just sleep with him, you know? Get it out of your system." Ginny grins at me, batting her eyelashes innocently. "Unless you already have, of course."

"How did you know that—"

"What the fuck? Azalea Jinx, did you just say that you fucked Shayde Glover?" Demi interrupts me, gaping in disbelief. Shit. I hadn't planned on telling her. I know exactly what she is going to say, and I don't want to hear it.

"One time," I grumble aloud, searching the crowded gym again. "That's it. And it was only because I was on this emotional high, plus an adrenaline rush, that I wasn't ready to let go of. I warned him that it might not happen again."

"That's why he's so obsessed with her!" Wren giggles.

"How long ago was this?" Demi sounds hurt, and I flinch at the thought of having a serious conversation about Shayde.

"And was it any good?" the triplets pipe in together, hanging on to my every word.

"Two weeks ago. And it was…" They want me to describe it, but how can I? It was everything I needed and more. It was more than sex, no less than madness.

"Mind-blowing? Phenomenal? The best sex you ever had?" Demi ticks off each sentence with a finger, smiling reluctantly.

Good; I really don't want to hear the speech. Anything she says will be something I've already told myself. "Sure. All of the above. It made me feel like an actual person, like I was more than just a side character watching my life from afar. Which is exactly what I wanted. But now? Now all of that is gone and there's no point in doing it again if I'm not going to get to enjoy it. Knowing what I'm missing out on, knowing it could be more than just the numbness…there's no way I wouldn't be disappointed. No way I could pretend to enjoy it as much."

"Are you for real right now? Shayde Glover gave you mind-blowingly good sex and you just said 'Nah, I don't need any more of that'? You aren't even going to try?" Ginny isn't the only one in disbelief, her mouth popped open in shock. Her eyes trail to Willow as she says, "If I had sex like that, I'd be foaming at the mouth for more."

"It was a one-night stand type of thing, okay? Can't you guys just drop it? You don't understand. You can't. I'm not interested in a relationship *or* a situationship. I…it was the first time I've had sex with anyone since Neil died. It was amazing, I enjoyed myself, and I hope one day I will be able to feel raw emotion like that again. But for now, it's over, and it probably won't happen again."

How am I supposed to have sex with him again when the first time felt so good? What happens if I do allow it and it isn't the same? What do I do then? What do I do when I've tainted that memory, ruined it with the realization that nothing will ever be as good again?

"Oh, you'll definitely get to feel something raw again," Demi quips. The laughter that follows is boisterous, drawing attention from the Conjurers surrounding us.

"Demi!" It's nice to be so easily distracted from such gloomy thoughts.

"How big was it? Like this?" She gestures with her fingers, then holds her hands wide apart. "Or like this?"

"I'm not talking about his dick right now." I manage out a laugh just as my eyes find his across the sea of people. His mouth quirks up into a smirk as he watches me shove Demi's hands down.

Demi turns to yell at me, surprise in her eyes. Then she notices where my gaze has landed, finding Shayde and his friends. She waves toward Arlo, grinning brightly as they sit with all of the other second-years across the room.

"I think he's trying to pick the second option," Reese says as Shayde begins stretching out his own hands, the others nodding and muttering in agreement.

"No, no. He's exaggerating. None of those are quite the right measurement. It was more like this." My eyes don't stray from Shayde's as I move Demi's hands again, and I can tell he's pleased as he begins grinning like a maniac.

"Oh, he knows exactly what we are talking about. She definitely isn't lying. Look at his face!" Wren bursts out, creating another avalanche of laughter.

The laughter cuts off abruptly when a large group of Conjurers enter the room. Silence envelops us all. The first thing I notice about the group is that half of them are dressed in all white, the rest in all black. I can hear audible gulps around me as their light steps echo around us, all ten Conjurers gleaming with a unique energy that screams *important*.

"The councils for each faction. Very, very important people." Demi confirms my thoughts from beside me, tense and aware of their every move as the chatter begins slowly arising once more.

"What's up with the whole faction thing, anyway? No one ever really explained it to me. Delarosa just said I would need to choose a side one day. Never really said why or for who."

"It's our form of government, basically. The leader of each faction is like a…like a…"

"Like a president?" I fill in, eyes falling on the pretty, middle-aged blonde in all white. She is definitely leader material. I can feel the confidence oozing off of her from here and can sense it in her self-righteous stance.

"Right! Each leader has a second, and the other three are basically advisors. Together, all five make the big decisions about each faction's rules and regulations. For things involving both parties, well, decisions become a little more tricky. Both councils have to work together to form a unanimous decision, and that is near impossible. The two practically hate each other."

"Why? Isn't the whole point for them to, like, work together for a better world?"

"That's the idea, yeah. You know the whole yin and yang thing? That's what they are supposed to be: two halves of a whole, just like their namesake powers. But the past few decades…well, from what I hear, both sides are up to some pretty shady shit. The Lights blame the Shadows for everything that goes wrong and vice versa. No clue what's going on, but it's big. They also get a say in our curriculum, which can make things a little tense. Sometimes they try to micromanage certain schools, but mostly they let the Deans make decisions. But they can come in here at any point and tell Delarosa that we no longer are allowed to teach certain techniques or use certain Charms and she would have to comply."

"I'm still not sure I get it. What's got them so tense? And what's the point of us choosing who to side with?"

"By choosing a side, we get to make decisions, too. We can be involved with the council by going to the public meetings and voting on things. It also means aligning your beliefs with one side over the other. The Shadows believe in freedom and choice. The Lights believe in rules and regulations. There's a balance in having both, but we get to choose whose beliefs we align with more.

"There's a lot more to it, but that's the gist. It would take forever to catch you up on the shit these guys pull behind the scenes. As to what's going on…well, if the whispers are correct…one of the sides is considering making a deal with the Grim. They want protection in exchange for giving up the other faction."

"The fuck? One of the factions is siding with the Grim?" Why would they do that? Isn't that the whole point of this world, to fight against him? Are they just…giving up?

"If rumors are to be believed."

"Well, which side is it?"

"Honestly, I have no idea. No one does. No one knows if it is even true, Azalea. It could be a seed planted to sow discord among us. Only time will tell."

"So, if I align myself with the right side…"

"Yeah, your life may be spared." Demi shrugs as if it's no big deal, and I suppose it isn't for her. She's used to this bullshit.

I'm not totally surprised by this revolution. Absolute power absolutely corrupts, after all.

"See that blonde in white down there? The one walking around like she owns the place? That is Haiden Bloodgood."

"Is she related to Jaymes?" I glance over at him, noticing the glare plastered across his face. A glare clearly aimed at Haiden.

"That's his *mother*." Demi practically bounces in anticipation, eyes flicking between the two Bloodgoods. "Yeah, she's the Light Faction leader. And once Jaymes chose to join the Shadow Faction…well, from what I heard, things didn't end well."

I can't stop myself from defending him, despite not understanding the situation to its fullest extent. "He's a grown man. He has a right to make his own decisions."

"Right? But she full-on disowned him. He went from golden child to black sheep like this." She snaps her fingers dramatically, sighing lightly.

"Her loss, I guess."

"It's sad. His dad died on a mission, like, ten years ago. He only had one parent, and now…"

"Try having none." I can't help but snort out, mouth snapping shut abruptly. Not everyone takes dead parent jokes well. "Sorry. Ignore me. You know I don't feel very strongly about parent death. Continue."

"You don't feel very strongly about *anything*," she grumbles in response, rolling her eyes. "Which should probably make me sad because that means you don't love me as much as I love you, but I am a forgiving and malevolent creature, so I will allow it. Anyway, as I was saying, that's his mother. Want to know what's even crazier? Arlo's dad, the redhead down there in white? Yeah, that's Leader Bloodgood's second. His mom, the blonde chick talking to his dad? Yeah, she's Light Faction, too."

"But Arlo isn't." I shake my head quietly in faint disbelief. Why would they do that? Why would they choose a different faction when their parents quite literally rule over the other? Wouldn't that put them closer to their goals of being council members? Wouldn't that gain them some kinds of perks, being the kids of such powerful people? Though, I suppose, they have gained power in their own rights.

"Yep." Demi pops her 'p' loudly, turning to me with a wide grin. "And guess what else?"

"Don't tell me Shayde's parents are also in the Light Faction?"

"Actually, I was going to say that Nox's parents are in the Shadow council. No one really knows anything about Shayde's lineage, now that you mention it. He keeps it pretty hush-hush. Most people just assume he's an orphan or a bastard or something."

I make a mental note to ask Shayde about his parents during our next lesson. Maybe, if he admits he's a bastard, I can be mean enough about it that he'll finally move on. "So three of the four Gravediggers have parents in the councils? But all four are aligned with the Shadow Faction?"

"That about sums it up," she agrees cheerfully. That's one thing I don't particularly like about Demi: she's always cheerful. "That's why they are so powerful. Powerful heritage and all."

"Good morning, Draxmere students!" Haiden Bloodgood speaks and the busy chatter dies down, the students' voices drowned out by silence. Haiden laps up the attention she receives, smiling and waving enthusiastically, and I can't help but notice the similarities between her and her son. Does it drive Jaymes insane to know that he looks like the monster who threw him away?

"Good morning, Leader Bloodgood," a chorus of responses echo around us.

A giant of a man steps forward to speak next, bald head gleaming in the light. "We are very excited to be here today!" The man subtly pushes up the glasses sitting on his crooked nose, brown eyes light and bright as they roam the student population. I notice that his dark skin is covered in even darker tattoos, and both arms are covered in full sleeves. Overall, for a middle-aged man, he's quite attractive.

"Excited to have you, Leader Fellows." Hoots and hollers ring out with the crowd's response, and I shift in annoyance. Obviously, this is a common introduction.

"Everybody here has so many tattoos," I observe, admiring the Shadow Leader's from afar.

"They cover the scars," Ginny says before shushing me.

"We are here today to talk to you about your futures," Leader Bloodgood begins as she paces, throwing up her hands as she speaks. "There is an importance in choosing your faction, a balance in picking the right side for you. Some of you may feel torn and unsure about what the right choice for you may be. This choice isn't only about powers; you can be a Dimineer and choose the Light, and vice versa. It's not only about family, and what your parents may have chosen. It's about you, your values, and which faction you believe will benefit you the most."

"What a fucking hypocrite," Demi snarks, and I have to agree with her sentiments.

"The two of us are going to essentially introduce our factions to those of you who are first years. We hope to provide you with insight on what, exactly, you can expect out of joining us. Keep in mind that you don't have to decide who to align yourself with until the end of your first year here at Draxmere. So, for now, these are just topics for consideration. Our speeches will be brief, as we have a few important announcements to discuss with the entire student body before we go visit our next school," Leader Fellows finishes, nodding toward Leader Bloodgood respectfully and allowing her to be the first pitch.

"Most people associate light and dark with good and bad. I want to state now, on the record, that that couldn't be further from the truth. We all have good and bad in us, and our factions aren't associated with our morality. Light does not automatically mean good, so don't join us just because you think we are the only good guys." Bloodgood is smiling, but Fellows isn't. His jaw tightens, his fists clenching. This must be a sensitive subject if his behavior is any indication.

"The Light Faction functions off of rules and order. We like to have a plan, a guide. We make rules for the rest of the world to follow. Some say we are strict and obedient, but we prefer to say we are protective. Careful. We like to have backup plans for our backup plans, and we want to do what is best for the Charmed as a whole. People in our faction tend to be smart, cunning, and willing to do whatever it takes to keep the peace and protect our people. If you want to read further about our beliefs, and the rules we adhere to, there are pamphlets available on the table by the exit."

"Leader Bloodgood is absolutely right: this isn't about good or bad, our faction is not corrupted or evil like many may claim, and we are not only meant for Dimineers. Our faction, like the shadows, craves fluidity. We don't want chaos, but freedom. We want to have fewer rules and more choices. Because what is life without choice?

"Our faction is responsible for your ability to choose a side today. Over a hundred years ago, our ancestors fought for your right to choose for yourself over staying on whichever side you were born into, and they won because choice is important. We don't seek out a world with no rules, rather, we seek options. We don't believe in one-size-fits-all. That doesn't make us destructive, power-hungry, or indecisive. People in our faction are strong, brave, independent, impulsive, and ready to make the hard decisions for their fellow Conjurers. As stated by Leader Bloodgood, there are pamphlets with more information on the factions available by the exit. Please, pick up one of each and carefully read them. This decision is important, and not one to be made lightly. Don't wait until the day before the Reaping to decide."

Leader Fellow takes a step back, allowing Bloodgood to step back into the spotlight. I don't miss the awkward pause as they brush against each other, nor the glares that pass between the councils. There's more tension between the two groups than I expected, considering they are supposed to work in harmony. I suppose that's exactly what Demi had hinted at, though.

"I'm sorry we had to be short and sweet today. Alas, there is some rather serious news that needs to be discussed. News that leaves us all with heavy hearts." She pauses to let that information sink in, allowing us to brace ourselves for her next words. "As you all know, Reapers tend to be lonely creatures and often choose to divide and conquer. Unfortunately, as of late, that is no longer the case. They no longer travel alone, and it has cost us dozens of lives in making this discovery."

The crowd breaks their silence, nervous chatter scurrying across the room. Demi glances at me with a raised brow, not surprised because I told her about the odd occurrence during my mission two weeks ago. But the triplets and Ginny? They're shocked. They look at each other with worried glances, biting on lips and sucking in breaths. I turn to watch the Gravediggers and nod in acknowledgment of their foreboding expressions.

"Reapers have been spotted in groups on multiple occasions, typically two or three at a time. There are no indications yet as to why this is happening, but we need our students to be aware that the danger is increasing. There are counselors available to speak to you today if you would like to reconsider your place here at Draxmere. We urge you not to, but we understand if any students feel as though they cannot, and will not, put their lives at such risk. Do what is best for you, and we will worry about the rest. Thank you everyone for your apt attention. We will stick around for a short while to take questions."

I stand along with everyone else, ignoring the uproar happening around me. I start to push my way through the crowd, descending the bleachers at a fast pace and ignoring my friends calling for me.

Something isn't right, and I'm about to find out why.

Why would the councils allow us to drop out just because the danger is a tad bit higher than before? This is what we signed up for. So why are they practically encouraging us to quit? Why are they putting the idea into our heads that we may not be good enough to handle more than one Reaper at a time?

"What the fuck?" It's all I can think to say to Jaymes when I approach, ignoring the rest of his friend group despite their sneers in my direction.

"What's the problem now, Jinx?" He barely glances at me, focusing instead on Stella approaching from across the room. I see her blonde hair swaying as she shoves people out of the way, her glare pinned on me.

"What was that bullshit about? Telling people it's okay to quit when the going gets hard?"

"How should I know? I'm not on the council."

"Yeah, but your mother *is*." His expression changes, eyes turning hard as his head whips back toward me.

"My *mother* and I aren't on speaking terms, Azalea. And I know *fuck all* about what she is up to. Do you want me to speculate? Because I have a lot of speculations. Other than that, information about the council's decisions is on a need-to-know basis. And guess what? *You don't need to know.*"

"Don't be such a hard ass, Jaymes. I'm not asking for specifics. I'm asking *why*. I'm new here. I don't understand how politics work in this place."

"All you need to know is that everything isn't as it seems within the factions. And I would advise you not to listen to the horse shit that my mother spews." He stands, stalking away before I can reply. Clearly, all good blood between the Bloodgoods is gone.

"Things are complicated, Azalea. You don't even want to know how complicated it truly is," Shayde says, taking my hand reassuringly. I squint my eyes down at the connection, my heart picking up its beat. The fuck is that about?

"Yeah, don't worry about Jaymes. He's still in his feels about the whole being cut off from his family thing," Arlo pipes in, while Nox stays silent as usual.

"Fuck off, Arlo. He's more than 'in his feels'. His mother betrayed him. Not all of us have safe and loving families like you do," Shayde spits angrily, hand clenching mine painfully.

"Whatever, man. We'll leave you and your girlfriend to it."

"I'm not his—" Arlo and Nox are gone before I can attempt to rip my hand away from his. "Have you been telling people we are together?"

"Of course not. They're just jerking us around. Are you okay? You seem a little worried about this council stuff."

"I'm not worried, just confused and trying to understand. None of it makes sense."

One of the issues with not feeling is that it makes you want to understand why people feel the things they do. When people do stupid shit, I like to know why. I like to puzzle out reasons for behaviors and reasons for decisions. It keeps me distracted from the fact that I'll never have those impulsive reactions others do. I won't ever jump in front of a gun for my best friend just because I'm supposed to, won't ever make a decision based on a love that may not even be reciprocated to its fullest extent. It fucking sucks, but at least I can pretend to have those things when I have a good puzzle to work through.

"That's because you can see things other people can't. You aren't ruled by emotions and blind loyalty, only logic and reason. My advice? Keep thinking."

Shayde releases my hand, jogging to catch up with his friends who are exiting the gym. Reluctantly, I make my way to the exit, too. I grab one of each pamphlet on my way out, clenching them tightly in my palms.

A tingling sensation is poking at my brain, an unease, an uncertainty. Shayde's right: I do need to keep thinking, to keep pursuing this puzzle.

Something majorly wrong is going on here.

CHAPTER 15

"In case of emergencies, every school has alarm systems set in place to protect you. If you hear these alarms, you must make a decision: fight or hide. I urge students to choose to hide and allow the professionals to take care of the issue. Do not fret, emergencies in a Conjuring school are rare and do not occur more often than once in a lifetime. As such, you will not likely face such a decision."
—*A Guide to the Charmed* (current edition), written by Glamourist Elias Kasper in 1907 A.G.

"In case of emergencies, every school has alarm systems set in place to protect you. If you hear these alarms, you must make a decision: fight or hide. I urge students to choose to hide and allow the professionals to take care of the issue. Do not fret, emergencies in a Conjuring school are rare and do not occur more often than once in a lifetime. As such, you will not likely face such a decision."

—*A Guide to the Charmed* (current edition), written by Glamourist Elias Kasper in 1907 A.G.

"What the fuck is going on?"

My eyes flash open after the first alarm rings, the sound blaring and irritating. My lights are flickering to the beat of the screams outside my door, mirroring the panic and desperation hanging in the air.

I pull myself out of bed, stumbling to my door with fuzzy vision. I blink rapidly, taking a deep breath and wiping my eyes until I can see clearly. Only then do I swing my door open, forcing myself out into the chaos that greets me.

Conjurers are everywhere, most still in their pajamas, surrounded by *dozens* of Reapers. My heart sings at the sight, but not in fear. No, a new, bright, exhilarating emotion appears: *excitement.*

I should definitely be panicking right now, or maybe even concerned about the bloody bodies lying in heaps on the ground. But I'm not. I should feel sick to my stomach, should be disgusted with myself for being excited while Conjurers' lives are being threatened. But I don't have a large enough emotional range for that yet, so fuck the shoulds.

I'm thrilled.

I want to fight Reapers, I want to *kill.* Fuck, there's something wrong with me.

I jump into the fray without a second thought, blasting my Light clumsily toward a Reaper descending on a crying girl with a Seer pin. She crawls away, weeping and terrified. I watch as she bangs on the door nearest her, begging to be let in. I can't hear the response, but whatever it is has the girl caving into herself as she tries to hide in plain sight.

Shouldn't these people be brave? Shouldn't they be strong and confident in the face of danger? I know I said to fuck the shoulds, but come on. I guess all of us should feel a lot of things that we don't.

I'm not the only one with fucked up emotions, huh?

"Go find your room and don't come back out," I tell her calmly, pushing on. If she isn't capable of doing the bare minimum in saving herself, well, I can't be to blame.

I step over a bleeding body, doing my best not to step on any limbs. I spot Demi up ahead, her lithe form flashing in and out of focus as she distracts the Reapers. I watch as she jumps onto one, snapping its neck in one fluid motion. It falls, allowing an Illuminoor to swoop in and kill it before it can rise back up.

Farther down the hall is a siren, screaming a tune so hideous that nearby Reapers and Conjurers alike hold their ears. I merely wince, gaze roaming over the dozens of Conjurers littering the ground. I'm not sure if the bodies between us are all dead ones, or if some students have merely been knocked unconscious. The smell of their blood is nauseating, my bare feet already slick and sticky from the sheer amount of the liquid that has leaked onto the carpeted floors.

On and on it goes as far as I can see, dozens of our own fighting dozens of theirs. I can hardly move from the amount of people fighting, can scarcely blink without a Reaper turning its empty eyes toward me. Close by, I hear Demi's voice shouting, "Azalea!" then she appears before me in a flash.

Her fangs have fully extended and her face is contorted in an odd shape. She looks more like a monster than I would have imagined her being, with blue-tinted skin and bulging eyes. Ironically, her features have transformed to seem much more bat-like. Her nose is misshapen, she has tiny little hairs growing all over, and her skin has been pulled so tightly that she looks more skeleton than woman.

"Demi. What's—" I start but am interrupted before I can ask what's going on.

A Reaper leaps for Demi, and I barely shoot off a jolt of Light in time. It's sloppy and uncoordinated, weak at best. The ball of Light hits the Reaper's shoulder, causing it to fall with a loud shout of pain. It isn't a fatal wound, but it is enough to hold it back for a couple of seconds.

"Keep doing that, Azalea. Just—kill them. I'll be right here to help you." Demi pants, licking her swollen and bruised lips. I nod, that newfound excitement bubbling up inside of me. I feel like an addict who is finally getting their fix.

Demi turns her back to mine and we press against one another, circling as we wait for the next attack. I try to drown out the screams of the students around me, try to push away the scent of blood mixed with that nauseating black goo permeating the air. I know Demi must be struggling more than I am, as the scent is much stronger for her than it is for me. She's told me before that blood is intoxicating, that it's hard to stop drinking once they've started. That's why they get it in little bottles instead of from the source: they don't want to overindulge and accidentally kill someone.

"Approaching!" I shout over the chaos, ignoring the wolf who slams into the wall next to us. This hall isn't more than ten feet wide, and we barely avoid being hit by the large body. I can't help my transfixed gaze as I watch the Shifter transform back into a man. He stands and stumbles away, wiping blood off his face as he approaches the same Reaper as though he didn't just have his ass handed to him.

I shout again as the Reaper who has set eyes on us swipes out at me first, sharp claws digging into my arm. I grunt as it rips the skin open, refusing to cry out in pain. I thrust my hand out and allow my Light to pierce its heart with more force than necessary, chest clenching as it turns into a pile of ashes at my feet. Fuck, that hurt.

"Azalea. Are you—is that blood? Are you—fuck, I'm sorry. I can't. I can't breathe in right now." Demi shakes against me, gasping for air as all of her resolve washes down the drain.

"When's the last time you fed, Demi?" Her face begins to crack and fissure, her nose twitching violently. If the blood is affecting her this badly, it must be near feeding time. How much power has she used while out here? Shit, she must need a fix by now.

"Yesterday at breakfast. I was going to have some more when we went downstairs to eat. I thought I would be fine, I'd barely exerted myself. I thought—"

"It's okay." I shush her, heart clenching in another new sensation: worry. I reach for her hand, stretching my arm out behind me. Our fingers clasp together and I hear her begin to sob. "Listen, I'll let you feed on me, okay? We just need to kill these fuckers first."

"I don't know if I can make it that long, Azalea. I don't—"

"You will. Because once you drink my blood, my powers will be so depleted that I won't be able to fight. And I need to fight. Do you understand? I don't see a lot of Illuminoors on this floor. There's, like, five of us right now at most. And who knows what's happening on the other floors? So you have to push through this, okay? You have to be strong. If I let you lick the wound clean, will that hold you over? It'll heal it, right?"

"Fuck, okay. Okay. I can do that. Yes, I can close the wound. My saliva is good for more than one thing." She tries to make a dirty joke, but her voice wavers and she lets out a pitiful whimper.

Our conversation is interrupted when she leaps away from me, yanking her hand away abruptly. I spin around just in time to watch her pull off a Reaper's arm, to hear it cry out in despair. The sound sends a shiver down my spine, the mutilated creature's roar haunting. I blast its heart as it spins to Demi, but another is on me before I can finish the blast.

I scream out in anguish as it tackles me, sharp nails digging into my spine and leaving deep cuts down my back. The wound immediately begins to burn, a sizzling pain that radiates throughout my entire back. It hurts more than anything I've ever experienced and stings more than any tattoo ever could have.

I attempt to throw the beast off of me, trying to flip myself around, but my hands are pinned beneath me and I can't get them out, can't perform a single Charm or get out a single blast to help myself.

My body begins heating up, an obnoxious energy inside of me rising that won't slow down. I scream again as the agonizing heat burns me from the inside out, painful tears involuntarily slipping down my cheeks. With one last wave of heat, I explode, a blinding light escaping from my body and burning every set of eyes within a ten-foot vicinity at the bare minimum. Once the light has escaped, the awful heat disappears, leaving a calm and contained spark in its wake.

I close my eyes, allowing my Light to do what it is meant to, allowing myself to feel at peace for these brief seconds. But seconds are all I get before the Light is gone, the three Reapers that were unfortunate enough to be in the proximity of the wave disappearing with it.

"Azalea! Are you okay? Fuck, that looks bad. Please, get up. Please be alive."

Demi is in front of me now, bent down with outreached hands. I grunt as I finally rip my hands out from underneath my own body weight, holding them out for her. My hands shake as I do so, my eyes pleading for her to help me up. She does so, gentle and strong as she pulls me to my feet.

"I'm alive," I say bitterly, glancing around. Fuck, that was a major slip-up on my part. I didn't hold control and it almost cost me dearly, and I can see how it affected those around us.

Conjurers are rubbing their faces, blinking down at the ashes littering the ground. More bodies litter the floor, and at least a dozen more Reapers have appeared. I try not to gag at the image of the ashes mixing with the blood; a disgusting sight to say the least. And the smell some of these Reapers are leaving behind is rancid, their black goo dripping down mutated limbs casually.

Some students are struggling more than others, fighting off Reapers without an Illuminoor nearby. It seems as though, despite the Reaper's numbers increasing, the Conjurer's numbers haven't. They are all either hiding, injured, or dead.

We are so fucked.

"Your back." Demi bites her lip hard, blood trickling down in a slow path.

"Yeah, I know. Fuck, that hurt." I reach back to touch it, wincing in pain as I do.

My tears have stopped leaking but they have already stained my cheeks, dry and obvious proof of my new vulnerabilities. The cuts are longer and deeper than I imagined, and one touch leaves my fingers coated in slick blood. I bring my hand back in front of me, still shaking as I take a deep breath through my nose. Demi whimpers at the sight of it, a hand coming up to cover her nose and mouth as her eyes shut tightly.

A scream sounds from next to us, another body hitting the ground. A leg slaps into mine and I stumble back, already woozy from blood loss. The person on the ground curses, pushing back up faster than I can blink. Darkness seeps out from their hands, surrounding the approaching Reaper in a cloud of ink. I lamely shoot out a blast of Light into the cloud, but it takes a toll on my body. I jerk forward, bile rising in my throat.

Shakily, I hold out my arm, offering Demi my blood despite my weakness. She nabs it gratefully, pulling it to her mouth in a flash. To her credit, she doesn't bite down or suck at all. She only licks at my wound, effectively healing and cleaning it.

"Almost there, Demi. Almost there," I whisper, stumbling as I try to take a step on my own.

"You are losing a lot of blood. Those are deep, Azzie. And your power usage…" Demi pulls away and wipes her mouth with her forearm, concern painted across her features. Then her lips waver, shaking, as she tries not to drool at the sight of me.

"Not much I can do about that."

"Here, take this." She bites her wrist hard, holding it out to me. "My blood has healing properties, too. I swear, it's not horrible."

"You're lucky I trust you," I murmur, holding onto her wrist tightly. "This better not turn me into a fucking vamp."

Hesitantly, I put my mouth to her wrist and lick. There isn't time for me to wait, or to be grossed out by what I'm doing. I just have to put my faith in her and trust that I will heal.

My licks quickly become sucks, and I moan and stumble back in shock as I feel the wounds tightening. It's as though someone is pinching my skin, pulling it tightly, and sewing the edges together. I arch my back at the strangeness, panting when heat and blinding pain spreads through my body. It's different from the intense burn from my Light; this burn is more like a second-degree one versus the third-degree one from earlier.

"It's okay. It's working. It just hurts because of the poison the Reaper left. You'll probably still have scars left because of that and the deepness," Demi whispers soothingly, grabbing my hand and supporting my weight with her own as I lean against her. I can only nod and whimper, eyes shutting tightly. I can live with the scars as long as I'm allowed to live past these moments.

"Okay. Good. Great. Feeling much better. Let's try to move farther down the hall," I say after a few minutes, when some of my strength returns. "I think the Reapers are staying away from us out of fear, but I also think they are smart enough to attack the Illuminoors. We need to—wait. Why does that one look…"

The Reaper standing only feet away from us looks much different than the others we have seen so far. Much more human-like than even the ones I helped kill all those weeks ago.

"It's been eating well," Demi whispers, looking at the discarded body beneath its looming form. "Isn't it uncanny how much they look like us? How they can pass as one of us without anyone knowing?"

"Yeah, it really—Demi! Watch out! Behind you!" Demi is only a few steps away, but my Light is sparking in my hands as if trying to start. It's like turning a key in a car whose battery is on the brink of death. Kicking, sputtering, but never starting.

Demi spins at my shout, kicking out with her unnatural speed and strength. The Reaper flies back several feet, landing with a thud and an unnatural roar. It shakes the entire hall with its anger, and several Conjurers pause to look over at us. Then it's rushing, fast and agile, as its eyes fall on me.

My Light streaks toward it, finally listening to my commands, but the thing easily dodges my power. I haven't practiced using my power on moving targets, and my aim is not precise enough to make contact. I throw beam after beam of Light at it, growing more and more frustrated with every wasted blast. I don't know what I am doing when it comes to battle, and it is costing both me and Demi.

She races forward, leaping and jumping onto its chest. She snaps its neck like she's done several times before, but this one doesn't fall. Instead, the Reaper slings her off, undeterred as it continues to race toward me. Not only is it more human-like, it's also stronger, faster, and a whole lot smarter.

I take careful steps back as I shoot more beams, careful not to trip over a body. My heart races the closer it gets, panic infiltrating my mind. This is the first time I've had to try to fight, the first time I've needed to really *focus*.

It's amazing.

I can feel every piece of tissue in my body, can pinpoint each new emotion racing up to meet me. Fear, panic, and nervousness are making me sweat, forcing my body into a shake as it tries to accommodate all of the new emotions.

I love it.

I go to shoot at it for what seems the hundredth time, but my Light is growing weak. I haven't practiced with it enough, haven't allowed it to grow and flourish in the way it needs. My beams aren't strong enough to create a hole in a creature this powerful, aren't powerful enough to damage it after being so depleted.

"Demi, I don't think I can kill this one. I'm too weak. I think—well, I think I've used up all my Light." My voice hitches, my mind wandering to new plans.

Distract, distract, distract.

I need to send Demi to find another Illuminoor while I hold this one off. What can I use to distract it? Will my Shadow powers be enough? Should I use—

"That's okay, Jinx. I've got enough for the both of us." I jerk in surprise at the leering voice, eyes wide as the Reaper dissolves into ashes before me. Jaymes steps forward into the pile, a cocky smile gracing his lips. That smile quickly slips as he notices my ripped and bloody clothes, as well as the tear stains on my dirty cheeks.

"Thank fuck," I breathe, too relieved to be annoyed.

"Are you okay? You're covered in blood."

Jaymes takes a step forward, hands searching my arm for the cuts that are no longer there. I shiver at his touch, stepping back in a hurry.

"I'm fine. Demi healed me already."

Cheers erupt in the hall as the students realize the Gravediggers have arrived with a group of professors. The chants and claps swallow Jaymes's reply. I look up to find Shayde racing toward me, and I find myself swallowed in his strong arms when he reaches me.

"Azalea, are you hurt? I'm so sorry, I thought we would be able to get here faster, but the professors were blocking everyone from coming up. It took a lot of convincing to be allowed up here. But we are here now, so we are going to take care of it, okay?"

I shiver under his touch, shaking as all of those confusing emotions from my first battle take over again. The lust, the want, and the absolute *need* to have him are all punches straight to my gut.

"Not much to take care of now. Only a few left," I gargle out, shaking for a completely different reason now. "Fuck, let me go, Shayde. You have to stop touching me right now. *Please,*" I beg, closing my eyes tightly. I'm not sure I will be able to control myself if he keeps touching me. The addict in me is coming out, and I don't trust myself not to rip his clothes off right here and now. Not if it means I get to quench this thirst, if I get the rush of emotion I so desperately crave.

"Oh. Oh, yeah. Sorry. I forgot what happens to you after a fight." He backs away, smirking and satisfied. "Listen, the boys and I are going to help the professors finish off these Reapers, okay? Just—wait for me. I'll come back and we can finish this conversation."

I notice Jaymes has already left, that he slipped away without saying a word to either of us. Shayde is leaving now, too, glancing back at me with a wicked grin full of promises.

We all pause to watch Shayde's Shadows expand across the ground, and the remaining Reapers all spin to watch him, too. There are probably less than ten left at this point, all of which abandon their fights to approach Shayde. Professor Slateman appears at his side, joining him in creating the large amount of darkness to tempt the Reapers.

Arlo is at the end of the hall in his wolf form, nipping at Reapers and encouraging them to move on. Nox stands next to Jaymes, eyes closed in concentration. When he opens them again, his body shakes, and the two men whisper among themselves. Another professor joins them, Professor Battle, and she shouts a command I can't hear. Other professors begin approaching students, crouching down next to bodies and giving out instructions to those who are still standing. In one large swoop, the Illuminoors begin killing Reapers. The efficiency with which they do so is quite startling, and I can't help but admire their strategy.

Eight. I count eight Reapers approaching, eight out of the nearly thirty that had to have been on this floor. How many lives had been sacrificed in the time it took for us students to kill the other twenty or so? How much longer would I have made it before I became one of those sacrificed?

Demi approaches and interrupts my self-deprecating thoughts, her face back to its normal, gorgeous state. Her fangs still protrude from her mouth, her tongue swiping out to lick her damaged lips.

"Azalea? I'm sorry, um…can I…"

"Of course. The Gravediggers and the professors are taking over, apparently, so…let's take a break. Let's take care of you." I turn my gaze away from the killing of the Reapers, focusing on her instead.

"Oh, thank the Grim." She groans, taking a step forward. "I promise it won't hurt. It'll leave you a little high if that makes you feel any better about it."

"I'm already high." I breathe out, eyes fluttering shut as I wait for the bite.

Demi leaps onto me, sending us both stumbling back. I groan as we hit the wall and reach up to grip her hips, thankful that the cuts on my back are no longer open wounds. Her fangs sink into a large vein on my neck, and I cry out in surprise. The brief pain turns into ecstasy, the high she promised me making its appearance.

My mind becomes a bowl of mush, my body light and airy. I can vaguely hear Demi slurping down my blood, but mostly I hear a light ringing in my ears. I let out an uncharacteristic giggle as my eyes flutter open, hands tangling into Demi's hair of their own accord. That's when she decides to push herself away, panting as she steps back. I pout as I open my eyes once more, finding her on the opposite wall.

"What's wrong? That felt so good." I drag out the word 'good', releasing a small moan and more giggling. I watch her hands move discreetly, blood disappearing from her body and mine.

"I know. I know, I'm sorry. I took just enough to hold me over. I didn't want to drain you, Azalea." She wipes my blood off her mouth, licking her fingers and sighing contently as she does so. "Not that I wasn't tempted. Your blood…there's something different in it. Probably the whole two-powers thing. Good Grim, I could get addicted to it if I'm not careful."

"You can get addicted," I urge her, taking a clumsy step forward. I've been drunk before, and this is very similar to that feeling; similar to the lack of control and the endorphins it releases in me.

"Okay. I think that's enough of that." Jaymes appears at my side, stepping forward to place himself between me and Demi. He puts a hand on my arm, stopping me from trying to continue my pursuit of the tiny vampire.

"But—" I try to protest but am distracted when Shayde appears behind me and whispers my name in my ear. I find myself squished between the two men, and my inebriated brain can't stop itself from going to sexual places.

"Oh. Is Jaymes joining us?" I question, reaching out and combing my fingers through his almost-white hair. Jaymes's eyes darken briefly, his own fingers twitching against my skin as he shares a knowing look with Shayde.

"No, thanks. I don't like to share." He brushes me off, stepping back and turning away before I can protest.

"Vamp bites do feel good, don't they?" Shayde questions as he leaves a trail of hot kisses down my neck, nibbling my ear and licking my wound. He doesn't seem to care that we are in the middle of a crowded hallway, or that Demi is still only feet away from us. I don't have the mind to care, either.

"I'm—er—I'm going now. Have fun, babe!" Demi practically shouts before speeding off, a blush staining her cheeks and fear hidden in her eyes.

"Uh-huh." I can barely form those syllables, much less words. Shayde is intoxicating, his presence lighting me up in the best way possible. And right now all I can think about is the last night we spent together in bed, the things that he did to my mind and body.

My one-track mind is focused and determined, one thought piercing through the fog. *I have to get Shayde Glover into my bed before this high is gone and I am left a husk once again.*

CHAPTER 16

"When there is little hope, a girl will rise.
A hero, a savior, a prophet;
she'll hold both light and dark inside."
—Prophecy found inside Seer Nova Howard's prophetic journals,
035 B.G.

I yank on Shayde's shirt, pulling him toward the direction of my room. We have to step over piles of ashes, puddles of blood, and way too many bodies. But I can't stop myself, and he doesn't want me stopped.

I am being devoured by this all-consuming lust willingly.

My hand slips out from underneath his shirt, though I'm not sure when it got there, and slams onto the front of my door. We slip inside the room, ignoring the calls of another Conjurer requesting help with moving injured students. Shayde only kicks the door shut, already ripping my tattered shirt off my chest.

"I fucking hate these shorts," he hisses, ripping them clean off of me.

Oh, yeah. I guess my "I heart Neil" shorts probably aren't what he wants to see right now.

I can't form the words to answer him. Only loud noises and harsh breaths escape my lips. I turn to approach my bed, tugging him along with me. I giggle as I stumble once more, falling into my mirror and grabbing onto its sides for balance. Shayde's hungry eyes watch me from behind, shadows rising from his body like flames.

My power reaches up to meet his, and it's unlike anything I've ever felt before. Using my powers is a cathartic release in itself, but having his powers mingle together with mine? Having them surround me, sinking themselves into the crevices within my skin? It's intense and deeply personal, like sharing a piece of my soul with him.

It's extraordinary.

I watch in the mirror as his hands wrap around my body and grip tightly onto my breasts, head ducking down to bite and suck along my neck. His shadows are everywhere and nowhere all at once, stroking my skin in soft caresses. It feels like his hands are roaming my body, like his hands are squeezing, pulling, and pumping.

"Fuck, Azalea. I don't know what you're doing to me," he manages out in a harsh whisper against my ear, voice cracking as he slams inside of me in one harsh thrust. I cry out, meeting his eyes through the mirror. A hand slips around my throat, pushing and clenching tightly until I'm truly gasping for breath.

"I did some fucked up things for you today." Shayde slams into me at a punishing pace, desperate and vicious. "Made some fucked up decisions."

I don't know what happened before he showed up, don't know what kind of things he had to do to reach me and keep me safe.

Anything that involves the Reapers is fucked up, though, and I don't want to know what he sacrificed for my safety. Or who.

I gargle out a response, my release hitting me over and over and *over* as he continues to ravish me. Something bubbles up within me, an unknown emotion I can't describe. Something raging and ready, filling me up inside and out. Somehow it brings this certainty, this clarity, that I won't get these intense emotions any other way.

Only Shayde can do this to me.

"Do you want to know the worst part?"

I nod feverishly, eyes rolling to the back of my head as his punishing pace turns into lazy strokes. As his thumb begins to trace circles around my clit, just as slowly and deliberately.

"I'd do it again."

Watching Shayde fall apart is beautiful and terrifying all at once.

The shadows are curling into one another, swarming the room like a mass of hungry sharks. They feed off one another, building and building along with our pleasure. Until we both come undone and lose control entirely. Until the room is swallowed in a darkness the same shade as his hair and the only noises are our heaving breaths.

I practically collapse against him, leaning back into his tattooed chest to keep myself standing and to prevent my knees from buckling. Shayde loops an arm around my waist, twisting me and dragging me to the bed. We fall while still facing each other, limbs entangling as the silence remains intact. His fingers swirl on my arms, my neck, my chest, all while his lips leave gentle kisses down the fresh scar on my arm.

Quietly, as if scared to disrupt this moment, he asks, "Are you going to leave again?"

"No. This is my room, why would I leave?" I swallow hard, eyes squeezing shut as his lazy touches move over a sensitive nipple. My heart is, remarkably, still racing, his presence still bringing out that insatiable lust.

"Are you going to give me another speech about temporary madness? About wishing you could offer me more than sex?"

"No, I don't think so."

"Thank fuck." His head buries into my neck, hair tickling my shoulders and cheek. We stay there, holding each other and enjoying the moment just a little longer.

I am the first to speak after a long silence, though I don't attempt to untangle our bodies just yet. "What happened? How did they get in?"

"It must have been an inside job." His voice rumbles against my skin, strong and sure. "From what I overheard, there's going to be an investigation. Somebody here had to have let them in, and they're going to figure out who and why. Most of the Reapers were contained to this floor, but a few managed to distract us on the lower levels. That's why it took us so long to get here, why the professors weren't here right away."

"They were mostly on this floor? Why? Why would they come here?"

"Because of you." He flinches as he says it, as if he can't bear the thought of me being the target of so many Reapers.

"Because of me? What do you—" Realization hits, and I pause, reconsidering. "Oh. It's my power. They could sense it, couldn't they?"

"You are going to be one of the strongest Conjurers we have had in a very, very long time, Azalea. Multiple Seers have predicted it. Dozens of prophecies have been about a girl with both light and dark inside her heart, a savior who comes to save us all. All very ominous, all very sure. I'm not sure if the person or people who let them in knew they would target you or not. I think mass chaos and murder was more than likely the goal."

"How did they sneak in dozens of Reapers?"

"Not dozens. Fifty, Azalea. Fifty Reapers. They had to have portaled them in somewhere on this floor, and the couple dozen who escaped went in search of easier targets. It would have taken a lot of power. That alone will eliminate suspects based on how many people can summon portals here. The boys and I were downstairs, as were a majority, if not all, professors. It won't be long until they find something, though. The whole portal thing is a huge mistake on the perpetrator's part, considering how obvious that is."

Shayde pulls away from me now, stroking my hair, my face, my lips. Then he leans forward, pressing his forehead to mine as his lips brush against my own in a gentleness he's never shown. "I knew as soon as I heard there were Reapers in the dorms that they would come for you. We got here as soon as we finished helping the other students on our floor kill the Reapers there, but the damn professors were keeping students away from this floor until they had more information on the situation. They wanted to assemble a team and, apparently, we weren't being considered for that honor. I was so fucking worried, Azalea. I thought I was going to come up here and find you among the pile of bodies. I don't—if you were dead—"

"But I wasn't. I'm not." I'm not sure how to handle a situation like this, or how to reassure him. But despite all odds, I want to.

"I know. But I need to tell you something, just in case something does happen to one of us."

"Well—"

"Don't try to argue about this, Azalea. Because in our line of work? It's way more likely we are going to die early. Sometimes earlier than the typical life expectancy dictates. So, please, let me just say my piece before you kick me out, okay?"

"Okay," I say quietly, bracing myself for the unknown.

Shayde takes a deep breath before cupping my face in his hands, staring into my eyes with a ferocity I hadn't known him to show before. He stares at me with an intensity that would pin a Reaper into place, and I get this odd twisting in my gut at the sight of it.

"I like you, Azalea Jinx. A lot. I know what people say about me. I want you to know that most of it is true. I've been called a player, a minx, a demon. But I want you to understand that I've never felt anything for anyone I've slept with before, never had this gut-wrenching fixation on someone who isn't you. I've never had a connection with anyone, never felt like a single person could handle me at my worst. But you? You are *exactly* like me. The kind of darkness the two of us share is more than just passion, more than a fledgling lust. I *know* you can be the thing I have been missing my whole life, the person who can finally fix me. Because I'm broken, and I don't care what I have to do to not be broken anymore. I think that's an ideology we share.

"I know you don't want a relationship. I know you don't want to be with me. I'm not trying to profess my love, just my hopes that you will let me get that far one day. There is this need inside of me when it comes to you. A need that takes over all of my senses and makes me do stupid, reckless things like take on ten fucking

Reapers all at once. I need you like I need air, Azalea. *I'm obsessed with you.* Your presence lingers in my mind, buzzing around like a fly that I just can't swat. I need to be with you, even if I can't be *with* you. Does that make sense?"

"You want to keep fucking," I clarify with a grin, surprised and somewhat happy at this revelation.

Neil never talked to me this way, as if I was a prize to be won. As if I was more than a wife, more than a way to produce a child. He was never obsessed with me.

"I want to keep fucking," he confirms, his own sly smile coming into play. "I was going to call it friends with benefits, but…"

"Friends with benefits it is, then. But, listen, Shayde. I truly mean it when I say I can't promise you anything. I can't tell you that this will become more eventually. I won't deny how I feel for you right now. I can't deny the way my Shadows sing for you or the way my body reacts under yours, but this feeling won't last. Maybe one day I can get there, and maybe I never will. But I think I owe it to you to try. To us. Because the experiences you have given me…those have been truly magical." I wink, laughing at the satisfied grin that fills his face.

Oh, how it feels to genuinely laugh again.

"Thank the Grim. I thought you were going to shoot me down again." He shakes his head, finally pulling himself completely away from me. I watch him pull his clothes back on, watch as he strolls toward the door confidently. "I'll see you later. I was probably supposed to hang around and help but, well, I couldn't *stop myself* from fucking you senseless."

"Don't let the door hit your ass on the way out," I call with a blush heating my cheeks, pushing myself onto my elbows.

"Quit staring at my ass, Jinx."

I let out another laugh as he slips out of the door, collapsing back onto my bed. I sigh loudly, that giddy feeling bouncing around inside of me. I'm not sure I can blame it on Demi's bite at this point. Beyond that, my emotions are lingering much longer than they did before. Even now, I'm still feeling more than has been allowed in years. And what, exactly, are these feelings hanging around?

Fear, because Reapers want to hunt me down for my exceptional powers. And because someone let those things onto campus with an unknown intent.

Relief, because I survived.

Dread, because I know these feelings will go away.

Lust, because, somehow, I still want Shayde.

But the best one of all? The one that is drowning everything else under its giant, cresting wave?

Happiness, because these feelings are lingering longer than they ever have before. Because I may not be the unfeeling monster everyone has always told me I am.

CHAPTER 17

"Beware a Grim who chose not to hide,
beware a friend who can not choose a side."
—Prophecy found inside Seer Katherine Valeriene's prophetic
journals, 2024 A.G.

I'm sick and tired of being followed by fucking Conjurers who think I'm incapable of protecting myself. If a Reaper appears right now, what the fuck do they think is going to happen? Do they think I'm going to weep and pray that I survive? I fucking killed half a dozen of those things last week! The least they can do is *act* like they respect my strength.

Dean Delarosa and I had a long chat about the attack in her office a few days ago, a chat in which she explained the increased security on me. According to her, she just wanted the trained Conjurers to hang around me for another week until they could finish their investigation. She tried to convince me I needed to be in a room on the bottom floor near all of the professors with the third-years, but I vehemently refused. Why the fuck would I separate myself from my peers who may be able to mask my strong scent enough to distract any rogue Reapers? Not that this should be expected to happen again.

Demi says this was the first time in Draxmere history that the Reapers have entered the school. The factions have made a decree that this is a call to war from the Grim, as though war isn't what's been happening for over two thousand years. Because of this new development, four full teams of Conjurers have been placed at the school by said factions; two from each side so as to remain impartial. One team for each floor, plus a team to roam the grounds.

During an assembly in the days after, Dean Delarosa also announced that our training would become even more vigorous than before. She says that we have to be prepared to protect ourselves to the fullest extent now that even this place is not safe. Then she fucking told us that midterms were still happening and to continue in our studies. As if we all weren't struggling through the deaths of our peers and the injuries we received trying to save them. As if some major history wasn't just made and nothing was out of the ordinary.

Midterms tend to be hard, but magical midterms? Yeah, those are *horrendous*.

The professors had coordinated the exams so that we only had to take one a day, but they weren't a walk in the park. During my Basic Combat Training test, I accidentally used my powers on another student. Then, during Charm Development, I managed to throw a desk across the room when I was supposed to levitate a piece of paper.

My Specialty Training tests went better, but my control is weak. I couldn't hold on to either of my powers for long periods, and my Light control was just outright pitiful. I can blast Reapers straight to hell, but I can't handle the amount of control it takes to form rudimentary shapes? Yeah, that's just pathetic.

The attack on the school hasn't slowed anything down, despite the waned strength and lack of morale it brought with it. Now that the midterms are over, we are finally getting to hold funerals for the fallen. It took the full week to identify all of the dead and contact their families. However, some of that time was also needed to get the families to Draxmere. The new security team did an intense background check on all of the families before they would allow someone from the teams to portal them here.

Ten students in total died: three Seers, two Shifters, two Il-luminoors, an Air Elemental, a Glamourist, and a Necromancer. Overall, it was a huge loss. Over triple that number were seriously injured, but vampire blood helped to heal a large majority of those tougher injuries. There were only a few who were sent off campus to specialized hospitals for help, and they were back within a week. Only those with broken bones are still out of commission, as they take large doses of vamp blood over a longer period to heal. A month, max, from what Demi told me. Luckily for them, they were excused from the Basic Combat test. Somehow, their "heroic performances" qualified them to pass, but the rest of us weren't injured enough to qualify for that category.

I squirm uncomfortably in my seat at the funerals now, pulling on my black dress absentmindedly. I shiver as I do so, wishing I had more than this thin sweater and a flimsy heat Charm to keep the freezing breeze at bay. I can hardly look at those glossy coffins coated in snow waiting to be carried by, can hardly stand the sight of all the crying people. Not because I'm sad, or even that I care about anyone else being sad, but because I hate death.

Death has followed me around my whole life, has lingered near my soul for what seems to be an eternity. Despite the way it haunts my heart, I can never be fully comfortable with its presence. Death is inevitable, I know that. But does it always have to make itself known in such grand gestures?

I'm not sure how they managed to preserve the bodies for over a week, and I'm not inclined to find out. I assume it has something to do with the Necromancers, but no one has said as much yet. Demi did tell me a few days ago that Necromancers will wake the dead before their burial, allowing them to speak to their loved ones one last time privately. That way, everyone gets a proper goodbye. If there are to be regrets after death, it won't be because you didn't get to say goodbye.

"For Grim's sake, Azalea. Sit still," Ginny gripes from beside me, sending a harsh look in my direction.

"Death makes me uneasy," I say, flinching as the low melody of a piano begins.

We all fall quiet as the wooden caskets begin floating down the aisle, one after another. Some a glossy red, others a deep black, a couple mahogany brown, and the last a vibrant pink. The families of the fallen stand on a makeshift stage, weeping on or near one another. The whole school is here to watch their sorrow—hundreds of students spread out in rows and rows of uncomfortable folding chairs in the front Courtyard.

The caskets slowly make their way to their prospective families, and I can see the Air Elementalists off to the side directing them. The caskets stay closed, hiding the faces of our fellow students from sight. I heard their bodies were mostly found in pieces, limbs ripped off and flung to the side once drained of all Charm Levels. I'd be horrified about that thought if any of the emotions from the fight still lingered.

Slowly, each family covers their caskets with white sheets, their sobs deafening in the silence. I didn't know these people, didn't know their names. I helped to defend them and tried my hardest to save them. But I didn't. I couldn't. My punishment is being here, listening to their families mourn.

Fuck, I hate funerals.

"May your Charms ward off evil. May your body find peace in the dark. May your soul find the Neverafter," the families chant, one after another, before beginning to talk about their children, their brothers, their sisters, and their cousins. On and on their sad speeches go, bringing tears to nearly every Conjurer's eyes.

Every Conjurer except mine.

"This is seriously depressing." I can't help myself as I whisper to Demi, offering her a tissue as her tiny body shakes with the force of her tears.

"Shh, Azzie. It's almost over."

"Before we light the pyres, we are going to read out the names of the proudly fallen." Dean Delarosa is the one to speak, and I catch the subtle wiping of a stray tear. "Lily Crow, Air Elemental. Griffon Cary, Light Elemental. Michael Travis, Light Elemental. Allison Nixon, Necromancer. Luna Landry, Glamourist. Frederick Fortier, Wolf Shifter. Calvin Hines, Siren Shifter. Davis Garrison, Seer. Savannah Teigen, Seer. Katherine Valeriene, Seer."

That's all their lives boiled down to in the end: their abilities. Some of these powers are perceived as better than others and are mourned more than the person themselves. All of these students were young, near twenty-two, and should have had more life ahead. They would have become strong Conjurers, would have become fighters in a war that's been ongoing for centuries. But now they are dead, and they are considered nothing more than resources lost.

Each coffin erupts as their respective names are called, flames rolling high into the sky. Families fall to their knees at this last gesture, screaming and crying impossibly louder than before. Wolves howl out, elements swirl around, and people clap and cheer for their friends and respective groups.

It's all over after a lingering bell chimes, allowing me to finally escape the suffocating atmosphere. Allowing me to get away from the overwhelming sadness that is beginning to infest me.

My emotions have been unsteady this week, rocky like a man-made wooden boat over the ocean's waves. Sometimes they hit me hard, punching my heart with their intensity. Other times it's a tiny pierce, a punctured hole that allows me to reach the outer ring of emotion.

I can feel a punch coming on now, a punch activated by the immense amount of emotions encasing this area. It's astounding the amount of feeling a funeral can bring, much less multiple funerals at the same time.

Just as I am readying to escape the vicinity altogether, I hear a calm, infuriating voice call out above the sliding of chairs and the murmured apologies: Haiden Bloodgood.

"Students! Before you take your leave, I would like to say a few words.

"I know this has been a hard week, and this day is even harder as we send your fellow students and friends to the Neverafter—may they find peace in the darkness where their souls now lie—but I want to congratulate you on your bravery, on your willingness to be here today. This loss was of great magnitude to our community, and we realize how this might affect your view of the future.

"We informed you during our last meeting that we would like for you to consider that future, to pull away if you feel necessary. Today we do the same. We urge you to consider the newfound danger the Reapers have introduced to our people as of late, to think about what it is we are doing here. If you are unsure at all, please reach out to speak to someone.

"The Reapers are growing stronger and more active; we need only the best when we face them. You cannot be at your best if your heart is not in it, if instead, you freeze in the face of fear. There will be no consequences for quitting. You did not fail us or yourselves. Please remember that over the coming days." Then she is gone, whisked away into a crowd of sad people and bodies desperate to be held.

Anger rises in me, fast and explosive. Then it dissipates, leaving just as quickly as it appeared. Now that all of my feelings have begun their return, the ones I am most familiar with are abandoning me. All a part of the healing process, I suppose.

I spot the Gravediggers across the yard, Jaymes's face lit up in the same anger that hit me. Demi is waving them over excitedly, beaming at Arlo. I groan, swatting her hand down.

Just as I open my mouth to condemn her, a woman places her hand on my shoulder. "Azalea Jinx? My goodness, look at you. You look just like your mother. Has anyone ever told you that?"

"Um, no. No, I've never been told that." I'm not sure I would recognize my parents.

"Well, I'm not surprised, I suppose. I'm sure a lot of the students here are too young to have known your parents personally. They only know the rumors about their powers."

"Yes, I have heard plenty about their power." I turn with squinted eyes, taking in the middle-aged brunette with scrutiny. "But you knew them? Personally?"

"Your mother was a dear friend of mine. When they ran away…well, it was a damn shame to lose powerful Conjurers like that."

"Hmm. Isn't it always?" I whisper, sighing inwardly. That's all anyone cares about here: power.

"Well, I saw you when you first walked in and I knew I had to come talk to you. I have something I think you might like."

"Oh?"

"Here. This picture is from many years ago when your parents themselves were students at this school. Don't they look so young?" I hesitantly take the picture from the strange woman's hand, gazing down at my parent's faces for the first time in over a decade.

My mother gazes up at my father lovingly, her short, deep brown hair grazing her shoulders. I can only see a sliver of her brown eyes, but even I can see the love hidden within them. My father is the polar opposite of us, his dirty blond hair tousled by the wind and his gray eyes glistening. He holds her by her slim waist, pulling her into his large body. Though she is taller than him, you can see he has control of the situation. The maze in the back courtyard is in the background of the photo, and I'm not sure I can spot a single difference between then and now.

"Yes. They do.," I whisper, blinking away a sudden surge of emotion. "Thank you for this."

"You're welcome, dear. I hope to speak to you again one day." Just as quickly as she appeared, the woman leaves, never even telling me her name.

"Are you okay?" Demi asks quietly, placing a hand on my cheek.

"Never better." I shrug off her touch, sitting straighter.

"Do you want to talk—"

"What is the Neverafter they kept talking about?" I interrupt with a question, praying it distracts her.

Demi sighs. "Our afterlife. It's supposed to be a place of calm and tranquility, a place with no Reapers and no worries. A growing darkness where we can be happy and together, a place for loved ones to reunite. Doesn't it sound lovely?"

"Oh, yeah. Dying is great." I mutter bitterly, sighing as the Gravediggers approach.

"Hi, Arlo." Demi smiles brightly, reaching out to brush her fingers against his arm. "I heard about the breakup. I can't believe she would do something like that to you. You deserve better."

Demi isn't really sorry about the whole situation. Apparently, his girlfriend slept with another Shifter, one who is a Senior. They had a fight, broke up, and then Arlo beat the shit out of the guy. Kind of hot, honestly. Demi is ecstatic at this turn of events.

"Ah, yeah. Thanks, Demi. You always know how to cheer me up." His smile is genuine, sharp teeth flashing as the predator is revealed. Playfully, he says, "Maybe you'll be the reason I don't drop out."

"Is Bloodgood being for real about the quitting stuff?" I interrupt, not wanting to hear the juvenile flirting.

"Unfortunately." Arlo sighs, shaking his head and rolling his eyes. "Some new policy that they are trying to encourage, I guess. They are saying that we choose to come here, so that means we can choose to leave, too. And both sides agreed on that policy, but it was way before any of this shit started going down. But now they are making everyone believe it was the Shadow Faction's way of getting people to quit, even though they just wanted us to have more choices than fight or die."

"What? Why would they—"

"We aren't discussing this with you," Jaymes grunts out, trying to push past me.

"Fine. But I have something to discuss with *you*."

"What do you want, Jinx?" Jaymes seems like he wants to be anywhere but here, which is fortunate because that's exactly what I want, too.

"You remember when you said you would give me extra training?"

Jaymes and Shayde both offered me extra training sessions after finding out my test scores, sessions which I readily accepted. I need more than the hour a day we already get, apparently. After burning out so quickly in that fight last week, I realized I needed to put in some serious work. My test scores only hardened that fact. Now that the midterms are over, I'm ready to put in the extra work.

Getting away from this sad little courtyard is a benefit to that training.

"Um, yes?"

"So train me."

Shayde is already nodding, always eager to spend more time with me. Jaymes, on the other hand, is much less enthusiastic about the prospect.

"Right now? You want to train right now?" he exclaims, almost exasperated.

"Yeah. Why not right now? You got somewhere else to be? Would you rather hang around here with all of *this* going on?" I gesture to the courtyard full of sad, wailing people. Some of whom knew my parents, apparently. I have more than one good reason to get out of here: I don't want to know anything else about the people who created me.

"No. No, I suppose I don't have anywhere else to be." His eyes roll up to the top of his head before coming back down to meet mine, accepting whatever he finds there. "Alright, fine. Get dressed and meet me in fifteen minutes on the West side of campus. Got it?"

I nod frantically, sending him a pleasant smile. "Got it. And what about you, Shayde?"

"If you aren't exhausted by the time Jaymes is done with you…well, then, I'll meet you after an hour."

"Perfect. See you in a few." I wink at Shayde before flouncing off, an extra bounce in my step.

Training is exactly what I need right now. Even with my current strength, my abilities aren't strong enough. I need *more*. And, unfortunately, I need their help to get it.

CHAPTER 18

"When the day comes for you to discover your powers, you must immediately begin to train them. The more you train, the faster you can control them. Without the proper techniques, your power will consume you from the inside out. You must Wield them, and Wield them properly. The following pages will be detailed descriptions for each type of power; read yours carefully and learn from them. Your life may depend upon it."

—*A Guide to the Charmed* (current edition), written by Glamourist Elias Kasper in 1907 A.G.

Jaymes's mood hasn't improved much since I last saw him fifteen minutes ago.

He approaches with a disgruntled look across his face, eyes flickering over to me in annoyance. He rolls the sleeves of his shirt up, flicking out his hands with a flourish.

"You're in a dramatic mood today," I comment, watching him wearily.

"I don't want to be here," he admits, staring off toward something in the distance.

"Is spending time with me that horrible?" Not that I care if he hates being around me; as long as I get what I need out of this whole ordeal, he can hate me all he wants.

"No. It's quite the opposite, actually."

I barely hear his whisper over the sudden wind. My eyes blink in confusion.

He runs a hand through messy hair, his blond locks much longer than I remember them being. How long has it been since he cut it? Or trimmed his beard? It, too, seems too grown now, his perfect appearance suddenly…disgruntled. Obviously, whatever is going on isn't because of *me*.

"Right. So you don't want to be here because…?"

"Because I have other things to do," he says dismissively, readying himself into a Wielding position: One leg back, slightly squatted, an arm pushed forward, and the other arm pushed back. Jaymes also tends to keep two fingers up when he Wields, with claims that it helps him direct the Light.

I think he just likes the dramatic flair it creates; I've noticed Jaymes excels in the dramatic.

"Right," I say again, unsure what else to do. So, I decide to try and break the tension with a joke. "By things to do, I assume you mean your girlfriend?"

"I don't have a girlfriend."

"Yes, you do." I crinkle my eyebrows together in confusion. "Stella Stargrove? You know, the blonde stick I beat the shit out of on my first day because she saw me talking to you and got all possessive?"

"We broke up," he says simply, eyes boring into mine. "Because of you."

"Because of me?"

"Oh, yes. Not that you're to blame for it, of course. The fault is entirely mine."

"What does that—"

He interrupts before I can question him further, saying, "Let's begin."

His Light bursts free with precision, blasting into a tree just to the left of me. The tree crackles, but doesn't fall. Jaymes has enough control to hold in his punches, to not destroy everything his Light touches. Unlike me.

"I need you to hit that tree without breaking it and knocking it down."

I decide to drop the subject of his ex-girlfriend, simply saying, "Okay."

I place myself in the proper position, closing my eyes as I try to concentrate. Jaymes's gentle hands land on my shoulders as he guides his Light into my own, heat seeping through my thin sweater. The heat is the prelude to the Light he pushes into me, a gentleness that I've never experienced with my own Light being shown in such simple actions. My Light is typically forceful and punishing, coming out in violent and uncontrollable blasts. To avoid that result, I attempt to guide it out using that gentleness, aiming for the same tree. I hit it dead-on, listening to the familiar soft cracks from before.

"Just like that," he whispers into my ear before taking a few steps back, gesturing for me to practice on my own.

I take a shuddering breath before trying again, aiming at the tree once more. My Light hurdles toward it at record speed, slamming through it and into the one beyond. Both trees snap, falling in a massive heap. Jaymes tackles me out of the way before they can crush me underneath their massive weight, our bodies rolling onto the damp grass as I release a loud *oof.*

"That didn't work." I pant, huffing in frustration.

Jaymes sneers, pushing himself up onto his elbows and glaring down at me. "Obviously not. Were you even trying? Do I have to hold your hand every time you Wield?"

A brief pang of anger strikes my chest, and I impulsively strike back at him. "I think that's the problem, Jaymes. You're too gentle. You like to hold my hand and reassure me. You like to give me soft pushes and easy moves. *You coddle me.*

"The Reapers are coming for us. They are in our backyard, in our own home. I don't need to be coddled right now. I need to become this great Conjurer everyone expects me to be, the kind of Conjurer my parents were. I need to know how to use my powers properly!" I breathe heavily as I finish yelling, chest heaving as I glare into those gorgeous green eyes.

Once again my anger dissolves, evaporating into the air as though it never existed to begin with. I want to hold onto it, to keep it there just so I have *something* inside of this black heart. But it's gone and there's no way to get it back now.

"You don't like it gentle, hmm, Azalea? Well, don't worry." He leans down until his lips touch my ear, whispering hoarsely, "I know how to play rough."

Jaymes is fast and agile, moving in a lethal dance as he leaps up and away to use his ability. "Block me, Azalea!" Light after Light stream is sent my way, beautiful masterpieces dealt with careful precision. I stumble back with the force of their impact, hissing out in pain with the rapid-fire burns infusing into my skin. I can't get a

Light shield up fast enough, the power too harsh and fast. I glare at him from my spot on the ground, scrambling up before he decides to throw more.

My first shield is weak, and my arm is set on fire when I am hit yet again. I hiss at the pain, flinging off my sweater and stomping on it to dissipate the flames. I send him yet another glare, a look I'm sure he's tired of receiving.

I can tell he is still being gentle, still holding in the true strength behind those punches. This time, I'm grateful for it. Light is seen as a symbol of purity, of good, of innocence, of healing, and it is those things. But it also fucking *burns*.

"Can't take it?" he purrs, eyes dark and heady. "I thought you said you liked it rough? Need a safe word?"

"Fuck you," I spit, ignoring his innuendos. I don't have time for his distractions. I need to learn, need to grow, need to improve. I need to be stronger.

I lose myself in the fight, time slipping from my grasp. Every once in a while, Jaymes will shout out instructions, telling me to picture a wall, telling me to make my powers bow, to show them I am the one in control, to hold my shield even while distracted. His Light is searing, and it gets more and more intense as time goes on and he begins to loosen up.

Half-way through the lesson he flips a switch, reversing our roles. Jaymes demands I shoot beams at him, demands I control the intensity of my hits. And damn if it isn't hard. All of my beams go out with a bang. I can't seem to make them gentle, can't seem to make them pliable.

By the end of our session, I've only managed one gentle hit and my aim is…well, not precise *or* accurate. I did rattle Jaymes's shield several times, though. It just wasn't enough to destroy one. Even if he did have to grit his teeth and force more power into them to keep them secure.

"Okay. Safe word activated." I pant, flopping onto the ground and groaning. "Am I supposed to be this sore?"

"Oh, yes. Being sore means you're doing it right." Jaymes assures as he strides over to me, lowering himself down next to me with an amused smirk on his lips. "Want me to help?"

"How?" I raise an eyebrow as he motions for me to flip over.

"Light is healing," he mutters as I flip onto my stomach, his long fingers lifting my shirt and baring my back before he crawls over me. "I can teach you that, too. Just…feel. You'll understand."

His hands brush against my bare skin, leaving little tingles in their wake as his Light brushes up against my spine. Then he's expertly digging those lean fingers into muscles, massaging the soreness away. Each dig of those fingers leaves behind a trail of warmth, little flashes I can feel deep inside my bones. I grunt in pleasure at the relief it provides, the aching and the burning dispelling as I allow myself to enjoy the healing nature of our power.

"That feels amazing. I think I'm going to need to hire a full-time Light massage therapist now."

"No need. Save your money. I'm available for you whenever you need me." His tone isn't as joking as mine was.

"Oh. Jaymes, listen, I—"

"Shut up, Jinx." My mouth snaps shut, my mind wandering. Instinctively my Light reaches up for his, and I gasp as I feel the merge. The joining of our powers is always strong, like jump-start-ing a car. It's magnetic and electric, and it always makes me feel powerful. "It's a very intimate thing to share powers, you know? I haven't done it very often. And it's not usually so…intense."

"Oh. Really? It feels like this with Shayde, too. Strong and undeniable. Like I can do anything." I don't apologize for the intrusion because I don't think he minds, and I don't care if he does.

"Mmm. Yes. I understand that feeling. It's because your powers are so strong. Shayde and I…our abilities are shared in that strength. It makes sense that your own powers want to share that with another, that they are seeking out strong connections. It may be their way of trying to help you with your emotional issues."

I like that he doesn't say "fix". Everyone always thinks I need to be fixed, including myself sometimes. I also like how he's not being a jackass for once; maybe our fight released the hesitations he's held for me all this time.

"Yeah. That makes sense. Is that how you and the boys got so close? Through your strong abilities?"

"Something like that, yes. Shayde and I found each other first. There's just something about Shayde that draws you in and pulls you under. He made my life…*electrifying*." The way he says it is so intimate, so pure. It's something I've said about Shayde, too.

"Are you…did you two…?"

Jaymes sighs at my blundered question. "Did we what?"

"I just—" Jaymes's hands stop their path abruptly, his Light jerking away from mine as he leaps up. It snaps as it separates, leaving me a little less warm and a lot more exposed to the elements. "What's wrong?"

"Azalea." Shayde's voice is the one that greets me, my eyes flickering open in surprise. He stands in front of us with crossed arms, a darkness clouding him. He looks positively angry. Downright *pissed*, to be honest.

"Oh, hey, Shayde. Is it time for our session already?" I hadn't realized how much time had passed.

"I thought it was, but you two seem a little busy at the moment. Maybe I should just come back when you're done putting your hands all over each other?"

Oh. Oh, I understand now. That's jealousy in his voice.

"Jaymes was helping to heal my muscles, that's all," I explain, reaching to pull my shirt down. I understand how it may look in his eyes to have another man on top of me, touching me. Although, it isn't as though Shayde and I discussed being exclusive. Or as if we are actually together.

"What is that?" He crouches down, hand reaching out to tug my shirt back up, revealing the pair of antlers stretching out across my lower back.

"Oh, you haven't seen that one? I assumed—well, you know. That you've seen them all." I clear my throat, not wanting to talk about our sex life in front of Jaymes.

"I'm a little too distracted to notice them all," is his curt reply, his finger tracing the outline of the tattoo. I don't mention the tiny heart that he noticed on my breast that Neil never did.

When he stands back up, his face is pale and his eyes unseeing. He almost seems…scared. "Where did you get that?"

"I've had it for years." I pull myself out of my lying position, opting to stand instead. "I got it in the human world at some random shop in Florida when I was, like, nineteen."

"Why those antlers?" Something is still wrong, even Jaymes's eyebrows curling in worry. He reaches out for Shayde, gripping his arm tightly as if to tether him to the moment.

"I had a dream about them. All of my tattoos came from my dreams."

"Those exact antlers?" They both eye me with suspicion, watching me wearily.

"Um, yeah? Is something wrong with them? Do they mean something?"

"No. No, actually. Nothing at all. Look, I need to go. It seems like you're worn out, anyway. Can I reschedule?" Shayde doesn't give me enough time to answer, fleeing the scene quickly. He rips his arm from Jaymes's grip, refusing to look at his best friend.

"Well, that was fucking weird," I say, turning to speak to Jaymes, "Wasn't it?"

"Um. Yeah. Yeah, I suppose it was, wasn't it?" He looks lost in thought for a brief second, mouth opening and closing before he finally comes to a decision and speaks again. "Listen, Azalea. It would be wrong of me not to warn you about him."

"What do you mean?"

Jaymes stares off toward the direction Shayde had fled to, pursing his lips as he tries to form a carefully worded warning. "Shayde is…one of my best friends. We are bonded in ways you can't even imagine and are closer than I have ever been with another Conjured. But because of that, I know things about him that other people don't.

"He is dangerous. When he wants things, he doesn't *just* want them. He becomes obsessive to the point of possessiveness. When things get to that point, well, let's just say things become detrimental. He will suck you dry and leave you wishing he would suck a little more. Every girl, or guy, he has ever been with wished they never had afterward. And yet, they couldn't help but want him back. He takes and takes and never gives anything in return. I love him, but…" He shrugs awkwardly, finally meeting my eyes once more. "There is a monster inside of him that seeks only to destroy."

The version of Shayde he has described is not the version I have already created in my mind. Shayde is dark and uncaring, rough and confident. Sure, he can be a little brass at times, maybe even a little rude. But he is also kind and sensitive, bold and sweet. I may not be able to have the same love-filled eyes as the ones that came before me, but even I can see the good in him.

So, I don't look away as I respond, "Maybe I need to be destroyed."

CHAPTER 19

"Her love ever fickle,
her heart ever sick.
If you manage to cage the savior,
make sure her loyalties stick."
—Prophecy recovered in the prophetic journals of Hart Albright,
1898 A.G.

"Good Grim, Azalea, what are you on today?" Demi huffs as she comes to a complete stop, bending over and putting her hands on her knees. Little scorch marks decorate her white sweater and dark jeans, and I wince upon noticing them.

"Sorry. I just know how important today is. They are going to be extra tough on us because of the attack on the school, and I have to prove myself worthy. I have to show the professors that there is a reason I was allowed in with no prior background. That my dead parents' legacy isn't who *I* am."

I usually don't let something as frivolous as other people's opinions about me bother me, but these opinions *matter*. I hear the rumors that are whispered as I pass, the little snarky comments Stella has spread upon the masses. The more I use my powers, the more these things begin to dig their way inside of my mind. It's…strange and not entirely comforting. But this is what I want, isn't it? To feel everything, including the bad stuff?

"I know, babes. It's just…do you have to be so damn good at it?" She laughs, standing straight again and patting my shoulder lightly. I allow myself to be comforted by her touch, a comfort that has slowly become something I can actually *feel* since the attack on the school a month and a half ago. I've been here for nearly four months and it has taken this long to get some tangible evidence that being here is improving my state of mind.

"You can thank Jaymes and Shayde for that," I remark with a grin, wiping my forehead of the gleaming sweat that's accumulated. One of the teams of security passes us, nodding in our direction as their eyes roam the woods behind us. I promptly ignore them, but Demi, cheery as always, smiles and waves.

"Mmm. I bet I can thank Shayde for the good moods you're constantly in, too," she jokes, shoving me lightly as we begin to make our way to the dorms. The sun is beginning to rise above the castle, the radiant beams lighting up the otherwise gloomy appearance of the Gothic architecture.

"He's to blame for some of them, I suppose." I shrug her comment off, fingering the hem of my shirt.

Shayde and I have an intense relationship, one that mostly relies on sex. We aren't dating, but we are constantly together. And when we do have sex, it makes me feel alive. It's the only time I feel like a whole person again, the only thing that makes the high last more than a few minutes. But outside of the bedroom, those feelings don't last. They flicker in and out of my body, trying to become corporeal but never achieving their goals.

I think my love for Demi is easier to grasp than whatever it is I have with Shayde, and it's confusing. I like to hang out with him, I like to be with him, and I have many moments where I think I want more. Then those emotions fade and drift away in the wind, disappearing and leaving me empty. It's a hard reality to face, one I'm not all that comfortable with. If all of these other things are coming back, then why can't I fall in love? What's stopping me?

Shayde would be the perfect guy to fall in love with, so why can't I just fucking try?

"Oh, come on. He's totally in love with you. The way he looks at you…girl, he wants to eat you alive. It totally gives me the shivers."

Demi is always so upbeat and quirky, honest to a fault. It's something I've found myself enjoying about her, but not something that is easy to get used to. Especially in situations like this, when I don't know how to explain myself.

"Well—I'm not sure about that—I—well—"

"Relax, Azzie. I'm not saying you have to be in love with him. He's crazy about you. Just…you know how *I* feel about him, but I also know how *you* feel about him. I may not like him, but I know you do. I just think you shouldn't string him along so much. Give a little, get a little, you know?"

"Yeah. Sure. I get it."

I shrug off her comments as we begin our ascent up the stairs, sighing heavily. I want things to be better with Shayde. Really, I do. Because if I can start falling in love again…well, then, I can be whole again, right? I won't need to be fixed anymore.

"Well, I have to say, despite me constantly talking shit about him, he *is* a good teacher. Jaymes, too. Your abilities are just…wow. Completely remarkable. Like, off the charts crazy. I've never seen someone build up so much control so *fast*. You should be totally proud of yourself."

"Thanks, Demi. Hopefully, the professors see the same thing in me that you do in these finals."

I don't mention Jaymes because I don't want to talk about him, either. After our weird training session a month and a half ago, things have become awkward between us. He won't look at me, touch me, or even speak to me some days. I suspect Shayde had a few things to say to Jaymes, but neither Conjurer will admit as such to me.

"You're welcome, gorgeous. I call dibs on the first shower, though!" Demi bounds off with a giggle, gone from sight faster than I can blink. Which fucking sucks, because I can't make the argument that she can go shower in her own room.

I sigh, smiling to myself. This is the kind of feeling I like; the little bubbling of happiness just ready to break free, the content dangling in front of me that I can almost reach. It's fast and fleeting, but oh so satisfying. I've never had a friend, never needed one. But I do now. If my curse makes a reappearance, I don't know what the fuck I'm going to do with myself.

Demi is my life raft, and some days she is the only thing keeping me from sinking.

Finals week is a time of uncertainty and nervousness for every-one, so I feel comfort in knowing I am not the only one holding on to such intense feelings. Though, I'm sure mine aren't near the levels as those around me.

I have seen students weeping over a pile of books, others dis-tressed as they attempt to perform Charms, and even more heaving in hedges after having way too many alcoholic indulgences. I feel more of a pulse, a flicker, as my nerves creep a path into my mind. This is one of the newer emotions I have, one I'm not inclined to like.

I don't know what to expect out of the final I am about to take. How do you test your skills in a Basic Combat class, especially after the amount of intense training we have endured since the attack? The midterm wasn't very difficult, but I also didn't have the added pressure of *wanting* to pass with flying colors. I just did it. Now, my mind is in the way.

"Alright, cadets! Line up!" Professor Donovan's booming voice pierces the air, and we all tense up before doing as told. Demi takes the spot on my right, Ginny on the left. We watch Donovan pace in front of us, muscles flexing as his jaw ticks.

"We all know what today is: Your final test for the semester. Next semester, you will be upgraded to a higher standard of training. If you thought this intro class was hard, then you may as well drop out now. Since you weaklings get a choice and all." He chuckles to himself, stopping briefly in front of me and giving me a 'you better not even think about it' look. I drop my head in respect, peering up at him from under my lashes until he seems satisfied I won't quit on him and continues down the line.

"Fuck, that's intense," Ginny mutters, grabbing my hand and squeezing lightly. My feelings for Ginny have changed, too. I don't see her as a nuisance anymore. I think…I think I actually like her now.

"Some of you have done exceedingly well in this class. Much better than even I anticipated." Those cold brown eyes meet mine again, and I feel a rush of pride at the compliment I know is meant for me. "We all know what is at stake. I know that things seem fine and that you believe the new security will keep you safe. If you do think those things…well…*think again.* Despite our endless search for the perpetrator, one has not been found. That means the bastard is still out there, waiting for their next chance to try and kill you. That's why we were instructed to teach you new skills, skills that you wouldn't have learned until your second year under normal circumstances.

"Today, we are going to test those skills. Your final exam is going to be a fight. If you win two fights, you pass. Lose two and you fail. I have already chosen your first partner. Lose, and you get to pick your next opponent. Win, and I choose for you once more. You will fight until I tell you to stop. Understood?" Nods and murmurs of "yes, sir" are mimicked across the room as we begin to migrate to the large boxing-ring-sized mat that has been moved to the middle of the room.

"Who do you think is going to go first?" Demi questions from beside me, shifting from foot to foot nervously. The stress of the exam plus the threat of the person who let Reapers onto campus still running around? Yeah, that'll make any sane person nervous.

"Stella Stargrove!" Professor Donovan booms, wasting no time. The plain-looking blonde pushes past her peers, a snarl set on her thin lips.

"I guess Stella," Ginny whispers, biting the ends of her nails. "Good Grim, I hope I'm not paired with her."

"Azalea Jinx." My heart does a little somersault, my head spinning. Stella had avoided me all semester after our cafeteria fight, and I had assumed it was because she realized I wasn't going to be the easy target she thought I would be. I guess Professor Donovan is trying to ignite the spark of competition he saw on my first day.

Stella and I take careful steps forward, approaching the large mat cautiously. Her blue eyes are cold and calculating as she sizes me up. I've lost some weight since coming here but gained a lot of muscle. I still look large and uncoordinated, and my curves are still prominent. Her lithe figure allows her a modicum of speed, a speed which I lack even after months of training. I'm sure she sees the same thing she saw when I first arrived: weakness.

I don't react to her, keeping my face in a neutral, bored expression. I won't allow her to see my nerves or even a hint of fear. I won't allow her to realize how important this is for me.

It isn't very hard to fall into that empty pit inside of me.

"Get ready, freak. I've been practicing all semester for this," Stella hisses as we approach one another.

I shrug, pushing my bangs out of my face and reaching out to shake her hand like we are supposed to. But Stella slaps it away, glaring. Gasps ring out, and I hear Demi shouting out in my defense. I don't need defending, though. I plan on beating Stella Stargrove so magnificently she never shows her face near me again. Her strong Charm Levels aren't going to save her in the ring.

"Begin!"

A whistle sounds nearby and Stella leaps, fists flying. I neatly dodge her attack, feet firmly planted in the soft cushioning. She stumbles at the lost momentum, and I use it to my advantage. My shoulder comes forward, fist flying with it. I land a powerful punch to her side, sending her sprawling onto the large mat.

She rolls once before jumping back onto her feet.

"I'm going to fucking destroy you, Jinx," Stella hisses, uncaring that everyone can hear her. She comes at me once more, blow after blow coming my way. I block them with little effort, but I'm unable to get in my own swings. She's too fast and wild, too unpredictable.

"What did I ever do to you, Stargrove?" I pant as I'm pushed closer to the edge of the mat.

I desperately throw out a leg, kicking her in the knee. She buckles, falling with an angry screech. Stella isn't satisfied going down alone, though. She swipes her leg under mine and I go down with her. The air is briefly knocked out of me as I hit the mat, and Stella uses that to her advantage. She leaps on top of me, aiming for my face once more. I use my forearms to block her, but it still hurts. Enough for me to let out a hiss and a grunt, enough to pull out a satisfied grin from the deranged girl.

"Jaymes broke up with me because of you," she seethes just before I manage to flip her behind me, giving me enough time to push into a sitting position. Stella tackles me from behind, shoving me onto my side. I squirm underneath her, spinning onto my stomach as I try to crawl my way up.

"It wasn't because of me." I pant through the lie, pushing up to my hands and knees.

Stella latches onto me like a backpack, hitting me in the face and sides. I let out a roar, flipping myself as hard as I can onto my back. I hear a crunch as we land, Stella screaming underneath me. I quickly scramble up and away, putting myself back into a fighting position. Stella is clutching onto her shoulder awkwardly, tears pooling in her eyes.

"*It was.* First I had to deal with him pining over Shayde after their breakup, and now you? The fucking idiot caught feelings for the very girl who stole his ex-lover away. Do you know what he said? He told me he was falling in love with someone else and it wouldn't be right to stay with me. Who do you think that someone could be?"

She comes at me again, releasing her grip on her shoulder. She grits her teeth hard, rocking on her feet as she tries to force herself into a run instead of a slow leap.

"How the fuck would I know?"

I make the decision to tackle her, not bothering to be gentle. If the roles were reversed, she wouldn't provide me with that kindness. I push her to the mat, pinning her down effectively. She screams beneath me, thrashing, but she can't get up. The sounds emitting from her are ear-piercing, bloodcurdling ones of pain. I weigh so much more than her, and it would take the use of that messed-up arm to even have a chance at getting out from underneath me.

"The winner of this match is Azalea Jinx!" The whistle blows once more, jarring me out of the intensity of the moment. I release the still-crying Stella, pursing my lips in annoyance as I sit up.

"You're too daft to see it, aren't you? What a relief. It's good to know he doesn't even have a chance. Don't worry, I'll be there to pick up the pieces when you inevitably break his heart." Her lip wobbles, her tear–filled eyes lighting up with unbridled fury.

Demi pulls me up and away, chattering about how cool my fight was and how horrible it is that Stella ended up with such a major injury. I don't tell her that it is an easy fix, that they just need to pop her shoulder back into place. I don't tell her that she will have to fight again on that shoulder if she wants to pass Basic Combat.

Instead, I ponder Stella's words.

She said I was too daft to see how Jaymes feels about me. Was Demi not just saying something similar about Shayde? Was she not just telling me I was blind to not see the love in *his* eyes? And what did Stella mean when she said she had to watch Jaymes pine over Shayde after their breakup? Is any of what she said true?

If it is…I have a lot to consider.

CHAPTER 20

"Light and Shadow will combine,
the Conjuring presented with a sign.
Heed the warning, heed the words.
Killing a Grim won't save the world."
—Prophecy found inside Seer Davis Garrison's prophetic journals,
2022 A.G.

"How did your last final go, Azalea? I heard Shayde administered your test." Wren is wiggling her eyebrows from across the cafeteria table, her sisters giggling with her.

"Oh, yeah. He did. He didn't take it easy on me or anything. Just had me perform all these little tricks we have been practicing to show off my control and resilience. At one point I had him in a cloud of shadow he couldn't escape from for ten minutes." I chuckle, remembering the look on his face when he finally emerged. Enraged, impressed, and, so he claims, completely turned on.

"And your Light Specialty final? Wasn't Jaymes the one…?" Demi tilts her head, gnawing on her bottom lip with worry.

She and Ginny overheard most of what Stella said to me on Monday during my first final, as did others. It has caused a tiny rumor to blossom into an uncontrollable inferno. I haven't talked to Shayde about it yet, and I don't really want to. I don't want to be the reason he and Jaymes get into a fight.

"Yeah, he administered that one. He was harsh. Like, tried to make me do things he hadn't even taught me harsh." I shiver at the memory of it, of the anger that had flashed in those bright green eyes. "Professor Battle pulled him aside at one point and told him to stop expecting me to perform third-year moves. Moves he only knows because he's so advanced compared to everyone else. I've only been here for, like, five months! I probably shouldn't even be able to do the things I can, much less the same things the seniors are doing!" I stab my fork angrily into a meatball, seething.

That one emotion has been flashing in and out of my mind all day: *anger*. I've been angry about Jaymes, Stella, the finals, the attack still going unsolved, and literally everything else. I'm used to anger, used to feeling a roaring rage. But now that my body is trying to balance itself out, that rage is burning an entirely unpleasant hole in my chest.

"Well, at least Charm Development was easy, hmm?" Demi tries to cheer me up, smiling brightly from beside me.

"Yeah, it was super easy. Five random Charms? It almost seemed too simple, especially considering how strict our coursework has been lately. Professor Canmore seemed to be in a generous mood, though. Maybe she knows we are all still on edge from the attack? Most of the Charms she asked me to do were from the first month of the semester, the simpler ones I was able to get in the first few tries. I may have shown off just a tad." I laugh along with the others, relieved that exams are over and I performed well in them. Everyone has been so tense, so cranky. Now things can go back to normal, back to being easy and breezy.

Except for the thing with Jaymes and Shayde, anyway. Oh, and this insatiable anger that is eating me alive today. And maybe the whole Reapers are pairing up and invading our school situation.

Other than that, though…easy and breezy.

"Hello, girls." Arlo approaches, hand plopping down onto our table dramatically.

Demi's whole demeanor changes, a gigantic smile stretching across her face. Her cute little fangs protrude slightly, and I notice Arlo's hungry gaze drift toward them.

"Hey, Arlo. What's up?" We let Demi speak, allowing her to have a moment with him.

"Have any of you heard about the party we are throwing tonight? Since no one had exams today, we thought this would be a great time to celebrate. Things have been intense around here, with the increase in training and the security people everywhere. We thought it would be nice for everyone to sneak out and relax for a while. You know, before they go home for the break."

I found out in October that the Charmed don't celebrate any-thing but New Year's. It was a little disappointing not to be surrounded by magical Halloween decorations, but I got over it fast when Demi told me that everyone goes home for a break at the end of the semester. That all but ensures I'll have a couple of weeks of alone time here at Draxmere.

Time when I don't have to work so hard to be something I'm not.

"Ooh, no! No one told us. A party is the exact thing I need right now. Is this an official invite?" Her flirty smile works, bringing a blush to Arlo's cheeks.

"That it is." He grins, rapping his knuckles a few times on the table. "I hope to see you all there. Especially you, Demi." He shoots her a wink before turning away, shoving his hands down into his pockets and whistling a merry tune.

"Wouldn't miss it for the world!" she calls toward his retreating form, eyes wide in disbelief.

"Ooh, Demi. Someone seemed very interested in our little vampire." Reese laughs, pointing at her with a fork.

"Probably because I've been mentioning her to him so much the past few weeks." I shrug, smiling sheepishly when Demi spins to me.

"You what?" she sputters in shock.

"Yeah, you what?" the triplets shout, all staring at me as if I had grown fangs.

"It's not a big deal. He's Shayde's friend. I'm around them all of the time." I stare at my plate to avoid their scrutinizing gazes.

"Wait a minute. Shayde is bringing you around his friends? That's a major deal." Demi is squeaking, cheeks red and aflame as she changes the subject.

"What's a big deal?" Ginny sits down next to me with a tray piled high with fried bat wings, eyebrows drawing in as she notices the weird energy around the table.

"How did your exams go?" I blurt, not wanting to talk about Shayde anymore. It's a good distraction, apparently, because Ginny starts babbling about her exams and the things she had to do for her Glamour Specialty one.

Demi squeezes my hand under the table, holding it there as we continue to gossip and eat our lunch. My heart lurches at the gesture, squeezing tightly as the brief pang of love hits me.

Demi is always here, never questioning, never assuming. She just holds and comforts; the way I imagine a sister would. I rub away the pain in my chest with unease, closing my eyes and pushing air out through my teeth quietly.

Fuck, that's a strong emotion.

Love strikes hard and fast, swift and agile. And if my sisterly love for Demi can do that? Well, maybe I'm not ready for the real deal after all.

"Knock, knock bitch! Open up!" Demi shouts from the doorway, and I can hear something jiggling. I drag myself to the door, already dressed in pajamas even though it's only late afternoon.

"What—? Oh. Alright. Come in." I reach for some of the items in Demi's hands, clothes and shoes that she carted all the way here from her room at the opposite end of the hall. In one hand she is clutching the handle from her big box of makeup, the other still clinging onto three more dresses.

"Makeover time," she coos, bouncing in cheerfully.

Demi is already decked out, her braids pulled up into a high ponytail and her makeup fresh. Her eyeliner is sharper than a knife, her foundation a perfect match as always. Her outfit is short and revealing, the pink ruffles of her skirt barely covering her ass. The black and pink top ends abruptly, showing off her stomach and the belly piercing I didn't know she had. I've never seen this much of her skin before, never realized how much of her skin is covered in those colorless spots.

Her boobs are practically bursting out of the top of her shirt, the thin straps barely holding everything in. The giant boots she is wearing elevate her by several inches, the thick heels on the bottom keeping her suspended there. She looks…*amazing*.

"I don't think I'm going to fit into any of your outfits, Demi." I try to object upon seeing the skin-tight black dress she is holding up.

"Relax. The material is stretchy. One size fits all and whatnot." She waves her hand dismissively, forcing me into my bathroom.

"Demi, I weigh a lot more than you. At least seventy pounds more." That's underestimating things, honestly.

My time at Draxmere has helped me to shed a little of the extra fluff I had from before, but it's quickly hardening into muscle. The numbers are basically the same, but the overall look is a little different. I don't know how Demi manages to look so slim and still be so strong. Probably the vampire metabolism, the lucky bitch.

"Relax," she repeats with a roll of her eyes. "It'll fit. I promise."

I sigh, allowing her to fall into what is usually our morning routine. It's something I find myself looking forward to most days, actually. Demi always wakes up early in the mornings to be here, and I love that about her. I love that she cares enough about me to spend extra time out of her day bonding with me and taking care of me.

"Alright. You look really beautiful, you know? Stunning, if I'm being honest. Arlo's going to pass out when he sees you. If he won't sleep with you, I will."

"You think so?" She bounces in excitement, laughing at my sentiments. When she bounces, I notice little lights glimmering off her, specks of glitter that decorate her skin.

"Definitely."

"So, what, exactly, have you been telling him about me?"

I laugh, and we fall into our usual chatter. Things are easy with Demi; she's just so nice. Around her, I feel light enough to laugh, feel safe enough to care. Fuck, first I was angry and now I'm sentimental? What's next, crying? Am I on the verge of a mental breakdown or something?

"Yeah, and then my parents grounded me for, like, two months!" She finishes her story at the same moment she finishes my makeup, hands quickly turning to my hair.

"What are your parents like? You never talk about them."

Demi falls silent at the question, hands stilling briefly. "Old and mean," she says plainly. "They had me later in life. My mom was forty-three and thought she couldn't have any more kids. I have four siblings, all of whom they like much more than me. Probably because none of them look the way I do. You know. *Imperfect.* For the longest time, I thought I would eventually earn their approval. Thought that all I had to do was try a little harder, be a little nicer, but nothing ever worked. I don't speak to them anymore. I'm not sure they even notice."

It's not often that Demi sounds like me, but right now, she does. Emotionless. Carefree. As if it truly doesn't matter. Maybe it no longer does for her. I forgot that normal people can feel that way about things, too. They can choose to be emotionless about certain subjects.

"I don't remember my parents," I admit carefully, watching her curl my hair in the mirror. Demi has been faithfully refreshing the purple chunks of hair over the months with Charms, and today they pop between the curls with such brilliant vibrancy. She has even trimmed my bangs once a month, keeping them perfect and bouncy.

"Oh. But weren't you five when…" She trails off.

"When they were brutally murdered by Reapers? Yeah, I was. I just…don't remember them. I should at least have a couple of memories, right? Maybe some happy ones where we all laughed and played? But I don't. I have nothing. They mean nothing to me. When that lady handed me their picture at the funeral, it was the first time I've truly seen their faces in over a decade." I shrug flippantly, closing my eyes as the heat of the curler gets closer to my cheek. That picture has been resting in my book bag, hiding away from my unstable mind. Out of sight, out of mind.

"That's so sad, Azalea. At least I have parents to remember."

"Yeah, but they're dickwad parents. You're allowed to be sad, too. Besides, if I can't remember them, I have no memories to mourn. That's one of the things I worry about sometimes, that when my emotions come back I will remember and suddenly feel this gaping hole in my chest that represents their absence. I don't want to feel those things." I shudder at the thought. I already have too many holes burning inside my chest; I don't need to add another one anytime soon. I'm a little too busy trying to rid myself of those that already exist.

"We all have to feel things like that eventually, Azzie. It's what makes you *real*. It's what connects us all. That humanity."

"I've never thought about it like that." It's the only response that I can manage.

"Well, try to from now on. Remember that it's okay to feel things you don't like to feel or don't want to feel. Maybe it'll help some of those emotions come back on their own."

"Yeah, maybe."

"Have you ever…wanted to find out what happened to them? I mean, people still talk about them and their love story a lot. Everyone always says how weird it was that they just disappeared into the human world. I mean, under normal circumstances, a Reaper never would have been able to kill one of them, much less both. I know their powers must have been weak after so long…but…don't you want to know what happened?"

"No," I admit, sighing softly. "I have a lot on my plate right now. The last thing I need to add to it are the reasons my parents left me with the humans. I haven't even looked into the history of this school, much less my parents. It's just not something I'm interested in right now. Maybe once my emotions are all back in place and working properly, I'll be more interested in my past. But for now…it's just not a priority."

"I can respect that decision. If you decide you *do* want to know more, I'll help you, okay? Just let me know when and where, and I'll be there."

"Thanks, Demi. You're a good friend."

"You know it, bitch."

We fall into a comfortable silence, one neither of us is eager to fill. All we need is each other's company.

Eventually, though, that silence is disrupted by the sounds of rummaging. As soon as Demi is done with my hair, she turns to the dresses. She holds one up, flings it. Holds one up, flings it. She pauses over the next one, nodding her head with a broad grin.

"Definitely this one. Put it on, Azzie. Chop chop." She lifts a short, glittering, blood-red dress. The straps are made of diamonds, the front dipping into a low 'v'. I stare, unsure if that will cover *anything* on me.

"Demi, we have a height difference, too. As well as the weight. And—"

"Fucking Grim, Azalea. Put it on. You're only a few inches taller than me. I swear, this dress is going to make you look like a goddess. Come on. Just try it. For me?" She bats her long lashes at me, pouting.

I sigh, yanking the sparkling dress from her grip. She discovered recently that I have one weakness when it comes to her: the sad, pouting face. "Fine. But the shoes better be just as cute."

I strip down as she digs through the pile of shoes, pulling out a matching pair of glittering silver heels with attached ribbons to climb up my calf. They are only a few inches tall, thank the Grim, and seem much more manageable than the monstrosities she's wearing.

"They're more than cute; they're sexy. Ooh, let me help."

The dress is stuck over my head, and no amount of movement is going to provide me with any relief on my own. So, Demi comes to the rescue. She shimmies the dress down over my body, gasping in delight once it is fixed in place.

"I don't know, Demi. This is really tight." I pull at the fabric, frowning. "I don't usually wear things like this. I don't think I'll even be able to wear underwear. These panty lines are horrific."

"Then don't wear any." She giggles happily, ecstatic at the sight of me. "Girl, you look *stunning*. Shayde is going to *die*."

I turn to look at myself in the mirror, shifting this way and that. I suppose Demi is right. I *do* look good. And, miraculously, the dress covers everything it needs to.

"He's seen me naked plenty of times," I murmur, a flash of embarrassment bringing a flush to my cheeks. "Surely that's better than this?"

"It's the anticipation that gets them, darling. The wanting, the craving, the need. Your goal is to have him on his knees *begging* before you even get to the naked part."

"Oh. Usually Shayde and I just…you know. Do it." The spark that ignites us is fast and furious. When we join together, we don't need or want admiration and foreplay. My emotional blockage only allows me so much time with him, so we get to it and enjoy it while it lasts.

"Let yourself be a little more open tonight, Azalea. Live a little. Enjoy the eyes on you. Make him a little jealous, even. I promise the sex is so much better when you're connected emotionally."

That's the problem, though, isn't it? Shayde already has that connection and I'm still trying to catch up.

Demi pats my shoulder lovingly, sending me a soft, sad smile as if reading my thoughts. "Alright. We've been lingering long enough. Let's go get our party on." She does a little shimmy, winking and smacking her ass before skipping to the door.

"Great. Can't wait." I sigh, tugging on my dress self-consciously once more.

Fucking Grim, I shouldn't have let her talk me into this.

CHAPTER 21

"The popular drink, Dragon's Breath, has won the award for Best Alcoholic Beverage for the tenth consecutive year. It comes as no surprise to this reporter, as it was created by the incredibly talented mind of Dakota Breather. Dakota Breather, a unique yet powerful Necromancer, gave up his career many years ago to instead focus on his business. And, wow, has it paid off!"
—Article entitled "Breather: the Dragon's Story", written by Glamourist Kelly Artega, 2023 A.G.

The party isn't in a dorm like I anticipated. Instead, it's in the woods. Deep, deep in the woods.

I grumble and complain to Demi the whole way; all she does is laugh and offer to carry me. I deny her offers vehemently, refusing to be carried by someone as tiny as Demi. It doesn't take true emotions to be embarrassed by *that*. At least she has the decency to cast warming spells over us, temporary but effective.

When we finally reach our destination, my heels are in my hands and my scowl is permanently etched into my face. I hurriedly slip them back on when I realize the party is already in full swing underneath the full moon's light.

Music blares through the woods, originating from a D.J. standing at her table off in the distance. I don't recognize the music, something fast and thumping with unfamiliar tunes. Probably something from this world and not the human one. They've somehow placed a wooden dance floor out here, the majority of the crowd pressed into the large area. I'm grateful for the reprieve it will provide my soon-to-be-swollen feet.

Lights flash all around us, hiding somewhere among the trees. I can only assume they've been Charmed to do so, as there's no way they have electricity in the middle of the woods; especially considering the damn school hardly has any, either.

Tables are scattered around with all kinds of refreshments, shiny drinks, and large vials of blood. A snack table is nearby, fucking fried bat wings laid out like gold. Demi is already drooling, her body leaning toward them enticingly.

The crowd on the dance floor is well on their way to being inebriated, hands in the air and bodies pressed together tightly. Everyone is dressed immaculately, with tight clothes and pretty shoes. Even the guys have put effort in, excluding the few who have decided to shed their shirts.

"Ginny!" Demi squeals, dragging her eyes away from the food and to our fellow friend. "Wren! Willow! Reese!" She calls them each by name, and the compliments begin. Hair is touched, shoes are admired. It all feels so *normal.*

I've never had friends like this, never felt the need for them. I've always known I would lose them, always known I would bring them death. And now I've slipped up and allowed people inside of my heart, exposing them to my wretched curse, which may still be present for all I know. No one I've been close to has died since I've been here, but these people are also much stronger than the weak humans I surrounded myself with most of my life. I love having friends. How am I supposed to go without them now?

"Come on, Azalea. Have you ever been to a party before?"

I shake my head, barely hearing my best friend above the music. "No. Only stepped into one to grab some coke from my dealer."

Demi pauses for a second, shaking her head with a sigh. "Girl, this is going to be so much better than a drug high. The music pumping through your veins, the drinks making you lose your damn mind, the anticipation of getting laid. It's amazing! Nothing better! Except maybe your blood." She giggles playfully, forcing me onto the dance floor.

Demi turns, her body lithe and nimble. She grinds on me playfully, hands winding through her hair as her body swishes around methodically. I can only bubble up a nervous laugh, unsure of what to do. Ginny slinks up beside us, hands in the air as she dances. Wren shoves a drink into my hands, and her sisters pass drinks to Ginny and Demi. As soon as I take a sip, I know there is something off about it.

"What is this?" I manage after forcing the sweet drink down, coughing a little at the tinge of a burn it leaves behind. There is some kind of berry mixture in it, the purple liquid bright and bubbling like a soda.

"Dragon's Breath," Ginny shouts over the music, moving to press herself against Willow slyly. "It has Dragon berries in it! Mash those suckers up and add a few things and mwah!" She presses her fingers to her mouth and kisses, downing hers in one go. "Drink it fast. It'll kick in faster that way."

I shrug, doing as instructed. It isn't easy to swallow in one go, but I manage. "Fuck. Okay. Great. How long before it kicks in?"

I found out ten minutes later.

My head is already becoming fuzzy, the buzz coming on faster than any alcohol I've ever had before. I'm not a lightweight, as I typically drank whole bottles at a time in the human world, but *fuck* is this stuff strong. I would go through bottles just to feel this kind of buzz, to feel this type of freedom from my own mind.

One drink has me melting into the music, dancing along with the girls like I can't bother to give a shit about anything else. They cheer me on, helping me move my hips in just the right way. That is until they spot something behind me and back away with wicked grins.

"You look beautiful, Azalea." Jaymes's rich voice is behind me, purring into my ear. I can hear the slur in his tone and can smell the alcohol on his breath. "Want another drink? You can have the rest of mine. Not a huge fan of this stuff." I eagerly take the cup from him, downing it quickly like before.

"Want to dance?" I shout, sending him a soft smile over my shoulder. Things have been tense with him since the whole tattoo ordeal, which neither he nor Shayde will discuss with me. The least he can do to ease that tension is dance with me.

I see Arlo approaching Demi nearby, and I shout out my encouragement proudly. Jaymes chuckles behind me, placing his hands on my hips. It sends a shiver down my spine, starting a pulsing low in my stomach. I ignore it, refusing to acknowledge such a treacherous emotion.

"I'd love to dance with you."

I swing my hips into Jaymes, laughing in delight as the beat picks up again. I've never seen Jaymes so relaxed, so willing to be around me. Demi was right; this party is great.

Jaymes's breath stings my neck as he presses himself closer, hands inching up only slightly. We move together effortlessly, sweat glistening down my arms and face as we dance. After what has to be at least thirty minutes, the second drink is bubbling around with the first, pumping its way through my body like the blood in my veins. It makes me a little reckless, and way too bold.

"Is what Stella said true? Were you and Shayde…together?" I feel him stiffen up against me.

"And if it is?"

"Are you in love with him?"

"I used to be." His movements slow, hands tightening on my waist. He stumbles in his steps only slightly, that alcoholic smell hitting my nostrils again as he speaks. "But there are things about Shayde I just couldn't accept. And then you came along…"

"I don't understand." My eyebrows crinkle of their own accord, my mind spinning slowly. Is he…is he saying that he cares for me…*romantically*?

"You're a nightmare wrapped in the prettiest package, Azalea Jinx."

"What's that supposed to mean?" I huff, spinning on him abruptly. Jaymes pushes himself into me, pulling me tightly into his chest.

"My best friend, who is also my ex, is in love with you, and I still can't stop myself from thinking about you. I can't stop myself from wanting you in the worst of ways. I've tried, Azalea. I've tried to put distance between us, tried to be a fucking jackass just so you would avoid me. But there's no avoiding the collision course we are on, and I'm a fucking fool for even attempting it."

"But Stella…" Jaymes shouldn't be saying these things to me right now, and I have this strong feeling that he wouldn't be if he was sober.

"Fuck Stella. I want *you*."

"I think you should know that I can't feel things like she can, Jaymes. She's totally obsessed with you. I don't think I can give you that."

"I don't need obsession." His lips brush against my ear, teeth scraping against my lobe.

"Maybe not, but you need someone who can feel. Right now, I feel a lot of things, but I think it's just because I'm drunk. This moment, these seconds? It may be the most I have to offer you for a while. Until I'm wholly myself again. If I am ever able to be that girl again." Not that I remember who she is.

"You're the only thing holding yourself back. The drinks don't change what you feel, Azalea. They only encourage those feelings to come out and play. This moment, these seconds? It's all you. The *real* you. So if you're feeling something you usually don't? It's because you won't let yourself."

His lips leave gentle kisses down my neck, his hands sliding down my back. Then those lips are on mine, gentle and slow. It isn't rushed and frantic, isn't hurried and forced. It just *is*.

I *wish* I felt more than lust from the kiss, *wish* I could offer more than this. But it doesn't feel like being with Shayde. It doesn't feel like bombs going off in my chest, like an overwhelming need that I'll never be able to satisfy.

Reluctantly, I pull back, wanting to explain. "Jaymes, I—"

"What the fuck, Bloodgood?"

Jaymes is jerked away from me, and screams of shock and panic release into the night air. Shayde launches himself at Jaymes, punching him square in the jaw before he has a chance to understand what is happening. But Jaymes isn't one to go down easy, and the fight turns into a full-on brawl. They fall to the ground, rolling and punching. I can barely register the growled-out threats, the hissed insults, the petty remarks.

"Stop it!" I screech, eyes wide in panic. This is exactly the type of situation I had wanted to avoid. "Stop it, Shayde!"

Instincts have me sending a blast of Light and Shadow their way, a multicolored ball that explodes between the two. Shayde was on top when the ball hits and is sent flying off, landing on his ass a few feet away. I scramble to get to him, placing myself between the two men.

People around us whisper about my dual-powered ball, but I can't bring myself to give a fuck. If I was sober, I would probably be pretty impressed with myself, considering I have no idea how it happened. I'm not sure I'll be able to replicate it, either. But I can't think about that right now; I need to focus on Shayde and Jaymes.

"Azalea," Shayde breathes, pushing himself up. My bottom lip quivers as I see the pain behind those light green eyes, the hurt written in every feature of his handsome face.

"What the fuck, Glover?" I repeat his earlier sentiments. He sends a glance over my shoulder, snarling at Jaymes one last time before dragging me away into the seclusion of the woods.

"Why were you making out with my best friend?" he seethes once we are alone, pinning me against a tree. His half-up hair is ruffled, the ends dripping with snow from rolling around on the ground with Jaymes.

"What, like you haven't done it?" I scowl back, my breath leaving at the anger overcoming his features.

"What Jaymes and I have done in the past isn't relevant to what happened just now. *Why. Were. You. Making. Out. With. My. Best. Friend.*"

"I-I don't know. He was just telling me that, well, he likes me, I guess. But I told him I can't give him what he needs. That I can't give him obsession like Stella can. But he said—" I'm blabbering now, but Shayde stops me with his lips. He is the exact opposite of Jaymes, harsh and bruising instead of sweet and gentle. And good Grim, why do I like it so much *more*?

"You want obsession? You already have it. I am beyond the point of obsession, Azalea Jinx. You occupy my every thought, fill up all of the dark and empty spots in my heart with your light. I look for you in every corner and hope for your presence in every dream. I am full of this constant, aching need for you, even though I know you don't feel the same way. The things that I would do for you, to you, over this crazed obsession is madness. Pure madness and nothing more."

His eyes are wide, his pupils enlarged, his words no more than a low growl. I can see every bit of that madness in him, can feel it in the tight grip he has on me. And suddenly that madness is in me and *I* am kissing *him*. My heart pounds in my chest, that low ache in my stomach drifting even lower.

"I want your obsession, your madness, your infatuation." I whimper helplessly.

I don't know how to feel the things I want to feel. I hardly remember what that desperate love for Neil was. I'm not sure if I ever loved him at all, or if it was just my mind grasping on to the one person who loved *me*. Convincing me that I *was* in love, that I *could be* in love.

Shayde is different. I feel things so intensely when I am with him, even if they are only brief. And the whole time I had another man's lips on mine, *he* was the one on my mind.

"Then let's go over the new rules." His movements are harsh, his body jerking with pent-up anger as he shoves me deeper into the tree.

"N-new rules?" I can hardly breathe as his lips brush up against my ear, can hardly think as his fingers dance at the hem of my dress.

"Rule one: We're exclusive now. No more kissing other people. You hear me? Especially not Jaymes." He growls, biting the spot between my neck and my shoulder possessively. I cry out, clinging to him for support in my weakened state.

"Got it," I whimper, shaking underneath his steady gaze.

"Rule two: You've got to start fucking trying, Azalea. You love Demi, but you can't hold any affection for me? You can have friends, but you can't risk having a relationship? You're holding yourself back because you don't want all of the negative things you've managed to avoid for so long. But you know what just happened because of it? Jaymes and I got physical. Over *you*. And you want to know the worst part? I'm not a good man, Azalea. If you chose him over me, I wouldn't honor that decision. I would have killed him so he couldn't have you, so that you would be mine."

I can only nod, hissing out as another bite pierces my neck.

"Speaking of killing people, this is rule three: If anyone ever puts their hands on what's mine, I kill them. Jaymes has been properly warned, but there will be no warning next time. Think about that, Azalea, before you ever do something like this again. Think about who you may get killed."

"O-okay," I whisper, arching into his touch. His fingers slip underneath my dress, grazing the tops of my thighs.

I ache, I burn, I *need*.

"You have no idea what kind of monster I really am, Azalea. I'm out of control when I am with you. I am so close to losing myself, to becoming something I never want you to see. A liar, a thief, a murderer, a villain. I'd do it all for you. No second thoughts, no doubts. Only this burning insanity connecting us."

I don't let myself think about the implications as his fingers dip inside me, don't let myself linger on the darkness inside of him.

I know that darkness; it lives inside of me, too.

"I don't care if you are a monster, Shayde," I whine as his fingers move slowly, teasingly. "I don't want to go back to the person I was before you. I don't want to be a shell anymore. I just don't know how to fix myself. I don't know how to be more than *this*."

"You don't have to be more, Azalea. You just have to let everything go. Stop focusing on the feelings you lack and start controlling the ones you have. You're mine now, and I don't plan on letting you go anytime soon." I shiver at his words, crying out as he picks up his pace. "Tell me you're mine."

"I am yours." I moan out, eyes fluttering close as he brings me to the edge. "And you are mine."

"Damn right, I am." He grunts, trailing kisses down my neck. Then his fingers are gone, leaving me on the brink of release.

"Shayde. Please." My eyes are wide open now, hands clinging to him as he tries to back away.

"I don't think so, Azalea." He wipes blood from his brow, blood I hadn't even noticed before. He runs a hand over the top of his dark hair, sighing softly as if disappointed. "You haven't been a very good girl."

"But—"

"As appetizing as you look in that dress—" He pauses, freely admiring my body. Slowly, tauntingly, he sticks those fingers in his mouth and sucks. I watch his eyes glaze over, listening to his groan of approval. "You hurt me and I'm not in control right now. And you're drunk."

"I have said yes to you many times, Shayde. Was I drunk then?"

He is slowly prying me off of him, pushing me away. Denying me. "The things I want to do to you right now, Azalea…the ways I want to punish you…you wouldn't like them. I need to get away from you before I let those fantasies come to life."

"Tell me!" I'm desperate, pleading, still on the edge. What could be that bad?

"I can't. You aren't ready to find out who I really am. And I'm not ready to show you."

Then he is gone, transporting away with the speed only a Charm can provide. Was he that desperate to get away from me? Is what I've done that bad?

I fall to my knees, holding my chest in disbelief as I whimper in agony. What is this feeling? It feels like my heart is cracking, little fissures forming within its depths. It feels like my heart is being ripped straight from my chest, being squeezed to the point of exploding.

Fuck, it hurts.

I can barely breathe at the sharpness of it all, at the sadness that is rushing over me. The heartache. A tear slips out of my eyes, followed by another. Before long, I am weeping, something I don't ever remember doing. But I let myself feel the pain, let myself weep. If Shayde is the one doing this to me, then I deserve it. It's only fair after what I made him feel.

I stay on the ground, crying into my hands, feeling the sadness inside of me take over. That's how Demi finds me, her warmth and comforting energy encircling me the moment she comes into view.

"Azzie." Her eyes are wide in shock, and she only pauses briefly before rushing to me. "What did he do to you? Are you hurt?"

I look up at her with tear-stained cheeks, my mouth opening. I try to form words but can't. Instead, I laugh. A weak, garbling laugh that quickly turns into a hysterical one.

I *am* hurt.

So impossibly, magnificently hurt. Shayde has done this to me, has created this weeping mess. But I'm not mad at him. I realize now that I am in his debt, that I will be eternally grateful for him.

He made me feel again. Really, truly feel in a way I haven't since well before Neil.

It's a fucking miracle.

CHAPTER 22

"In danger, she shall lie
if you let her walk out of sight.
Beyond campus lines,
a Grim plans to release his spies."
—Prophesy recited to Demi Lockwood by an unknown Seer, 2024
A.G.

Demi isn't one to forgive and forget.

The fact that I'm not upset with Shayde was a hard pill to swallow, one that lodged in her throat and choked her until she spat it back out. Her dislike for Shayde morphed into full-on hatred, her anger only increasing when I told her that he dropped off a letter at my door instead of coming to speak to me in person.

She reads over that letter now, glaring up at me through her lashes.

"Dear Azalea," she says, eyes rolling to the back of her head as she reads the overly formal words he wrote. "I have spoken at length with my father about you, and he wishes to make your acquaintance. I'm sorry I can't ask you this in person, but we would love to have you over at the house during break. I will be spending my break at home with my father, and it pains me to be away from you for so long. Please accept? Yours and yours alone, Shayde G."

"I know what you're going to say. Please, hear me out. The fact that Shayde wants to bring me around his family, that he wants to include me in this secretive part of his life…it makes me feel *wanted*."

"I understand why you feel that way, but I'm not sure about this, Azalea. I'm being so serious right now. Don't do this." Demi is blocking my door, arms crossed across her chest.

I huff, slinging my purse over my shoulder. We are five days into the break and, so far, Demi is the only person I have interacted with. I have been withholding this letter from her for a week now, scared of this exact situation. Now that the time has come to leave, I didn't have much of a choice in telling her.

I miss Shayde, I ache for his presence constantly. I'm ready to see him, even if Demi doesn't want me to.

"I don't understand, Demi. It's just his dad," I whine, trying to step around her.

"Azalea, no one even knew Shayde *had* a dad. Isn't that a little weird? It gives me the heebie jeebies. I just—I know I'm not a Seer, okay? But I don't like this. Something feels wrong." She shivers, her whole body shaking.

"I trust Shayde. And he trusts me enough to bring me around his family. I'm trying to take our relationship more seriously. What's so wrong with that?" I hiss, glaring back at her. I'm not sure what is going on, or why Demi is being so cagey. She seems on the verge of telling me something, her mouth constantly opening and closing. It's driving me insane. "If you have something to say, just say it."

"I know things about those guys." She presses her lips together tightly. "About Jaymes and Shayde, anyway. I can't...I can't tell you what I saw. But I can tell you, the things they get up to? They're terrifying. My dreams are haunted by the night I saw—well, it doesn't matter what I saw. All that matters is that Jaymes and Shayde are not these innocent lovesick boys you think they are. *Please, Azalea.* Don't go off campus with him. I know things have been really quiet, but they still haven't caught the person who set the Reapers loose here. Not only that, but Reapers are hanging out together now! It's dangerous going to an unfamiliar place. At least if you were here, we could take care of each other. Protect each other."

"I trust Shayde," I say firmly, despite the guilt that grips my heart. I don't care what they get up to in their free time; to be honest, I'm in too deep now. Quickly, I add, "And you don't need protection. You're a badass bitch who Reapers run away from screaming."

Demi closes her eyes tightly, face pinching as she says, "I can't talk you out of it?"

"Nope." I pop my 'p', smiling brightly. "Shayde would never let anything happen to me." I haven't told her about the things he said to me that night in the woods, the magnificently horrible things he confessed in the dark. I know exactly what kind of man Shayde is.

"Okay. Right. Well then—I—ugh! Please?" She bats her lashes at me, pouting. I'm close to caving, but I can't. Not even for that horrible, guilt-inducing pout.

"Sorry, Demi."

"You aren't. Okay, let me give you 'the talk' before you go."

"Whoa! No need for that! Thanks though!" I shake my head furiously, blushing. That's new, too. *Embarrassment.*

"Not that kind of talk, silly. I just wanted to provide you with a few affirmations. You know, tell you that you are a badass double Wielder and that the world should fear you. That you have more power in your pinky than most Charmed have at all. That kind of talk."

"I know I'm powerful, Demi. That's why I'm not scared."

"Well, you don't have complete control over those powers. You're still learning. Quickly, sure. But still. Just…just be cautious, okay?" Demi has been telling me to be careful for days and keeps saying that she has a bad feeling in her gut. Then, today, when I told her I was leaving campus with Shayde, she had a total freak out. I think a Seer may have said something to her, but I have no idea *what*.

"I will be," I reassure her just as a knock sounds, three hard raps. I shove Demi aside playfully, swinging the door open before she can stop me. "Shayde!" I launch myself at him, wrapping my arms around him tightly. He stumbles back in surprise, arms sliding around me carefully.

"Wow. Okay. That's new." His deep chuckle reverberates in my bones and the ache I have felt since our encounter in the woods finally eases.

"I missed you," I say simply, sighing loudly before allowing myself to inhale his scent. Smoke, leather, and something I can only describe as *darkness*. It's the first time I've noticed he has a distinctive scent, and it creates a rolling boil inside of me.

"Is she on something?" He aims his question at Demi as he lets me settle back down.

"No. She's been like this since the other night. You've done something to her. You would know that if you'd been around any," Demi quips, eyes squinting.

"I *feel* like I'm on something. Really, I've just been feeling so many things," I say excitedly, proud of myself for coming so far. "I still have several hours of the day where everything is just gone, but…"

"That's great." He smirks, pleased. "You seem so…"

"Happy?" Demi answers for him, still glaring. "Yeah, a little distance from you seems to have been good for her."

"Demi, stop. I'm done with this hostility from you. Let's go, Shayde. I'll be back late tonight, so don't wait up." I push Demi out of the room and into the hall, slamming the door shut behind her and clicking the lock. I hear her screaming at me, telling me that she'll get back at me for this later.

"Did I do something to her?"

"She's just mad you made me cry. I tried to explain to her that you gave me the reality check I needed, but…" I shrug, not sure how to tell him the truth: Demi doesn't trust him, and never has.

"You cried over me?" Excitement lights up his eyes, hands reaching out to cup my cheeks.

"Wept like a fucking baby," I reply, body arching into his instinctively. I missed his warmth, his touch, his taste.

"Good."

Shayde devours me, pouring a liquid fire inside of me that only he can create. I melt against him, eager and pleased.

"You want me crying?" I manage out, tangling my hands into his long hair.

"I want you to feel the things I do, to feel so intensely that you weep at the *thought* of me." His grin lights me up, expression intense and daring.

"Why did you stay away?" I finally ask the question I've been pondering ever since he left me alone in the woods. He had made his point, leaving me there like that. So why did he have to take so long to come back to me?

"I had to go home. I needed to take care of some things. I just—I couldn't come back to you until I was myself again. Until I no longer wanted to kill my best friend and make you watch me do it." The admission is quiet, his head leaning forward to touch mine. He shut his eyes so he didn't have to watch my expression, didn't have to see if I was horrified.

I let out a deep breath, unsure of what to say. "I'm sorry. After the amount of things I've felt this week, I think I can understand how you must have felt when you saw me kissing Jaymes. You can go kiss Demi if you want. Will that make you feel better?" I joke, hoping it will help if only slightly.

"My lips were made for yours, little flower," he whispers, pressing them to mine once more. It's slow and sensual, the first meaningful kiss the two of us have ever shared.

"Can we hang out here just a little longer? Your dad wouldn't mind, would he?" My hands are slipping under his shirt, lips brushing against his neck. But Shayde takes a step away from me, shaking his head and running a hand through his dark hair. The mere mention of his dad seems to have sobered him up, his expression turning cold and hard.

"No, unfortunately, we can't." He twists a lock of my purple hair, tugging on it lightly. "I think I need to warn you about my dad."

"Warn me?" My stomach bubbles, something akin to nervousness rising. Was Demi right? Is there something off about this situation?

"My dad is…strange. He's a control freak, very strong, and very opinionated. When he asks for something, he rarely gets told no. Don't let him talk you into anything or convince you to do something you normally wouldn't just because you want to impress him.

"He's a secret I have hidden my whole life, but he's been insisting I bring you to him from the moment he found out we were together. He is good at prying into minds, at finding weakness. He's a Seer, so sometimes he knows things nobody else does and sees things that nobody else can. Most people don't like it. I'm not sure I do, either. But he's the only family I have, so…" Shayde shrugs limply as if resigned to the fact that he has no choice in being in his father's life.

"Oh. That's fine, Shayde. I thought you were going to tell me he's a serial killer or something." I laugh, but he doesn't. He only turns away, heading to my mirror.

The silence is suffocating, and I can only watch as he forms the portal. A few weird hand motions, whispered words, and a startling clap. Then the portal appears.

My mind races as I stare wearily into the glimmering liquid, fear trying to work itself into my mind. The fact that he isn't denying anything is a little disconcerting and a whole lot creepy. Demi was definitely on to something.

Maybe I should heed her warnings more often.

"Hold my hand, Azalea. And if you can shut your emotions off, I would do it right now." Shayde grips my hand, pulling me into his arms. I swallow hard as I spot the worry gleaming in his light eyes, his lips tight and his body stiff.

Shayde is scared. *For me.*

"It doesn't work that way. Once they're on, they're *on.*" I shake my head, allowing him to press his lips to mine one last time. It's a desperate, breathless kiss that leaves me at a loss for words. He kisses me as though he'll never get to do it again.

"Yeah. I was worried you would say that."

I'm wet and sticky, the jelly substance clinging to every inch of my skin. I hold my breath, attempting not to gag. I fucking hate portals, and I don't think I will ever get used to this feeling. I don't know how the Gravediggers can stand creating them, how they can casually travel in this way all the time. Just the thought of a portal makes me queasy.

Luckily, the torture is over within seconds.

Shayde and I emerge into a dark and dingy room. A mildew smell permeates the air, paired with the distinctive scent of something old and rotten. The walls are supposed to be a cream color but are littered with yellowing patches. The carpet is a matching shade, covered in scorch marks and ashes.

Shayde's father must smoke.

We stand in a living room, vintage frames hung upon the walls. There aren't any pictures of Shayde, though. All of the frames are empty. Completely and utterly empty.

A dirty, brown leather couch sits on one wall, a matching recliner facing away from us. A TV sits on a broken, wooden stand, stained black but discolored with age in several spots. Trash litters the ground, and I spot several bugs crawling around inside the carpet. I swallow and try to mask my expression, not wanting Shayde to see the disgust in my eyes.

"I'm home, Father, and I've brought Azalea as you requested." Shayde's voice is different as he speaks to the father I can't see, transforming into something deeper and darker. His face has changed, too, a carefully placed blank slate he is wearing like a mask to cover the man beneath it.

I think I underestimated exactly what kind of situation this is.

"Nice to meet you, sir," I say brightly, going for a gentle smile as I search for him. I don't tell him he has a lovely home; I think we would all sense the lie.

Shayde's father stands from the recliner, turning to face us. His returning smile is anything but gentle. It's unsettling, unstable, unkind. And fuck is it creeping me out. That smile reveals teeth that are yellowing, with several gaps inside where teeth are missing. And although at first glance I wonder if this can truly be Shayde's father, it's harder to hide upon closer inspection.

His hair is short, but the same deep black as his son's. His eyes are a deep brown, the opposite of Shayde's light green ones. He has the same honey-colored skin and the same angular face. He's even the same height. He's missing the long scar across the cheek, but the similarities are still striking. It's strange to see this older version of Shayde. Though…this version looks the worse for wear. His skin is stuck to his bones, dark shadows underneath his eyes. He looks…sickly, to say the least.

"Azalea Jinx." His eyes bore into mine, the grin glued to his face.

"That's me." I clear my throat, glancing at Shayde unsurely.

"I've heard many things about you." He approaches us with little caution, hand reaching out shakily. Shayde slaps it away, the sound echoing in the silence that follows.

"Don't touch her."

"Tsk tsk. I'm not going to hurt her. I just want a peek." He cackles, and I gasp as his fingers brush against my palm. He had slyly slid his opposite hand in the space between us, desperate for that contact.

His touch is cold and leaves this horrendous feeling behind, similar to what it would feel like if bugs were crawling underneath my skin. Then it's gone, and Shayde is shoving the man in a rage.

"We agreed that you wouldn't touch her." He seethes, pinning his father against the back of the recliner. He holds him by the collar of his dirty gray shirt, growling in his face.

"You don't know what you have." He cackles again, eyes wide in delight. "Do you know the amount of power she possesses? Son, she could feed an army of Reapers for weeks!"

"The fuck I will," I spit out, anger burning me from the inside out. He looks all too delighted at my reaction, all too delighted at the prospect of what my power could mean.

"Don't talk about feeding her to those beasts.," Shayde snaps, leaning down to whisper something into the man's ear. Whatever he says seems to settle him down, enough so that Shayde releases him.

"My apologies, Azalea. Please, have a seat." The crazed man is gone in a matter of seconds, replaced by a sane one. The transition is fast and spontaneous, the evil grin gone as a complacent one takes over. But I've seen the crazy underneath, and I know now what to watch out for.

I follow Shayde to the dingy leather couch, wincing only slightly at the creaking that ensues. He wraps an arm around me, pulling me tightly into his body. His scent wraps around me again, enveloping me in a comforting haze. Shayde's father sits back in his recliner, watching us with amusement.

"Shayde mentioned you are a Seer? Was it a shock when you found out he had the Shadow element?" I begin the conversation after a pregnant pause, unsure how to navigate through the weird tension invading the air.

"Oh, yes. Lots of things surprise me about Shayde. He's not at all what I raised him to be."

Shayde's fists clench tightly beside me, nails digging into his skin.

"I'm sure that's not true. Shayde's a wonderful person. He's smart, powerful, very social. What else could you want him to be?" I smile hesitantly, tilting my head at the man.

"Bah. Those things mean nothing when he possesses no loyalty. When he won't take care of his old man's business."

"I told you I'm still undecided on that front. I don't want to take over the business." Shayde is uncomfortable and on edge. I'm missing something important here, I just don't know *what*.

That's the second time today I've felt like someone close to me is hiding things

"What kind of business do you own, Mr...?" Neither one has given me a name for the unfamiliar man.

"Just call me Mr. G, Azalea. All my friends do. As for the business I run, well, it isn't one meant to be brought up near such delicate ears."

"Oh." I'm too stunned to say anything else.

Is Shayde's father dabbling in illegal things? Is that why he never talks about him? I mean, what kinds of things are considered illegal in this world? Do they, too, have banned drugs and weapons like humans? Or can it be something far more sinister?

"Enough." Shayde grits his teeth, glaring at his only family.

"I've heard lots of things about your power, Azalea. I've seen a lot just from this brief encounter. You're very strong."

"Oh, yeah. That's what everyone keeps telling me," I reply lightly, sitting straighter as I feel Shayde squeeze my arm tightly in a warning.

"Tell me more about it, won't you? How does that work, having both light and dark inside of you? Does it not drive you mad?" He leans forward, eyes wild and interested.

"I was mad long before I got here." I flinch at another dig of Shayde's nails.

"But surely there must be more to it? I mean, how exactly does it work? Do you—"

"That's enough," Shayde repeats himself, releasing me. "Change the topic."

"So protective," Mr. G whispers, the wild grin returning.

I watch Shayde, my heart pounding as fear begins to build a tower within me. Why doesn't Shayde want him to know about my powers? About my emotional problems? What is going on here?

"Well, are you at least learning anything useful at that damn school?" Mr. G starts again, eyes following my every move.

"Oh, yeah. I'm catching up fast." I don't say anymore. If Shayde doesn't want me to give him any details on my life, then I won't.

"Thank the Grim they saved you from that miserable place." He pulls out a cigarette, lighting it with a quick Inferno Charm before putting it to his cracked lips.

"Miserable place…? You mean the human world, I suppose?"

"Ugh. Yeah, that place. It's horrible. Full of those filthy, powerless humans. Oh, and they stink! They reek up their entire world with their Charmless odor. I'll tell you now, I won't let them reek up mine!" He begins to laugh, sputtering and coughing briefly. Then he blows smoke in our faces, smiling with little to no worries.

"I don't necessarily agr—"

"Actually, I think we need to be going now, Father. Azalea's friend is waiting for her." Shayde interrupts, stopping me before I can interject for the humans.

"Bah. Kids are always in a rush these days. They never slow down to see what's around them. Always going from one place to the other with little consequence," Mr. G mutters absentmindedly, watching us with empty eyes as we stand and take quick steps back to the wall we had sputtered out from.

"It was nice to meet you, Mr. G," I say, attempting another smile. I can feel my emotions draining, making it hard to force the cheeriness from before into it. Whether it's a result of his touch or my own volition, I don't know.

"It was very enlightening," is the only reply I receive.

Shayde is quick to form a portal, creating it and pulling me through before I can glance back one last time.

"Thank fuck that's over," he says as we step out of the mirror, taking a few confident steps into the room. We hardly spent ten minutes with his father, but Shayde seems to think it was too long of an encounter.

"I know you said he was strange, but that? That was *bizarre*, Shayde. What was going on? I feel like I am a chess piece in some massive game you two are playing."

"My father isn't around other people a lot. And as Seers get older, sometimes their minds become a little more jumbled. He babbles on about nonsense a lot. I know he's weird and creepy. I'm sorry I had to bring you around him."

And he *does* sound sorry; that's the worst part of this.

"What he said about the humans—"

"You'll find a lot of people feel that way here, Azalea. Don't take it personally."

"It's hard not to when I thought I was a human for over twenty years! When I was fucking born there!" I exclaim, annoyed. When I heard what he said about the humans, it seemed as though he was talking directly to *me*.

"You're right. I'm sorry. He's just an old man, Azalea. Can't you forgive him? Forgive me?" He flops onto my bed, pouting.

"What about the weird stuff with my powers? You dug into me kind of hard." Now that my emotions are slipping and my rationality is kicking in, I have more questions. I'm not ready to let this go. Not yet.

"The abilities my father possesses are a little strange. He can touch you and see things. Not a lot of Seers have that. He gets…obsessed with powerful people because he can touch you and see that power, can sense your Charm Levels. He wants power like that for himself. If he was able, he'd suck every person in this world dry to make himself more powerful. But he can't. So, instead, he stalks them. Follows them around, digs deep for their biggest secrets. He likes knowing he holds leverage over powerful people. Just…just don't let him find anything to hold over you, okay?"

"Alright." I shiver, wrapping my arms around my body as I process the information. "Tell me what kind of business he is running."

"Don't worry about the business, Azalea." He huffs, shaking his head. "It's all bullshit. It isn't *really* a business. Just a list of lies and betrayals and secrets in his head that he thinks are important. Don't worry about it."

"Why didn't you tell me any of this before?"

"I wasn't sure you would care," he admits softly, picking at the comforter. I nod softly, satisfied.

"He's just a weird, creepy, loony old man," I tell myself and him, allowing myself to approach him. I crawl over his long body, smiling down at him as my hair curtains around us.

"Exactly." His whisper hits my neck, managing to send shivers down my spine.

"You do know that this was our first date, right? It kind of sucked. We need a redo" I kiss his neck gently, changing the subject away from crazy fathers and my lack of emotions.

"Are you asking me on a date, Azalea Jinx?" His fingers tighten on my sides, hips thrusting up as I bite down on his lobe.

"No, I'm asking *you* to take *me* on a date. A proper one."

He pulls away just enough to look into my eyes, green clashing with brown for a tantalizingly long time. "Ask me for anything and it is yours, little flower."

The words reverberate deep in my soul, bouncing around in my head until they are lodged deep inside. Sitting here, seeing the deep affection on display in his eyes, I know *exactly* what I'm going to ask for first.

Chapter 23

"The Slithering Bite has, yet again, been applauded by citizens as the best restaurant in Maladara. I conducted interviews with customers while investigating these claims and managed to flag down a group of men widely known as the 'Gravediggers'. These men describe the restaurant as 'delectable', 'delightful', and 'romantic'.

Maybe there is something to these claims after all!"
—Article entitled "To Bite or Not To Bite, That Is The Question", written by Glamourist Kelly Artega, 2021 A.G.

I haven't been on a proper date since I was married. I haven't felt the nervousness of a *first* date since long before that.

Shayde insisted on taking me out after my joke last week. I think it's his way of asking for forgiveness, of trying to reclaim the "first date" title he had lost. Honestly, I don't mind. There are only two days before the new semester begins, and I would like to end our break on a good note. I don't want to think about Reapers, their sudden groupings, or the havoc they raged on my school. I don't want to remember that someone let them in to hunt me, or the ever-growing pressure laid upon my shoulders to become the savior everyone thinks I should be.

That's why I didn't tell Demi I was going out.

I know she will be upset, that she will make this a much bigger deal than it needs to be. I also haven't told her about what really happened last week with Shayde's dad. I mostly just shrugged off all of her questions and told her that it was awkward but meeting the parents always is. I told her that Shayde is embarrassed by his dad and that Mr. G lives in a dirty old house, on top of being a creepy old man.

Demi said, quite plainly, "Ha! I knew something was wrong!" Then we moved along as though everything was right in the world, as most of us have these past few weeks. If we ignore the looming danger, we don't have to think about the consequences of said danger.

I stand before my mirror as I prepare for my date, turning this way and that to admire the sleek black dress I chose to wear. It's plain and simple, but it's the same dress I wore on my first date with Neil. It's a little looser, but it still holds sentimental value. Well, it does now, anyway. I only kept it because I couldn't afford new clothes.

I left my hair down in its natural waves, not curling it for the first time in, well, since I arrived at Draxmere; Demi is always here before breakfast, fixing it for me. I've become so accustomed to her presence in the mornings, never questioning her early arrival. I'm grateful for them now that I can be grateful.

I've never been skilled in the makeup department, but that's okay. Demi always makes me look like a model, but I'm not. I'm just a girl. Not a normal girl, but a girl all the same. With that mindset, I decided to keep the makeup simple, too.

I want this date to be a good memory, one where I know I showed up exactly as who I am. Unlike with Neil, when I dressed the way I thought *he* wanted. When I said the things I knew *he* wanted to hear. I had been ensnaring him, desperate for someone to attach myself to.

A lot of good that did for either of us.

"Hello, little flower."

I screech in surprise, spinning around with my Light at my fingertips.

Shayde takes a step back, the edges of his lips turning up only slightly. "Well, aren't you a little jumpy today?"

"Fuck off," I breathe out, trying to seem angry despite the smile on my face.

Shayde is donning a black button-up and jeans, sleeves rolled up to his elbows per usual. A long chain dangles from his ear and back up, a cute accessory I haven't seen him wear before. He wears a pair of square, black glasses; glasses I didn't know he needed or owned.

"Alright, I'll fuck off and take my gift with me." He smirks, turning and shoving his hands down into his pockets.

"Gift?" I can't stop myself from taking the bait. It's been so long since anyone got me a gift.

"Yeah. In this box." He waves around a small black box, whistling.

"You can stay. As long as the gift stays, too, of course."

"Of course. I hoped you would see reason."

I like this side of Shayde—playful, unserious, romantic.

I watch as he lifts the top off of the box, gaping at the sparkling jewel inside. It's a ring, entwined in a chain that transforms it into a necklace. The ring has one large teardrop diamond in the middle, the silver band covered in more tiny ones. I'm not sure what to say at first. It's huge and gorgeous, and definitely expensive.

But it's also a *ring*.

"This was my mother's." His voice cracks at the end, and he quickly clears his throat. He's never mentioned his mother to me, never even uttered her name. "And it was her mother's before that. After she died, it became mine. Now, I want it to be yours."

"Shayde—I—well, I'm not sure—"

He holds a finger to my lips, shushing me. "Take it, Azalea. Wear it. I—well, I need to explain some things to you. One day. For now, I want you to know that I don't expect to be alive for a very long time. I can't guarantee you a future, can't guarantee you tomorrow, even. And when I die, I don't want my father to have this. This one thing that has gone untouched by his special brand of evil. So take it. Wear it and don't ever let it go."

I don't get a chance to respond before the chain is looped over my head, the heavy ring falling into the depths of my breasts. It's cool and heavy, weighing me down with its importance.

"Are you sick?" I don't know what I will do if he is. I'm finally coming to terms with the fact that I have the capability of falling in love. My curse has been blessedly quiet since coming here, but maybe I was too hopeful for my future. Maybe I allowed myself to become complacent.

"No. Oh, no. Nothing like that. I just—it's my father's work. It's dangerous. And I can be called back to him at any moment, may be forced into doing things that will put me in the line of fire. If I decide to take over the business, well, that danger passes on to me, too." He avoids my gaze, shifting uncomfortably on his feet.

"Then don't take over." I shrug, running my fingers over the ring cautiously. It's sharp and bumpy, prickly like me.

"If only things were so simple." He runs a hand through his long hair, ruffling it to the point of disheveledness.

"Do you want to talk about it?"

Shayde has refused to bring this up again; refuses to tell me the full story about what business his dad oversees. I know it's something bad—that it's wearing on him and his father's relationship. I know it must be something illegal, and I understand why he might not want to admit to being involved, but I want him to trust me. It's a little disheartening after all I've been through in trying to face my truth for *him*.

"No. I don't want you to be involved. If he knew *you* knew…" He leaves it at that, trailing off before clearing his throat.

"Okay. That's fine. Totally fine." It isn't, not really, but who am I to make him feel uncomfortable? What we have now is new territory for both of us, and I'm not going to push us apart by prying.

"You're stunning," he remarks, tracing a knuckle across my cheek.

"I don't look different?" To me, it seems like an astronomical difference.

"No. You're always this beautiful." He shrugs, beginning to form the portal in my mirror. Casual, as if his comments do nothing to my still-learning heart.

"T-thank you." I swallow hard, trying not to jump him.

I want to learn how to be slow, want to learn how to enjoy his company. I don't want to keep rushing as if the world is ending. I don't want to constantly be on edge, worried I will lose everything

I ever felt for him. Maybe, one day soon, I won't have to worry any longer.

"Come on. You're going to like this." Shayde takes me by the hand, pulling me through the portal and into a blinding light. I gag as we emerge, shaking off the sensation of slimy goo touching my skin.

When I finally adjust to the light, I gasp.

I've lived in big cities my whole life, but I've never seen *anything* like this. All around us are color and motion, street signs flashing and erupting into fireworks, flying objects zooming around every-where. All of the nearby shops have large windows, showing off their crazy inventory.

Shayde chuckles at my amazement, tugging me along after him. I watch a shop full of flying fabrics in wonder, audibly gasping once more as we pass a shop with popping drinks and hopping burgers. The third store we pass is a store only meant for cats, with several roaming around outside. I stoop down to pet one, its slick black coat shining underneath the sunlight.

"Why cats?" I whisper, hesitantly leaving it behind.

"They're a Charmed favorite. They've got little carts for them, backpacks with shelves for them to perch on, and a million different types of treats. I had a cat once, and it loved their bat delights."

"Conjurers and their bats." I shiver, eyeing a jewelry store adver-tising never-fading, never-aging pieces.

The more stores we pass, the wilder they get. A bookshop with books that literally read to you, a gift shop where the gifts wrap themselves, and a tailor's shop that didn't seem to have a single worker inside. Everything you could want or need is right here, waiting at your fingertips for a steep price from the looks of the tags.

Everywhere I look, there's power in the air.

The people along the sidewalks glide along without taking a single step, and everyone is dressed immaculately. Fancy ballgowns, nice suits, gorgeous shoes cluttered with jewels. Everyone wears an array of colors, even the shops are bright and luminous. My eyes can't focus on one singular thing because every bit of it is *new*.

"You're right. I do like this." I nod my head reverently, eyes wide in wonder.

Shayde only chuckles, watching me with hooded lids. "This is the city of Maladara. The city where the rich go to get poorer." He gestures widely as we narrowly avoid a flying package.

"Maladara," I repeat, testing the word on my tongue. "Is it close to the school?"

"Yes, actually. It's the area down below us, the lights past all of the trees?"

"Oh. Oh, yeah. I've never given much thought to what's past those gates, if I'm being honest. I haven't even wondered how big this place is or even if you have your own separate countries like the humans. I don't know anything about this world at all."

"Draxmere is overwhelming to those of us who have been training our whole lives for it, much less for someone who didn't know of it or the Charmed world's existence. You've not had much need to worry about what's in our world, just that it needed to be saved. Which is very valiant of you, might I add."

"I didn't accept the school's offer because I was being valiant," I admit sheepishly, slightly ashamed now that I know what, exactly, I am fighting against.

"Oh?"

"I accepted because I had hoped that using my powers would be the thing that brought my emotions back, that my abilities were the missing thing I had searched for for so long. That the school could repair my broken soul." The admission rings through my ears, honest and true despite its selfishness.

"You shouldn't feel bad about that. It worked." He shrugs, as if my being selfish about something so serious was okay.

"I kind of do now. That's the bad part of getting my emotions back, I guess. Things that didn't bother me before do now."

"Well, you stayed, didn't you? You didn't quit once reality hit and you realized the dangers of being here. You just embraced it."

"I like it. I like to kill." The words slip off my tongue, coating my mouth with a foul taste.

"So do I." I meet those light green eyes and know that his words ring true, that he isn't trying to placate me. He and I are so similar that it is eerie sometimes.

"That's what made the emotions *really* hit," I admit, looking away. "The kill. And when they did, all I could feel was this hunger for *you*." I ignore the satisfied smirk creeping onto his lips.

"Like calls to like," he says simply, as if murder is inconsequential.

As if the Reapers weren't once people like us.

"But shouldn't we have some hesitation? Some remorse? I mean, they used to be people, right?"

I have morals, and I hate it.

"They were people." His body language shifts, his large form stiffening. "Some of them chose to be Reapers. A lot of them did, actually. Because if you can keep yourself fed, it's a lot of power. A lot of strength. Some Charmed only have a tiny amount of power within them, a useless amount. They can't even perform simple Charms, much less be considered true Conjurers.

"They want to be powerful, and the Grim convinces them that this is the only way to do so. Power is seductive, Azalea. It's mesmerizing and thrilling and dangerous. Conjurers are attracted to power like moths to the light. I'm sure you've heard people tell you that our world runs off the stuff. That's why me and the boys are so well regarded, so respected. That's what power does for *us*. But it's not as easy for those less fortunate. I don't feel bad for killing them. I don't have remorse for dwindling the Grim's army. They chose to be Reapers; I choose to kill them."

"And those who didn't choose?"

"Then death is a gift."

Shayde's point of view makes sense. It's logical and rational. But this new part of me mourns for the souls inside of the monsters.

"I'm not entirely sure I understand the Grim's motives. I mean, what does he get out of this? Everyone talks about him like he is some crazed god, but I don't get it. Why can't they find him? After centuries of hunting him, there's not been a single person to find him? It shouldn't be that hard, because once they find him, then all they have to do is kill him. It'll stop the creation of Reapers for good."

I've never thought to question the way things are here, but as the guilt for killing people creeps its way into my heart, so does the doubt. Now that I care more, questions are stirring.

"I don't think he has motives, Azalea." Shayde's eyes meet mine, his steps pausing only briefly. "The Grim is pure evil. He lives for chaos, thrives off it, even. And the more Reapers he creates, the more power he gets. He's too strong to just be killed, too smart to just be found. I think he gets off on the destruction he creates. It's mindless and all-consuming, a need he must fulfill. There's no more to it."

"Oh, that's…well, horrible." I shudder at the thought of a monster who cares so little, who kills so freely. But wasn't I something similar not all that long ago?

"Mmm," Shayde murmurs, agreeing. Then he stops, reaching out and yanking on an iron door handle in the shape of a serpent suddenly. "This way, m'lady."

I glance up at the large sign hanging overhead, reading:

"Well, that's an interesting name."

"Nothing bites in the food, I swear." He winks, gesturing me forward.

I take a tentative step in, darkness swallowing me. I blink rapidly to adjust to the difference, a few dim chandeliers the main source of light. A neon serpent squirms along the wall opposite to us, blinking in and out of existence.

"It's very dark in here." I state the obvious as Shayde steps in behind me.

"It's romantic mood lighting," he argues, sending a charming smile to the host who is quickly approaching. "Reservation for Glover."

"For two?" The host looks down at her tablet before meeting his smile. When Shayde nods in confirmation, she turns away. "Right this way."

Her steps are light and fast, much faster than I anticipated. I practically jog to keep up with her and Shayde, silently fuming in frustration at my short legs. She leads us deep into the restaurant, twisting and turning around way too many bends. Then she stops abruptly, pushing back a curtain and revealing a singular table in a small room.

A private room.

"Shayde!" I spin on him once she places the menus down and leaves, eyes wide.

"What? You don't like it?" He looks genuinely concerned for a few moments, eyebrows raising in confusion.

"How much did you have to pay to get a private room? You don't need to waste—"

"Oh. You're worried about the money?" He chuckles, placing his hand on my lower back and pushing me forward lightly. "Don't worry, little flower. Private rooms are a privilege that comes with being a Gravedigger."

"But—"

Shayde spins me in a matter of seconds, pushing his body flush against mine. My tongue stops moving, my mouth gaped open in surprise.

"Don't worry about the money." His voice is deep and strained, eyes flashing in anger. "I have plenty of money. Money I don't know what to do with. I can take care of you. This isn't even a drop in the bucket."

"So you're rich?" I blurt out, snapping my mouth shut frantically. That's *definitely* not any of my business.

"Very." He purrs, releasing me. "Does that change things for you?"

"It makes me like you a little more."

He laughs, taking a few steps back. He reaches over and pulls out one of the dark, cushioned leather chairs and gestures for me to sit. I do so, rubbing my fingers along the darkly stained wood table. There is an engraving of a serpent in the middle of the table, the logo from what I've gathered. Though, this one isn't wiggling around like the neon signs.

White napkins are gingerly placed with dark silverware on top, the white napkin being one of the only things that stand out within the dark decor. The walls are a deep gray, with strange Polaroids of weird shadows and blurry movements in crystal frames decorating them. The lighting is just as dim, with candles lit around the room in beautiful sconces.

Shayde was right about this place: it does have romantic mood lighting.

"Welcome back to the Spiced Bite, Mr. Glover!"

I jump in surprise, my Light hitting the tips of my fingers in a flash. A server approaches, having snuck inside without my noticing. Fuck, I need to be more alert around Shayde.

"We'll take my usual, Josh." Shayde sits, nodding at the man.

"Of course. I'll have the drinks out in a jiffy, and I'll go ahead and put the order in." Josh scoops up the menus, breezing away as if he was never there.

"Your usual?" I question with a raised brow. "How many dates have you brought here, exactly?"

"Does Jaymes count as my date? Or Arlo? Or Nox?" Shayde chuckles, leaning back and crossing his arms across his chest in amusement.

"I don't know, how many of them have you kissed after?"

"That happened one time!" he insists, holding up his index finger. "I cannot believe Arlo told you—" He stops abruptly at my bubble of laughter, glaring.

"Arlo didn't tell me anything. Shit, Shayde. Arlo is so not your type." I can barely get out the words through my laughter, can barely breathe through my snorts.

"We were drunk," he grumbles, glaring. "And he wasn't even a good kisser. All of the girls rave about him, but he is severely lacking in skills. The guys I'm usually into are much better looking, anyway. Roguishly handsome, if you will. Like Jaymes."

"I didn't realize the two of you dated until Jaymes mentioned it after the funerals. I mean, I knew you were into guys, that's not a problem! I just—well—" The way Stella had spoken about the two, I suspected, but I hadn't known for sure until Jaymes stated so quite plainly. Shayde hadn't mentioned anything about it, but I suspect things may have been a bit more serious than he let on.

There's so much I don't know about him, so many things I haven't even begun to unravel.

"Yeah, but it was several years ago. We ended things on a good note. I mean, he is still my best friend." He huffs, fingering a napkin before changing the subject to *my* dating habits. "Have you ever dated a woman or do you only like to admire them?"

"I've slept with a few. But, well—I mean—I—well, mostly I admire. How did you know about that?" I stammer, surprised.

He shrugs, eyes bright and playful. "I catch you looking down Demi's shirt all of the time."

We both laugh, my sides beginning to ache from the foreign movements. This side of Shayde is one I heartily enjoy.

"Here you go, Mr. Glover. Two Slithering Dragon Bites." The waiter appears again, dropping off two blood-red drinks before darting away once more.

"That guy's quick," I remark, eagerly taking my drink. One sip is all it takes to realize I've never had anything so delicious. "This is so much better than that stuff at the party."

"Better quality," he says simply, running a finger around the rim. "You've only had the cheap stuff."

"Shit, this is good." I practically moan, taking another long swig. "Does this have as much alcohol in it as the other one did?"

"Not *as* much." He grins cheekily, and I notice for the first time that he has a singular dimple on his right cheek. How had I never noticed that before? I guess I've been avoiding looking at the scar that ends just above it. Not that I don't enjoy all parts of Shayde; I quite enjoy his soft yet angular face, his honey-colored skin that glistens in the candlelight, his long black hair that's always falling in perfect waves. I like to admire his body when we are alone and enjoy studying his tattoos in the dark.

So far I've noted broken chains around his biceps, the words "Good Grim" written across both sets of knuckles, an actual Grim Reaper holding a scythe on his chest, a book with the interesting title of *How to be Evil* on his left forearm, bats dancing across his neck, and a shit ton of branches in between everything. I haven't had much time to notice those on his legs; I tend to get distracted in those few moments I do have to examine his naked form.

I take a shuddering breath, trying not to focus on those thoughts about what lies below his waist. "Should I even ask what food you ordered?"

"Just a special pasta. You'll like it." He seems so confident that I believe him. He's been paying more attention to me than I realized.

I finger the ring around my neck, speaking before thinking once more. "Why didn't you want to save this for your own kid?"

"Because I'm never going to have kids." The statement is simple, as if it doesn't matter. But it *does*.

"Demi said that this world practically revolves around child-bearing." I swallow my fear and my worries. "Everyone here wants kids."

"I don't." His tone is harsh, the decision final.

"S-so, if I couldn't have kids…that's not a deal breaker?" My voice goes up an octave at the end and I wince, turning away so I don't have to watch his expression. I don't want disgust or hatred, but I especially don't want pity.

"You can't have kids?"

I see his head tilt curiously out of the corner of my eye. "I was a murderer long before I came to this place," I say, adjusting myself nervously, "Though, my therapist said I shouldn't think of it that way."

"I'm not quite sure I understand."

I take a deep breath, finally turning to face those unassuming green eyes.

"I've been pregnant three times, and not once did the fetus survive longer than eight weeks. I thought—I *think* it was the curse.

I knew that I would kill anyone who got too close to me, but I had this insane notion that a baby could survive. I thought…I thought that the thing my body created would be immune. I was wrong."

I shrug, face pinching as I try not to think too deeply about it. I'm glad I don't have a kid now, but the pain and the heartache that comes along with this conversation…it's something I haven't experienced in a long time, if ever. After being numb for so long, this wound feels fresh.

"But now that you're here, and using your power freely, the curse is gone. Don't you think you might still have a chance?" His voice is soft, gentle, and kind, and his eyes show only concern. He's curious, not insistent.

I understand the logic and the reasoning behind the question, but I shake my head sadly, exhaling slowly through my mouth.

"No. My last pregnancy was ectopic. I didn't realize it, didn't have symptoms until it was too late. Or, at least, the symptoms seemed normal. It—well, it ruptured. I was rushed to the hospital, but—" I shiver, remembering the blinding pain, the lack of sympathy from every nurse who spoke to me. "Well, they ended up removing the Fallopian tube because there was just too much damage. I almost bled out on the table."

"And the other tube?" Shayde reaches out and grabs my hand, grounding me in the moment. His own face is pinching now, concern and pain written across his features.

"Something went wrong in the surgery, and it got infected, so…"

"They took it out, too," Shayde concludes, a sliver of shock flashing across his face.

"Yeah. I haven't told anyone here about it. Not even Demi. I know that my worth as a partner is tied to my ability to have children. It's one of the reasons Neil and I had such major problems.

"I wanted that first child, was nervous for the second, but by the third time? I knew it wasn't meant to be, and I was over the heartache. I was over the false sympathy and the people who only cared about that baby, not me. I was over the little support and the lack of answers as to why it kept happening. I was over the people whispering behind my back, telling each other I must have done something to kill the fetuses. I was over the people who told me, 'Well, at least it was early! Imagine if it happened in your second or third trimester,' as if my loss wasn't still a loss. I was over the tears and the disappointment. I didn't want that third baby. But Neil did.

"Afterward, when the doctors told us what had happened, he freaked out. He didn't hold my hand and cry with me, he didn't hug me and tell me things were going to be okay or that we had other options. Instead, he told me that he couldn't see himself living a life without children. I tried to talk to him about adoption or even getting a surrogate, but he wouldn't listen. He didn't want to hear it. Neil said that it had to be me, that it had to be natural. That all he ever wanted was a kid of his own. So, I said, 'What about me? What about what I want?' That just pissed him off even more.

"I tried to tell him how I almost died. I told him about the disappointment that I went through each time I found out I was pregnant, only to start bleeding a few weeks later. About the fear inside of me every time I went to the bathroom and had to check the toilet paper after I wiped just to make sure everything was still okay. About the anxiety that consumed me as I tested over and over again, desperate for the lines to grow darker. The panic as I called doctors and fucking *begged* them to help me. To do something, anything, to help me keep the pregnancy. The pain as I sat over a toilet, pushing out a dead clump of cells that lost the potential to be anything more. The anger as I blamed myself over and over, as I cursed the curse I was born with. All because I was sure he would leave me if I didn't have a kid, and not even necessarily because I cared about having a kid myself. In the end, my pain wasn't enough.

"When he died, we were nearing the point of getting the divorce finalized. All because I couldn't have babies the natural way. Because that's all I was to him: a baby-making machine. By that point, I couldn't feel anything anymore. Already, for most of my life, I was numb, and the only time I could feel was in incredibly painful situations like the miscarriages. But when he told me we were done? I didn't feel love or loss or regret; I was numb to it all. That dead baby was my last straw, the thing that snapped me in half permanently."

"What a fucking asshole." Shayde seethes, grip tightening on my hand. He doesn't seem sad, only angry on my behalf. It strikes my heart hard, and I rub my chest absentmindedly to ease the intensity.

"Yeah, he was." I sniff, blinking away tears. I don't like this feeling—this grief, this agony, this wave of sadness.

"I don't want kids." He repeats himself firmly, meeting my eyes. "I don't want to pass on my genes. I don't want to become like my own father, drowning in power and forcing his kids to do things they don't want to do. I don't want to be someone I can't recognize, latching onto my heir for the sake of having one. I *won't* do it."

"You don't want to pass on your power?" I question, relief flooding me.

"Grim, no," he spits, shaking his head furiously. "I have a monster inside of me. It's ugly and violent, uncaring and unkind. I won't pass that on to a child. I refuse. No, the Glover line ends with me. That I will swear to you."

"Okay. Good. Great." It's all I can think to say.

"Is that why you killed him?" he takes a sip of his drink casually, watching above the glass with amused eyes.

"What?" I whisper, heart racing.

"Is that why you killed him?" He repeats, sitting straighter and tilting his head curiously. "Because he was such an asshole about the kid stuff?"

"Why do you think I killed him?"

Fuck.

"I know you did."

I totally did. "How?"

"I know more about you than you think, little flower. More than you know yourself, if I had to guess. So, tell me. *Is. That. Why. You. Killed. Him?*"

"That was part of the reason," I whisper, cheeks flushing in shame. "I just—I couldn't stop myself. He had been saying all of these horrible things, and I had to live with him because neither of us could afford to be on our own. And he kept bringing girls home, kept fucking them in *our* bed. We had agreed to go on dates and meet new people since we were over. Not that it mattered to me, because I hadn't been the most faithful person in the duration of our relationship. But, I mean, he didn't have to fuck them in *our* bed!

"When I confronted him about it, he hit me. He hit me so hard I passed out, and when I woke up my arms were tied behind my back, and tape was slapped onto my lips. Do you know what that fucker did? He brought home some bitch and fucked her in front of me, just to prove a point. I couldn't see, I was so angry. But killing was the one thing I hadn't done, the one line I had drawn in the sand. I didn't even think about it, not in a legitimate way.

"We were walking the next day and he was being so horrible. Once we broke up, he began acting so mean, so vicious. I hardly remember what he was saying, something about my dead parents being the reason I'm so fucked up. I just couldn't take it anymore. I didn't know why my curse had stopped working, didn't know why it hadn't taken him yet. But I decided that if the curse wouldn't do something about him, then *I* would. It was a rash decision. I just…stuck my foot out. He tripped and stumbled right into oncoming traffic. The worst part is I didn't even feel bad about it. I still don't. Does that make me an evil person?"

"No, just a relatable one. You're not going to kill me if I make you mad, are you?" He grins playfully, snorting at his own joke.

"You'd never treat me the way he did," I whisper, smiling softly. "So, no, I wouldn't. You don't hate me now, do you?"

"Don't beat yourself up about your past, Azalea. You don't have to worry about telling me anything. You're perfect in my eyes. Nothing you say or do will make me hate you."

"You can show me the monster inside of you," I say in response, closing my eyes tightly as I repeat his sentiments. "Nothing you say or do will make me hate you."

"I'm going to hold you to that, Azalea Jinx," he mutters, stroking a thumb across my hand just as Josh arrives with our plates. My eyes pop open and I grin, stomach fluttering.

I don't care what lies in wait inside of Shayde. Whatever is in there, I can handle it. I'm beginning to realize my mind and heart are hopeless when it comes to him, that this thing I'm feeling isn't leaving anytime soon. And this thing?

It's more than obsession, or madness, or infatuation.

It's love.

CHAPTER 24

"A jinx has come into play,
a Wielder born to save the day.
Two choices lay ahead,
two choices may save the presumed dead."
—Prophesy recorded inside student Seer Allia Jordan's Prophetic
Journal, 2020 A.G.

"Azalea, I don't know if I should call you stupid or romantic." Demi shakes her head from beside me, frowning at the new tattoo on my wrist.

It's small, hidden among my other tattoos, but it's there. Two little letters in a twisting font Shayde wrote: *SG*. It took me the usual week to gather the courage to finally show her.

"Both?" I shrug, grinning as the triplets peek over her shoulder to see.

School has resumed as though we never had a break, but we are still under tight security measures. Everyone who stayed off campus went through an intense search and questioning, leaving a sense of unease among the students. As harrowing as it is to no longer be alone, it's been nice to see my other friends again. Somehow...I missed them.

"And he has your initials, too?" Ginny raises her eyebrow questioningly, hands on her hips.

"Yep. Same spot. He talked me into it after our date. It's the first tattoo I've gotten that I haven't dreamed about first." I was nervous when he first brought it up, but then it felt right. Everything with Shayde is *right*.

"That's...something," Reese says, earning laughs from us all.

"I know it's a little crazy," I say sheepishly, "But I'm crazy for *him*."

"I don't know, Azalea. You know how I feel about him. Shayde exudes bad vibes. I swear, something's wrong with him." Demi has forgone the gentle approach, getting decidedly more harsh when it comes to Shayde.

"Nothing's wrong with him." I hiss, glaring.

Demi flinches back, and I feel an ounce of regret. "Sorry. Just voicing my opinion." She shakes her head, glancing knowingly at the others.

"What? Do you all feel like that?" I look around in disbelief, suddenly unsure.

"It's just—well—" Ginny starts, wringing her hands.

"It's just what?" I narrow my eyes, fingering the ring he gave me.

"Shayde is dark, Azalea. All the Seers say his aura is scary. And nobody really knows anything about him or his past. We just love you, and it makes us nervous to see you so infatuated with somebody so mysterious. His hooks are way deep in you, and you have no chance of escaping. Shayde tends to devour everything in his sight; don't let him swallow you whole." Demi's speech is eerily similar to the one Jaymes gave me months ago.

"Why would the Gravediggers keep him in their little group if he's so bad, huh?" I question, anger rising like the tide. Everyone keeps warning me about Shayde, even fucking Shayde himself. But I *know* him. I know him better than anyone on this damn campus ever will.

He's kind and caring, despite the bad things he has claimed to have done. And more importantly, he doesn't care about the bad things *I've* done. We are each other's equals. We complete each other in a way only two pieces of a puzzle can.

They're wrong about Shayde.

Everyone is.

"I can't answer for them." Demi shifts, looking away. I huff, glancing around. I spot Jaymes walking across the courtyard, heading towards the dormitory.

"Fine. Then I'll go ask Jaymes." I sprint away, ignoring their objections. They don't realize that he, too, warned me away from his best friend. Was it jealousy or something more?

"Azalea," he says in surprise, stopping abruptly as I reach him.

"Jaymes." I nod, plucking up all of the courage I can muster before continuing. "What's wrong with Shayde?"

"What? Are you two fighting or something?"

"No! No. Quite the opposite, actually. I'm just—I'm confused. Everyone has deemed it important to warn me about him, and it's only getting worse. My best friend keeps telling me that Shayde isn't what he seems, that there's a darkness surrounding him. *You've* told me that. So what's wrong with him? I'm ending this debate once and for all.

"He told me there's a monster inside of him, that something dark lies within him. I understand that and I accept it. I would even venture out to say that I have something similar within me. So, I don't really care about that. It doesn't upset me. But something else has to be going on. What am I missing? What has he not told me?" I don't miss the flicker of surprise that flashes across Jaymes's face.

"He told you about the monster inside of him?"

"All the time." I roll my eyes, crossing my arms over my chest. "Honestly, he's always so broody about it. I don't get what the big deal is. We all have darkness inside of us. This whole world is full of it, and we have to harness that to use our Shadow powers."

"His monster is different, Azalea," Jaymes says solemnly, bright green eyes hardening. His eyes are the dark to Shayde's light, a remarkable difference for such a similar shade. I still haven't told him those striking green irises are etched into my skin; how can I after that night in the woods?

"Um, okay. How so?"

"Ask him to show you. Just—ask him to be honest with you, okay? I know you've chosen him, that you want him, that you love him. But he needs to be honest with you about a few things. Because if he can't be honest, then he doesn't deserve you." Jaymes's earnest tone sends a brisk chill down my spine, sending a deep realization straight to my core.

There *is* something wrong with Shayde.

But what could be so bad that it has everyone this terrified of him?

I raise my hand, knocking on the dingy white door in front of me. I didn't know where else to look for him, so I started here. Classes are over for the day, he wasn't with Jaymes, and dinner ended over an hour ago. So, if he isn't here, I'm not sure where else to go.

"Azalea? I wasn't expecting you." Shayde opens the door and leans against the doorway with crossed arms, a smirk playing across his lips. I ignore his shirtless form, ignore the sinking stone in my gut.

"Can I come in?" I'm pushing past him before he can answer.

"Of course you can." His hands brush against my ass as I walk by, sending heat straight to my core. But I can't give in to his charms right now.

"I'm not here for a booty call." I roll my eyes, turning to face him as the door slams shut behind us.

"What a pity." The heat pooling in his eyes almost makes me cave. *Almost.*

"Everyone keeps telling me that there is something wrong with you." I get straight to the point, pressing my lips together tightly when I see the irritation that crosses his features.

"Do they?"

"Just today I have been told that you have a dark aura, that you're too mysterious, too dangerous. Oh, and I've also been told that you are hiding things from me. And that's all *today*, Shayde. I'm sick of feeling out of the loop, sick of defending you when I don't know what I'm defending you against. I feel like I'm missing a lot because I haven't known you as long as everyone else has, like I'm missing something because the only version of you I know is undoubtedly good despite your morally gray tendencies. I need you to be honest with me right now. I need you to trust me."

"I trust you."

I search his eyes for the truth, hoping I'm not believing him just because I *want* to. "Then show me your monster."

Shayde freezes, a stony expression stuck on his face. "Did Jaymes tell you to say that?" His voice is light and lofty, but I sense the anger lingering behind the words.

"You're not being honest with me about something. When we talked about it last week and I said you could show me your monster, you said you would hold me to it. So hold me to it now. *Show me.*"

"Fine." He hisses, grabbing a black button-up laid out on his bed and slipping it over his arms. His nimble fingers begin to clasp the buttons, a scowl on his lips as he snags a jacket off of the ground. "If you're so desperate to see the evil inside of me, then so be it."

Shayde grabs me by the hand, and I don't have time to let loose a shocked scream before we are transported.

CHAPTER 25

"A Grim will hide in plain sight,
a curse, a jinx, may change its mind.
If all else fails, a savior will rise,
but only through ashes will we survive."
—Prophesy recorded inside Seer Isabella Langdon's Prophetic Journal, 2012 A.G.

I yank my arm away from Shayde angrily, wrapping them around me as the cold seeps in. We have emerged somewhere in the woods on the outskirts of campus, somewhere far enough that I can't see the large and looming buildings anymore. It's snowing, as usual, but the past few months have hit all-time lows according to Demi. I'm not dressed accordingly in a t-shirt and leggings, my feet clad in thin socks and running shoes.

I'm shaking in a matter of seconds.

Quickly, I begin waving my hands. I form the shape of a triangle, holding them above my head before throwing them down in a fury. My body warms instantaneously, the Balmy Charm a success. It's one of the more difficult Charms I've learned because I must contain the heat to myself while not setting anything on fire. The

Charm can be useful for that, too, if an Inferno Charm would be considered overdoing it.

"What the fuck, Shayde?" I fume, taking a step forward. He has his back to me, body twitching. Above us, the sky is dark. A loud noise cracks in the silence, a flash of light blaring not long after, illuminating us briefly. It's then that I notice that Shayde's not only twitching.

His body is changing.

"Y-you wanted to see the monster," he pants out as his body stretches skyward, head whipping around violently.

"What's happening? Are you okay?" I take another step forward, fear penetrating my heart. Fear *for* him.

He continues to climb, clothes disappearing the larger he grows. When I see the horns, my heart stops completely.

Shayde's height reaches at least twelve feet tall before he stops growing, his skin tight over the bones underneath. That skin has turned a deep shade of gray, the veins eerily black and throbbing underneath. I can see claws extending from his fingers, long and sharp. When he turns, he fully exposes me to the truth and to the monster that lives inside of him.

I take a step back, stumbling and falling onto my ass as my hand flies up to my mouth. I try not to scream, try not to whimper in fright. This is *Shayde*.

His face is skeletal, similar to that of an animal. It's elongated and large, with a few chips and broken areas on the outer edges. A crack runs through his cheek in the exact spot his scar does, a wound so deep even this monstrous form holds on to the life of it. Where those beautiful light eyes are supposed to be are now black holes, two empty caverns watching me from high above. My eyes trail away from those empty eyes and up to the shockingly large horns, or antlers, or whatever they are, that are fully present now. Two main ones are branching off the top of his head—one to the left, one to the right. Smaller horns protrude from those diverting points, and it reminds me briefly of a tree and its branches. My heart starts again as a horrifying realization sets in: *I know these antlers.*

They're tattooed on my back.

This is the reason Shayde freaked out about my tattoo, the reason he has refused to bring it up again. He didn't want me to know the real reason he was upset, didn't want me to find out about this version of him.

"Are you happy?" Shayde asks, taking a step toward me.

His voice is even different now, deep and dark and *terrifying.* Every word is a growl, every syllable a promise of violence. When he opens his mouth and lets out a roar, the very sound shakes the trees and competes with the thunder crackling in the air.

"Your antlers," I say, breathless. He nods in understanding, crouching down next to me as a long tongue slides out to lick my cheek. I stiffen, refusing to move.

This doesn't look like Shayde, doesn't sound like him. But it has to be him in there, right?

"On your back." One claw reaches out, tracing down my spine gently.

The touch is what drives me to move, and I scurry away frantically. My eyes widen as I stare at the thing in front of me, the thing that is supposed to be Shayde. He doesn't move, only sighs loudly as though frustrated.

"How?" I whisper, confused.

"I don't know. When I saw them, it really freaked me out. It had me questioning everything you've ever said to me, had me wondering what sweet little lies you had told us. But you didn't know. How could you have? If you had, you would have never stayed with me. Would have never fallen in love with me."

"You don't know that. Everything here is new to me, Shayde, and I've accepted all of the insane things that happen here. What makes you think I couldn't have accepted you?" I snap, flinching afterward.

I've never felt anything like this. This fear, this dread, this hope. Everything rages inside of me, every emotion threatening to burst right out. It *hurts*.

"Look at you," he spits, standing abruptly. I find myself scrambling up, too. I use a tree for momentum, swallowing hard. "Jaymes couldn't accept me either."

"I'm not Jaymes," I whisper hopelessly, eyes wide. Jaymes told me that there were things about Shayde he just couldn't accept. Is this what he meant? He knew about this; I'm sure of it. His reaction to my tattoo was just as obvious as Shayde's had been.

His monstrous head tilts down and back up as he glances me over, that deeply dark voice murmuring, "No. No, you're much more deserving than he ever was."

"I don't know about deserving." A bubbling laugh escapes me as I shake my head vehemently. "Do I deserve the fear you are trying to instill in me right now? Do I deserve to be driven away by your insecurities?"

Shayde takes a threatening step forward, hissing, "You deserve the world, little flower, and I can't give it to you. I'm not the hero in your story; do I need to prove it to you?"

"What are you going to do, huh? Are you going to chase me around until I'm pissing myself on the forest floor? You won't hurt me, Shayde."

"Would you like me to chase you, little flower?" Even in this form, with this voice, Shayde manages to make my body come to life. Heat floods my core, my breath coming uneasily.

"And if I would?" I'm not sure what compels me to say it, considering the unhinged version of Shayde standing in front of me will hold no reservations about hunting me down. But I like the idea of a hunt and am thrilled by the very thought of the adrenaline rush it may provide.

"Oh, how you torture my soul. You, who was created to be my worst enemy and my better half." Shayde bends down, growling in my face with a sudden anger I can't comprehend.

I shake under his searing, empty gaze, a little terrified and a lot turned on. "I-I'm not sure what to say. What to do." It's barely a whisper, a series of desperate words.

"I'll tell you what to do, Azalea Jinx. *Run.*"

The lack of emotion in those empty sockets, the lack of expression on the stony face; it's too much. Something in that new, deep voice is unfamiliar and I have this gut instinct to just *listen.*

I run.

I've never been a fast runner but, shit, I'm going to try. I'm not sure if I'm running from Shayde or the feelings he's stirred up, if I'm scared *of* him or *for* him. I just know that I need to listen to my instincts for once, that I need to go. And, fuck, it's exciting to be chased through the woods, exciting to be hunted. It's a thrill I wasn't expecting, a gallon of lust tossed into the storm brewing within me.

"Shit!" I cry out as I stumble, turning my head behind me to see that Shayde hasn't even begun to chase yet.

When he sees me watching, he takes a single step forward and I immediately understand why he gave me a head start. The ground *shakes* underneath his steps, his stride covering *triple* what mine does.

I have no fucking chance.

I take a deep breath, pushing myself forward again. I won't make this easy for him, won't be a sitting duck. If we are going to play, I'm going to make him work hard for the win.

I zigzag through the trees, using my momentum to sling myself to and from each one. I'm not sure where we are, not sure if we are remotely close to campus or not. I don't know how deep I am in these woods, or if I even have a chance at escaping. Shayde wouldn't have risked allowing someone to see him or hear me, so we have to be far out. My guess is somewhere below campus, between it and the city of Maladara.

I swallow down my anxiety, breathing deeply. I can't allow those thoughts to penetrate my mind, can't allow myself to slow down.

I keep running.

"Azalea," Shayde sings in that deep, monstrous voice. It's chilling, and I shudder along with the ground.

I turn my head briefly, crying out a string of curse words when I see the distance he has gained. Just a few more of those long strides and he will be here, capturing me. I'm not sure what he's going to do, or if he plans on doing anything. Was this all to scare me? Or is there something more sinister running through his mind?

"Fuck you!" I shout decisively into the howling wind, glancing up and begging the sky not to come crashing down around us.

I'm already stumbling over the shaking ground and the thick roots jutting out everywhere; rain isn't going to benefit me in the slightest.

I hear his answering growl and push myself harder, panting at the exertion. I don't make it much farther.

Shayde swipes out with one of his clawed hands, pushing me gently. I scream out in frustration as I am pushed into a tree, his claws not leaving a single scratch on my skin. My clothes, however, aren't left unscathed. My shirt is ripped clean in half, exposing my naked skin to the cold air.

I groan against the tree, disoriented. My whole back is now exposed, my shirt dangling off of me. I can feel Shayde's presence behind me, can feel the ground still as his footsteps hinder. I close my eyes, sucking in the cold air as I turn to face him.

"Look at me, Azalea."

At the sound of his normal voice, I open my eyes, the harsh tone a reminder of what he is. The monster is gone now, replaced by the man I know.

The man I love.

"Shayde, I—"

"Look at me!" he screams again, hand gripping my throat suddenly. I wince at the bark that digs into my back, surprised by the wild and frantic eyes staring back at me.

"I see you," I say quietly.

His head drops down to meet mine, breathing unevenly as his rage releases him from its grip. Above us, the sky cracks and the torrential downpour begins. This moment is too important to do anything but ignore it, though.

"I'm cursed with this beast inside of me, cursed to always be a burden on those I love. How could anyone ever love a monster? How could you ever look at me the same? I'm the monster haunting your nightmares."

"You have haunted my dreams since the day I met you, Shayde Glover. As long as you're there, what does it matter which kind of dream you're in?" I whisper, desperate to keep him here with me. I can feel Shayde's whole body stiffen, muscles twitching as his head lifts once more.

He shoves me harshly, grinning wickedly as I fall to my knees. I make a move as if to crawl back a few inches, confused, fearful, and extremely horny.

"Don't move," he snaps, slinging his jacket off. I can only nod, my heart racing as I watch him. He unbuttons the ends of his sleeves, pushing them up to his elbows before crouching down in front of me. I suck in a breath of anticipation as that wicked grin returns, back arching as he rips the rest of my shirt off.

"You wanted a monster? I'll show you one."

Shayde leans into me, lips meeting mine in harsh and frantic movements. He holds me like I may slip away from his grasp, like if I move even an inch it'll all be over. I arch into his touch, desperate for him. All of the fear, the anxiety, and the lust have turned me on more than I ever could have imagined. Vaguely, I hear a zipper sliding down, hear the rustling of his jeans as he stands fully once more.

A hand slips into my hair, pulling tightly on the roots. The other hand reaches down and grabs my chin, forcing my mouth open with an audible gasp. He thrusts inside of my mouth in one quick movement, not gentle or easy. I choke and gag at the intrusion, tears forming at the corner of my eyes, but I don't relent. I take every bit of him, accept every inch. It's blissful agony, and it sets every nerve inside of me on fire as the thrusts pick up their frantic pace.

I almost have an orgasm from the pure wildness of it all.

"Fuck, Azalea." He groans, yanking me up by the hair.

I'm slammed back into the tree, his fingers ripping at my lace bra with little care. He isn't satisfied until I'm left bare from the waist up, until my nipples pebble up in the cold, wet air. My body goes rigid as I wait for his next move, my mind emptying.

Shayde watches me for a long moment, eyes glazing over. Then he's ripping at my pants, my shoes, my socks. Every bit of clothing he gets his hands on is ripped off, every inch of skin exposed to the elements. My Balmy Charm has almost completely worn off, but the heat from our bodies is enough to keep me from shivering.

When he pushes himself inside of me, I scream. His movements are harsh and punishing, his thrusts unkind and just as frantic as before. He grips my breasts hard, nails digging into my skin until little droplets of blood are exposed. My own nails dig into his back, scratching, pulling, devouring.

It's the roughest sex we have ever had, and I love every second of it.

I am vaguely aware of the rain, of the bark digging into my skin, of the pain in my breasts as he claws and bites down harshly on a sensitive nipple. But my skin was already on fire, my heart full to the brim with each touch.

I don't leave him without any marks, though.

Each time I feel my release coming I bite down on his shoulder, his neck, his chest. I leave him covered in bruises, long scratches raking down his back. I manage to rip every button off his shirt and leave hickeys all down his perfect chest. It's pure instinct, pure rage, pure love that drives us now.

By the time he releases me, I am a shaking mess, unable to stand on my own. Shayde only chuckles, tucking himself away before pulling me into his arms.

"I don't care if you're a monster," I whisper finally, my breath leaving little clouds in the cold air. "I was a monster before you. An uncaring, unfeeling monster. And you didn't care. You still pursued me, still helped me become more than the curse I thought I was. Let me help you, too."

"I'm afraid my motives weren't as pure as yours are, little flower. I pursued you because you denied me and because I thought fucking you would give me some leverage over this beautiful, powerful Conjurer who was going to come in and ruin everything for me and my friends. But my plan backfired when you wedged yourself into my mind. You caught me in your trap, Azalea Jinx, and I don't think I'll ever be able to escape it."

"I don't care what your motives were. Please, Shayde. *Let me help you.*"

"No one can help me." His whisper is broken and sad, and my heart aches to heal his.

Before I can reply he is lifting me into his arms, transporting us right back into his room. He carries me to the bathroom and turns on the shower, silent the whole way. The warm water burns my skin, the dirt and blood washing from my body as though it was never there.

He doesn't speak as he steps in behind me, doesn't make a single sound as he bathes me and cleans my wounds. He doesn't ask for anything in return, either. I can't make myself form any words, can't make myself move on my own accord.

Shayde is gentle and slow as he dries me off, scooping me up and laying me in his bed softly. He curls up behind me and wraps me in his warmth, our soaked hair dampening the pillows.

Eventually, we fall asleep, not a word spoken between the two of us. We stay that way, interlocked together and desperate for the other's touch. I dream of him again, dream of his touch and the feeling of him inside of me. When I wake up, I'm excited. I'm ready to tell him that my dreams of him aren't nightmares even knowing what he is, that he doesn't have to worry about me hating him.

But by the morning, he's gone.

PART THREE

AZALEA JINX AND THE GRIMS

CHAPTER 26

"When two sides cannot align,
and all else fails, then we must find
the girl who hides her powers inside."
—Prophesy recorded inside student Seer Allia Jordan's Prophetic
Journal, 2023 A.G.

Shayde didn't just disappear from the bed; he disappeared from the campus entirely.

After a day, I was worried. After a week, everyone else was, too.

The first day, I tried not to be. It's not unusual for him to be with his friends or in class, not unusual for him to be gone most of the day.

By day two, I was hesitantly asking around. When Jaymes found me that day, asking *me* questions about Shayde's whereabouts, I became nervous.

By day three, I was panicked.

A week in and I am scared.

Had someone seen what he became? What if they turned him in and he's now being tortured in some dank cell way below campus?

What if an angry mob hunted him down and killed him because they were scared?

Worse and worst-case scenarios flash in my mind, each more unbelievably unrealistic than the last. Yet, fear still sits in my heart. It's heavy and unbearable, suffocating and silent. I know in my heart that something is wrong.

I just don't know what.

"Chin up, Azalea. They're sending out a search party for him," Demi tells me, her usual perkiness absent.

The air today is cold and damp, clouds rolling overhead with cracks of thunder and flashes of lightning accompanying them. Today marks a week straight of storms. It's as though the very atmosphere misses him, as if a warning is rolling along over our heads.

I'm no Seer, but even I can sense the urgency in the air. I sense the wrongness of this whole situation.

"Why haven't the Seers been able to find anything yet?"

"That ability is so unpredictable, Azalea. It's really hard to see something so specific. Actually, I'm not sure anyone's *ever* had a prediction involving Shayde. It's kind of weird, honestly. Most of us have heard several predictions by the time we make it here."

"But—"

"Listen, Azzie. You need to quit worrying. Do you know how powerful that man is? He's insanely strong and insanely smart, just like you. And very, very capable. I'm sure he's fine. Maybe he just needed a little bit of air or something, you know? Maybe his dad needed him and he didn't have time to tell anyone." Demi sounds unconvinced, not that I blame her. First Reapers broke onto campus, and now a student is missing? With the insane amount of extra security at this place lately, someone should have seen something.

Shayde had just revealed a major secret to me, one that he was hesitant to let go. He wouldn't have just *left*.

Unless he didn't trust me to keep it.

"I'm going to go find Jaymes," I say, stumbling off without another word.

Jaymes knows all about the monster inside Shayde. He kept that secret as if it was his own. He'll know if that's why Shayde left.

He has to.

After ten minutes of searching, I find Jaymes in the library. I've only been in this room a few times, mostly when Demi wants to study for Charms. The whole place gives me the creeps and hides an unnatural presence behind the scent of old books.

Demi claims a lot of the Seers say similar things.

"Jaymes." My voice cracks as I say his name, and it's enough to jar him. He looks up from his book, standing from the table in haste.

He puts a hand on my cheek, searching my face with concern. "What's wrong? Did something happen to Shayde?"

I hate how he knows me so well when I know him so little.

"He told me." My voice drops to a whisper, body shaking as I try to form the words. "He showed me the monster. The night before he left. Would he have—"

"No! Grim, no, Azalea. He wouldn't have left because of you. If anything, he would have left *for* you." Jaymes reads me like the book lying on the table, strong arms enveloping me in a hug. "He trusted you completely, or he would have never shown you."

"Where did he go?" I whisper into his shoulder, sucking in a deep breath as my heart cracks open.

Only Shayde can induce such intense feelings inside me, can bring these fears I've never had before to the surface. I think Jaymes is the one person who can understand exactly why. He's been avoiding my touch since that night in the woods, but we need each other right now. We both love Shayde, and we both know exactly who he is inside. We can bond over that, at the least.

"I don't know." His voice is pinched with uncertainty, his body stiff as he holds me.

We stay like that for a while, wrapped in each other's comforting presence. Neither of us cry, and neither of us let go. I'm not sure I want to until I remember that Jaymes and Shayde fought over me, that Shayde might not want me running to his best friend for comfort the moment he is gone. So, I let go, smiling sadly before turning and fleeing the scene.

Where are you, Shayde?

CHAPTER 27

"Urgent: Shayde Glover, a junior at Draxmere Academy of Conjuring, has been reported missing. Shayde is a member of the popular group known as the Gravediggers and is a Dimineer. If you have seen Shayde, or know of his whereabouts, please contact the school."
—Article entitled "Urgent: Missing Gravedigger", written by Glamourist Kelly Artega, 2024 A.G.

A month has passed and there are still no signs of Shayde.

I had hoped for an update after the search party, but they found nothing. No signs, no clues, not a single item out of place in his room. But Shayde can create portals quickly and efficiently. There is no way to regulate portals, so…he could be anywhere.

He could also be dead.

I try not to imagine that, though. I don't want to picture Shayde floating in a body of water, or his bloody, bruised body dumped off a cliff. I try not to think about his father and the family business, try not to worry about someone hurting Shayde to get back at his crooked father.

The worst part is that all of those are legitimate possibilities, and no one can find anything to hint otherwise. I told the missing person investigators that his dad was shady and involved with some dark stuff, but they never found him. They said they had no records of his father, and I was never given an actual name. I didn't know the location of the house I visited, didn't know what city or what part of our world we were in. I was useless.

I still am.

CHAPTER 28

"Light and dark will combine
in the girl who has no time."
—Recovered notes from the prophetic journals of Seer Jaylon
Brown, 326 B.G.

The world moves on without Shayde.

Classes continue, security increases, relationships bud, and our powers strengthen.

But he's still gone.

Two months and still *nothing*.

What do I do? What do I do? What do I do?

CHAPTER 29

"There has never been a single sighting of the Grim, though we know him to exist because of the creatures he leaves in his wake. Do not get any silly notions in your head about being the first to find the Grim; he cannot be found. He is an evil mastermind, and our species must come together as a whole to rid our world of him."
—*A Guide to the Charmed* (current edition), written by Glamourist Elias Kasper in 1907 A.G.

Each month that passes sparks a new series of stabs to my chest, each stab accompanied by a dagger buried to the hilt that twists and turns further and further into my heart.

Three months without Shayde has been utter agony. Before him, I felt nothing. After him, all I do is feel.

And I'm back to feeling all the wrong things.

I am consumed by fear and anger, by tears and anguish. I've never felt something as horrible as this. I am constantly worried, constantly looking for him. I've spoken to every Seer, to every investigator, to every student. No one knows where he went or even if he left willingly.

The world is still moving on, albeit slowly.

I'm not sure I want to move on with it.

CHAPTER 30

"When the Reapers begin to swarm,
the end is near, be forewarned.
The Charmed cannot evade the storm
unless the dark and light have joined."
—Prophesy recorded inside Seer Brock Mighty's Prophetic Journal,
1607 A.G.

A whole semester has gone by and I don't know how I got here.

I know I attended classes and that I've grown stronger. I remember practicing and getting better, stronger, faster. But it's all a blur.

There are Charms in my head now, swirling around waiting to be picked, but I barely remember learning them.

I took my exams, but they were so fast. I know I did well and that I scored high. But I'm not sure I was really there.

My mind is doing what it does best: keeping me numb.

"I can't believe we are already done with our first year." Ginny squeals as we push our way past large groups of parents and even larger groups of students.

We shove, poke, and shout to get to our seats, frustration building within me. We are currently in the back courtyard and already had to wind through the large maze to make it here. I'm pretty sure I've got twigs and leaves in my hair, as they managed to somehow expand the middle and push all of the walls within half a foot of each other. We had to walk in a single-file line, and I'm certain most of us were left with holes in our clothes. We weren't allowed to transport inside because of security reasons, and I've already seen a few people tackled by security when they suddenly appeared inside.

A large stage has been placed in the middle of the maze, with rows upon rows of cheap white seats in front of it. The seniors get the front rows, followed by the juniors, then us. Parents are scattered on the outskirts of the stage, jumbled in among others as they wait for their children to cross the stage and graduate with a degree from the most prestigious school in our world.

"Me either," I say quietly, less excited.

Shayde should be here, too. But he's not. And no one gives a damn about him anymore.

Just as we are finally approaching our seats, black dresses drifting together, I see something out of the corner of my eye. There, in the shadows. The figure of a man, hiding in the alcoves of the west wing. Something about the man draws me in, his presence familiar. My heart stops when he holds his fingers above his head, giving himself a pair of antlers.

"I have to go. I'll be right back," I say abruptly, taking a giant risk in transporting away before they can respond. As soon as I arrive at the alcove, I'm tugged into the darkness, away from prying eyes and any security who might have noticed.

I recognize his touch immediately.

"Azalea." His voice is a comfort, grounding me in this new reality. Shayde is here.

Shayde is *alive*.

"What the fuck, Shayde?" Anger boils in me unexpectedly. I thought I would be happy, relieved, excited. But I'm *furious*.

"I know, I know. I should have come sooner." He rushes it all out, holding his hands up complacently. "I just couldn't get away. My father—"

"Fuck your father," I grind out, shoving him hard. "You just *left*."

My tears hit hard and fast as I register the truth. He had a choice this entire time. He wasn't lying dead in a ditch, wasn't being held captive, or devoured by a Reaper.

He could have come back to me and he didn't.

"No, no! I swear, I didn't! I wouldn't have left you like that if I had a choice, Azalea. Believe me, please," he begs, his hands clutching onto me in desperation.

I swallow my pride, taking a deep breath before speaking again. "What happened?"

"The morning I disappeared, I woke up before you. I usually can't sleep past sunrise, so I got up and went for a walk, like usual. But one of my dad's goons grabbed me and took me to him. He's kept me locked up for the majority of the time, refusing to release me until he was sure I would do what he wanted. Until he could trust me out on my own. He—well, I've been working for him."

"What have you gotten involved in, Shayde? I thought you wanted nothing to do with him or his business?" Confusion wracks my brain. I don't understand why he would willingly stay after all that shit he said about not wanting to be like his dad.

"I can't tell you yet. I can't tell you why or how or what's going on. I just—" He pauses to run a hand through his hair, chewing on his bottom lip. "I came to warn you."

"You disappear for *months*, willingly choose not to tell me you're *okay*, then come back here to fucking *warn* me? Are you for real right now?"

He reaches out to grab my shoulders, fingers digging in tightly. "You need to leave right now, Azalea. Take your friends and go. Take *my* friends and go. I'm serious. Something bad is about to happen. I can't tell you the details or how I know, but you need to leave. I won't let you get hurt." His grip tightens painfully, his eyes wide and frantic.

Yeah, he's for real.

"I'm not going to leave," I hiss, jerking away from his harsh touch. "If something bad is happening, I can help. *Let me help you.*" My words hang between us, an echo of the past.

"You don't understand, Azalea. You can't help me. No one can." The familiar words sting my ears, embedding into my mind. He's never believed himself to be worthy of redemption.

"That's why you joined your dad, isn't it? Because you don't think you have a chance at being something else, at being something more?" I can't read the expression that flashes across his face, can't understand the pain hiding there.

"Just listen to me, Azalea," he begs again, falling to his knees before me and bowing his head low. "Please listen to me. *Please leave.* If you want to help me, then this is how you do it. Help me keep you safe."

"How am I supposed to deny you?" I whimper, crouching down to wrap him in my arms. It feels so good to touch him, so nice to have this familiarity.

"You're not." His lips are harsh and fast as they crash into mine. A goodbye kiss. I cherish it, devour it, consume it. I memorize the taste of him before I disobey his commands.

"But I am."

The words are barely formed against his lips before I am gone.

Demi lets out a little squeal at my sudden arrival, laughing and scolding me as I plop down between her and Ginny. The triplets are farther down, chattering away with the rest of our class. I glance around with creased brows, looking for security, but none seem to have noticed me in the large mass of people.

"Where did you go?" Ginny raises a singular brow, flipping auburn locks over her shoulder.

"I thought I saw somebody I knew." It is the quickest excuse I can come up with. "Listen, guys. I need to tell you something."

"What's wrong?" Demi is the one to sense my urgency, my panic. Because I know if Shayde risked coming here to warn me, then whatever is about to happen is bad.

"I've been told that something major is about to go down. I don't know what. It may be bad. Just…be prepared." I choke out, scanning the crowd for any obvious signs of distress.

"Do you think it's the factions? Do you think there's about to be a fight?" Ginny chews on her bottom lip, hands wringing.

"I don't know. I don't know what's happening. Shayde said—" I flinch, clenching my mouth shut.

"Shayde? Shayde's here? What the fuck? You weren't going to say anything?" Demi is practically screaming now, eyes wide in disbelief.

"Look, I don't know—"

"Welcome to Draxmere Academy of Conjuring!" The booming voice of Dean Delarosa interrupts me, cutting our conversation off swiftly.

"This isn't over, Azalea," Demi hisses under her breath, clapping politely along with the crowd.

"This year's graduating class is truly impressive. It has been an honor to stand by their side on this journey, to teach them and refine their skills. I have—" Dean Delarosa only gets a few sentences into what I'm sure was a well-rehearsed speech before she, too, is interrupted.

A large crack splits the air, a swirling darkness forming beside her. The growl that emerges from that darkness is sickening, terrifying, and all-consuming. The dark hides whoever is within it, and all we can hear is the continued noises coming from within.

In a flash a hand reaches out, grabbing Dean Delarosa by the head. I see claws, gray skin, sharp teeth, and then nothing. Her scream is cut off short as she is yanked into the darkness, her body disappearing right before our eyes.

Panicked cries ring out from the crowd, murmurs echoing across the rows. We all begin to stand and push at one another as we try to understand the threat, as we move closer to examine the stage being swarmed by security. Is this real? Is this a joke set up by the Dean?

Our questions are answered when Delarosa flies back out, landing hard without so much as a groan. When she stands, the screams begin. Because, even though the figure looks like her, it's no longer Dean Delarosa.

It's a Reaper.

The Grim is here.

Demi is one of the first Conjurers to react, her speed aiding her in getting to Delarosa's side. The security members below the stage begin to fan out, moving in all directions to try and herd the crowd away from the Grim. I'm not sure if Demi plans on finding someone on that team to help her kill Delarosa, but I need to get up there to her anyway. I will do it if they won't.

More screams sound and I look to the left, where a giant portal hangs in the air. Bodies topple out of it, clumsily hitting the ground the same way Delarosa's had.

More Reapers.

Chaos erupts around me.

Conjurers transport away left and right, scared and unsure. The Grim still growls at us inside of his circle of darkness, reaching out and grabbing unsuspecting Conjurers who are trying to escape. So far, three new Reapers have been created. I'm pretty sure one of them is a senior who was supposed to be graduating today.

Ginny grips my arm, eyes wide as she scans the area. "I don't know what to do," she admits, barely breathing.

"Don't create any glamours. It'll confuse everyone. No one will know what's real and what isn't." It's all I can think to say as I search for Demi once more.

"Obviously! I just don't know how to help."

She is scared.

"You fight," I say, turning toward her. "You help the others. You can create small distractions to help lure Reapers into isolation. Find an Illuminoor. Team up. Do what you can."

"Where are you going, Azalea?" She clutches onto me, refusing to let me escape so easily.

"I'm going to go find Demi."

"Oh, shit. Where did she go?" She spins around wildly, trying to find her among the chaos.

"To Delarosa like an idiot." I grind out, moving away from her and leaping onto chairs. They sway and creak underneath my weight, but I keep my momentum going. It's too dangerous to transport with a large amount of moving people around: I could land on someone or in the line of fire. I'm going to have to go the long way.

"Come back to me, Azalea," Ginny calls, and I watch her scuttle off into the crowd. She has no weapons and no Light abilities. Fuck, I hope she listens and finds an Illuminoor quickly.

I shove past students, hissing at cowards hiding under chairs. I send Reapers to their ashy deaths and doom Conjurers who need me to stick around. But I can't stop myself from moving on, can't focus on anything but Demi right now. She is all that matters in this situation, not the dumb fucks who aren't even attempting to flee if they can't fight.

I should have listened to Shayde.

I should have known that Demi would jump into the fray without me.

"Demi!" I shout over and over, desperately looking through the crowd.

At least a hundred Reapers are here, grabbing and sucking the life out of any Conjurer they can touch. And the Grim still hides behind the shadows, creating more and more and more.

"Azalea!" I hear her voice for a precious second, see Delarosa swinging at my friend. My voice distracts her, and she doesn't see the swing coming.

"Demi!" I scream again, fighting my way forward. I'm so close, but it's not close enough.

I watch the impact, horrified as Demi's eyes widen before emptying. She falls, her tiny body hitting the hard ground. I'm close enough to blast my Light at Delarosa, screaming in anger and despair. I don't know how I hit her heart so perfectly, how I manage to miss everyone else. But it's enough to kill her, enough for her body to turn into a pile of ashes. Many will mourn her, and it's going to be my fault.

My fault, my fault, my fault.

I can't focus on Delarosa, can't focus on anyone but Demi. I have to get to her. She's alone and unconscious, her body ripe for the reaping. I have to—oh fuck.

I hadn't noticed how close Demi had gotten to the Grim, how close she was to becoming his next victim. But I see it now, and fear races through my heart as I pray he doesn't notice her. I push my body harder and faster, tears springing to my eyes as the heart-wrenching scene unfolds before me.

Demi is limp before the Grim, and his hand is reaching out to grab her.

I'm not going to make it in time.

CHAPTER 31

"Evil lurks just beyond our sight
a beast, a monster, a Grim who hides.
When we find the evil at home,
know it's been there all along."
—Prophesy recorded inside Seer Anastasia David's Prophetic Journal, 707 A.G.

My Light escapes me in a giant blast, a large beam directed at the outstretched hand of the Grim. The beam hits its target, and I hear the howling scream of pain within the darkness. It gives everyone pause, all heads turning in his direction. But I don't stop, refusing to let him take Demi.

I blast my Light into the darkness with a fury I didn't know I possessed, screaming in determination with each bolt that escapes me. Over and over and over, I shoot, face contorted in agony. The cries of outrage following each successful hit fuel me, burning my soul in just the right way.

I don't stop until I feel a tap on my shoulder.

I'm spinning, Light blazing to life in my palm. I barely stop myself from blasting a grim Arlo into oblivion.

"Azalea, you're going to burn yourself out." His red hair is much darker than before, and with a sick realization I understand why. It's caked in blood. Most of him is, actually.

Jaymes and Nox stride up from behind him, their clothes and hair in similar states. Their faces are solemn, but they seem to be in a state of calm that I haven't yet managed to find. Guilt slams into me as I watch them approach, my chest tightening. These three have been fighting for their lives and the lives of others, as we have all been trained to do, and I've been wasting my power on trying to defeat the undefeated.

"Demi," I whisper weakly, gesturing to her fallen body that is still much too far away.

Reapers are beginning to surround us, and I see so many more unconscious bodies littering the ground. At least, I hope they're just unconscious.

"We will try to get to her, but we have to fight right now, Azalea. Teams are being dispatched as we speak, so they will take care of the Grim. We need your help. We need you to focus. I know it's hard to stay calm in the heat of battle, but you need to get a level head. The Reapers will probably assume Demi is dead, okay? That's going to work in her favor. In the meantime, help us." Jaymes is harsh and strict, a leader doing what he does best. Arlo looks shaken at the sight of Demi's limp body, but he nods in agreement.

"I'm only fighting so we can push *forward*," I clarify, looking between the three so they all understand clearly.

"Agreed." Arlo is quick to speak, determination setting in his features.

"Alright then, team. Let's go."

Jaymes leads us into the sea of bodies, and we stumble into a Reaper unbelievably fast. These Reapers are strong, their bodies so similar to ours. It's obvious they haven't been missing any meals.

Jaymes reaches out to blast it immediately, but it swings hard and fast. He's sent flying into the chairs, tumbling into another Reaper.

"Fuck!" Arlo is leaping after Jaymes, transforming and sinking his teeth into the one descending upon them.

Nox can't transform into another form like Arlo, but I watch in amazement as he begins to use *my* Shadow ability. Nox leaps toward the Reaper, swinging onto its back in one fluid move. The Shadows swarm its head, blinding it briefly. The Reaper howls and reaches up with both hands to pry at his hands and feet, pulling and tugging in an attempt to free itself. I rush forward, blasting it straight through the heart. Nox has the good sense to jump before the beast bursts into ashes, rolling onto the ground with perfect form.

We don't have time to congratulate each other, don't have time to tease. Another Reaper is already approaching, grabbing Nox before he can take a single step forward. Arlo appears suddenly, ripping at it with razor-sharp teeth from behind. It's enough to force the creature into letting Nox go, enough to allow a blast from Jaymes. His aim is perfect and his accuracy impeccable. He misses Nox by an inch, effectively hitting the Reaper and killing it in seconds.

To our right, a siren begins screeching. Three nearby Reapers wail in response as they turn their attention to him. An Illuminoor slides up behind the middle Reaper, blasting it while it is distracted. The other two begin to turn, but not before the Illuminoor kills another. The last one is too fast, though, and leaps for the woman before she can send one last blast of Light. The siren tries to scream again, but the Reaper ignores the ear-shattering sounds. I gasp as it rips the Illuminoor's arm off, bringing the removed limb up to its mouth. I hold my arm up, despite our distance, preparing to take the fucker down. But the Illuminoor woman still has enough sense to send out one last parting blast, collapsing in time with the Reaper's ashes. I turn away as the siren rushes for her, taking a shaky breath so I don't have to see the blood coating the ground.

"Push forward!" I screech, eyes darting to the space Demi occupied only moments ago to avoid the dying woman nearby. But now her body is gone; disappeared in the frenzy of battle. I don't know if she woke up and left, or if the Grim has her. I shut my eyes tight, shaking my head.

No. No, that isn't a possibility.

As my eyes search around us, I notice the lack of Conjurers. It's mostly Reapers, and over half the students are gone. A majority of the parents left, too. Rescue teams still haven't arrived, but our ten security teams are spread out killing as many Reapers as they can while also sending those who can't fight away. It's felt like hours of fighting, but how long has it really been? Minutes? Seconds?

"Where did everyone go?"

Jaymes searches the crowd at my question while Arlo tackles another Reaper, Light lazily blasting into it. "The Light Faction is gone." His brow crinkles at the realization. "Everyone here is either undecided or Shadow Faction. The fucking cowards told their people to leave." Anger encapsulates him, radiating from his body like a noxious gas.

"Or they organized this."

The thought I recite aloud is a treacherous one, but it needs to be considered. There has been a lot of tension between the factions, and the Light has been known to do shady shit according to Jaymes. He's repeatedly told me that things are going on behind the scenes that I can't understand. What if this is one of them?

"No. No, she wouldn't…she wouldn't." He shakes his head violently, adamant. He doesn't think his mother is capable of such brutality.

We never think our loved ones can betray us until they do.

"Fuck, okay. We don't have time for this shit right now. Let's just find Demi."

As a group we push forward again, finding more Reapers. The one directly in front of me slashes out with its claws, cutting me quick and fast. I stumble back, blood gushing from the wound on my cheek.

"Azalea!" I swear I can hear Shayde's voice, but he isn't here. I can't see him in the crowd, can't spot that mop of dark hair.

"Little flower!" I hear him again just before I fall, and I swear the Reaper's lips move.

The ground is hard and unforgiving, my head bouncing on the grass. I watch as Jaymes kills the Reaper who cut me, blinking way too many times as I try to comprehend the situation. I'm disoriented and confused, unsure if I had really seen a Reaper speak with Shayde's voice. Then I feel Jaymes's touch as he assesses the damage, fingers tracing along my cheek. He's gentle and focused, prodding along the edges of the scrape. His fingers come back slick in blood, but he wipes them off on his white shirt with little care.

"They're shallow. Does your head hurt?" I can only nod, still blinking away the fogginess. "Alright. Stand up, Azalea. We have to keep moving."

As I'm pulled to my feet, I fight the urge to vomit. It's a fight I lose.

I barely turn my head in time, emptying my stomach onto a pile of ashes on my right. Surprisingly, it makes me feel better. My head is still stuffy, and my vision is still swimming, but it's better than being entirely disoriented.

I wipe my mouth with the back of my hand, sending a thumbs up to a concerned Jaymes. We decide to throw ourselves forward again, but the Reapers abruptly fall still. Several get blasted with Light in this moment of hesitation, including the one directly in our path, but most Conjurers are too stunned to continue. We all watch in astonishment as they turn and retreat, their strides long and purposeful. Jaymes and I blast a few on their way out, but our powers are weakened. Neither one of us wants to waste any of our remaining power in case the Reapers turn around and begin the fight anew.

I glance around, taking a shuddering breath when I realize how close to failure we truly are. Bodies litter the ground, screams render the air. Most of us are bleeding or limping, injured in some way or another.

I still can't see Demi.

The scent of blood invades my senses. A shattering silence envelops us. Something is about to happen, something important, but none of us know *what*.

It isn't long before we find out.

The swirling darkness onstage dissipates, leaving a lone figure. He's covered in a long, dark cloak, hood drawn tightly over his face. He's hunched over, but I can tell he is tall.

We watch in anticipation, confusion growing with each passing second. No one moves to strike the Grim: We don't know what can kill him or *if* he can be killed.

The Grim reaches up, hands clasping around the fabric of his hood and sliding it off of his face.

No one gasps in surprise or recognition, no one screams in disgust. Only I have a physical reaction, my body stumbling back as I clutch onto my chest. I can see Jaymes's face harden as he looks on, and I realize he knows exactly who that is, too.

Mr.G.

Shayde's father.

CHAPTER 32

"If you find yourself being tempted by the Grim's offers, do not cave. Once you are turned into a Reaper, there is no going back. There is no known cure. If things get too bad, and you see no other way to survive, please contact the Agency for the Charmless. They can help you gain access to employment, shelter, and food. Please consider this before making such a life-altering decision."
—*A Guide to the Charmed* (current edition), written by Glamourist Elias Kasper in 1907 A.G.

The truth hits me like a bullet.

This is why Shayde didn't want to bring me to meet his dad. Why he wouldn't tell me about his father's business. Why he was so adamant about not having children. Why he didn't want to follow in his father's footsteps.

The monster inside of him… it isn't just a *curse*.

Shayde is a Grim.

The son of a Grim.

There's not only been one Grim this whole time, living for centuries upon centuries. There have been multiple Grims. It's an ability that is being passed on from generation to generation, a curse that they willingly took on. A curse they continue to pass on to their children.

All except Shayde, who didn't want that life.

So what changed? Why did he decide to start working with his dad? *What happened?*

"Hello, Conjurers." The Grim cackles.

Before our eyes, he changes, transforming into a beast that is all too familiar. His Grim form is so much larger than his son's, though. He's over fifteen feet tall, his antlers wild and chaotic. They branch apart like the roots of a tree, looping over and under each other in a senseless pattern. His skull is not cracked and chipped like Shayde's, but it's still utterly terrifying. And when he begins to speak again, his voice is deeper and darker than even the worst things my imagination can create.

"Nice to see that some of you survived." The wicked laugh erupts again as he looks down upon us with those empty sockets. "I have to say, none of this would have been possible without my son. You have his betrayal to thank for this. Most of you should know him, he's really very popular here. Maybe you will know him by his great ability to create portals, an ability that gives me such easy access to this school." The grin that cracks across that stone–like face sparks screams of terror in the crowd.

My heart races in disbelief. It can't be. Shayde didn't—he couldn't have…*unless he did.*

"A stellar introduction, father." His voice pierces through my thoughts, drawing my attention to his form.

Shayde now stands next to his father, arms crossed with a solemn look gracing his handsome features. Gasps and shouts ring out, and

I can't help but look at Nox and Arlo's faces. They seem surprised and devastated, shocked and angry. Jaymes just looks pissed.

When I turn back to the stage, the sight that meets me makes me want to gag.

Demi is awake, eyes wide and fearful. The Grim has her in his arms, pinning her tightly to his body. Fear sinks into me, wrapping around every bone inside. I can't breathe, can't think, can't move.

Why would Shayde do this?

Why, why, why?

"I have a message for the Conjurers!" The Grim snarls at us all, shaking Demi's lithe body. "I'm getting sick of the runaround, sick of you killing all of my creations! So, I am going to propose a deal. One that I am only offering because my son is so benevolent that he begged for your species' survival. Go on, son. Tell them."

"The deal we offer you is this: We take the human world in exchange for saving yours."

Gasps ring out, cries of outrage resounding. I can barely breathe, barely think, barely see over the rage that engulfs me, over the fear that douses my flames.

"You have until the end of one year to decide." Shayde continues as though everything is fine, as though he didn't drop the biggest bomb in existence on us all.

We don't only have to fight for ourselves, but we must fight for the humans, too. I *was* a human. I was married to one, raised among them as their own. And now we have to decide to save ourselves or them? To let these beasts run rampant in their world just so we can survive? It's madness. Utter madness.

"And in case you were thinking about not taking the deal…"
The Grim grins, hoisting Demi up. "Here is our promise to you:
join us or die. Any last words, little vamp?"

Demi's dazed eyes meet mine, and her mouth opens to form
gargled words. "Don't let them take the deal. Don't let them
eradicate the humans." She sucks in a breath as the Grim squeezes
her tighter, her fierce glare piercing Shayde.

"Stop!" I scream, pleading and begging. "Please, Shayde, please!"
Jaymes holds me back as I surge forward, Arlo joining in when I
almost escape from his grip.

Demi opens her mouth, her lips twitching in a gentle smile as she
says, "I don't think you were my doom, Azalea. I think you can still
be my savior."

I don't recognize the scream that is ripped from my throat. I
don't hear myself over the ringing in my ears. Everything is in slow
motion, the world spinning softly in front of me. I leap forward
again, screaming and snarling at the hands wrapped around me. It
takes three pairs of arms, three people to keep me from racing to
save my best friend.

Tears pour from my eyes before I understand completely: He's
not outright killing her like I expected him to. Instead, he turns her
into a Reaper.

Demi's dark skin lightens to a sickly shade of gray, dark patches
of discoloration littering her body in the spots where it should have
been white. Her brown, doe-like eyes turn a harsh shade of black,
eradicating her gentle gaze. I whimper at the sight of it, weeping
as my friend's life is forfeited to create this creature.

I can only watch in horror as her hair fades in color, the vibrant
hues now hideous blacks and blues. Her belly is not yet bloated,

but I know it will be the moment she consumes someone's powers. Her cute, tiny fangs turn a sickening shade of black, seemingly rotten. My heart drops into my stomach as her head whips around frantically as she attempts to understand her surroundings, her nose sniffing the air as she hunts for food.

With a sudden snap of her neck, her eyes land on mine.

Demi's body shudders and shakes, eyes wide and frantic as she leaps. The Grim keeps her in his grip, though, refusing to let her escape. His dark eyes meet mine for the first time, a wicked grin spreading across his stony face.

"Azalea Jinx," he purrs, cackling. "I'm sorry, does this belong to you?"

Demi thrashes in his arms, desperate to get away. Desperate to get to *me*. Maybe some part of her recognizes me, remembers my taste. Mostly, I think she may sense my power.

"You motherfucker," I hiss, all fight draining from my body.

"The only reason you are alive right now is because my son has chosen you to be the one who produces his heirs. Be grateful, little savior. You'll have the honor of bearing my grandkids one day."

"I'd rather you killed me," I shout angrily, eyes drifting back to Demi.

My tears fall harder as I sob. I can't bear to look at her anymore, can't bear to look at the thing that used to be my best friend. I can't kill her, either. I can't bring myself to do that. Maybe she can be saved. Maybe I can find a way to reverse the Reaper process.

Maybe Shayde can—no. Shayde can't help me right now. Not anymore.

Demi had warned me over and over again that something was wrong with him, that she didn't think it was a good idea to start a relationship with someone so dark. It's my fault that she was turned; I'm sure of it. The Grim knew what she meant to me; Shayde knows what Demi is to me. She stayed by my side from the moment I stepped foot on this campus, determined to make me like her. And, fuck, do I. She saw something in me no one ever has before, saw me as worthy of friendship and love despite my many flaws. She wasn't turned off by my emotional turmoils, wasn't afraid of the evils lurking inside of me, and now I've lost her. I've lost the one person who kept me grounded, sacrificed my best friend in the name of a love I can't be sure exists anymore.

I turn to face Shayde, hand over my mouth as I weep. He stares back at me, but he isn't there. Whatever is in his eyes isn't love or adoration or worry: The only thing that lives behind that gaze is a Grim. Shayde doesn't acknowledge me before he and his father leave, taking Demi with them as well as the many Reapers still left. Will he protect her for me? Will he keep her safe until I can figure out what to do?

I'm not sure how I'm supposed to survive after this. How does a heart carry on after such betrayal, such loss?

My boyfriend and his father just turned my best friend into a Reaper.

Why do I crave his redemption even now?

Can a monster like that even be redeemed?

EPILOGUE

"It has been reported that over four dozen deaths occurred as a result of the thirty-minute battle at the Draxmere Academy of Conjuring's graduation ceremony. These deaths do not include those who are now missing, confirmed Reapers, or limbs that have been found without their bodies. This loss is a major one to our community, and we must prepare ourselves for worse news."
—Article entitled "Grim Appearance at Draxmere Academy", written by Glamourist Kelly Artega, 2024 A.G.

The number of fallen is too high, the Charmed hopes too low.

How do we recover from such devastation? How do we hope for a better future? How do we defeat two Grims?

These haunting questions brought on a faction meeting, and it's why we are now gathered in the Basic Combat classroom debating our options. This meeting allows all of the student survivors to participate, a dangerous and possibly unwise decision for the Light Faction who abandoned us in our time of need. I can see Jaymes's mother from my spot in the bleachers, can spot the vein throbbing in her forehead. Whatever she's arguing for, she's passionate about it. She has determined her answer is the right one.

I can almost guarantee it won't be.

In the end, the silence is too much to bear. Jaymes is the one to start the meeting, impatient and angry.

"What are we going to do?" he shouts out his question, a chorus of voices crying out to encourage an answer. I watch on numbly, choosing not to join in.

"Okay, everybody. We have two options." Haiden glares at her son before pasting on a beautiful, award-winning smile.

"Yeah, die or be enslaved!" Arlo shouts out angrily.

"No, Mr. MacLaren. The Light Faction proposes this option: We give in to the Grim's demands."

Outrage fills the gym, the students angry and confused. The other official members of the factions aren't present for this meeting; no, their official council will come later. This meeting is meant to placate us, to offer their sympathies and their guidance.

It's bullshit.

"Listen, everybody!" Leader Fellows bellows, quieting us all. He nods at Leader Bloodgood, encouraging her to continue speaking.

"The humans are insignificant. Our race is far superior, and between the two, we must save our own people. The humans will only fill the Reapers for a time before they will, undoubtedly, grow weak. Eventually, we will be able to attack them with little struggle. Our suggestion is to give in to the demands and wait it out."

"Is that even going to happen in our lifetime?" Ginny shouts in exasperation. I send a tentative smile to my friend, nodding in agreement. No, no it wouldn't. The Light Faction's solution is no solution at all.

"Should the people who bailed on us even get a say in this decision?" Nox shouts next. Jeers and shouts follow his statement.

"There was a miscommunication," Leader Bloodgood states simply, as if it is of little consequence. As if over fifty students didn't die because she and her faction chose to abandon them. And that number doesn't include the family members who died, either.

"Miscommunication my ass! You're working with the Grim!" Someone else shouts, which causes the crowd to erupt once more.

"Enough!" Leader Fellows bellows again, causing another wave of silence. He takes a long breath before speaking. "The Shadow Faction's solution is this: we fight. We don't give in to the demands of the Grims, and we choose to fight for both our world and the human world. This will mean more dedication, more training, more strength. We will need to be prepared for attacks anywhere, anytime. We will need to be prepared for many more deaths before this is over."

"I'd die before I gave in to a Grim!" Ginny shouts, and a lot of people agree with her. Including some of the students who are active members of the Light Faction.

"We aren't here today to choose. We are just here to announce our options, to let you think about your choices," Leader Bloodgood interrupts.

"We are also here to tell you that the Reaping ceremony has been pushed off. We don't think now is an adequate time to choose a faction, not in the middle of such chaos. So, we are giving you around six months to make a final decision. And you *must* choose. Along with any first-years attending next semester."

Gasps ring among the crowd. We get a longer period to decide but they get their dates moved up? It's a tough decision, one not all of us have agreed upon. Especially not now that the Light Faction has made such a public statement by abandoning their own to the Grims.

"Oh fuck," Ginny whispers, rubbing her arm. A large bruise is still present there, purple and angry. I send her another weak smile.

I like Ginny, I do, but…

She's not Demi.

"What about the traitors who were friends with a Grim?" someone else shouts.

I tense, my eyes drifting toward the Gravediggers.

"Yeah, or the one who fucked it?"

I stand abruptly, but Ginny yanks me back down before I can blast the fucker with my Light.

"They will be questioned thoroughly to see if they knew anything about the Grim beforehand. Otherwise, they are innocent until proven guilty. Now, tomorrow we will be holding the funeral pyre for your fallen comrades." The second one of the year. "Afterwards, we can worry about the Grims and the repercussions of not caving into their commands. Until then, mourn. Allow yourself to grieve. Heal. Then come back next semester with hope renewed."

Leader Fellow's eyes flicker to me, mouth closing tightly. Does he think I knew about Shayde before he revealed himself? Well, I guess I kind of *did* know; I was just too naïve to realize it.

"Meeting adjourned!" Leader Bloodgood smiles brilliantly one last time, waving goodbye as though she didn't just tell us all we should sacrifice an entire world for the sake of ours.

I silently follow the other students out of the gym, making my way to the dorm rooms. I don't want to eat. I don't want to hang out with Ginny or the triplets.

I want to disappear into my bed, to be swallowed whole, and never emerge. I want the darkness inside of me to rage, to eat me alive and never spit me back up.

Upon entering my room, I collapse by the door. I can't even make it to my bed. I am blessedly numb, my eyes heavy and clouded.

Good.

The Charmed version of a chill pill is finally kicking in. Ginny gave them to me, hoping it would help. And, fuck, they do. Sleep is all I need, all I want, all I hope for. To drift away into slumber and never wake up from this nightmare is better than the alternative: actually living it.

If only my dreams weren't haunted by my reality, too.

I blink rapidly up at the ceiling, finally coming to. I wonder what time it is. I wonder how much more time I can waste away if I take another pill.

The thought is a motivating one and I sit up, deciding to search for one. My eyes drift to my book bag where I left the pills when the door behind me begins to shake, the banging violent and angry.

"The fuck?" I whisper, rubbing my eyes wearily.

The answering voice is so clear it's as though it is coming directly into my ears. "Good. You're awake."

Oh fuck.

"Get out of here," I hiss, banging back on the door weakly as I struggle to stand. How am I hearing him so clearly? What Charm has he cast?

"Please. Please, listen to me."

I can't stand the pleading in his voice, the desperate whispers. "What can you possibly say to make this better? After what you did to Demi? I—"

"That was never supposed to happen."

I sway on my feet as I stand, gripping the door for support. I should transport out of here, should alert someone that a Grim is on campus.

I should, I should, I should.

I've never been one for those.

"It did," I say plainly, if only to keep him talking. If only to hear him one last time.

"My father grabbed her because she got too close. Then, when I tried to plead for her life, he decided to use her anyway. He said that my compassion makes me weak. That he will destroy everything I love so that I will no longer be powerless in the face of the Conjurers." He bangs on the door once more and I flinch, taking a step back.

"I just want her to be alive," I whisper.

He hisses as though I stabbed him. "She's alive. I don't—I don't know if I can fix her. I've never tried. Come with me and we will find her. We can try to fix this." The worst part of this whole situation is that he truly sounds as though he believes his own lies.

"Go with you? Are you insane? You're a *Grim*." I hiss "Grim" as though it's a curse. To most people here, it is.

"Yeah? And you *fucked* a Grim, so what does that make you?" He bites back, somehow knowing the exact thing that had upset me only hours ago.

"A Grim fucker." I shrug callously, unable to continue this line of talk any longer.

"You won't come with me?"

"I—"

The banging starts anew, this time strong enough to burst the door down. I screech, scrambling back as far as I can. I throw myself toward my pile of clothes, digging for a belt that's hiding daggers inside.

Fuck, fuck, fuck.

"Azalea!" The pounding doesn't slow down, the door threatening to burst from its frame. "Azalea let me in! Azalea, open the door! Azalea! *Azalea!*"

I've never heard Shayde sound so angry, so desperate, so scary. It doesn't sound like him, doesn't feel like him.

This is the Grim that's been hiding in plain sight.

I shakily wave my hands, casting a one-way window through the door.

I almost collapse upon seeing him. Why does the light have to hit him just right? Why does he have to look like a dark angel come to save me? Unfortunately, I know he is anything but an angel: No amount of pills can convince me otherwise.

I finger my ring necklace and stay silent, hoping he'll believe that I transported away. I probably should do just that, but...seeing him here, listening to his voice...I'm an addict who needs one last fix.

"Azalea, I know you're in there." He presses his cheek to the door, voice soft and gentle once more. "Please, we can fix this. I know we can. If you just open the door—"

"N-no!" I finally get enough sense to pull free a dagger, clutching it so tightly my fingers turn white. I stand, watching the door as I shake in fear and desperation.

"Azalea, please." I see the look that passes across his face, the scrunching of the nose, the twitching of the lips. He reaches out and traces a finger across the door, pressing his hand flat to it. "Don't make me come in."

"Oh, shit." He's too calm right now, his green eyes alight as he chuckles darkly.

With one defiant shove, he's bursting in, throwing my door open even though I'm supposed to be the only one able to unlock it. Fuck, did he Charm the door at some point? He must have.

I can't move as he towers over me, hand clasping around my throat. He shoves me harshly into the wall, scowling into my face.

"You won't come with me?" he repeats, angry and hurt.

"Why did you do it?" I ask instead, a single tear slipping out. "I don't understand why you would do this."

"Which part?" He has the decency to look ashamed.

"Let's start with letting Reapers onto school grounds. The first time, I mean." The fact that there was a first *or* a second time still shocks me.

"It was the only way I could be with you." His angry voice has grown to desperation, his eyes wild as the grip on my throat tightens. "Don't you understand? We fought those fucking Reapers and it brought you to *life*. I tried to protect you, don't you remember? I licked you, put my scent on you so they wouldn't attack you.

But Jaymes fucked up and smeared blood over my saliva and they found you, and I can't be more grateful. It was the first time you looked at me like you gave a shit about me! Before I slept with you, you were a game, a trophy, a way for me to hold some leverage above a powerful Conjurer's head. But then we slept together and everything changed.

"Fuck, little flower, I am *obsessed* with you. I am obsessed with the way you feel wrapped around my cock, the way you breathe when I'm inside you, the way you scream out my name when I make you come. Every bit of you was meant for every bit of me. I am in love with you, dammit! So, yeah, I let those Reapers in. I let them in and gave you the fight you had been itching for, the fight you *needed*. And then I found you and gave you what you needed to come alive again.

"You're so fucking addicting, little flower. I couldn't stay away. Sleeping with you one time doomed me. This never-ending madness has consumed me. My obsession led to possession, just like it was meant to. You are *mine*, and I will do anything to keep it that way."

He's panting now, gripping onto me with such enthusiasm. I've never seen him look so deranged, so imperfect, so insane.

Why the fuck do I like it?

"There were over fifty Reapers released, Shayde. Why would you do that? I could have died! Other people *did* die!"

"My father wouldn't let me do it unless I made a statement. I had no choice in the matter. Besides, I made sure that some of them would come find me and the boys. And it wasn't that many deaths! They knew the risks when they agreed to attend Draxmere."

"I love you, Shayde, but that's insane. You can't just *kill* people for me. Because of me!"

"I can and I will!" he barks, leaning into my face and growling. "*I am.* I'm killing off a whole species, a whole world for you. Just so *he* doesn't kill you first. Can't you see that? I'm protecting you!"

I can barely breathe, can barely get words to slip from my lips. "Shayde, that's…" Crazy? Horrific? Incomprehensible? Twisted? *Fucked up?*

"Come with me," he begs, nuzzling into my neck as he releases me. "Please, come with me. I can protect you if you stay by my side. My dad will understand; he told you that I've chosen you to bear my children. He was going to kill you, you know? He made me bring you to him so he could determine how powerful you really were, and he was going to kill you and feed you to his Reapers for that power. Now he thinks that you and I will produce the most powerful Grim in history."

It's as though there are two different versions of Shayde, one sweet and one violent, and I don't know which one is going to end this conversation.

"Shayde, you know I can't—"

"He doesn't have to know that." His lips trail gentle kisses down my neck and it would be all too easy to give in, to allow him to convince me to leave. But I can't. I won't.

"Shayde, you did make me come alive. And I fell in love with you because of that. But the person you brought back to life is someone who can feel. And all I've felt is betrayal, and anger, and hurt, and *pain* since you showed up here two days ago. It's horrible. It feels like my whole body has been submerged in water and I'm barely managing to keep my head up. And then I think about you, or

Demi, and I slip back under. I keep fighting just to break the surface again. How am I supposed to keep doing that? How am I supposed to just get over it?"

"We can work on it. We can talk and work it out! I know we can. Please, Azalea, just—"

"Shayde, I know right from wrong. I have a moral compass. The only reason I am here, at this school, is to kill the creatures you and your dad keep creating. I thought that's why you were here, too. Isn't there some part of you that understands that what he does is wrong? You have a chance to make things right.

"I know you offered up the humans to save me. *I know that.* But that doesn't change things. That doesn't make this situation better, or easier. And all the lies you told me…I don't know if I can move past them. Telling me your dad is a Seer, that you have a curse, that you don't want to be in the family business. None of it was real! I can't wrap my head around this, Shayde. *You hurt me.*" I pant as I finish raving, waiting for the anger within him to rise to the surface once more.

"He *is* a Seer!" He latches onto the last part of my rant, frantic and wild. "He is! I am, too. That's why the other Seers can never find us. Seers can't see things about other Seers." He offers up the information, lapping up my surprise greedily. I didn't know that about Seers, didn't know that he had dual powers like me.

"That's one thing, Shayde. One!" I scream, exasperated. One truth won't make up for the dozen lies.

"We are meant to be together. You can pretend to not be just like me, but you are!" He shakes me in a crazed state, and I cry out in pain as my head hits the wall. "We are puzzle pieces! Our edges have melted together, fused to create one person! That is who we are. Cursed dual-Wielders who only have each other to rely on!"

"*I had Demi!*" I screech, shoving him away from me. "I had Demi, and you took her from me! I can't forgive you for that, Shayde. Not right now."

I watch him deflate, watch him change once more before my eyes. He slams down onto his knees, hands clasped together as tears run down his cheeks.

"Please, Azalea. Please, come with me. *I love you*. Please, little flower."

A small noise escapes me, my hand covering my mouth. Shayde is on his knees, crying, begging for me to leave Draxmere for the second time in such a short period.

But I can't. I still can't do it.

"No."

Shayde is up faster than I can blink, pushing into me with so much force that I gasp. I know he sees the fear that flickers across my face, his teeth gritting accordingly. He grabs me by the jaw, jerking my face toward his. I take a deep breath, doing the only thing that there is left to do.

I stab him.

"Did you just fucking stab me?" He wheezes, stumbling away from me. The blade slips out cleanly as he does so, his hand moving to grip the gushing wound.

"I did," I whisper, watching in horror. "Don't make me do it again."

"Okay, little flower." He chuckles humorlessly, eyes lit up with a coldness that doesn't belong there. "You want to betray *me* now? That's it? Fine. So be it. But I am going to make sure you feel every ounce of hurt with me. Your petals are going to fall off and decay, your leaves are going to die of thirst, your stem will never grow, and your roots will burn before they ever latch into the dirt. You will crawl to me and beg for water, beg for the sunshine you crave. And only then will you get it, not a moment before."

"Shayde, don't do this. Please, don't leave like this." I can barely see through my tears, can barely hear over the sound of my heart cracking into a million tiny pieces.

"Find me when you're ready to get on your knees and *beg*, Azalea Jinx."

A Reaper's State of Mind

I don't know who I am.

I'm scared.

I'm alone.

I'm hungry.

I whip my head around as my eyes flicker open, taking in the unfamiliar sights. Back and forth I look, but nothing here is recognizable. Except…what is that smell? I tilt my head back, sniffing hard as I try to remember.

When I spot the girl, somehow, I know it is her scent that is so intoxicating. She looks so familiar, but I do not know her.

She is a weak, weeping mess. Screaming and thrashing in someone's arms, shouting out a strange name.

Demi!

I do not like the name.

But I do *love* her scent.

I am so, so hungry. Just by her scent, I know she will be tasty. Just by her scent, I know she is full of the thing I need: *power*.

It is a pure instinct that has me leaping, preparing to take what should be mine. Except, something stops me. Arms are wrapped around me, too. I glance up, snarling and growling. Ah!

My creator.

I fall silent, tears stinging my eyes. My creator cares enough to hold me, to comfort me during my time of transformation.

Now who is a weak, weeping mess?

I don't know how to speak, don't know how to communicate with my creator that I need the girl. Her scent is stronger than any other being in this entire place, which must mean she is the most powerful.

I need that power.

I am so, so hungry.

You can't eat Azalea.

It's treacherous words in my mind, accompanied by an unfamiliar name. Is that the girl? Azalea? The delicious one? Yes, I can remember her taste now. Unlike anything I had ever had. But when did I taste her, and why?

I can't remember, I can't remember, I can't remember.

My thoughts are sucked up into oblivion as I am whisked away to another place, a strange building that is too small for a creature like me.

"Give her to me. I have the perfect place to take her."

I turn toward the voice, snarling at the thing that is not my creator. I do not want to leave with him. I do not want to be away from my creator's arms.

"She's all yours, son. Go with him, my darling, and listen to what he says. He'll make sure you eat." My creator has spoken to me! He has given me my first orders: I must obey.

The man with long hair takes me, guiding me away.

We vanish again.

This time, we appear in a cold, dark place.

"I'll keep you safe, Demi. I don't know how to fix you. I don't know if I can. But I'm going to try."

The man is backing away, swinging a door shut. A clicking sound follows, and I hear his footsteps fade away.

I approach the door, twisting the knob. Am I not supposed to eat now? Was I not promised food?

The door is not opening.

I've been locked in a cage.

I rage at the man, hissing and growling and shaking the door. It doesn't move even the slightest. So, I ram myself against the cold walls. They are hard and unforgiving; they do not cave.

I'm so hungry.

I need to get out, to eat, to restore my power.

I'm hungry, I'm hungry, I'm hungry.

"I'm sorry, Demi. This wasn't supposed to happen."

There's that name again: *Demi.*

Is my name Demi?

Acknowledgements

Where do I even begin? Thanks to my husband for supporting my dream and listening to my many rants about these characters and their many, many flaws and wrongdoings. Thank you to all of my beta readers who offered amazing advice. Without them, this book would not be the same. Thank you to my amazing editor Sage for such amazing work and support. Thank you to my street and arc teams for supporting me on this crazy journey. And last, but not least, thank you to you, the readers, for taking a chance on a small indie author. Without you, I could not do what I do.